FOR LOVE OF LIEUTENANT ARGAMENTINE

An item in a report had been bothering General Fry for weeks. It was just a fragment from the frozen memory of a cadaverous kzin warship that had drifted aimlessly in Centauri space to be discovered only recently for intelligence analysis. Perhaps, if it had not been for his unhealed love, he would not even have noticed this trivial detail buried in a routine document. Gibraltar's computer had long ago broken some of the old kzinti war code. The deciphered minutiae, quaint and chauvinistic, read like a commendation list given by Julius Caesar to his centurions, useless to any practical reader who found it.

It praised kzin warriors. Supply lists, orders, codes, command lines, strategy, contingency plans — all had been erased. But true warriors did not erase the deeds of revered warriors.

It was heroism which had caught the attention of General Fry in one sudden adrenaline rush . . . an ambiguous line in the role of commendations referred to the intrepid capture of a UNSN scoutship . . . and the capture of a single, unnamed prisoner.

Can a heroine rise from her grave? Hope kept jumping out of the strangest places. Only one UNSN ship was unaccounted for in Centauri space — the hyperdrive scoutship *Shark*.

His emotions had their priorities all wrong, he knew. It was the capture of an operational hyperdrive vessel by kzinti warcraft sixteen years ago that was his primary intellectual concern. A missing soldier was irrelevant compared with the terrifying vision of a hyperdrive-equipped kzinti naval armada. Still, uppermost in the general's mind were thoughts of a charming woman and schemes to hold her again in his arms. . . .

MAN-KZIN WARS VI

Created by

Larry Niven

with

Donald Kingsbury

Mark O. Martin

and

Gregory Benford

Man-Kzin Wars VI

A Baen Books Original

Baen Publishing Enterprises
P.O. Box 1403
Riverdale, NY 10471

ISBN: 0-671-87607-4

Cover art by Stephen Hickman

First printing, July 1994

Distributed by Paramount Publishing
1230 Avenue of the Americas
New York, NY 10020

Printed in the United States of America

CONTENTS

CONTENTS

THE HEROIC MYTH OF LIEUTENANT NORA ARGAMENTINE

Donald Kingsbury

• Chapter 1

(2435–6 A.D.)

He was a five-year-old human boy without membranous ears or fur, or even claws to defend himself, a boy severed from his family. For days in space he had been segregated, inspected, prodded, pricked, scanned, examined, and questioned by an unnerving assortment of kzin. He endured these strangers dumbly, fear having muted every word of his Hero's slave patois. Hushed, he recited his mother's name to himself again and again, as if the inner sound of it would force her to stay alive. He didn't want her to be dead. He called his mother by the kzin word for mommy, *Prrt*, the most comfortable word he knew—having forgotten that she had once told him fiercely never to forget her name, Nora. "Prrt!" he ordered her in his head like he sometimes did when she wasn't paying attention. Often she didn't pay attention.

But she only came to him in his dreams.

He was bewildered. Where had his colossal protector gone? Mellow Yellow would *never* desert them! Why had their master turned funny and started calling himself by the name of a lord, Grraf-Nig? Where had their mother gone? Where had the babies and his five-armed Jotoki friends gone? What kind of world was this W'kkai place? But finally an officious orange kzin corralled the whole family together, younger siblings and mother. The room was gray but it shone with relief because *she* was there. "Prrt!" he purred. Her children were excited to see each other again. He was excited to see them again. The babies wailed. Their kzin guardian glowered.

This enormous kzin with large nose and lips that never quite covered his fangs was not like *their* kzin. He was too tall and he was a deep hue of orange with disfiguring black spots. He was foppishly dressed in an unknown cut of garment with lace. And he was mean. The boy watched him with alert eyes. The boy had known only one kzin, the master, but he could read every kzin gesture, every expression, every throb of a kzin's hairless tail. This one was annoyed, a twitch of a grin on his lips. It was not his pleasure to deal with human slaves. Danger.

Without warning, the kzin cuffed Prrt for not controlling the squalling and squeals of her infants while he did his record-keeping. The boy flew to protect her . . . and bounced off a vicious backhand, thumping against the wall. Instantly, from the mother, an unspoken grimace of warning passed to her eldest son—*freeze!*—causing him to freeze into an unwanted posture of obeisance. The large-nosed kzin did not notice the exchange because he could not read human expressions. He merely noticed the monkey's sudden calm, which probably saved the boy's life in the minutes before Hssin's lord Grraf-Nig arrived in a rage to hiss and spit his offense at having his *property* maltreated by a mere Record-Keeper.

The slave name of the boy, given to him by master Grraf-Nig, was "Kz'eerkttt," said with a glottal gnashing at the end to distinguish it from "kz'eerkt." The tree-bound kz'eerkt, a quasi-primate native to distant Kzin, featured in kzinti mythology as an animal of trickery who will always best those who lack bravery and, afterwards, will raucously advertise his joke from the trees. Kz'eerkttt (with the glottal gnash) referred to the tricks themselves. The name is best translated as Monkeyshine. His twin sister was Furlessface.

Monkeyshine had no memory of the human name his mother once whispered so fondly in his ear when he was a baby. It seemed natural to him that females like his mother and sisters spoke with emotion and expressions and could not understand words, except the simplest words, even when spoken loudly, firmly, and slowly. Not like his brother, Fastanimal, who chattered with the agile Jotoki and teased old Mellow Yellow until he told them stories. The third brother, the baby, was still practicing his screams and growls with Monkeyshine's encouragement, but was not yet able to string them together to make sense.

Monkeyshine could chatter nonsense with the baby boy, he could make up words with Fastanimal, hisses and sibillated snarls—shared secret words for kzinshit and farts—that no kzin could comprehend. But his sisters never caught on. His twin, Furlessface, remained as silent as his mother. The girls made noises, especially if they were provoked or teased, or hungry or curious, but they never made much more sense than a baby.

Monkeyshine's younger self did hold on to three sacred human words which he repeated to himself like a mantra during both moments of peace and of danger, words from a past life of unremembered tenderness: "cookie," the name of a sweet food made in the stars; "Earth," the name of a planet bigger than Hssin with better air; "centipede," the name of a worm with 512 legs. Monkeyshine wasn't sure how big a centipede grew but he was sure that it towered at least big enough to eat a kzin in one bite.

After their journey from Hssin, the revival from the hibernation bin, the transfer from tiny ship to the bustling space station, the confusion and the reprieve from doom, life settled into an easier and more exciting routine. Mellow Yellow seemed, day by day, to be gaining in stature, and that was good because slaves rise with their masters. But it was a strange new place, different, excitingly dangerous. Monkeyshine was fluent in the slave language of the Jotoki but he knew enough of the Hero's Tongue to pick up pieces of the conversation around him. He wasn't sure he liked the implications. This was no minor kzin outpost! Their station was circling a major kzin world. Zillions of kzin down there! Surely not all of them were to have master status!

Once a splendidly dressed warrior had demanded an audience with Monkeyshine, inducing in Mellow Yellow an overwillingness to please. Such a deportment of his master amazed the young human. A master making slave gestures! Who was this Si-Kish? There was no time to contemplate such a behavioral wonder; Monkeyshine was hastily presented to the W'kkai Hero with a cautionary/threatening admonition to be respectful. Intently, the boy read the monster's emotions, his eyes scanning kzin ear posture, lip tremors, muscle tension, tail position, and the erectness of hairs around the neck.

"So here is the little man whose fleet blockades our star?" he said to the five-year-old boy.

This elaborately beclothed kzin didn't seem to want an answer. He was neither angry nor ready to attack. He just seemed to want to look, so Monkeyshine, who was warily afraid of the warrior, said nothing, letting him stare.

With a vague sense of unease, Monkeyshine had deduced that they—his mother and his brothers and sisters—were not only slaves of the kzin, but that they were *enemy*. The slave part seemed natural, but the enemy part was uncomfortable. In the following days his cautious questions about this were unproductive, limited as his inquiries were by an immature mind which had to twist around the grammar of a slave language that was ill-suited to questioning. Grraf-Nig's loyal Jotok, Long-Reach, hinted with several of his underarm mouths that the boy's monkeykind was a race of warriors, that his mother was a ferocious warrior—but that was absurd, a typically wild Jotok fantasy. Bonded slaves did not know how to make war. And his mother had neither the wits nor the sharp teeth to be a Hero. She had the grinding molars of a vegetarian.

Sometimes his Prrt seemed to sense his confused astonishment, and ambled over in the peculiar kind of gravity that the kzin maintained on their ships of space where feet were heavier than heads. She combed her fingers through his hair, then playfully bounced him in his sleeping constraints until he was having fun again. Once she pulled him past a kzin guard to the viewport to look out over the vast moving orb of night-shrouded W'kkai. He knew that she could stare at the lights of space with endless patience, never losing her fascination. He wondered what her simple mind could be thinking to hold her eyes so steady. The sight certainly didn't frighten her. Did she even *suspect* that there were zillions of kzin down there, each needing his ceremonial *wtsai* polished?

A crescent of light began to glow along the horizon. He'd never seen a sunrise from space before, only sanguine R'hshssira rising huge in the dusty atmosphere of Hssin. The viewport darkened in response to the new sun. It was *small* compared with immense R'hshssira! And bright! Even through the darkening viewport it was too bright to look at. Didn't they freeze with a sun that small? Well, they had fur and maybe their sun made up in dazzle what it lacked in size.

The dawn area of W'kkai grew as they watched, rolling like a surf of light beneath them. The mottled blue and green smoothness would be sea. Their massive space structure overtook a vessel that passed above them. He found himself as fascinated as his mother.

***

Another change. They were shipped to the planet's surface. While floating trucks bounced them through low hills to a distant destination, Monkeyshine had time to watch the sky and wonder where its supports were hidden. At the homestead site they were set up in military prefabs. It was worse than Hssin. There were bugs that crawled through the prefab doors and flew noisily. The small ones bit. Things changed too fast to resent the discomfort.

Little by little the troop of refugees, kzin and slaves, were taking up a new life. Mellow Yellow seemed to command vast wealth. Monkeyshine was awed to see construction crews build a mansion for the mighty Grraf-Nig, surrounded by an airy palazzo for his kzinrretti. Groomed, coy females came to the lord, offered by fathers who sought favor. At each of the numerous wedding feasts the boy competed with the ambling Jotoki to serve the live beasts, or run errands on the hunts, proud in his new livery. The elaborate celebration tents gave way to more formal affairs within the partially completed mansion. They had all risen to a level of importance. Once they had been servants of a grumpy kzin warrior who scrounged through the war ruins of Hssin for bolt and copper wire. Now they served his females milk in tooled platinum dishes within the corridors and feast halls of a palace!

• Chapter 2

(2436 A.D.)

Major Yankee Clandeboye scowled at the travel orders on his infocomp. Now *that* was being hauled off to Gibraltar on pretty short notice! A brief mnemonic executed by quick fingers called up his almanac of the Asteroids. He punched in Egeria and Gibraltar and zoomed. At the moment Egeria was 80 degrees out of phase with Gibraltar Base—so it would be a long trip in a tiny can. If it was business that couldn't be conducted over the network, it was going to be trouble. Again. And for a man on disciplinary probation, any kind of trouble was bad news.

Flies in the cow dung!

He swore like a flatlander because he was a flatlander, though he had never touched a cow or smelled dung in his life. Once he had pushed his cousin Nora into a sim-space manure pile when he was nine and she was three. His parents believed in education for their children and had put *Old Macdonald's Farm* in his library because they believed everyone should know something about Earth's past. His cousin, who was from an Iowa farm city, had been lording it over him in his own sim-space; it was *his* farm, filled with *his* colors and sounds and smellies and more pets than he'd ever want to own, *his* pets. It was *not* her farm. So he had pushed her into the manure pile. The cows scolded him. Usually they only sang with the pigs and the ducks and the horse and the dancing geese.

What kind of scolding was it going to be this time?

These Belters were never going to leave him alone. Nervously, he looked around his small office. It was free of unauthorized chemicals. There wasn't anything blocking the air vent, nor dangerous floating things—his mermaid charm on a string didn't count. If you were a flatlander, to survive in space you had to be twice as good as a Belter or they harassed you to distraction. You had to notice everything. If you weren't being chewed out for playing hazardous games with their hallowed air supply, you were being chewed out for having too much nefarious hair . . . or something, even for the way you smelled.

But this time it was going to be big. They didn't drag a man a quarter of the way around the Belt just to rap his knuckles for neglecting the air filters. He patted his faded lucky charm and she bobbed in the ventilation breeze wiggling her tail. "Gonna need you, pretty baby." His mermaid was his one reminder of Earth and her seas. She was a plastic antique with a blue bra, which dated her to the twentieth century, and she'd gone to war with him against the kzinti and brought him home.

Major Clandeboye had been in space for a full nineteen of his forty-seven years. He'd been farther from Sol in a marauding hyperdrive than any of these arrogant Belters he met—brave men who panicked if they had to travel farther than five meters from their pressure suits. With the infocomp still in his hand, Yankee toggled back to his orders. Signed by General Fry. Another holier-than-thou Belter who'd never been out of Sol System. What could this flasher have on him?

Ever since the inquest into the Virgo fiasco, Yankee had slavishly cultivated all the aspects of a model military administrator—even to the point of making and filling out daily self-evaluation checksheets. He knew they'd never forgive him, not after five years, not even after hell froze over. For Finagle's sake, he'd been *devoted* to his behavior. It was *hard* work keeping his ass so clean.

Well, almost clean. Oh, oh.

But nobody knew about *that*. He slumped for a minute, which makes you look like a limp rag in space, and then grabbed a bulkhead handle and slithered through the lock, kicking himself down the narrow fallway, adrenaline ready for a major confrontation. Could Smelly have betrayed him? His best friend? It wasn't impossible. After all, Smelly (whose real name was Smeegie) was a lanky Belter of low morals. He slipped his infocomp into its holster.

While he sought out Smeegie, he had time to cool down. Yankee and Smeegie had not started out as friends. They were assigned to the same combat flight when the Virgo Volunteers were thrown together for a probing dash deep into kzin space. Smeegie had openly resented serving under a flatlander of insecure demeanor. He valued his life. But danger forges bonds and by the time Clandeboye, the only surviving senior officer, brought them back alive none of his men cared that he was a flatlander.

He found his friend in the workshop with their orange kzin warrior, who was even taller than Smeegie and grinning at him while a furry arm was being operated upon. To divert himself from his untactful suspicions, Yankee took the opportunity to grab the kzin by the nose with one hand. With the other he pulled on the fur of the jaw to pry the mouth open. He ran fingers over the teeth. "I think his teeth are too sharp," said Yankee. "We should file them down."

"Why?"

"He might hurt someone."

"He already has."

"Yah. That's what has suddenly started to worry me," grumbled Yankee, watching his comrade closely for signs of betrayal.

"You don't think your, ahem, *colleagues* are going to complain, do you? They wouldn't dare admit to being mauled by a *mechanical* kzin. They'd be laughed out the airlock. Who's to know you were the teleop? *I* know, but I like my private jokes. You're not even supposed to know how to run a waldo, much less know how to fight from an op-suit. Your reputation as a rough and tough fighter is piss-in-a-bladder-sack and always has been—except, of course, among us surviving Virgins." Smeegie grinned while he did something to the kzin's arm with a whizzing tool. He was remembering the gruesome outcome of the original fistfight at the officers' mess, tormentors against flatlander. A very beat-up Yankee had had time and reason to work out a careful revenge.

"I overdid it."

"Just because you gave them a week's vacation in the autodoc?" Smeegie suggested, slyly. "That was bugs in the equipment." He smirked. "An unadjusted damping coefficient." Smeegie lied well. "You know how waldos are; they aren't good at picking up an egg without breaking it. I'm fixing that, aren't I? Right now. Maybe you did them a favor. When they meet a real kzin, he's not going to have his damping coefficients adjusted down to 'play.' You make a great kzin, sir. That pair will be reminded about the consequences of flailing with their fists on that day when they meet a flesh-and-blood ratcat."

"They don't think there's going to be another war."

"And they can prove it, too, by punching out the face of the nearest flatlander who contradicts them."

"My father never liked my temper," mused Yankee. "He always told me that revenge was an option—but that no matter how sweet the revenge, revenge was *never* the end of the story. He was a programmer; to him revenge was an escape routine that called up an endless loop of violence."

"Well, go ahead and feel sorry for those two rockjacks pretending to be soldiers. I saw both fights and I'm still laughing." He paused. "You sound worried."

Clandeboye was feeling guilty that he had suspected his friend of ratting on him. Mystery was unnerving. What *did* they have on him and from what source? "I'm fertilizing my suit right now. I've been called in to Gibraltar. It sounds like I'm going to be relieved."

"Naw. Yankee, sir, you're the best Training officer we have. They've always had enough on you to court-martial you to lighthouse duty on Titan, but they never do. If you really want to worry, think about the upbeat stuff it could be. Maybe some stone-brained general thinks we might field a regiment of kzin waldos and they want to run the notion past you. Generals get ideas like that. How would you like to head up a regiment of orange waldos?" He grinned.

"Let Finagle toast God's Death!" exclaimed Yankee, horrified.

"Speaking of Finagle, you know what Finagle said; he said reality can outbid your worse nightmare every time."

"Maybe I should do some quick research on this guy. Smelly, all you Belters know each other. Tell me about General Fry. He's the name on my orders."

"Never met him. We were out there fighting. He was sitting in an office. He's an ex-goldskin. As a young man he sat at a telescope and watched for torchship exhaust-placement violations. Developed an algorithm for catching offenders. Came up through the ranks. Administrator. He was a goldskin who *liked* catching smugglers! Got a hotjet name in logistics during the second kzin assault. Cops make the best thieves. He could smuggle *anything* through a kzin blockade."

"All I know about him is that he's a womanizer. He had an affair with my cousin, then sent her off to Wunderland to be killed."

"I've never figured out why it bothers you flatlanders when a man has more than one woman, or a woman has more than one man."

"He's in Intelligence now," grumbled Yankee, changing the subject.

"And you, you paranoid, think he is onto our little caper."

"Yah."

"Maybe I'm not as impressed by ex-goldskins as you are. It has always been an old rockjack tradition to bypass Ceres's thirty percent tax with an occasional display of fancy shipping. Rockjacks get away with it all the time."

"Rockjacks get caught, too, and then the tax is one hundred percent. If I remember correctly our Commander Shimmel was an old rockjack who liked to take impulsive risks." Commander Shimmel had died some forty-four light years from home, at 59 Virginis on the far side of kzin space, taking twelve hyperships with him. And seven hundred and eighty men. The official United Nations Space Navy story was that he'd died valiantly in battle.

"That's my point," said Smeegie. "The UNSN still believes he lost all those ships because you refused to support his attack maneuver. Now if that's the best that Intelligence can do, how do you expect them to track down a little practical joke that was done invisibly?"

"Smelly, for a Belter, your systems check out green. Wisdom personified. You can be my valet in prison."

"What's to worry? They don't convert nuisances like you into spare body parts anymore. We'll send our furry ratcat in after you, sir."

"You guys would."

"Sure we would. We were there. We know what happened."

***

The loyalty of Clandeboye's comrades didn't reassure him. He shipped out to Gibraltar via Farmer's Asteroid in a little supply truck, huddled and cramped where the vegetables would be on the return trip. Belters never thought in terms of the elegant transport that a flatlander took for granted—the distances were too great. They flitted about in light, cheap ships and took the inconvenience for granted. In such a primitive can, Yankee could hardly connect with the man in himself who had piloted a hyperdrive probe on an interstellar journey to the back of the Patriarchy, farther than any man had ever reached.

After three days, and still only halfway to Gibraltar, he was a tired tourist fascinated by the truck's approach to the awesome mirrors that fed sunlight into this vegetarian's bubbleworld. The mirrors grew during sedate docking maneuvers until they filled half the starry sky. At a berth, far up the long axis-mount, he debarked with the truckers and wandered through the fallways—for the docks were not rotating like the rest of the world—until he found a reception area. He was reluctant to insert his infocomp at a terminal, to reconnect with society.

The machine put him through to military service, which read his orders. He waited. An automated voice confirmed hotel reservations at Farmer's and told him that his infocomp would be called as soon as transportation to Gibraltar was located. Click.

Three centuries ago Farmer's had been blown up like a balloon out of the substance that had once been an asteroid, then filled with people and farms. The pioneer days were long gone. He had a full day in one of the hotels, resting in the gentle centripetal gravity. It was as near as he'd been to an earthlike environment in years. The smells were right, but he could never get used to a sky paved with farms. He thought about his singing cows and dancing geese—and his cousin, Nora Argamentine, who had once lived in a real farm city in Iowa.

• Chapter 3

(2436 A.D.)

The old Patriarch had failed. The Patriarchy belonged
to whomever could restore the glory and the order. When
a father weakened, his son had the heroic duty to reclaim
his heritage. W'kkai was the son of Kzin. In a mansion of
the sprawling central metropolis of W'kkai, a magnificent
kzin, taller and heavier than an ordinary kzin warrior, had
a plan to break the blockade and conquer the galaxy under
a new dynasty. It all depended upon how he was dressed
tonight and the subtlety of his perfume.

Si-Kish wore the high brocades and lace of evening
wear that kept him warm during W'kkai's lengthy night.
Passing from his mansion's dressing room to the mezza-
nine he stole glances at himself in the gold-tinted Reflec-
tion Glass that lined the walls to the stairwell. He had no
wish to outdress the young and inexperienced Voice of
the Patriarch.

It was a good choice to be seen in the bold colors of the
Design of Zealous-Power. Lesser kzin he would have to
deal with might be impressed—if he couldn't simply avoid
them. He liked the effect of the lace fins down his sleeves.
Yet there was an austerity to this outfit, a proper respect
for the Voice. Such a fuss, these evening styles. But fashion clearly established dominance/dominated roles. In
that, they were useful. Si-Kish had no time for ranking
fights. The war with the man-beasts had grown to govern
his time and mind in an all-consuming passion.

So obsessed was he that he no longer hunted his own food, but had it brought into his office freshly killed. He let his best officers service his harem so that he might have sons. He had long been a neglectful father, relegating the training of his sons to others, even to slaves. He did not think he was a better kzin for his neglect, there was no help for it. He missed his hunt, and sometimes even missed his harem duties. Most of all he missed the sparring matches in the tournament ring with his kits.

He was not known to miss the entertainment circuit—on W'kkai, business was conducted as an afterthought of theater gossip, as bantering across the game boards, as haggling at the market stalls—sometimes even during the hunts if one could stand the group hunts where whole families turned out in colors and breeches with pompous lackeys carrying banners that did little more than scare the game. The bargaining was done with all the formality and skill of a tournament match, sometimes even with the viciousness of the killing ring.

Si-Kish lightly powdered his multi-braided mane, choosing a scent that was the barest illusion of sweat and hard work and slaughtered game. Ready, he swept down the broad stairway of his mansion's hall, his personal pride of splendidly dressed kzinti falling in around him as an escort. They had been ready long ago. A star-white limousine was floating above the driveway and ready for the journey across the city.

It was a city carefully laid out to give the illusion of space. The gravitic floater raced over grassways that blended into masking treescapes. Dikes seemed to be hills. The wandering hunting parks were designed as much to block the city from view as they were for feeding. Supply trucks which brought in thousands of animals a day for the parks arrived unobtrusively underground. When a building did reveal itself among the foliage it seemed to be the only structure within a day's hunting range. W'kkai's architects were masters of landscape art.

While they traveled, Si-Kish activated his ear/nose implant. He was checking the ongoing deployment of his special forces—a warrior to this ministry, a triad to that hierarch, warriors to a "sixteen" of the most influential patriarchs who had decided to spend the evening at home, some whom he would have to rouse out of bed. Other "ambassadors" were in the process of contacting lower-echelon nameless ones who had shown an acute aware-ness of the danger and *must* be recruited as allies. All law and policy supposedly came from the Patriarch's Voice on W'kkai. In fact laws came out of lengthy battles of influence and argument and pressure that went on for weeks. Si-Kish preferred a well-organized blitz built around the paradigm of a naval battle.

The target of his personal contingent of Heroes was the Leaping Palace.

There were many entrances to W'kkai's greatest cul-tural establishment, all hidden from each other. Even during an important dancing event, hosting hundreds, the immense Palace gave the illusion of being the abode of a single mighty kzin who was entertaining only a few select friends. The white limousine dropped them off at the sunken portico of the Lurking Entrance—and vanished on automatic.

Si-Kish led his admiral's pride past a stone column that housed an ornate blue and gold vial done in the design of the Riit seal; the Patriarch's urine had been imported for the dedication of this proud edifice and sat here now to announce to all his suzerainty over this hallowed ground. Then they were inside, marching through a frescoed corri-dor. For the last time Si-Kish briefed each of his splen-didly robed aides, sending each warrior to his private battle on some balcony. All had a special contact mission.

The dance was already in progress when the High Admiral of W'kkai parted the curtained entrance to the gallery of the Patriarch's Voice and took a seat at the Voice's table. The male attendants of His Fierceness remained attentive to the choreographed prancing of the kzinrretti. The Voice was mesmerized by their beauty. Si-Kish watched only the Voice. Quietly he removed a jeweled breast-banner that outranked one his master was wearing. He had entered a ring of combat, perhaps even a friendly sparring ring. He had to expect anything. The Voice ignored him.

It was a dangerous opponent who pretended you were not there before he struck. This elaborately dressed Hero was a powerful kzin—Si-Kish would not have relished challenging the youth physically. He was an enigma. Sometimes he was even wise. He was as apt to kill fools as he was to tolerate them, but he never challenged his best advisors, even when they told him what he did not want to hear; he tested them ruthlessly with verbal jabs and intellectual leaps. It almost made him great.

Yet the magnitude of the disaster that had befallen the Patriarchy had hardly penetrated his skull. A calamity of such immensity was beyond his comprehension. The Voice had noticed the silence of Kzin—but it was as if he had no need to listen; he had noticed the absence of trade, but as long as the warriors of Si-Kish kept the human devils at bay beyond the boundary that their ghostships could not penetrate, and as long as he could watch his kzinrretti dance, the predicament of the Patriarchy did not seem to impress him. He had been born among the elite and his weakness was overconfidence. He could not imagine the kzinti as the hunted.

At some pivotal moment such a deadly conceit could be used to overbalance and depose him—but this evening's festivities only marked a preliminary bout.

Si-Kish dared not *lose* tonight's event, but tonight there was no way he could *win* his liver's ambition. His aim was more than to depose the Patriarch's Voice; he desired the role of Patriarch itself and he expected to move the seat of power from Kzin to W'kkai. Every warrior's skill was demanded of him. Even patience.

Alert, mentally limbering himself, Si-Kish waited for the attack. The Voice would not be able to comprehend his ambition and therefore could not counter it; nevertheless he was a kzin who *enjoyed* each and every minor skirmish with the nobles he dominated. The secret of survival in his court was to let the Voice win—without ever acceding defeat. It was like having an aggressive student who liked to spar with his nameless weapons master; the master had the duty to teach the student without destroying the student or being destroyed. For now.

The kzinrretti on the terraced stage were attired in mock battle armor and leapt through a formalized battle, trained to perfection. The delicately arousing scent of estrus—being piped into the gallery by a dance master more interested in female sales than in art—clashed with the old warrior's battle sensibilities. Though he hardly approved of such perverted sexual displays as kzinrretti in armor, Si-Kish had no real problem with them intellectually; a kzinrret who could perform in the more intricate military dances produced sons with fast reflexes. Being a battle master it pained him to imagine the vivid slaughter that would befall such innocent females in a real fight— but fraudulent dances were popular and he knew enough not to interrupt the Voice's rapt attention.

Overtly the Voice had his eye on a lithe specimen and would probably buy her for his harem—to the vast financial advantage of Dance-Master.

Covertly the Voice was preparing to knock Si-Kish off balance.

Suddenly, the Patriarch's Voice tipped his head to Si-Kish while his eyes remained on stage. "That small one is very quick," he breathed. "I'm struck by the shape of her nose, so long and arrogant." She was removing her silver armor, which was a silly thing to do in the middle of a battle, but it made her the center of attention. The flavor of estrus in the air subtly increased. "Such power!" the Voice exclaimed.

"We could send her out against the man-beasts," said Si-Kish in the mocking tense of the Hero's Tongue. It was a riposte to redirect the conversation to military matters where Si-Kish was far more prepared than the Voice would ever be.

The Voice growled disparagement with a slight flap of his fanlike ears, turning the riposte to his advantage. "You promised me a plan of action tonight. Is that your best device, to send tiny beauties out to their deaths in ornamental light armor?"

Si-Kish flipped the table top to a convenient angle for the Voice's eyes and entered a code. "My second best plan, in case our kzinrretti fail in their bravery, is to go ahead with the building of five hundred and twelve hyperdrive warships."

For a moment, off balance, the Voice's eye fell from his favorite kzinrret. "The mechanics of the drive have been mastered already?"

"No. All is as it was. But we cannot wait. Time is critical. We already know enough of hyperspace to design the hyperdrive mountings. When the ships are ready, we will have motors in production. Better to have the ships ready and no motors than to have the motors ready with no ships."

Choew-Aide, immense, taller and more ponderous even than the Voice, had been scanning through the war plans like a weapons carrier selecting an appropriate weapon for his waiting lord. Other aides activated other screens. The Voice continued to admire his favored kzinrret. In time Choew found what might be a flaw in the war scenario and whispered to his master.

"Your warships have a strange design. Lean," commented the Voice. The implication was that they would not be able to fight a sustained battle.

Si-Kish countered with the fable of Reoll-Riit and the sthondat. The kzin warrior, who was as swift as all Riits of fable, could resupply himself from a distant waterhole. The sthondat—massive, powerful, but slow—had to hoard his water within his own body. In the fable, victory went to the swift. The implication was that ships faster than light could be resupplied quickly. A subluminal kzin warship retrofitted with a hypershunt motor would not fight as well as a W'kkai warship *designed* to strike from hyperspace.

The aides continued to search their flatplates for flaws in the major plan. They concentrated on the lightning assault against Procyon and Barnard's Starbase. With human control of the hyperwave and strangulation of kzinti trade, was there enough man-beast spoor to make intelligent strategy? How would W'kkai be defended during the assault? Si-Kish was expecting the UNSN to pull in their ships to regroup against the planned W'kkai attack—but could he *depend* upon that?

The aides moved around the gallery almost as if they were on a tournament mat as they consulted each other and formed defensive groupings against the High Admiral of W'kkai. On the stage the kzinrretti were now floating through a multicolored dream sequence. The Voice paid no attention; he was leading a more interesting foray.

Si-Kish had an easy answer for everything—the lace fins of his waistcoat gestured in emphasis and sometimes in mock parry—it had all been thrashed out long ago.

The Admiral had asked the same questions of himself until the answers shone—but he let the Voice's staff feel that they were giving him a good workout. What they didn't understand was that the attack against the man-beasts was a feint. It was an opening gambit not meant to defeat anyone.

Neither human nor kzin understood what Si-Kish had winnowed from his assiduous analysis. The man-beasts were artificially strong. The Patriarchy was artificially weak. The purpose of his fleet was not to conquer the humans in a bloody interstellar battle but to *reestablish* the Patriarchy's nervous system and trade. *Then* the galaxy's Heroes could turn to crush the monkeys and reduce them to useful slavery.

In the middle of a particularly tail-thumping debate, the spotlights swung to the Voice's gallery. It was time for the assembled multitude of male kzinti to rise. They rose as one. Two petite kzinrretti rushed in through the balcony curtains—his favorite dancer and another—placing a magnificent helmet upon his head. He stood—the Voice of the Patriarch for all to see. Then the lights dimmed upon him but brightened everywhere in all of the galleries, allowing the dominated kzinti standing there to be *seen* by their Voice as they gifted their master with the slash-across-face salute. The kzinrretti, half his size, were at his feet, and he was tickling his favorite behind the ears, contented by the accolade of his subject males.

The mood of discussion and contest was over, as suddenly as it had begun, broken in the middle of an important argument. The Voice remained pensive under his grandiose helmet. When the entertainment resumed he watched kzinrretti stalk across a stage of fog boiling from witches' pots. He glanced at Si-Kish. "Let me watch." He was no longer interested in war. He brought out his seal and electronically imprinted all of the programs with his approval. He had established to his satisfaction that the conflict was in competent hands. Let the hierarchy of hierarchs vex over the details.

That was *the* breakthrough for Si-Kish. The rest of the evening could be conducted as a mop-up operation. He tuned his ear/nose implant to the high command codes and asked for a status report while his eyes watched the kzinrretti stalk a brilliantly feathered beast through the fog. The online reports came in, sector status at a time. The greatest resistance was coming from the Production Hierarch. An amused warrior admiral preened his ears. The geezers in production would be balking at abandoning their standards, some of which were thousands of years old.

Quietly he backed out of the gallery, into the corridors of the Leaping Palace, still listening to what were essentially battle reports. He left the Palace by the Northern High Entrance, feeling the need for a walk alone. It had been three Kzin days since sunset and the air was frigid. His breath steamed. The hair around his mouth frosted. Even some snowflakes were drifting. He passed through a narrow-walled street of cut stone laid out like a canyon, night-flowers blooming through the cracks. He was not yet willing to call for transportation.

He could go anywhere in the city to reinforce his minions, but he should probably go into the catacombs of the Production Hierarch and bring his full prestige to bear. His whole plan for W'kkai's dominance of the Patriarchy depended upon the rapid deployment of *new* standards throughout a Patriarchy so starved and desperate for hyperdrive technology that they would abandon their age-old commitment to Kzin technology.

Standards *never* supported the most advanced technology, and standards which could only be promulgated at 80 percent of the speed of light were *lifetimes* behind what could be done. Kzin was crippled in that its power depended upon standards that were not good enough to fight the man-beasts. W'kkai had no such constraints. With a hyperdrive fleet it could promote its technology to Meerowsk, to Hrooshpith-Pithcha, even to Ch'Aakin or Warhead, faster than Kzin could keep up. And where the center of trade was, there would sit the new Patriarch.

A daunting dream—with a single suck-fly in Si-Kish's ear.

W'kkai's physicists had not yet built their first hypershunt motor.

The High Admiral hated to channel all his hopes through one kzin. The failure of that one kzin was too dangerous. And it galled him in the liver where it hurt that his one kzin, Grraf-Nig, wasn't a known W'kkaikzin but an outer barbarian who, the Fanged God help him, needed a valet to dress him properly and, worse, whose loyalty to the reigning Patriarch was set into him with the mindlessness of a berserker to whom distant Kzin was some kind of mythical warrior's Valhalla.

The simple-minded Grraf-Nig would never be persuaded to believe in a power shift from Kzin to W'kkai. Never. Not by wit. Not by cunning. Not by torture.

You had to be *of* W'kkai—belong to a family that had been grossly tithed for a thousand years by the Patriarchs of Kzin, be master of a colorful art that balanced ferocity, be *superior*—to understand Si-Kish's ambition.

• Chapter 4

(2436 A.D.)

The lights flickered. General Lucas Fry's eye was distracted from the tiny framed face for a moment. Why were they switching over to Gibraltar's emergency power source? But before he had time to fret, the regular power returned. Then he had to reach out and catch the miniature, which had drifted away from him. He did so with the economical ease of a born Belter who never made unnecessary gestures in space. But there was a thoughtfulness in his reach—as if to snare all that he had ever lost. It had been her only vanity to have commissioned a tiny painting of herself as a gift to him before she shipped out for the Battle of Wunderland.

Just another ship's crew missing in action so long ago. It had been sixteen years since the rout of the kzinti at Alpha Centauri. Had it really been so long? He still remembered the scent of her full flatlander hair, the little auburn ringlet she pulled before asking one of her impudent questions. Missing-in-Action. He thought he had forgotten her—deaths are forgotten in a war with so many deaths. Now he had been reminded.

An item in a report had been bothering General Fry for weeks.

It was just a fragment from the frozen memory of a cadaverous kzin warship that had drifted aimlessly in Centauri space to be discovered only recently for intelligence analysis. Perhaps, if it had not been for his unhealed love, he would not even have noticed this trivial detail buried in a routine document. Gibraltar's computer had long ago broken some of the old kzinti war code. The deciphered minutiae, quaint and chauvinistic, read like a commendation list given by Julius Caesar to his centurions, useless to any practical reader who found it.

It praised kzin warriors—all Heroes had to be honored for their deeds, even in the middle of a desperate battle. That was the way of war: take a moment here and there to praise vanished warriors for their immortal deeds of courage, which would go unremembered soon enough.

That kind of detail was all that the Gibraltar team had been able to abstract from the records of the wreck. The really sensitive information had been prudently expunged during the death-throes of the warship. Supply lists, orders, codes, command lines, strategy, contingency plans— all had been erased. But true warriors did not erase the deeds of revered warriors. Warriors sang the songs of their Heroes from skeletal mouths buried in trenches and the floating hulks of war. Heroes were immortal—so Heroes believed.

It was heroism that had caught the attention of General Fry in one sudden adrenaline rush . . . an ambiguous line in the role of commendations referred to the intrepid capture of a UNSN scoutship . . . and the capture of a single, unnamed prisoner.

Can a heroine rise from her grave? Hope kept jumping out of the strangest places. There was no hope, of course. A man could deal with Killed-in-Action. There was no way to deal with Missing-in-Action.

Only one UNSN ship was unaccounted for in Centauri space—the hyperdrive scoutship *Shark*. General Fry had a moment of grief, a dropped tear on the report. Nora had been the *Shark*'s observer. He thought he had forgotten her by now. He thought it strange that he should still remember her so vividly. Until today, he hadn't looked at her miniature in years, but he had known exactly where he had hidden it from his latest girlfriend.

His emotions had their priorities all wrong, he knew. It was the capture of an operational hyperdrive vessel by kzinti warcraft sixteen years ago that was his primary intellectual concern. Had this been a brief kzinti victory, wiped out by the carnage of the battle that followed the capture? Or had the UNSN's superluminal scout somehow made its way back to the techcenters of the Patriarchy? A missing soldier was irrelevant compared with the terrifying vision of a hyperdrive-equipped kzinti naval armada. Still, uppermost in his mind were thoughts of a charming woman and schemes to hold her again in his arms.

"Major Yankee Clandeboye to see you, sir!" said the sergeant's voice from the speaker tacked to the bulkhead wall.

The appointment was for the hour—and would have been scheduled days earlier but physics permitted no hypershunt travel this close to a sun. A glance at his chronometer showed ten seconds to the hour. "Send him down. Better not take the usual route; the grunts are moving machinery."

Clandeboye was a find—even though the search to uncover suitable candidates for this mission placed him a distant last in a field of twelve. General Fry reordered the list to place him as first choice. Clandeboye alone was the cousin of Lieutenant Nora Argamentine. He must have known her well because it was his recommendation that had taken Nora off clerical duties on Earth and sent her out to the asteroids for combat training with Intelligence.

The old note, resurrected from the archives, had been ambivalent—a reluctance to recommend her for dangerous duty was in it, but also an intense admiration. (Nora

had probably done some of her blatant arm-twisting on
that one. Fry could almost hear her voice speaking to Yankee: "I want that assignment! You're going to do this for
me." Then coyly, while she fiddled with her ringlet, "I'll
be good at it! You'll be proud that you recommended me!")

The machine expert that had done the personnel search
had placed Major Clandeboye dead last for good reasons.
His record was uneven. It was clear he would never make
it above major in spite of his talents. But none of these
faults appeared to be fatal. Lucas Fry was a master
machiavellian who never assumed that he was dealing
with perfect people. Strengths were essential but weaknesses provided the pressure points from which to manipulate a man.

His record:

The *measurements* of Major Clandeboye's administra-
tive accomplishments gave him high marks but the officers he worked for were hostile in their appraisal.

There was a peculiar mutiny charge against Major
Clandeboye two years before the end of the war, in Sep-
tember 2431. It had never gone to court. The evidence in
his ship's automatic log was damning—clearly he had refused to carry out direct orders—but none of his superior
officers remained alive to testify against him and the survivors of the Virgo Volunteers he brought back with him
had flatly refused to do so.

Even though Major Clandeboye had mutinied, his
automatic log suggested that he had fought brilliantly *after* Commander Shimmel's fleet had been destroyed and
it was too late for him to carry out his support role.

Major Clandeboye was under probation for a recent
fistfight unbecoming of an officer.

For footnotes to the official file, General Fry always
tapped the gossip mills. The major was rumored to be a
stiff-necked moralist. No, he would *not* approve of a

curmudgeon general having an infatuated dalliance with a young lieutenant half his age while he abused his power to give her what she wanted. (She had wanted danger.) The trouble with moralists, who were always right, was that they weren't always good at taking orders that disagreed with their consciences. Moralists were hotbeds of mutiny. They took their orders from a higher authority.

The number one rule for manipulating a moralist was to use him as a channel to interview his "higher authority," then to speak to him in the language of that authority.

Why did this misfit even stay in the UNSN? That was the key to working with him.

The man had written articles for the extremely conservative *Belter Factnet* and one ranting article for the datarag of the Isolationist Party of Wunderland. Fry could understand why his views had annoyed his fellow officers. With his temperament he might have become a flatlander media firebrand and gone far with the unpopularity of his opinions, but as a military man it was suicide to be so outspoken. However sympathetic Fry was to those who feared a kzinti resurgence, he had no use for the young major's bluntness in deriding the patrols and the peacekeeping.

Clandeboye belonged to the small minority of officers who believed that the kzinti had *not* been trounced in the recent war and would return with a terrible ferocity—a preposterous belief while mankind's hypershunt ships patrolled kzin space with impunity. The UN's Amalgamated Regional Militia had imposed a three-hundred-year peace on a fractiously warring mankind, until mass-man hardly understood war, and the navy in alliance with ARM had no reason to believe that they couldn't do the same with the kzinti. Everyone, except maybe Clandeboye and the Wunderlanders, assumed that this was exactly what would happen.

The major's viewpoint was preposterous, certainly, but his speculation about the strength and determination of a humbled Patriarchy was an alternate scenario that *should* be taken seriously. No harm in that. Hannibal's march through Europe's Alps had also been preposterous from a Roman point of view. The generals at Pearl Harbor had rejected the preposterous notion that the blips on their radar could be Japanese warcraft from a disappeared fleet.

Fry was coming to the conclusion that the way to this miscreant's heart was to give him help with his eccentric ideas. (With friendly guidance, of course.) Wasn't this pariah a man in desperate need of allies? Fry would, of course, stay in the shadows of the bunker while he played his multiple games. It was prudent to cultivate officers inclined to plan for a resurgent Patriarchy. A card up the old sleeve. Cover all bets. A Clandeboye with power might even be useful in the Belter effort to take out General Buford Early, a flatlander who needed a little cement in his jets.

What about mutiny? At first sight this disgraceful mutiny thing seemed to disqualify Clandeboye completely from a sensitive mission. But the more Fry investigated the inquest, the more fascinated he became. Men are loyal to an officer for a reason. The inquest had not found out why. Clandeboye might carry the psychological nature of a mutineer—a man who always thought he was being put upon—but none of the men who sided with him even remotely fitted that profile. There were other aberrations. It was highly irregular that the inquest had come to the conclusion of mutiny, had placed that in the major's record—and then refused to prosecute him. Here was a rich arsenal of weapons available to Fry, stacked both against Clandeboye and his enemies. It was a situation that could be worked both ways.

What particularly attracted Fry was his candidate's

brilliance under fire. The man could improvise against the kzinti faster than a computer. That was rare. There was no record at all of Shimmel's brilliance.

When all items in the major's record were weighed against Lucas Fry's purpose, the fisticuff fight was the blackest mark against Clandeboye. These fights had become too common of late, as if young soldiers had taken out-of-control kzinti kits as their role models. Why admire the ferocity of the enemy you had just defeated? Modern youth was becoming incomprehensible. Human males of Fry's generation, even as children, had *not* settled their differences by physical combat. In space, with a vacuum on the other side of the bulkhead, such behavior was deadly. It seemed that war had been short-circuiting the morals of the young; fist makes right, it told them. So Clandeboye liked to fight, did he? Well, he could, and would, be nailed to the rack and stretched for that one.

To Lucas Fry it was self-evident that the ability to clobber someone did not make one right. If men had destroyed the kzinti war machine, that was a matter of survival, not of rightness. Fry had gone into the war as an adult, already knowing that. But the younger men and women had seen the war won by force and not by philosophy. They did not have the long view of history. Force seemed dominant to them; they had been born into it.

How does one pass one's wisdom on to the children? (To men as mature as Fry, 66, men as young as Clandeboye, 47, were still children.)

His parents, he reflected, had been horrified when he left the goldskins for the military. They had tried to teach him that the kzin could be handled nonviolently. They had implored him to study man's history to understand where violence led. He had ignored them. Now he had his own wisdom to teach—force must be balanced with compassion. But he had no children of his own to listen.

They had been killed in the war. He had only his cadre of young officers.

He wasn't going to let Clandeboye's temper disqualify him. A man's weaknesses could be turned to advantage. Weakness was non-Medusan—if a man could look at weakness directly, he became strong; if he dared look at his failings only obliquely through a mirror, he became ossified. Fry was sure enough of his role as a martinet to believe that he could teach the sons of Zeus and Danae to face their Medusas without a mirror.

The heavy bulkhead door swung in, enough to let the sergeant's head through. "We found a way down past the kitchens. I didn't let your boy get lost."

In person, Major Yankee Clandeboye turned out to be a rumpled flatlander who had a flatlander's unbalanced way of giving a snappy salute in freefall. He was slightly awkward and ill-at-ease. He did not have the charisma of a commanding officer. He had too much hair; it even covered his ears. No matter—one did not judge flatlanders by their size, color of skin, grace, or cleanliness. They had other virtues.

"You'll be wondering why I hauled you in from Egeria. Convince me that you are the right man for my mission and I have a high enough priority rating to get your transferal processed immediately. We're in Intelligence here; I suspect you already know that."

"Sir, I'm happy in Training," drawled Yankee with a quizzical grin.

Fry appraised his recruit. This Yankee was going to be a man who sniffed his soup before he drank it. "A negotiator, are you? Why would you be happy in Training, for Finagle's sake?"

"I don't see a more important job than training elite fighters. With all due respect to ARM, sir, I think we did a very sloppy job in the war. We won more by wild good luck than with steady competence. Chuut-Riit was assassinated—Buford's what-the-hell shot-in-the-dark. The Outsiders happened by at just the right time to sell us the decisive hyperdrive. By chance we woke up a Slaver from his billion year sleep just in time to disorganize the kzinti before our attack. That's a lot of luck."

"In war one seizes luck and uses it!"

"Agreed. But after the Battle of Wunderland it was thirteen years of slugging. Our luck was dry and our leadership mediocre, begging your pardon, sir."

"Have you read Chumeyer's *Tactics of Interstellar War*?"

"Of course Chumeyer was a genius! He demolished the Patriarch's supply lines and communications brilliantly. Yet his book is already obsolete. That was the last war! Chumeyer had hyperdrive ships and surprise against lumbering kzinti transports who had yet to hear about the Battle of Wunderland! We owe the war to Chumeyer. Yet his victories were in interstellar space. What about the assaults on kzinti strongholds? We have to go back to the Great War of 1916 to find parallels to such stupidity. Many heroes; staggering casualties; ill-trained leaders. For the next war we dare not depend on luck. We'll need better discipline, much better discipline. We'll need planning and a radically new strategy. It's the training we do now that will forge the navy we'll need sooner than any of you veterans think."

"That from a man who starts fistfights he can't win?"

"I didn't start that fight, sir. I raised my voice."

Fry was grinning. He knew how to hit a man hard without raising a finger. "And, of course, they hit you first?"

"Yes, sir."

"You're very good at training, I hear."

"I think so, sir."

"I have a better job for you."

"There isn't a better job, sir."

"What's this? You're going to refuse to take orders from me?"

Yankee knew very well that the general was referring to mutiny. It was a delicate point and he hesitated, beginning an answer he didn't have the words to finish—so he started over. He was damned if he was going to kiss a Belter's butt. "Yes, sir. I do what is in the best interest of the navy."

Fry garumphed in his throat. "In that case, I'll have to clock you in the crotch to persuade you. Everything is fair in a fisticuffs fight, right? Are you ready? Stick up your dukes. How would you like to rescue your cousin?"

Clandeboye had to repeat that last sentence to himself. He was dumbfounded. "Nora?" Even after he said her name, he was disbelieving, checking his memory frantically for other cousins he might have forgotten.

"We have information that Lieutenant Argamentine may have been captured."

"Is she alive?"

"We don't know. She was captured with her hyperdrive scout. We'd really like to find out what happened to it."

"Where is it?"

"We don't know. Your assignment might involve a tour of duty inside the Patriarchy."

"I don't think anyone in the navy would trust me inside the Patriarchy."

Lucas Fry smiled enigmatically while he rubbed his hand through the strip of white brush topping his side-shaved skull. "The men you brought back alive trust you."

This conversation was unnerving Clandeboye. "But do *you* trust me, sir?"

"Of course not! What I'm interested in is the look on your enemies' faces when you come back with evidence that the kzinti are building an armada of hyperdrive dreadnoughts."

Clandeboye sucked in his breath. "We don't know *what* happened to Nora's ship, sir?"

"But we have to find out, don't we?"

"Yes, sir." Yankee was too stunned to say more.

"So it's *yes* then, is it? You start today." Immensely pleased with himself, General Fry brought out the miniature of Nora Argamentine. "And, if we can, we'll try to find her, too. If our heroine is alive we can't leave her out in the boondocks with only ratcats for company. Ungentlemanly. Soldiers take care of each other."

• Chapter 5

(2436 A.D.)

Yankee Clandeboye had nostalgic waves of emotion on his return to interstellar duty even though he was stationed at a different star and the war had been over for three years. He was ever the provincial flatlander gawking at the new sights. Then it had been the brilliant white dwarf companion beside Procyon in the sky of We Made It, now it was Beta Centauri floating beside Alpha from the viewports of Tiamat. Only a flatlander connected by megayear ties to Earth would be awed to be a tourist in a binary system.

The Wundervolk, having suffered during the war as slaves of the kzinti, treated him differently than had the crashlanders—they carried their slave history as a kind of martyrdom that allowed them to feel they had won the war all by themselves. They almost resented the presence of UNSN personnel. He could sense it in the way they handled his requests for information. The aloofness of Interworld Space Commissioner Markham was typical.

Yankee's UNSN Intelligence team were all Belters and they had set up shop in Alpha Centauri's Serpent Swarm, on the asteroid Tiamat where his men were comfortable because it had originally been tunneled and tamed by Belter colonists. Yankee promised himself a side trip to more earthlike Wunderland but there was work to do first, sorting through the wreckage of kzinti warships, checking the reasoning of other teams but with eyes primed for a different theme.

On his tenth day in Tiamat, in a mood of angry frustration, he ran into an old crashlander friend from the era of his Virgo mission. The man was unmistakable, a seven-foot-tall albino, slender with almost skeletal limbs stooping in an archway that was too small for him.

"Brobding!" He wasn't sure it was his friend Brobding Shaeffer—all crashlanders looked alike to him, and when the pale eyes stared at him without comprehension, he was sure he had made a mistake until a sudden smile cupped the large nose.

"Yankee! Didn't recognize you—all flatlanders look alike to me! I thought you were rotting in irons!"

"They didn't know how to pin my sins on me!"

"Finagle is sending you on another wild chase?" The Virgo mission had jumped off from the naval yards of Procyon's We Made It. Yankee remembered the underground warrens of Crashlanding City and had become fond of his albino mechanics and the tall willowy women who liked to touch a real flatlander. In those days of war, not so very long ago, the nervous crashlanders took very good care of the soldiers who defended them. "Where to this time?"

"You could call it a wild chase; I hope not as far as the nether regions of Virgo."

"Then you like it here among our Wunderland hosts?"

"Not really," mused Yankee ruefully. "They're all so sure they won the war single-handed—don't seem to appreciate the part Sol and We Made It played in their liberation."

"But they make good Vurguuz."

"Haven't tried it. Hear that it's like a hand grenade that sneaks up on you with a sugar coating."

"I know a place. It has authentic antique Landholder

artifacts on the walls glorifying the good old days before
the invasion when Landholders were Landholders and
the volk, respectful."

That was how they came to find themselves in one of
Tiamat's after-hours trunkshuppen, sipping Vurguuz and
reminiscing about old times. The crashlanders had fought
the war from a different perspective than the Wundervolk.
Unknown to man or kzin the outpost world of We Made
It had been settled inside the nominal kzinti frontier.
When the small We Made It colony woke up 300 years
later to the fact that they were behind the lines of an
interstellar war, they appreciated allied comrades in arms
like Major Yankee Clandeboye. The camaraderie was still
there.

Eventually the talk, now slightly voluble, turned to the
kzinti.

The Patriarchy had once probed Procyon, Yankee
informed Brobding conspiratorially (drawing upon his new
Intelligence sources). The probes returned with a negative report about a nasty F5 star sixteen times as brilliant
as Kzin, almost a subgiant, its only usable planet having
an axis in the orbital plane which made for unacceptable
seasonal violence. The planet was uninhabitable.

"They fielded smarter probes than ours," the
crashlander commented wryly. "When was this?"

"Long ago. At about the time we humans were questioning the validity of our early interplanetary efforts.
I've read some of the old texts." He sipped his Vurguuz
from a goblet blown from green glass. "The wisemen of
the time were sure that an interstellar civilization would
be benevolent." He began to grin. "Sometimes the
wisemen were monkey-arrogant in the belief that
humanity was alone in the universe and invulnerable
behind the light-speed barrier. You should read their
proofs that we are alone in the universe. All of these

proofs seem to be based on the statistical analysis of a sample of one."

They both had a laugh at the expense of their naive ancestors.

Yankee continued. "Fortunately for you guys, the frontier kzin lost interest in Procyon—or your original slowboat would have walked into a kzinti outpost hungry for skinny slaves to brush their fur."

"Lucky for you, you mean," retorted Brobding, trying to fit his legs under the little table. "What if the Outsiders had arrived to sell their hyperdrive tech to the *kzinti!*"

It was the luck of the draw for the crashlanders. When the Conquest Warriors attacked the fourth human slowboat bound for We Made It, their exploring warfleet had already bypassed Procyon. Strangely they had never probed Centauri, a binary that promised to be barren. There were so many stars—and a sub-light culture moves slowly. The kzinti literally stumbled into the resource and slave-rich Alpha Centauri system. A shock to both sides.

Yankee was very mellow as he twirled the stem of his goblet, staring at the luminous play of light on the bubble flaws in the glass. "But you haven't told me why you are here. I thought you were happy wenching in the warrens of Crashlanding City? Here you can't even kiss a woman. You'd need two of them, one standing on the back of the other!"

"Then I'll have to settle for a kzinrret—if they are willing to stoop down to kiss me! That's not so far from the truth. I'm here trying to make some sense out of kzinti gravitic designs." Brobding Shaeffer was a hypershunt engineer. He did not have any formal training. Hyperspace technology had come so suddenly to We Made It that anyone with talent at understanding the weird technology had advanced rapidly in Stefan Brozik's organization. There were no degrees in hyperspace engineering.

"What's a hyperspace illiterate like you doing trying to understand gravitics? You don't have any training in gravitics, either."

Brobding laughed. "Maybe that's why Brozik sent me. Kzinti gravitics is hairy stuff. Living through the cloistered life of orthodox physics schooling seems to pile up sand dunes that my esteemed colleagues can't seem to wade out of. I'm the wind that scours the dunes down to bedrock."

"Ah. The Devil's Bellows." The crashlanders had dozens of names for their winds.

"Yah."

"So you're here sticking your screwdriver into the various gravitic devices that the kzinti left lying around, are you? If you learn anything, tell me. I've become a kind of military historian. I'm raking over the coals of the war to figure out why we lost so many battles when we had the decisive weapon. It always seems to turn on the fact that their gravitic ships were able to operate to advantage inside the hyperspace singularity."

"Brozik thinks so, too. He's been building hyperdrive experimental ships equipped with salvaged kzinti gravitic drives."

"I could have used one of those! Hypershunt or no, try running from a ratcat who is closing in on you at sixty gees! Scares the be-jesus out of you!" Yankee had done space battle with kzinti warriors at light-minute distances which was as close as he ever wanted to get. "I hear the kzinti drive is a murphy to duplicate."

"It's the energy containment."

"Not much to learn at Centauri," mused Yankee. "Wunderland physics went to hell during the war. The Scholarium was decimated. First the kzin. Then ARM. Wunderland lost five of its top physicists during the assault on Down."

"Brozik told me to talk to the experts. I was thinking of chatting it up with some of the resident kzin. Must be some of their gravitic technicians left around."

"You're braver than I am." Talking to a kzin whisker-to-whisker was unthinkable to Yankee.

The crashlander was grinning now, his large nose about to fall into the devil's charm of his smile. "If you are into pub-crawling we could move on to Tigertown."

The hero of the Battle of 59 Virginis paled. Tiamat's Tigertown was kzin territory, only nominally under human law. It was even policed by kzin. Not a place for the innocent.

There should have been no kzinti left in the Wunderland system; kzinti do not surrender. But wars only laugh at the rules of heroes. There are always survivors. A culture based on strict rules of bravery has its disgraced combatants, its failures, its eccentrics. Kzinti were wounded—to recover consciousness in human hospitals. Young kzin, who considered the Centauri system as home, had taken over the families of their heroic departed patriarchs. Kdaptists, deranged by humiliation, were using Centauri as a safe haven in which to formulate a new religion. There were kzinti who knew that however hard life was under human domination, they dared not go home.

Many of them had no home to go to. Some had found a niche on Wunderland—some skill, a human contact, the hope of reconquest kept them there. But most, upon release from the POW camps, had collected among their kind on Tiamat in a volume of the asteroid that had been outfitted for kzin during their fifty-three-year rule of the Serpent Swarm. Tigertown.

"Come on," said Brobding, "I know a place."

Yankee had always liked to pub-crawl with his albino friend. But this wasn't the maze underground of

Crashlanding City where twists and turns led to secret pleasures known only to the natives. He hesitated. He was afraid of the kzin. He wanted to stay in his seat. He had led the team that built a waldo kzin and he knew exactly the strength of a kzin and his temperament and quickness in a fight, and he had teleoped that simulated kzin against two humans, nearly killing them while all the time restraining the force he had at his command.

Brobding was looking at Yankee now, waiting, the minutest smile on his face. "When you see a grin, just apologize quickly."

Yankee got up and followed. The two of them, alone, were going into Tigertown. *Why am I doing this?* he thought—but couldn't stop himself.

• Chapter 6

(2436 A.D.)

The hour was quiet and the main trophy room almost empty. A lone kzin snatched a vatach from the snack cage, beheaded it with his teeth and squeezed the fresh blood into a cup with a dash of spiced brain sauce. It was just a steel cup—the splendid golden goblets were gone. He tapped his tail. He sat by himself under the mounted gagrumpher head which had once given some kzin a challenging six-legged chase back in the good old days when the huge Wunderland estates were governed by kzinti rule. The trophy was groomed with an oil that made it smell alive.

Hwass-Hwasschoaw was forever trying to get himself repatriated—to Kzin preferably. He had nothing else on his mind. This rodent hole in an asteroid was driving him crazy; the disability from his healed wound, its pain, was driving him crazy. It wasn't easy to be stranded in an alien land after losing a war. His family had always been in the Secret Service of the Eye of the Patriarch; he had messages from his grandfather and his father that it was his sacred duty to deliver to the Patriarch. He had his own messages to report. And he was stranded. At the least he had to get back to W'kkai, where his father's network would still be in place.

Hwass also carried the added burden of Kdapt's teachings, his own self-imposed burden, important teachings which he must spread to the stars to ensure the victory of the kzin over this race favored by God. Who but Kdapt-Captain had understood the defeat at Wunderland and the path that must be traveled henceforth?

The gagrumpher trophy was not a good replacement for Leiter Obensim Frankhausen, who should be up there staring down at his masters. He had been captured during a kzinti foray into the Serpent's Swarm. Times were deplorable!

Long ago, while Tiamat was being sieged from within by maddened man-slaves, the Club had shredded its mounted guerrilla leader, Obensim Frankhausen, disposing of him hastily down the excrement turbines. The Club had only survived because of the need for a holding area to confine kzinti prisoners. It had been the logical place to put them. As times mellowed and honor agreements were accepted by released kzin, the Club became the nucleus of the future Tigertown.

Leiter Obensim Frankhausen was never replaced in the Club's main display room, although there was now a superbly stuffed kz'eerkt discreetly located in the urinal, where it served the same purpose. The grinning kz'eerkt was frozen in the act of reaching from the branch of a fruit tree for a luscious persimmon. These days it was affectionately referred to as "Ulf Reichstein Markham," never in the presence of humans.

After an endless groveling petition to Markham, in which he'd had to concentrate to suppress his lip twitching to the point where he sometimes couldn't even think straight, Hwass had been granted passage on a UNSN ghostship to Kzin. A hope since dashed. Markham had been a devious sore, more devious than any other monkey this miserable kzin had ever dealt with, frustrating, enraging. Finally Hwass had extracted passage from him by accepting an exchange offer that seemed to work.

It didn't make sense—he was to deliver a message of

goodwill and peace to the Patriarch—but it was something he *could* do. Still, the Ferocious Father would wiggle his ears in amazement to hear that humans were offering subservience to the Patriarch and tribute to seal the offer. Before the offer had been withdrawn, he had been hoping the Patriarch could take such a joke calmly and not execute the messenger!

Peace from Markham!—a man who had harassed and slaughtered kzin all his adult life, who had been the abject slave of a thrintun, and who now treacherously professed to admire kzinti discipline. The monkeys not only lied, they didn't even understand that their lies were transparent. He had put up with it out of loyalty to the Patriarch. So much humiliation, now suddenly for naught!

Vegetable-eaters beneath dignity, these humans—and yet the God was on their side.

It was a kind of torture-by-false-word, unknown to an honest well-bred kzin of integrity. These men told a lie to kindle hope—then layered on a new lie to douse the hope. Such low treachery and teasing and lying continued like malicious play without rules. They tortured in teams. As soon as repatriation passage had been granted by Markham, the arrangements made, the humiliating medical tests completed, another monkey with the unpronounceable name of Yankee Clandeboye had appeared to cancel his papers.

Markham had apologized. He pleaded "higher authority." Evidently monkey field commanders did not have field authority. Would the endless play repeat—promise and then betrayal? "Bullfighting," they called it; tease with banderillas and lance until the bull was weak enough for the cowardly matador to kill it—a game that only kz'eerkt could enjoy, because they had no self-respect. Tonight God required special supplication. God must be a masochist to so love these hairless wonders.

He didn't mind delays. Heroic journeys were always delayed by hardship. He belonged to a race that was impulsive at short range but patient over distance. A Hero was made steadfast by the agonies of trial. If he couldn't carry out his duty, he could pass that duty on to his sons. If his Kdapt revelations reached only clogged noses, his sons would still be able to smell. But it wasn't in his nature to deal with the duplicity, lying, inefficiency and inconsistency of monkeys to whom he had shown his throat in defeat. They brought out the irrational choleric in him. It displeased him that such creatures should have been given the true form.

There was no help for it. It was God's way of speaking to kzin in the Dominant Tense. One could only reply in the Dominated Tense. Truth was truth. An earlier generation of kzinti had been equally shocked to discover that Kzinhome was not the center of the universe.

Killing Markham was no solution. He was Dominant. It was God's challenge to Hwass that he find other means to circumvent this man's treachery.

The Club-Master approached him. "Hwass, honored Dominance."

Hwass-Hwasschoaw growled acknowledgment. He was not in a good mood.

"The humans are here."

"Here? Throw them out!"

"Sire." Club-Master stood his ground. It was clear that he was not going to obey this impulsive order.

"Then keep them confined below. In the holding room. Who is it this time? That breakable pink pole who would steal our knowledge of gravity? He's become like a tigripard after the sheep." Hwass had grown up in the sheep ranching territories of Wunderland.

Club-Master spoke in the most respectful tense. "Not

to contradict your Dominance, but they have requested only drink. They are drunk already."

Hwass swiveled on his attendant. "Learn that they lie with their every breath! They are not honest warriors like you and me! They are weak in gravitics and seek to improve their skills so that they can kill more kzin. Their ghostships do not operate near the mass of stars and it is only the gravitic superiority of our warcraft that keeps them at bay. They control only *interstellar* space. We still dominate the stellar realms. I have spoken with this man before."

"There are two. One is the lean monkey known to you. The other is a Major Yankee Clandeboye." Club-Master had a hard time with the name because it did not translate properly into the hisses and sibillated snarls of the Hero's Tongue.

"That one?" Now the play was clear to Hwass. To obtain his freedom he would not only have to deliver a message of peace to Kzinhome, which would cost him nothing (maybe), but he must also act as a hunt guide in the hills of gravity, which would cost him dearly. What else would they demand—his hide for a rug? "Bring them here," he said reluctantly.

"What shall I offer them to drink?"

"Banana pulp mixed with orange juice!" At this reply, Club-Master's membranous ears went into shock. Hwass remembered that this servant had no sense of humor. "They will take kahlua with cream. Charge them triple." He tapped his furless tail three times.

When Club-Master departed via the dropway, Hwass surveyed the great room to see that it was in presentable order. Much kzin carousing went on here and it wasn't always tidy, but the present hour was a quiet one with few celebrants. These simians could be entertained with some propriety. The Hwasschoaw family still retained some of the more elegant manners of the inner worlds, spot-worn like the rugs but serviceable.

He stooped at the entrance to view the room from a dwarf's height to see it as a kz'eerkt might see it. He straightened the kudlotlin hide rugs, all of which had been imported in the holds of Chuut-Riit's armada and now showed signs of wear. They could not be replaced. There were no furry kudlotlin to hunt on Wunderland—the planet was everywhere too warm for that beast. No matter. How would he seat such midgets? Kits were not allowed in this room of Heroes and so there were no proper sized furnishings. His membranous ears waggled. It would do these monkeys good to look silly with their feet dangling.

When they finally arrived, after Club-Master had delayed them as long as one could possibly delay a Dominant, the tall pole with the pink eyes was his usual disgustingly ingratiating self. The lesser man showed all the signals and smells of monkey fear that Hwass had learned to read from years of owning human slaves. He did not look like the hero of 59 Virginis who had "defeated" a local kzin fleet, but that's what the records said.

Hwass had carefully researched this major since finding his name on the orders that countermanded those of Markham. "Defeated" was probably the usual primate exaggeration. Humans lied even in their records. Their dishonest officers routinely told their commanders whatever the commander wanted to hear. The record probably meant that Major Clandeboye had "escaped."

"And how iss that I must serve you?" He was frustrated that he could not put irony in his voice but was relieved that he did not have to speak the Hero's Tongue—the humiliating circumstances would have required him to use the Dominated Tense. These barbarian human languages were fortunately deficient in the nuances of tense. "Iss you able understand my accent?"

"Major Clandeboye has a pocket device that compensates for the distortions—and I don't need one." The white-haired human led them to a table as if he had built the Club himself, and accepted his kahlua with cream as if he had a full name. His friend behaved like a servant, following, watching Brobding before he acted. He twiddled uncomfortably with his pocket device.

Hwass accepted a kahlua and cream for himself in a kzin-sized cup. He was tempted to push his muzzle close into the major's space, to play with the fear he smelled there, but such behavior would not advance his cause. He restrained himself admirably and sat down across from the table, rather than next to the major. "You," he said, "iss the man-thing I am interested in for you iss failed approve my return to Kzin."

The major seemed startled. "You're the heroic Hwass-Hwasschoaw?" He glanced up at Brobding Shaeffer in mute appeal, then returned his gaze to the eyes of Hwass before he shuddered and dropped it to the watery ring that his infant's cup had made. "I apologize for that."

It was the second astonishing apology Hwass had received for this act of human duplicity. They promised you freedom, whacked off your head—and apologized. He gazed at this marvel who could not have survived for a heartbeat without the aid of the Great God who seemed to have a fortress in his liver for sniveling weaklings created in His image. "Continue."

"I have no desire to abort your journey to Kzin."

Kzinti nostrils flared. That was the first lie. The next sentence would contain the second lie. The warrior waited.

Major Clandeboye was struggling with the simplified, non-idiomatic grammar used to converse with the kzin. "I have determined that you have information we need and have been looking forward"—he shuddered—"to a friendly conversation."

"I iss not gravitics expert," Hwass replied curtly. "I fly ships; I not build them."

"Gravitics is Shaeffer's concern, not mine. You were in Intelligence?"

"All carnivores iss intelligent," grumbled Hwass, misunderstanding the statement.

"Excuse me. I meant that you are a student of spoor."

How had the UNSN guessed that? The kzin used his tongue to flip a taste of his drink into his toothy mouth. "Yess, I iss been known to be observant. Iss you expect me betray my Patriarch?"

"No. We are at peace. It is in both our interests to cement the peace with acts of goodwill."

There they were again—peace and goodwill. Hwass-Hwasschoaw did not quite understand what he was being told. The only translation he had for the human word "peace" was the word from the Hero's Tongue for "subservience." The nearest translation he had for "acts of goodwill" was "tribute." He replied carefully. "What information that you wish as tribute to ensure my voyage toward Kzin?"

"I require nothing of you. I only wish to ask you a few questions."

You lie! thought the kzin, enraged, his lips twitching as he tried to suppress a smile.

Brobding nudged his companion. "You are being unnecessarily polite."

Yankee retorted, "I'm allowed to be polite to a kzin—especially when he is so much bigger than I am."

"The tense is wrong. Interworld is deficient in tenses. So far as a kzin is concerned, the direct tense is the only 'tense' it has. I'll explain to you later." What Brobding meant to say, and what he was not going to say in front of a kzin, was that politeness required the use of the Dominant/Dominated Tenses, and since the humans were the victors, they would only be able to speak insults while Hwass, who was the defeated, would be restricted to the groveling politenesses. He could see that Yankee was lost. "Recall, my friend, that politeness in the Direct Tense is a form of lying." Yankee paled.

Brobding Shaeffer turned his attention casually to their kzin host to smooth the conversation. "My companion was using an idiom that you do not understand. Humans have been lying for so long that we have standard lies which everyone understands. Since the second meaning of such a lie is known, it is no longer a lie." The crashlander had the kzin's full attention. "Let me illustrate. When my companion said that he required nothing of you, he was using an idiom to tell you that if you do not answer his questions, he will never allow you passage to Kzinhome."

Hwass calmed at this clear truth and his claws, which he had kept hidden, were retracting naturally. "You iss already promised me the passage. Now you retract your promise. You iss without honor."

The crashlander spat out a phrase in the Hero's Tongue which roughly translated as, "The victor has room to roam." Then he resumed in Interworld, "I believe the basic nature of the promise remains intact. Answering my companion's questions may taste like leaves but there will be no trickery in them. Am I correct, Yankee?"

"My questions do not form a conundrum prison. They are answerable by an honorable kzin. Is it not true that an honorable warrior will not abandon his warrior mate in battle? Some of our warriors feel the same. I seek information about a fallen comrade."

"I iss not the God who iss seeing every fallen warrior."

"But you were a member of the Third Black Pride at the time of the Battle of Wunderland?"

"I be."

"And the Third Black Pride captured prisoners."

"We capture prisoners. All iss destroyed when our Pride iss destroyed. I not know details."

"But there *were* survivors. You, for instance."

"I not know details. You iss recall that the climax of battle occurs as I iss the unconscious companion of my laser-fried companions, and furthermore iss dying in damaged spacesuit. I not recover consciousness until weeks beyond the battle ending."

"The Third Black Pride was the first to capture a prisoner—long before the Pride left its station to reinforce Traat-Admiral."

"The records iss destroyed."

"Not all of them," insisted Yankee. "We are still piecing together records from your burnt-out hulks. The old codes are no longer secure. Your security officers did an excellent job of sending sensitive information to computer heaven, but not all ghosts make it to heaven. I am interested in your first prisoner."

"Yess, I iss remember her much well." Hwass was thinking furiously as he talked. They were *not* interested in the prisoner; she was the one captured with a more-or-less intact hypershunt three-man scout ship. They *were* interested in the fate of their ship.

Yankee interrupted. "You just used the word 'her.' Kzin tend to make mistakes with that word. Are you talking about a female prisoner?"

"Yess. I remember such detail much well. We iss all astonished that humans try use females in combat role."

"What was her name?"

"I iss not remember such detail like that."

"Was it 'Nora Argamentine'?"

"I iss not know."

"What became of her?"

As long as this monkey was asking only about the female, Hwass was willing to answer. "She iss be destroyed in the battle." Along with the hyperdrive scoutship, alas.

"But you have no personal knowledge of that?"

"No."

"What happened to her after she was captured?"

"Chuut-Riit is establish the unit to study animal behavior. She is put in thralldom to animal-trainer who iss been given authority conduct behavior research."

"Ship-based, or on Wunderland?"

"Ship-based. That iss why I say she iss destroyed. All kzin ships iss destroyed in battle. None does surrendered." He spoke with pride.

"But you have no personal knowledge of this?"

"How iss I know such thing? I iss critical wounded before battle iss taken to disastrous end."

"To what ship was she assigned? Our records are complete on the fate of every one of your warships. We can determine her fate."

"Our Third Pride has large mother ship"—large enough to hold the hyperdrive scout in her maintenance womb. "Trainer-of-Slaves worked from there. I iss not recall its title."

"Was it a . . ." Yankee paused. He was thinking "drydock," but there was no equivalent word in the Hero's Tongue. The continents of Kzin were all linked by narrow shallow seas and the kzin had evidently gone to space before they had a strong seagoing tradition. Eighty percent of their space naval terms were not related in any way to basic kzinti sea lore, and did not obey the normal rules of kzinti grammar, showing strong fossil evidence that the kzin had been taught their spacefaring skills by an alien race. "Was it a ship used to overhaul other ships?"

"Yess. This be mother ship."

Yankee called up a word on his infocomp and showed it to Brobding. "Could you try to pronounce this for me?"

"*Nesting-Slashtooth-Bitch*," said the crashlander in his best growling-hiss.

"Was it that ship?"

"Yess."

"No such ship has ever been recovered." Yankee posed the statement as a question.

"*Bitch* warcraft ordered to battle-zone."

"It never arrived," Yankee insisted.

The mind of Hwass raced. This was news. Then Trainer-of-Slaves had actually carried through on his determination to take the hyperdrive scout back into the Patriarchy! He couldn't have done that, of course. He was under arrest and in suspended animation. If he had, he deserved a full name. Could his captain have disobeyed orders and revived Trainer? Probably not. That old Hero had never had an original thought in his life.

Mystery. That's what this monkey was tracking down. Now Hwass was interested! Was a hypershunt motor actually in possession of the Patriarch? That changed everything. He felt a curious elation.

"I iss help you. Then you iss help me go Kzin?"

"It's a deal."

• Chapter 7

(2436 A.D.)

The landscape could have been anywhere in the universe and nowhere. A triple-cross rose out of the swirling fog at dawn. It was an illusion, of course, built within a tiny chapel inside a distant corner of Tigertown. The bulk of a kzin warrior purred his supplications to the triple-cross. He wore a mask of steam-stretched human skin. The mask was all bushy eyebrows, scowl, and beard, its human face too large because it was there to hide a kzin's muzzle.

The purring words, couched in the Dominated Tense, were for the invisible Grandfather on the left, to the Father off stage on the right, and to the Son in the middle. They were exactly those words prescribed by the teachings of Kdapt. The mask honored the true shape of God and made Hwass-Hwasschoaw bold in his thanks for the fortune of the day. He was dedicating himself to the goal of finding the lost hyperspace shunt.

An interesting challenge. Hwass had contacts within the kzin community that no human could match. Clandeboye had access to hyperwave communication and hypershunt transportation and to the naval records of the humans. Neither man nor kzin could succeed without the other, yet at the same time each dared not help the other. It was a puzzle subtle enough to intrigue a W'kkai Conundrum Priest.

In the days that followed, he prowled Tigertown, trying

to find any surviving crew member of the *Nesting-Slashtooth-Bitch* at the time of the battle. Not a trace. Then he began to put together a compendium of stories about Trainer-of-Slaves, who had disgraced himself by insisting, probably correctly, that the human scoutship *Shark* should immediately be shipped back to the naval yards of Kzin. Hwass had not known the slave master at all, and was aware of him only because he was a favorite of Grraf-Hromfi, the Dominant of Chuut-Riit's Third Pride. By now Hwass was very curious about this nameless barbarian from Hssin.

He used his new authority with the simian navy to obtain a restricted visit to Aarku of Beta Centauri where Trainer-of-Slaves had been stationed as a slave breeder before being assigned to the Third Pride. He was evidently a superior trainer of the nasty Jotok slaves. But Aarku had been more than a slave factory. Aarku was still used to maintain kzinti-equipped vessels of the Serpent Swarm. The technicians were all kzin and many of them had known Trainer.

Hundreds of wrecked kzinti battle craft were beached on Aarku. It was a mine of information about how kzinti weapons performed against their human counterparts. He had time here to expand on the Wunderland Battle analysis he intended, someday, to deliver to the Patriarch. If he could not deliver the message in person, then his sons or grandsons would. While Clandeboye was using him, he was using Clandeboye.

He spent much of his time at Aarku setting up a Kdaptist cell. The kzin salvagers had found a desiccated man-beast in the wreckage of one of the ships and Hwass showed them how to skin the corpse so that its leather could be used to form masks for their Kdaptist services. Carved, the beast's bones made excellent altar pieces and candelabra.

Through his contacts on Aarku he learned that most of Trainer's surviving associates were on Wunderland. That was convenient. Hwass was granted a second restricted travel pass. From Aarku, he went to Wunderland. No Kdaptist had more freedom of movement to spread the word.

Hwass's questioning around the kzinti tenements of Munchen fed him many tales. Trainer had achieved a reputation in the animal world through a devotion to the chemistry of the human brain. The simians had mawkishly converted an orphanage, which once supplied some of his experimental subjects, into a memorial commemorating the martyred children, hundreds of them, each child's name engraved into an eternium plaque. Kzinti documents were on display, some in Trainer-of-Slaves's compact dots-and-comma style. Descriptive drawings of brain operations, Trainer's bad poetry, the skull-clamps from basement test rooms, the saws and micro-fluid taps were all there.

The collectors of the memorabilia for this holocaust museum had been thorough. But Hwass (cynically wearing a black ribbon of contrition so that he could gain admittance) noticed one item that he was sure the humans didn't understand. It was labeled as a little three-dimensional puzzle used by Trainer-of-Slaves to amuse himself while long experiments were in progress. But it wasn't that at all. Hwass-Hwasschoaw, whose patrilinial ancestry was rooted in W'kkai, recognized it as a wooden puzzle built by the Conundrum Priests. But it was much more than that to a Patriarch's Eye. It was a covert datastore.

Hwass shopped around in the back streets of Munchen until he found a real Conundrum Puzzle in a curiosity and antique shop. He repolished it to duplicate the sheen of the other, then returned to the museum and switched the two. The locks on the display cases were human-primitive. From the engraved markings on the original he traced it to a now legless kzin who had originally given the device to Trainer-of-Slaves as a present of respect for a problem solved.

The crippled warrior restored obsolete kzin electronic devices for a living—hundreds of thousands of them were still in circulation. He had no trouble in reading the datastore. The solution to the puzzle itself was the codekey. The database proved to be an encyclopedic compendium of the neurochemistry of the human nervous system bought by the lives of slaves and orphans. Interestingly, among the poisons were micro-dose gases that would stop a human nervous system instantly but not affect a kzin at all.

From his malfunctioning gravitic chair, Trainer's friend shared a wealth of stories about his polyvalent comrade and thus it was revealed to Hwass that this Trainer-of-Slaves had excellent credentials in gravitic maintenance and, even though he was not qualified as an engineer, he was more knowledgeable of gravitic mathematics than his duties required.

The extensive discussion provided fresh meat for Hwass's speculative chewing. Trainer knew chemistry and gravitics—an unusual technical versatility. Difficult problems never seemed to bother him. Where another ship's captain might be baffled by hyperdrive mechanics, Trainer would be inclined, at the least, to try to restore the function of a misbehaving hypershunt motor. Had he succeeded?

Did he have the courage? That was always important. Grraf-Hromfi's youngest son had survived the battle and told stories of how Trainer-of-Slaves had served as an instructor for Grraf-Hromfi's kits and had even killed several of them for lack of discipline. Hwass knew that challenging and killing a kit of one's dominant superior was a very dangerous act—if the kit wasn't victorious the father might be so incensed as to challenge the instructor himself. And no Hero had ever survived a fight with Grraf-Hromfi. Yes, the courage was there—even if he had a reputation as a "grass-eater."

It was not probable, but it was possible for such a strange warrior to have challenged the captain of the *Nesting-Slashtooth-Bitch* to a duel—but to win? Had he had an ally among the crew to bring him out of hibernation? Two against a full crew? Preposterous! But the ship *had* escaped Alpha Centauri. How? It was useless to speculate.

This Trainer-of-Slaves was a Hssin barbarian, recruited when Chuut-Riit's armada passed through R'hshssira on the last leap of the crusade to Wunderland. *If* he had achieved command of the *Nesting-Slashtooth-Bitch*, where would he have taken it? To nearby Hssin. He could not have abandoned the *Bitch* and proceeded in the *Shark*—the human scout had been badly damaged when captured and subsequent analysis had shown that it had only been captured because its drive unit was malfunctioning. On-board repair was impossible, even on a superbly equipped repair vessel like the *Bitch*.

Hwass had much time to review and check out and correct his projection of events. By human reckoning Hssin had been sacked in 2422. The *Bitch* could not have arrived before 2423. That had been thirteen human years ago. Trainer-of-Slaves would have required elaborate facilities at Hssin to reoutfit and re-equip the *Bitch* for another interstellar hop. The *Bitch* was not a vessel that could flit from star to star. Could it have pushed on from the ruins of Hssin? Not likely. Was it still there?

Such a delicate decision. Hwass could sniff out no way to reach Hssin without being taken there by Major Clandeboye on a human ship. Clandeboye would not help him unless he received some kind of cooperation in return.

So he would have to be a valuable assistant to Clandeboye. Then he'd have to destroy the human expedition and proceed to Kzin on his own. Perhaps they'd never notice if he smuggled aboard a tiny capsule of Trainer's neural gas.

Could he succeed? He thought about it for only a moment. A Hero might attempt such a coup—but if there was anything to be learned from the debacle at Wunderland it was that a warrior would not win without the aid of the Bearded God. To claim God's favor in a contest with the favored humans required the greatest of Kdaptist skills. No simple prayer, no wordy supplication would be enough.

This hunt was in fresh theological territory! Perhaps a sacrifice? But the most ferocious fighting animal of Kzin delivered on a golden altar would not impress *this* God when His precious humans were at stake. A Kdaptist must ceaselessly strive to understand God's needs and His view of the universe. Certainly a sacrifice had to involve great fighting bravery and skill—but it must also be *appropriate*. Would a wise herbivore proffer a gift of rare grasses to the Patriarch!

What was it that God seemed to desire most?

• Chapter 8

(2436 A.D.)

The lord called Grraf-Nig was out for a solitary hunt on his W'kkai estate, naked in his fur, seeking a little relaxation while he tried to make order out of what he was up against. One of his more adventurous wives, in estrus, had been following him at a discreet distance, watching his every move with cool yellow eyes, patiently waiting for his attentions. She was the daughter of his most powerful W'kkai sponsor, Si-Kish the High Admiral. He let her tag along, but ignored her, his alertness elsewhere. The pungent scent of a zianya distracted him into a marvelous chase up along the rocky crests, where he trapped the animal in a ravine, killing the beast after one sudden leap while it tried to escape. His blood lust satiated, he had time to climb the talus to the top of his world.

His year and a half on W'kkai had been exhilarating, yet Grraf-Nig felt deceived.

He had been swept into direct contact with the best philosophers and tool makers. He merely had to grope aloud with a question and a work force appeared with tools to master the answer. He was flown across continents to hunt with W'kkai's best mathematicians who gloriously tore apart the fabric of the universe while they tore apart their meat by the light of all-night campfires. He had been flown to space often, where a whole shielded laboratory was being built to study hyperspace. He had been given females and honors and servants to manage his estate—but he had been deceived.

At first the sashes and clasps and pinned-on ruffles of W'kkai clothing had intrigued him—now they felt like a straitjacket. He was often close to killing his valet. His servants were spies. His closest associates were guardians. If his co-workers spoke the truth they also told him only what the W'kkai patriarchs wished him to know.

The brilliantly slow sunset was worth watching from high on these ridges, though it hardly seemed natural standing here on broken shale, exposed to the sky, without pressure walls to protect him, without even the walls of a ravine to hold in the air. He had lived in space too long ever to adjust to a planet. But the orange play of light on the scudding clouds was a worthy battleground for his imagination. Aboriginal plains kzinti could have evolved their protective coloring hunting among such clouds.

The sunset would bring night. He shuddered. The weather here was harder to get used to than his overstocked harem.

W'kkai was too close to its K2 sun. Tidal friction had slowed W'kkai's rotation until there were only two seasons—seventy-nine hours of light and seventy-nine hours of night. The huge sun broiled them by day, steaming them in their fur, sapping the energy of the hunt. After dark a cloud cover formed and the rains came, dumping heat into the atmosphere, retarding nighttime cooling. Even so there was a skin of ice on the puddles at dawn and, sometimes, snow.

Orange W'kkaisun seemed to have twice the diameter of Alpha Centauri as seen from Wunderland, but it was not nearly as immense to behold or as red as R'hshssira, the brown dwarf that had warmed Grraf-Nig when he was the young Trainer-of-Slaves. Why, amidst the luxury of his own estate, should he suddenly be nostalgic for the tiny hellworld of Hssin, for the hunting caves of its Jotok Run where he had taken refuge as a nameless hunted kit?

A furless tail lashed.

He was aware of his wife's overpowering attraction, the beauty of her black fingers clinging to the red rock below him, but instead of responding, he threw to her the remains of the zianya. She must have been hungry for she ripped into it with a coy glance of thanks. He did not move to her; he talked to her instead, coaxing her closer, knowing she would not comprehend an iota of what he said. Because he did not have to make her understand, he omitted the inflected growls and hisses, the spices and smells of language, hearing them only in his mind's ear. He rambled, dredging up memories he would not have bared before a male.

How to tell her that out there alone with only slaves he had dreamed of his own harem of lovelies? He had dreamed of her. He lapsed into the simple patois of gestures and grunts that a female could respond to. "Love you. Lust your fingers," was all he could manage within her vocabulary. It was not enough. His wives were a burden; he had been without females too long in the wretched emptiness of space ever to get used to the attention they required.

One almost had to be raised as the spoiled son of a W'kkai lord to have the energy to deal with female demands.

Her response to his musings, obviously cast in her direction, came as a tilt of the head and a raunchy smell from the erect fur of her haunches. A female always understood *something* but never what was meant. Absently he turned his great orange-yellow head out over the ridge and the bushes that clung there in the wind. He flapped his fan-like ears. He spoke forcefully to the God of Air and Wind and Smell. "With my own eyes I found the W'kkai star in the firmament and dreamed, wishing myself here." His voice chose for its message the Mocking Tense with which the Hero's Tongue derided victims.

First he had escaped from Hssin to Wunderland, joining the armada of Chuut-Riit. Then after the disastrous Battle of Wunderland, after slinking back to Hssin at less than light speed with a captured UNSN scout, he had scrabbled through its war-smashed ruins for twelve years, talking to ghosts—like he talked to his wives now—repairing the damaged hyperdrive unit, despairing of a second chance to escape gloomy R'hshssira, rejoicing when the opportunity came. Rejoicing when he reached fabled W'kkai.

That which is possessed is never as important as that which is lacking. Had it always been thus? In brief reverie he flashed on a peaceful hunt through the forested caves and domes of Hssin's Jotok Run, a day he could never have again. He remembered his passion to escape the claustrophobic horror that had once been his birth world, but the memory no longer carried passion. It only reminded him of a smelly UNSN cabin stuffed with slaves and a cantankerous hypershunt motor and the irony of picking W'kkai as his destination. Nothing was easy.

The trouble he had taken to get himself transferred from *that* prison to *this* prison!

The warrior Grraf-Nig was more and more certain that the Lords of W'kkai were holding him as a guest prisoner—and didn't want him to know about it. He had tested his hypothesis delicately, in ways too subtle for his enemies to detect. Grraf-Nig had expected better—he had expected adulation, exposed throats even—but he had arrived here with mere slaves, with Jotoki and human slaves, not a warrior among them, and so he should have anticipated an unpleasant fate. No matter that he had also arrived with an extraordinary prize of war, one of the humans' fearsome spacedrives that shunted their ships through hyperspace.

It wasn't enough. To the W'kkaikzin he was Trainer-of-Slaves, though they did not dare call him that to his face. His claws unsheathed. He suspected that once his stolen machine had been duplicated by W'kkai's naturalists and engineers, he would be no more than chopped zianya liver, an outcast kzin who had wandered into the wrong hunting park. W'kkai was not his territory. He had no territory.

Hssin was irretrievably gone.

His mouth twitched to show his fangs while he recalled how Hssin had been destroyed by the raping monkeys. He owed it to those tree apes to blacken the stars with a fleet that would convert every human warren into a hunting park. But his plan was going awry.

The W'kkai thought it would be *their* fleet breaking the blockade and humbling mankind. Well and good—but they also thought it would be *their* grand fleet which would humble the present Patriarch. They thought a re-invigorated Patriarchy would rise from the grass of W'kkai. They were dreaming a monopoly of hyperdrive power. He could taste it; he could smell it. They were dreaming of dominance for W'kkai. There it was, a raw wound: the need to dominate, coexistent with the necessity to submit—the bane of all kzinti.

Ships of the Patriarch had been collecting taxes from the W'kkaisun system for longer than humankind had known the nature of their sky, and—for as long—the nobles of W'kkai had resented parting with those taxes. Why should the culturally superior world of W'kkai deliver their wealth to degenerate Father Eaters! Now W'kkai physicists were examining the only hyperdrive ship in kzinti claws. For the first time in their history they had the longer swipe. And Grraf-Nig was in an ideal position to catch glimpses of their response. They were recklessly planning to build a fleet of warships that the Patriarch's admirals couldn't match. They were, in fact, building it.

Self deceivers! Only once during the war had they fought! Their local naval collision with a light reconnaissance of fighting ships from Procyon during the Humiliation had been bloated into an Epic Saga. The haughty W'kkai Warriors of this *minor* skirmish, led by Si-Kish, remembered themselves as the Heroes who had saved W'kkai. In fact they were losers. Had they witnessed the Battle of Wunderland they would not be so eager to throw together their fleet of hyperdrive ships and defy the infamous MacDonald-Rishshi Peace Treaty without even bothering to inform the Patriarch whose very life might be sacrificed by their impetuousness.

In a universe of sub-light warships, it was the duty of a Conquest Commander to act independently, of necessity informing the Patriarch of his heroic deeds only later through laggard time; at sub-light speeds the Patriarch could not be involved in time-sensitive decisions. But Grraf-Nig was uneasy about applying such a doctrine to a battlespace dominated by hypercraft. It seemed to him that warfare had been redefined.

Grraf-Nig found himself strangely loyal to the Patriarch. Why? He didn't know. On the tiny frontier backworld of Hssin, the Patriarch had been a distant myth. Nobody on Hssin had ever shown their throats to the Patriarchy, they'd hardly been touched by taxes, and they had been blind to its splendor until the fleet of Chuut-Riit had passed through on the way to Wunderland. Still, distant as Kzin had always been, a lowly slave-trainer could not help but envisage W'kkai ambition as the most terrible of treasons.

The whole problem had been a moot point as long as it

was impossible to build a hyperdrive shunt. Grraf-Nig and his Jotoki technicians had had a hard enough time just repairing and tuning the one motor they had captured. He had assumed that it would take generations of secret probing to learn how to build a copy. He had pictured a covert network of kzin worlds dedicated to the task, secretly running physicists back and forth through the human blockade in a united conspiracy directed by the Patriarch.

The brilliance of the W'kkai mathematicians had never occurred to Grraf-Nig, who knew mathematics but who was, himself, hardly more than a glorified gravity-polarizer mechanic. That they had been able to construct a working theory of hyperspace within a few years had astonished him. That engineers were already building hypershunt test beds was a stunning breakthrough.

Yet the advance was uneven. Grraf-Nig saw the superluminal technical march being grafted onto a conservative military strategy that had evolved over millennia against a constant background of subluminal transport—faster-than-light claws attached to slower-than-light minds. The Patriarch had to be told what was going on—and soon. Otherwise, another disaster.

Grraf-Nig had begun to toy with the details of an escape to Kzinhome. Yes, I will; no, I won't. Visions of sharing zianya with the Patriarch alternated with his knowledge of W'kkai dungeons. Like any nascent schemer he dreaded the hard decisions.

How he would recapture the *Shark* or commandeer one of the newer experimental ships he didn't know, so he began by dreaming about his piloting skills. It was probable that he would find the relevant kzin navigation tools denied him—but he had investigated the human navigational paradigm on Hssin before rebuilding Lieutenant Argamentine's unnatural mind to the female-norm. Early on he had understood the necessity of deciphering the human navigation computer in order to steer his captured vessel to a friendly port. He doubted that his W'kkai allies were aware of the function of a certain coded box, so focused were they on the nature of the hyperdrive shunt.

The monkeys referred to W'kkai's trifling K2-star by catalog numbers BD+50° 1725, or HDraper-88230, or Gliese-380. Under those names there had been neither helpful listings of less-than-giant planets nor listings of nearby interstellar hazards—the humans were woefully ignorant about kzinspace. He'd had to fly blind on his near approach to W'kkaisun. But the human system was usable. He had already deduced that they cataloged Kzinsun as 61 Ursa Majoris. Its hyperspace coordinates were in the box and would be accurate enough even if the fine details were missing.

Then he sobered. Everything on W'kkai had been reduced to a fine art—even torture. A W'kkai dungeon was a Conundrum Puzzle that took a lifetime to solve. Its stones were sculpted by vow-sworn priests into shapes of beauty and balance and engineering. A finger might liberate you—or reshape your dungeon into a tinier cell or feed you to the fish.

Fighting his own kzinkind was worse than fighting humans. As a barbarian from Hssin he had been brought up to believe that W'kkai was one of the great centers of learning and wisdom. In fact it was parochial. The local lords were too far away from Kzin to share directly in the awesome power of the Patriarch, and too far away from the war to have been bloodied by any other battle than their petty internal duels.

The dangers inherent in escape came from W'kkai's naval strength. He was a trained fighter pilot and knew what he was up against. It would be harder to evade the gravity-driven dreadnoughts of the W'kkaikzin than, after escape, to outmaneuver a lethargic superluminal ship whose monkeycrew had yet to master the tech of the gravitic polarizer. These UNSN treaty enforcers hovered outside the W'kkai system, beyond a spherical hyperbarrier generated by W'kkaisun's mass, looking down at kzin military might from a height of three light-hours— like monkeys in a tree throwing nuts at the prowling carnivores below. They had not dared come in toward W'kkaisun for a real fight.

Their silly blockade of military trade between the kzinti worlds was no big shake of the tail. A few kzinti hyperdrives could break it. The Procyon planet, the one that named itself by some incomprehensible human pun, could build starships for a millennium and still not have enough of a net to snatch each fish from the stream. Space was bigger than ignorant treaty-makers could dream.

Grraf-Nig did not doubt that, once beyond the hyperbarrier, he could slip past the monkeys. He was a veteran of deep space. Already, by himself, he had leapt halfway to the legendary world of Kzin. And he had done this, after the war was over, when the blockade was already in place. What was another fifteen light years? He could *see* Kzin from here, shining at magnitude 4, twelve degrees off galactic north, a proud hilt in the Constellation of Swords.

The trip had to be risked. There was no way around it. By the terms of the MacDonald-Rishshi Peace Treaty the humans insisted upon retaining control of all superluminal communications. The Patriarch, light years to the galactic north, would not yet even know that a hyperdrive ship had been captured. No human was likely to tell him.

Escape was a matter of timing. If he stole away *before* the physicists of W'kkai fully understood the nature of the hyperdrive shunt, and if, by unluck, the Patriarchy's only working model was captured or destroyed on the way to Kzin, then his premature decision would have left the kzinti in thrall to the humans forever. Patience. That was the lesson Chuut-Riit had taught. That was the lesson his name donor, Grraf-Hromfi, had tried to teach, and had not quite learned himself.

Timing. Too soon or too late. If he waited too long to carry his gift to the Patriarch, the W'kkai might become so strong as to be deluded into waging war by themselves. And that, too, would leave the kzinti in the thrall of victorious humans. There was no such thing anymore as a "local" war. W'kkai could attack human space, but the humans would simply bypass W'kkai and destroy a helpless Kzin. All kzinti worlds would have to be armed with the hyperdrive shunt. If Heroes were to undo their humiliation, as one pride they would have to hunt and kill the man-beasts and their women and their children.

And where was the pride that could command that kind of interstellar loyalty? Only the glorious Patriarchy!

Later, returned from the hunt, walking along the balcony of his mansion, Grraf-Nig watched one of his human slaves play with his younger brothers. The Lieutenant Nora-beast had proved to be excellent breeding stock. The way her sons showed their teeth to each other, a naive kzin might think they were about to attack but they were only laughing.

He was genuinely disappointed that he would have to leave them behind. Leaving his wives he didn't mind, but good slaves were hard to come by. *The older male-beast might have made just the right slave gift for the Patriarch*. Life's regrets!

• Chapter 9

(2436 A.D.)

Because Hwass-Hwasschoaw was on Wunderland, he had not dared bring with him his masks of human hide—there had been no secure place to conceal them on the tiny shuttle craft from Tigertown, staffed as it was by kzin-hating animals. That made difficult any communion with God.

Kdapt's forms had to be observed rigorously.

Hwass went into retreat above the cluttered electronics workshop in a room that was often used for secret meetings by Munchen's Kdaptists. He meditated in this claustrophobic space built to human size. How was a devout kzin to appeal to a Bearded God who had given the Patriarch thousands of years of victory—but who thwarted every kzinti attack on His newly discovered tree-climbing pets? Noseplugs attached, he fasted alone in darkness among the salvaged junk, thinking.

Where was the logic behind God's bias?

Hwass, a noble of the Patriarch's Eye, was here in a crumbling slum while *they* were being resurrected in prosperity all about him. Strange. God never interfered with a kzin who made an ill decision; such a kzin was respected as a noble intelligence and allowed to grow wise—or to die—by living the consequences of his decisions. Not so with humans. Why?

A master crafter, Hwass reasoned, only interferes in his creation when it is moving awry of his intention. A mechanic repairs only after his machine begins to fail. A potter touches clay only when he sees imperfection. God was an artisan. When he ceased admiring the beauty of His work, how did He choose to interfere?

In all of God's universal masterwork, the man-beasts, molded in God's perfect image, seemed to be the only imperfection that disturbed God. God interfered ceaselessly for human salvation. Let a man-beast make a mistake, and God rushed in to save him. God's simians might lie and cheat and beat their females, they might run in battle—but He was always saving them. Let a man make a lethal decision, and God invited him to be born again. Some divine author was not allowing the men to lose no matter how iniquitous their behavior. Saved from blunders, mankind was never allowed to grow wise . . . as a kzin became wise through the blunders of his youth.

It was told by men that they had mightily offended their God by eating vegetables from the tree of knowledge. Perhaps God's purpose in saving the man-beasts was to keep them in their animal state—naive, innocent, lacking in wisdom. What better way to cage an animal from knowledge than to save him from the consequences of his acts?

Hwass was beginning to understand. The sins of men caused God pain; He interfered to put things right. Men tore down His work wantonly; God rebuilt their homes. While God demanded bravery and discipline and honesty of His kzin because he respected them, He *spoiled* His simians out of love. In their writings did not men see Him as one who raged at their sins but who was always merciful? Was not this Bearded God obsessed with the salvation of those He had created in His image? There, *that* was the path to His liver!

Understanding salvation was the key to understanding God. And the Son of God was the key to salvation. Kdaptist rigor had found the way. His mighty frame stirred in the attic, shaking spiders into their cracks. Through His Son, Hwass could reach God.

Clandeboye had planted on Hwass a homing device no more sophisticated than those the ARM used to map the wanderings of criminals. In the Munchen workshop he showed his legless electronics Hero how to remove it and how to plant it on a young Kdaptist of the correct height and color who was to proceed to a safe house farther south—and stay there until Hwass returned.

He chose a time before the rising of Beta, in the dark of the night, to slip from the back of a truck into the forest outside of Munchen, intending to place himself far from any city. The holy quest for the Son of God began as a kind of reverse hunt, avoiding everything, loping quickly, silently, tirelessly, always out of sight and smell—hiding himself by day, moving by night and by the pale ardor of Beta—until he was totally beyond human habitation. The journey was endless joy. Many times he broke his trail so that it could never be followed. It was joy to hunt the Son of God.

Each evening the quetzbirds gargled on their night hunt. They hunted only when Alpha had set but were most active when brilliant Beta dominated the night sky of stars. Once he saw one on a log munching a luminescent fungus, its brilliant feathers eerily glowing. The smell of the bird and the tang of broken fungus was a forest poem. How could he ever give this up again for civilization?

On the third day he sniffed the smoke of a human bonfire and thought he might have found the Son. He smelled burning oak from Earth, mixed with slightly green bundlestick. Fresh meat on the fire was too hot and charring; blood was ablaze. He could detect human sweat and sour beer, a background of spicy insect pheromones, moist soil. But long before he was close enough to see his prey he smelled its female scent. Not the Son of God. Avoiding the woman, he came to a steep slope that overlooked the stars. He reveled in the stars, then plunged on, silently swift.

At dawn he found a grassy meadow being grazed by a small herd of six-legged sprinters, hardly taller than the grass itself. He was tempted and hungry but he did not attack. This was a religious mission and hunger drove a keener spirit. Now he was well beyond the boundaries of human settlement. It made the hunt venturesome because his prey was a man. Beta was now the only star in the dawn sky.

Two days later, still deliberately fasting, eating only the odd rodent, ravenous, he found his first spoor, fish skins by a stream. By that evening, at Alpha-set, he had located the cabin, its log walls twice the length of a man, made from thin logs one man could haul and notch. The roof was pond reeds. Best of all was the smell of male. Hwass had saturated his orange fur in pond muck for the sake of invisibility. He could have attacked the recluse and killed him then—deadly claws against an ancient hunting rifle—but for religious reasons it was necessary to capture the Son of God alive.

He waited. Animals moved in the forest, breaking twigs. Insects whistled and sprayed the air with their mating scents. A Terran squirrel warned the forest with indignant quarreling. Hwass remained silent, his thin, winglike ears extended, listening for the man to settle in for sleep, nose relishing the night air, waiting. But he had to act before Beta-rise.

Darkness. Wide pupils. The human stirrings ceased. Time to act. Only the cloud-diffused starlight and his flared nostrils guided him noiselessly across the lightless moor. It was so dark he had to finger-feel his way across the logs to find the opening. Carefully his mind measured the inside of the dwelling so that his strike might be quick and accurate.

Hwass reached an arm deep into the open-shuttered window.

Rudely he dragged the naked man through the opening with a hand tightly closed over the man's mouth. "Hey now, easy does it," mmmphed the struggling hermit. But the kzin was trussing his prey before the victim was fully awake. Surprise over, adrenaline surging, the lamb of God fought with a silent clawing ferocity until he could no longer move at all. Immobile, his mouth free, he snapped, "I didn't do it. I'm not responsible! Gimme my clothes!" He glanced furtively at bear-black ghosts spread over a nearby bush. His patched shirt and utility trousers were molded from forever fabric, frayed beyond the bounds of forever, now recovering from a wash and clubbing by the stream's shore. They were valuable to him.

"You iss Son of God," Hwass answered gently, relieved that he had indeed captured a male. If it had been a female he would have had to put it back, or to kill it for the sake of silence.

"Hey, you've got the wrong man!" came a desperate croak.

"No. You iss His perfect Son."

"Not me. My grandfather came to Wunderland to get away from that mouth-flap."

"Your Grandfather iss everywhere at all and once," said the kzin. "He iss with you now. You iss holy."

"Tell Myrtle. To her I'm *teufel*. Already I've skipped out on two wives. I'm a mean cantankerous no-good who likes to fish and to rot in the woods by myself. Peaceful like."

"I iss captured God's Son," Hwass hissed threateningly, a theologian daring to be contradicted.

The hermit was surprised that kzin were still loose in the woods after sixteen years. This one had gone crazy after all that time. Still, the panic in him forced him to argue. The cantankerous wife-deserter said the first inane thing that came to his head. "My teeth are rotten. You can't believe the Son of God would be plagued by rotten teeth," he suggested hopefully.

"All male mens iss the Son of God, teeth or no. You iss the Son of God I hunt. Men's Bible iss say that the Son of God may be found anywhere in any disguise, even in dungeon. Matthew 25:40."

"Finagle save me!"

Hwass hissed. "Finagle iss atheist devil-beast. Cannot touch Son of God."

The hermit took a moment to consider screaming at the top of his lungs—but there was no one to hear. With his arms tied to his sides, his only weapon was reason. "Whatever you want, you've got. Tell me and I'll give it to you. I'll kiss the ground you pee on."

"You iss the true-form."

"What does that mean?"

"You iss beautiful and iss shape in the image of God."

"My mother used to stare at me like that."

"Not to talk of mother. The mother of the Son iss soul-less animal!"

"Does that mean you're not a Catholic?"

"Tonight we converse only importantly with Father of Son."

The old hermit was beginning to feel sarcastic. "Hey Dad!" he shouted over his shoulder. "Company!"

"Silence!" Hwass snarled. "Serious matters iss upon us. Your Father iss stressed at sins of all humankinds, men's lying, deceit, vanity, cowardice, and dishonorable scheming as you mens iss talk out of two sides of your head! Mens iss the greatest sinner of all sentients. A great sorrow

He has at your sinning in His liver and iss wish to help you mens, all too much, for you iss been made in true-form of God. He weeps at men's deviations from true path. He wishes to help you to path of righteousness. He iss obsessed with helping you. Sorrow iss pain to bear—even for one who iss God. He iss so filled with crazy driving sorrow fixating His attention that He iss neglect His other kittens. *This you iss will correct.*"

"Riiight!"

"You iss now to lay God's liver to its ease."

"If you'll untie me, I'll gladly go to my knees and pray to God fervently. Say your prayer and I'll say it with you. I'm praying already!"

"You iss not pray. You iss take all mens sins to your soul with courage of true warrior, thus relieving God of His grief for mens. You iss be guilty for all sins. You iss accept all punishment. You iss forgive all mens their transgressions, wipe them clean with your suffering and make God glad again. This iss duty I require of Son of God."

While the trussed Son of God peered helplessly into the gloom, the devout kzin used his torch to fell a straight tree. Flaking muck flickered on slick fur. The giant cut his log into two parts. He notched them and lashed together a sturdy cross. He measured the man's arm span while the man pleaded hysterically, now aware of his fate. Holes were drilled at the right place on the crossbeam. Holes were drilled in his wrists which carefully avoided all major arteries and veins. The kzin used ironwood pegs to secure the Son of God to the cross and raised him to the night, higher than a kzin's eye. It began to rain.

In the pouring rain, Hwass cheerfully cut and built two smaller crosses which he erected to the right and left of the crucified Son of God, one for the invisible Grandfather and the other to call God to the scene so that He would know He was wanted. When the clouds began to clear, Beta was rising through the misty trees and the hermit, in the first delirium of his pain, could actually see his enemy sitting on the wet moor weaving—what was it? a basket?

Hwass-Hwasschoaw was weaving a human mask of pliant bark to replace the mask of human skin he had not been able to bring with him. Basket weaving was one of the skills he had ordered his father's slaves to teach him as a youth. His patriarch had not allowed him to observe a slave without learning how to do all that the slave was doing. Once he had killed one of his father's metal-working slaves for refusing to teach him the art of variable alloying. His father commended his act by sharing in the bloody meal—even though he had lost a valuable property.

It was predestined from birth that Hwass was to become Patriarch's-Eye, an unmentionable name he was to carry in priority to all other social names he might be known by. Eyes sometimes led quiet lives of observance. Sometimes their lives became lively affairs of survival by wit where even the most impractical skill might be the key to survival. His father had *ordered* him to learn everything.

While he wove, he recalled his father's words. "A master who cannot do what his slaves do has become like an unskilled animal. A kzin is owned by his slaves if they are more clever than he." His father was born on W'kkai of the Kzin aristocracy, nominally a member of the W'kkai aristocracy, but more of Kzin than of W'kkai. He had only contempt for the W'kkai habit of letting their slaves be the custodians of their gestalt.

He did not have to kill his father's basket weavers for they were enthusiastic in teaching him all they knew. The mask shaped up nicely. The skin was finely woven with shaped cheekbones and cleft chin and protruding eyebrows. The eyes were of stream-polished quartz. The hair was of fine plant fiber which he pounded clean while the Son of God was dying with his awful burden of sin.

Day came and night, and the pallor of Beta, and the dawn of Alpha. In his delirium the hermit was taken to a ghostly remembrance of Munchen in the spring of a year when Beta was an evening star. It cast shadows the length of Karl-Jorge Avenue and set the steel steeple of St. Joachim's cathedral ashimmer against a purpling sky. Some kind of Mass was gathering, and his grandfather, whom he loved far more than his father, was holding on to his hand with the kind of vigor that adults use to protect children from Calvinists, nearby kzin, and other evils.

The hermit was remembering this now because as a child this was the first time he had ever seen a statue-man nailed in agony to a cross. The cross was larger than life-size and it rose above the massive entrance to St. Joachim's. He had not asked his grandfather about it but his grandfather had sensed his consternation and volunteered an explanation.

"Son. Don't be scared. The kzinti don't do that to people. Crucifixion is peculiarly Christian—the kzinti have only been here nine years; they haven't had the time to be reborn again. Give them fifty years to convert and then we'll get some real atrocities."

The Son of God had not spoken for a day. Now, suddenly awakened to the present by his vision, oblivious of his pain, he shouted wildly down at his kzin. "You reborn?"

"Ratcats iss live eleven lives?" The giant's ears waggled in amusement as he used a monkey's demeaning term for kzinti. He meant nine, but Hwass had never managed to master decimal mathematics. He got it garbled when he converted from base eight.

"Born once of mother! Born twice of Christ!" shouted the hermit in explanation.

The kzin remained puzzled.

"Finagle's censored balls! Are you a Christian convert? I'm trying to explain to myself what you're doing! Crucifixion is a *Christian* sacrifice!"

"I iss Kdaptist," explained Hwass patiently to his victim.

The hermit's sight was wavering again. He followed his grandfather's eyes to the St. Joachim cross of his hallucination. His dry lips were raving. "My grandfather warned me about people like you!" he screamed at the kzin. Then he was gone again into delirium and vision and revelation.

"Christians!" his grandfather was lecturing with a booming voice that traveled all the way from Munchen to the Wunderland backlands, "they delegate their wrong-doing to Christ who suffers for them in proxy. 'Let Christ do the suffering,' that's their motto. 'Let Christ be punished in my place.' Christ earns God's grace the hard way, and all they have to do is drink Christ's blood and eat His flesh on Sunday. Christians acquire God's grace secondhand. For this service they are grateful and worship him. Been a popular sales pitch for thousands of years. Christians are the ones who get indignant when *they* get nailed to a cross; they think God's been falling down on *His* job and hire a lawyer to sue Him."

High on his cross the hermit was in a rage of indignation. He *wasn't* Christ! It wasn't his job! Why should he have to suffer? It was sacrilege!

Below, Hwass was busy honing a theological point. Since God had granted to these animals the gift of superluminal communication, surely their awfulest sins had the superluminal ability to fly from all the realms of man, here, to the poultice Hwass had made from the body of the Son of God.

Hwass had completed his mask. Wearing it, he was permitted to gaze directly into the eyes of the Son of God. He smelled the fear and the agony. The true face was tormented in pain. Sometimes the pain was so great that the Son fainted but then he would slump and choke, unable to fill his lungs, and had to awaken, to stiffen his legs so that he could breathe. The sacrifice was working. The sins of mankind were arriving, a new one with each gasp and groan, and with them the punishment that went with sin. Kdapt had truly mastered the nature of the simian form and mind.

St. Joachim's was gone but the grandfather had brought with him a spinning Munchen hotel, made shabby by the fist of the kzinti occupation, horribly fuzzed by the delirium. Grandpa was trying to convince his grandson not to abandon his first wife. The guy could be a bore! What did it matter so many years too late? Cindy-belle was bones under a kzin factory. You can't go back. Finagle, what did all that matter when a kzin had you nailed to a cross? *Die. I want to die*.

"You can blame Cindy-belle all you want, son, for your own incompetence. It's a painless way to go, to pass off all your sins on to her, to make her guilty, to attribute to *her* the source of your own stupidities. That will make you feel good. You'll be absolved. You'll be saved—for the moment. But Finagle knows it won't do you any good in the long run. Your sins aren't transferable. In the long run you get nailed to your own cross. Christ never saved a single soul but his own."

Shut up, old man! The universe wasn't supposed to be *literal*.

The grandfather held tightly to his grandson's hand and

they were back in Munchen with the painted wooden
Christ. "He wanted to take on the world's sins. He wanted
to suffer in your place, and he suffered. But he didn't
save anyone. A sin is something even Jesus can't take from
you. A sin is something you can't give away. You can't even
run away from it."

Shut up. Let me die. He was dying of regret. *I could be
with Cindy-belle now, and the boy grown up, and my
mad kzin would have found someone else, some other sinner. Too soon old; too late wise.* Why didn't the raving old
ghost just shut up!

From parched lips almost too stiff to speak, he asked
for water. If the damn ratcat had read the Bible, like he
claimed, he'd hold up a rag soaked in vinegar. The man
fainted. He woke. He found a cup of stream water in
front of his face . . . attached to a pole that went all the
way down there to a crazy kzin wearing the outsized mask
of a man's face. Why water and not vinegar? Did the rat
kzin want him alive to suffer longer? He smiled through
cracked lips. He was warm and cozy. Pain was its own
anesthetic. He was floating. Still, he wanted the water
and slurped at it awkwardly. The water revived him but
he wished it hadn't because his grandfather was still chat-
tering away. That damn old man was never going to give
him any peace; somber advice right up to the end. They
were having beer in a trunkshuppen in wartime Munchen.

"The road you're taking, son, running away from your
wife, letting father handle it—that leads nowhere but to
death. No matter where you run, son, all you'll find there
is your own deathbed, and the faster you run, the quicker
you'll get there."

The cantankerous hermit was choking again. This time
he was grown-up and at the end of his life. When he tried
to stiffen, his legs refused to obey. He couldn't breathe
with limp legs and he couldn't talk his legs into helping

him. He was pleading with his legs to raise his body when
he blacked out.

The kzin was watching intently.

At the exact moment of death the man-beasts would
all be saved, at least temporarily. Every man, across all
the realms of men, would be in a state of grace. Their
suffering would die as the Son died. And God would no
longer be distracted by the pain emanating from their
multiple true-shapes.

He prayed. Grant the Bearded God tranquillity! The
Great God's Patriarchal courage and bravery and strength
were about to be restored by the sacrifice of His Son.
Rejuvenated, He would be alert and ready to listen to *all*
who called upon Him, not just the whining of His favorites.

The body on the cross slumped, convulsed, was still.
Hwass turned to the smaller cross, God's antenna. Now!
The mask respecting the true-form was firmly upon his
muzzle. He composed himself. In the air were the songs
of heaven and the smells of glory. His hunter's senses felt
the full attention of God. He delivered only one request,
a resonant, powerful request, carefully phrased in the
purrs of the Dominated Tense of the Hero's Tongue:

"Mighty Patriarch, Son of the Grandfather, and Father
of the Son," he began formally, "the aroma of Your piss
emanates from every star. As Your feces was dropped into
the mud of Earth to bring forth the true-shape, I throw
my soul to the mud of Kzin to bring forth loyalty to God's
purpose. Obedient children I promise You."

Hwass was remembering a lost life on the sheep estates
of Wunderland. "A fanged dog may be ugly in Your eyes.
An untamed dog may kill sheep. But a fanged dog who
has been bred to the faith is a shepherd."

Then he made his plea. "Place in my loyal claws the

hypershunt drive so that my brave kzinti may move freely
to their destiny! Let us guide Your true-shaped children.
We will discipline their behavior! In the whole of the galaxy, You command no greater race than the race of Heroes.
Use us. I ask no more."

After a respectful silence, Hwass-Hwasschoaw feasted
upon the body of the Son of God so that he might share
in the grace of the true-form, as God had commanded in
Matthew 26:26, and drank of the blood, all of it, which
was shed for the remission of sins as commanded in Matthew 26:27–28.

• Chapter 10

(2436–7 A.D.)

When Major Yankee Clandeboye tried to organize an expedition to Hssin he discovered just how many naval officers he had alienated. He had full authority to mount such an expedition, but it took more than authority; it took cooperation. Whatever request he made was referred to some other naval department. Clearly Admiral Jenkins was not cooperating.

From the scuttlebutt he learned that Admiral Jenkins, in command of the Eighth Fleet based at Wunderland, had been involved in a running internecine war with General Fry for years, a covert war involving character assassination by secret ballot, redirected supplies, gerrymandering, reluctance to share ideas and innovations, officer sidelining—and an overt war over budgets and weapons procurement. They had policy quarrels, philosophical differences, and they belonged to competing power blocs. A sort of simmering truce had been in place since their last open conflict during the invasion of Down.

One informant thought it was funny. "He actually enjoys his little wars. Keeps about six or seven fronts going at the same time. He once tried to have Buford Early court-martialed. Didn't succeed but sure kept the volcanoes puffing."

"Admiral Jenkins did that?" Yankee was incredulous.

"No. General Fry."

"And the ARM just lets my boss get away with it?"

"What can they do? Fry has goldskin roots. The goldskins and ARM collaborate reluctantly. You know, Belter and flatlander rivalry."

"And I thought *I* was unpopular!"

The higher authorities of the ARM had done their best to keep such disputes compartmentalized. Yet the very structure of the Amalgamated Regional Militia exacerbated such conflicts. The ARM had never been designed to wage war against the kzin or mediate between alien races. For 350 years it had shaped itself to find and *suppress* military technologies rather than to use them. The ARM's military response to the kzinti had been hastily cobbled together out of the wrong pieces of bureaucracy.

Yankee's men suggested that they bypass Jenkins and go back to Sol and pick up a ship. Besides the fact that this option put a ten-light-year (thirty-day) dogleg detour into the Hssin trip, it wasn't the kind of failure that Clandeboye had the courage to pass on to Fry to fix—the old game player had doubtless moved him into this hotseat quite deliberately.

He was left crawling from rumor factory to rumor factory, grasping at wild stories for some kind of lever into his problem. Perhaps, he thought ironically, he could lay charges of mutiny against Jenkins. Good idea; bad odds. It was in such a mood that he accepted Brobding Shaeffer's invitation to dinner at Tiamat's Star Well. Brobding was always a good source of gossip.

The Star Well was more formal than Yankee liked, complete with a flatland headwaiter with black suit and oyster-sized turquoise jacket buttons who actually escorted him to the Shaeffer table on one of the tiers overlooking the well. His eyes fell off the rim—down to the beginning of the universe. It was vaguely disconcerting to know that a structural failure in the "skin" would suck him through the floor into an even better view of the stars. If you hadn't noticed that Tiamat was rotating, its motion was brilliantly obvious here; the constellation of Pavo was just slipping across the bottom of the well. He recognized Peacock from his days as starstruck navigator. Binary giants, period 11.7 days. Minds were filled with such useless detail.

True to form, Brobding Shaeffer immediately began to pass on the latest gossip—while Yankee was still standing. He was ensconced in a cushioned crescent overlooking the well, his lips happily assaulting his nose in a pincers maneuver, long arm happily around a young lady. "I just got it straight from the ISC Adjunct that Sourface Jenkins considers your mission to be a direct violation of Eighth Fleet territory. A pointed insult. He was raving at 3D soccer last night that a mutineer has been given sweeping authority in *his* bailiwick."

"And here I thought he was happy," Yankee said sarcastically. "The last time we talked, he was grinning like a kzin."

"Sit down. Meet Chloe." Shaeffer turned to Chloe and jerked a thumb at his friend. "That's Yankee. He's a mutineer."

Yankee sat down. "Knock it off."

"That sounds like a *real* adventure!" exclaimed Chloe with the skill of a young woman who has read about how to get a man talking. There was an artificial spring to her loose black curls. She was either a naive twenty-year-old on her first date or else a very sophisticated sixteen-year-old pretending to be twenty. Brobding could be trusted to date underage girls or to get caught in his spacesuit without underpants or to drink too much in Tigertown. The girl, and she was a girl, continued to stare at Yankee. She actually batted her eyes. "Well?"

"Just another war story," grumbled Yankee.

"Tell us. I've never asked you what happened," said Brobding. "I'm too polite."

"That's what I like about you."

"Aren't you going to tell us?" Chloe sighed. "Please, I'm a navy brat and I like war stories."

"No."

"What can I bribe you with?" she flirted.

"A ship, sweetheart." He smiled kindly and she chewed her lip.

That was when Brobding announced happily that he had brought in a kzin mechanic from Aarku to share some of the black art of gravitic drive maintenance. "I'll be taking him back with me to Procyon."

"I hope you have a rage-proof cage," mused Yankee.

"Don't need one. He lost his legs in the war. That's the deal; he helps us. We grow him a new pair of legs."

"Are you sure he's going to buy that? Kzin wear their wounds proudly."

Brobding grinned. "They're not all the same. This one would be humiliated to ask a kzin for legs. He'd never do it—even though he wants legs now more than life. He's old. But he reasons that humans have no honor—so he can ask us. He comes from Ch'Aakin. We'll send him back home once Brozik's boys are through pumping his brains."

Yankee remembered that Ch'Aakin was a neighbor of Procyon—nine light years. It was a lousy M2 star, not worth a gold-plated lead napoleon. The crashlanders had tried to take it during the war—it was too near for comfort—but Ch'Aakin had turned into a bloodbath and one of the defeats the navy didn't like to talk about.

The next evening Yankee was invited to the naval mess for dinner. There he had to endure a different kind of formality. The gray bulkhead walls were decorated with stiffly mounted brass portholes salvaged off the bottom of Earth's Pacific, and, at the head of the main table, a coral encrusted propeller from some ancient pursuit plane which had overshot its mother carrier. These were flatlanders, importing their ties to Earth. The officers were seated by rank, their placeholders Chinese ivory military weapons.

Yankee had hoped it might be an informal gathering to break down whatever obstacles were impeding an unorthodox intelligence mission. Instead it was an ambush.

"The Clandeboye articles" had not been published in major datamags. Nevertheless they had been widely circulated and frequently condemned. Often the critics had read only other reviews. His dinner critics were ruthless. They wanted to *prove* to him that he was wrong, that the UNSN patrols had a vise grip on kzinti space.

Every single man at the dinner had combat experience from the ferocious thirteen-year offensive that had followed the Battle of Wunderland. An average of four percent of their ships had been destroyed on every mission. These were the hardened survivors, some of them brilliant combat officers, some of them just lucky men. None of them had a good reason to discount kzinti strength, yet all of them did.

It chilled him. This was the core of the navy that would have to repel the next kzinti attack. The hyperdrive performed some strange perversion on men's minds. It gave them the *illusion* that they commanded space. Yankee remembered Vice Commander Yoni Marshall's parable about the fleas who rode first class on Earth's supersonic aircraft, thinking they were lords of every nook and cranny of the Earth—the same Marshall who had taught him three-dimensional attack strategy, the same Marshall who died with the attack forces trying to penetrate the defenses of Down.

"The UNSN patrols don't even cover the top end of the Patriarchy!" Yankee exclaimed in frustration.

"They don't have to," said a confident rake eight years his senior.

While Yankee politely listened to the nonsense the man was using to justify his statement, he had his own thoughts. He had been further into kzinti space than any officer here. There were worlds out there. There was a rumored world called Warhead that the kzinti had controlled since about the time of Genghis Khan. The UNSN didn't even know where it was and wouldn't even know that it existed except for a quirky case history in one of Chuut-Riit's volumes on military strategy.

Yet Warhead was the forward base in a subluminal war being conducted against the Pierin that was still going on as of this very moment. Who were the Pierin? The kzinti warriors fighting that battle probably hadn't yet noticed a Man-Kzin war. The kzinti had been interstellar warriors since before man had beaten his first iron swords from red metal, since before bronze, since before Ur, since maybe before even beer. That was a lot of time in which to build a network of bases.

How many kzinti worlds were out there? How many kzinti armed rocks hidden in interstellar space? How many miserable little kzinti fortress worlds like Hssin? How many factory worlds? Hundreds? Thousands? No one knew.

These young men who had lost so many comrades could not even admit that they had been fought to a standstill. The hyperdrive was a great logistics and transport weapon. It had allowed the reintroduction of blitzkrieg warfare. The UNSN had been able to surround and isolate the main kzinti worlds. But the hyperspace singularity which enclosed every stellar mass in a "forbidden zone" was as good as any medieval wall at stopping a hypershunt-equipped invader.

In the wicked days before the ARM, horse cavalry might sweep across a thousand miles of Earth and lay siege to the mightiest cities of a domain—but the horses couldn't walk through walls. A mechanized Wehrmacht might race across the steppes of Russia in tank and armored halftrack and truck and motorcycle—but it couldn't take the streets of Stalingrad, where tank and armored car and truck were useless.

In thirteen years the human hyperdrive fleets had done brilliantly at smashing kzinti interstellar trade. That didn't make much difference. The Patriarchy had long ago adjusted itself to supply lines that moved at 80 percent the speed of light. Send off to Kzin for a replacement part and it might arrive half a century later. As a consequence, even a kzinti minor outpost was a more-or-less self-sufficient manufacturing center. A kzinti attack force was a lumbering, ill-supplied adventure. But a kzinti-defended star under siege was almost invulnerable.

The gravitic acceleration of kzinti warcraft allowed them to outmaneuver anything the humans had been able to field, and almost every class of kzinti warcraft was superior to its human counterpart inside the singularity. Long range beam-weapon duels were ineffective; at subluminal beam velocities an ablative shielded kzinti vessel could dodge faster than the response time of the beam generator. Intelligent missiles were the best way to get through but they were *very* subluminal and could be picked off by alert defense crews.

The siege record was poor. Down and Hssin were the only clear victories.

The assault on Down had been a massive surprise attack on a world whose star was so small that its singularity extended only to eighteen AU, less than the distance to Uranus. It was an anomalous outpost, sitting well inside human space, farther from Kzin than any other known world of the Patriarchy, poorly supplied, lightly taxed, underdeveloped and underpopulated. Still the warriors there had destroyed a quarter of the human fleet sent against them before being exterminated.

Yankee listened patiently. An officer whose place was held by a charging armored battle-elephant of the finest carved ivory began reminiscing about his elite unit's landing on Down while he neglected his plum chicken—but not his slivovitz. "I was caught in the tower with no way to get down and my best cover man was blown ass over head into the canal where he was stuck in his disabled armor. He couldn't run so he just sat there popping off every ratcat as they jumped over the canal while I was shitting bricks because if they got him, I was dead meat. He swatted about a dozen of them, one by one, coming over the rise because they couldn't see him."

Yankee was reminded of the gambler who enthusiastically gave his audience a blow-by-blow account of how he won a hundred "big ones" early that morning—while forgetting to tell them about the thousand "big ones" he had just dropped at the tables. The kill ratio on the ground at Down had been three men for each kzin. Victors don't remember details like that.

Down had been considered important because it was behind human lines. That was nonsense. It had zero strategic importance. Probably it had been a target of frustration. None of the bigger worlds were falling, so get the weakest one.

On the other hand, the conquest of Hssin in 2422 had been an absolute necessity. It was only two light years from Wunderland and 5.3 light years from Sol and had been the original staging area of the kzinti thrust at humanity's heart. Theoretically it made an easy target. R'hshssira was a failed star with a singularity that extended out only eight AU, less than the distance to Saturn. Alpha

Centauri was a mere week away by hypershunt, an optimal staging area from which to supply the assault. Yet fierce Hssin warriors managed to destroy a third of the UNSN fleet before the Wunderland marines were able to carve out their first beachhead.

Thirteen years on the offensive. Two victories. Thousands of kzinti starships destroyed in interstellar space. Hundreds of raids. Dozens of unsuccessful sieges. Stalemate. The MacDonald-Rishshi Peace Treaty had given both sides what they needed. The Patriarchy needed a breathing space. Humanity needed to stop beating its head against a stone wall. To call it a human victory was wishful thinking.

What humanity wasn't doing was using the time that the Treaty gave them.

The dinner served its purpose. It reconvinced the hosts that they had won the war and were maintaining the peace. It convinced Major Clandeboye that he wasn't going to get to Hssin by orthodox means. His hosts were gentlemen. Having been victorious over their guest verbally, they toasted him with Vurguuz. He raised his glass, too, wondering who these cardboard men were. They had no substance. He was never going to get to know them. It left him with a kind of desperate despair.

When men are desperate they wander alone, deep in thought. Yankee took the long way home. He was already outside his apartment door before he noticed that Chloe was waiting for him, huddled on the hallway's red carpet, arms around her legs. "Chloe!" He stuck his thumb in the lock and it opened. "Hi," she said. She followed him inside.

"It's past your bedtime, young lady."

"Good idea," she replied demurely, "let's go to bed." With the tiniest of smiles she watched the shock hit his face. She waited just exactly the right amount of time.

"Gotcha!" she triumphed. Then with a bob of her springy black hair she went to his console and called up the codes for a tinkly kind of beating music that he didn't understand. "Cornucopia," she said by way of explanation. He didn't understand that either.

"Where's Brobding?" was all he could think to ask.

"I never go out with a man again after he's let me 'tuck the George.' How could I ever respect him?"

"Uh . . . what was that? I think I missed something."

"What's the flatlander word for it?" she asked in a tone that left him wondering if he was being teased or not.

"I think I should be taking you home."

"You're saying that through clenched jaws. *I* think you need a relaxing massage . . . all the way down your back to your bum."

"Strangling a few people I know is the only thing that would relax me right now," he growled. Since he was looking directly into her eyes she became momentarily frightened. That upset him to the point of hasty denial. "Not you!" He laughed at himself to put her at ease. "Actually you have a pretty neck. Breaking would ruin it. What I mean is: I don't need a massage. What I need is to get you home before it is too late . . . before your curfew."

"I just got here. You're throwing me out already?"

"Yes."

"No. I'm here to interview you for the school paper. You have to tell me about the mutiny. I'm writing you up."

"No, you're not."

"Then could we take a shower together instead?"

"Young lady, I have to tell you something about myself. I don't need any more trouble. I'm up to a giraffe's eyeballs in zoo-doo already."

"What's a giraffe?"

"It's just an expression. An extinct animal, I think."

"I'm no trouble. I swear I've never ever gotten a man pregnant; cross my heart."

"Your father is probably a chief petty officer with shoulders *this* wide. Petty officers enjoy making pulp out of me. They're not supposed to hit majors, but with me they get away with it—and I get blamed. It looks terrible on my record."

"That's all very well and good but my father is *not* a petty officer. He's a rear admiral."

Yankee grabbed for her wrist. "Young lady, you are going home *right* now!"

"No-I'm-not!"

"Yes you are."

"Nope."

"I may carry you every millimeter of the way."

"In that case it's a deal. But we have to take a *long* detour so you can buy me an ice cream. There isn't any good ice cream place between here and home."

"If that's the best deal I can get."

So he took her home and bought her ice cream. He asked her if her father ever worried about her. He was too busy, she replied. Well, didn't her mother ever worry about her? No. Chloe was born on Tiamat just months before a mob liberated it from the kzinti during the Great Battle. Her mother was an axe-wielding member of the mob and had been killed. Chloe still wore her iron wedding ring on a chain about her neck.

"Ah, so you're all of sixteen," he said gently.

"No. I'm going-on-seventeen," she replied stiffly.

Yankee was quite willing to drop her at her door and run but she dragged him inside to meet her father. "Daddy! I got him! Don't blame me if it took all night! He wasn't home!" In a quieter voice to Yankee she said, "Now you'll have to tell me about the mutiny. Daddy's going to wring it out of you."

A bony but handsome Wunderlander appeared in a spidersilk bathrobe. He shook hands in the old flatlander custom. "I see you survived my little *teufel*. She was raving about you at breakfast this morning. *The* Clandeboye. I think it was a diversion so I wouldn't question her about that no-good crashlander she's taken a fancy to, but no matter. I decided it was time we met."

"Make him tell us about the mutiny, Daddy."

"All in good time." He dismissed his daughter impatiently and refocused his attention on Yankee. "I've been hearing that you want to take a ship to Hssin? Is that true?"

"It's an Intelligence matter."

"I, too, want to take a ship to Hssin but lack the authority. I have the clearance to look at your orders if you wish to show them to me. It is possible that we might strike a deal."

Puzzled, Yankee brought out his infocomp.

Rear Admiral Blumenhandler talked while he perused. "Well, well, well," he smiled. "I have ships but no orders. You have orders but no ship." He grumbled, continuing to read the fine print. "Now this is what I call an airtight order. If you commandeered one of my ships, I don't see how I could refuse you. I might be upset; I might be enraged at the imposition, but I couldn't refuse you." His eyes twinkled. "Of course, I'll want a favor in return, just a gentlemen's agreement, mind you; nothing in writing."

"And Jenkins?"

"Jenkins has made *suggestions* on this matter—but I don't believe a *suggestion* has ever carried the same weight as an order, now has it? Let me be plain—off the record. Jenkins is a foreigner. I am of the Wundervolk; my family has served the Nineteen Families for centuries. Jenkins serves the ARM. I've sworn loyalty to the ARM—but my heart lies with the security of Wunderland. Let's assume for my peace of mind that there is no higher contradiction between my sworn loyalties. Loyalty to Wunderland, even loyalty to the ARM, doesn't require me to kiss the seat of Jenkins' power. Do we understand each other?"

"I'm sworn to carry out my naval duties. My orders are clear." It was Yankee's polite way of saying that he was not interested in exceeding his authority.

"Of course. Let me tell you where my interest lies. Hssin calls up a special dread in my heart. Many powerful Wundervolk feel as I do. Hssin, the ARM tells us, has been destroyed. I believe them because I was there. But has it been reinfested? Jenkins scoffs at the idea. Kzinti supply ships long en route to Hssin have been intercepted and destroyed. There have been flyby patrols. These quickie patrols have found nothing. What does that mean? There are thousands of places to hide on a planet. If you were given the assignment, could you hide yourself on Hssin?"

"I don't think it would be difficult. I intend to find out."

"What you intend to do on that planet does not interest me. It's an Intelligence matter I don't want to know about. The favor that I'm going to ask you *does* interest me and will ensure my full cooperation. I want a thorough study done of Hssin. When we left it in '22 there was not a kzin left alive on that world. When you leave it I want to be sure that the same is true."

"I'm bringing a kzin with me. I had to make a deal."

"You'll be bringing him out again. Right?"

"The deal is that if he comes with me, I'll rubberstamp Markham's repatriation release. He wants passage to Kzin."

"And good riddance. I don't expect you to find kzinti on Hssin. If you do I don't care if you kill them or bring them out with you—so long as Hssin is dead when you leave it. I'll send ten Wunderland marines with you, experienced men, men who were there. If they give it a clean bill of health, I'll believe you when you say you've done the job. This is a gentlemen's agreement. No orders, no talk, no paperwork."

Yankee did a quick scan for catches. He didn't like to take on high risks without careful evaluation, but sometimes an immediate call was the only way. "It's a deal."

The admiral was smiling. "Not so fast. I don't put one of my ships in the hands of a coward. You'll have to tell me about your mutiny."

"Yes," said Chloe enthusiastically. "Adventure time!"

"What are *you* doing here?" Yankee groaned. "It's your bedtime. Scram."

"No. I made a *deal* with my father."

Trapped. "It's simple." Yankee was angry now. "I disobeyed orders."

The admiral paused. "There's more to the story." It was a command.

"We were horsing around in the kzinti backwoods where no man had dared go before. We didn't know anything. We were looking around for signs of life. At 59 Virginis we found it. A major kzin world. Commander Shimmel planned a deep probing raid. Surprise was assumed. No electromagnetic message could have told them that they had a hyperspatial enemy. Shimmel went in. I held my wing back against orders. His twelve ships disappeared. The official story is that the kzin got him because I wasn't there to cover him. What *I* think is that Shimmel rammed his ships into the singularity. I think his officers followed him against the wall out of blind loyalty. I didn't. I told him his math was suspect, he was cutting it too fine. He got mad and ordered me in. I dallied. When he disappeared I was pretty freaked and went in, on my own calculations, at my own entrance point, and tried to find him. I didn't find anybody. The kzin found me and the wing had to fight its way out again."

"Why didn't you trust his calculations? He had standard UNSN computers and standard code. We all used the same code."

"A commander has discretion about how fine he's going to cut it. You trust the code. I don't. For Finagle's sake, nobody understands that stuff. It's all ad hoc. It's rules of thumb. The simplest rule of thumb is that the singularity is a sphere with radius, in AU, of thirty-six times the root of the mass of the star in solar masses. Would you bet your ship on that? Damn right you wouldn't. The code takes a thousand things into consideration to come up with a better answer. Do you trust that answer? I don't. I know it's *not* based on a theoretical understanding of hyperspace. It's based on experience and a bit of mumbo-jumbo distilled out of that incomprehensible manual the Outsiders sold us. When I was training at We Made It, one of the trainees walked his ship into the wall. He was using the then current code. What we found of him was a string of vapor three AUs long. The motor is probably still in hyperspace. Who knows? Scared me out of my mind. I *studied* singularities. Made up my own rules of thumb, and I'm damned if anybody will tell me not to use them. Yes, they are *conservative* rules but I'm still alive."

"Your loyalty to *yourself* is greater than your loyalty to the *navy*?"

"Daddy! You promised to be diplomatic! It was part of our deal!"

Yankee couldn't help himself. He rose to the bait. "I'm more loyal to the navy than you can imagine, sir. If I had my way men like Jenkins and Buford Early would be composting the shit of the newest recruits. With shovels!"

"So you think there is a time when a loyal officer must disobey orders?"

"I couldn't say. I wasn't thinking at the time. I was *reacting*. It was a judgment call. I was trying to keep my men alive to fight the kzinti. Going through the wall didn't make sense on any counts. Sometimes you have to sacrifice—but it has to count. When I came home I found a poem. I know it by heart. 1854. October twenty-fifth. The Battle of Balaclava. Tennyson. The British were better at obeying orders than I'll ever be." He closed his eyes.

" 'Forward the Light Brigade!
Charge for their guns,' he said;
Into the valley of Death
Rode the six hundred . . .

"Someone had blunder'd:
Theirs not to make reply.
Theirs not to reason why,
Theirs but to do and die.
Into the valley of Death
Rode the six hundred.

"Cannon to the right of them
Cannon to the left of them,
Cannon behind them
Volley'd and thunder'd;
Stormed at with shot and shell,
While horse and hero fell,
They that had fought so well
Came through the jaws of Death
Back from the mouth of Hell,
All that was left of them,
Left of six hundred."

• Chapter 11

(2437 A.D.)

The Wunderland crewed frigate *Erfolg* had been commissioned in '22, its first fight at R'hshssira. Badly damaged during the unsuccessful assault on Ch'Aakin in '25, it was rebuilt in '26 with an extended midsection to house the most powerful of the redesigned hypershunt motors coming off the We Made It assembly lines. From '26 to '33 mankind flooded hyperdrive warships into kzinti space. During that time the *Erfolg* had been an agile part of Admiral Chumeyer's fleet while the Patriarchy's supply lines were being decimated.

Yankee laconically referred to the MacDonald-Rishshi Peace Treaty as the "Truce." For the first year of the Peace the *Erfolg's* seventy man crew had patrolled kzinti worlds until forced into a less active role by a newer class of smaller and more economical (and less warworthy) UNSN patrol vessels. But Blumenhandler, with Wunderlander paranoia, had managed to keep the *Erfolg* out of retirement. She was war ready.

As Yankee boarded the ship through his shuttle's umbilical he remained apprehensive. Admiral Blumenhandler sympathized with a military readiness that went beyond patrol duty, but were his men as imaginative? Yankee was met by a thin young officer with an adam's apple and the nametag "Claukski" who took him through a cramped corridor that was stuffed with pipes and boxes and leads; most of them from the '26 retrofitting. The officer, who couldn't have been more than twenty-five, apologized solicitously for the inconvenience, pointing out possible hazards as they moved along. But where else could they have found room for new equipment but in the corridors? Military vessels are not designed for comfort.

He was led to a claustrophobic gunnery stuffed with five companions of Claukski, most of them too young to have been veterans of the war. Clandeboye expected bland camaraderie and a stash of beer but they seemed to know him and to be more interested in discussing his writings than in drinking. Such enthusiasm was heartening. Better yet, they were eager to show him what mischief they had been up to.

The *Erfolg's* battle stations were spliced into a simulator that could put the whole ship into game mode. They showed him software "saves" of recreations of the original Battle of R'hshssira, which had been refought with full crew participation. The tactics which had evolved from their practices were a radical departure from standard UNSN procedures.

Brilliant. Yet Yankee was depressed by their approach. Like hundreds of generations of military men before them they were preparing themselves to fight the Last War.

He tried to express his concern diplomatically. He had no intention of dampening such ardor. "Haven't you been unnecessarily restricting yourselves? Suppose war broke out again, might not UNSN ships themselves be equipped with gravitic polarizers? There *is* some effort being extended in that direction. War is never static."

Six men just grinned and immediately showed him a wilder scenario. Ship specifications—from firepower to performance—were modifiable with an initialization table. Already tactics were available for several specification upgrades. The recorded simulations on the battle screens appealed to Yankee's trainer instincts and he found himself grinning, too.

Ensign Tam Claukski, the youth with the adam's apple, was the first to sober. "We have a big problem we all want to discuss with you, sir."

They did have a big problem, he thought—they hadn't equipped their kzinti warcraft with hypershunt capabilities. That would turn out to be a major oversight if their intention was to ready themselves for some future war. "Problems? What kind?"

"When we tried to simulate a kzinti hyperdrive fleet we ran into major problems with our model."

Yankee was not used to naval types who could accept the obvious, and it startled him, suddenly, to find out that with these boys he was not going to have to cajole and convince. They already *knew*. He felt relief. He nodded and let Claukski continue.

"It turns out that our basic model is an efficient tactical analyzer, but that is more by accident than by design. In it we know everything about our own fleet and what help we can bring in from outside the battle. Without hyperdrive the kzin are limited to what ships they have on site. That makes the number of unknowns manageable. Tactics dominates over strategy." Tam made a face. "Assuming that the kzinti have hyperdrive changes everything. It connects any local battle to the whole Patriarchy. The number of unknowns, escalates. Strategy begins to dominate tactics. We thought . . ." The ensign trailed off. Obviously what he had once thought had proved incorrect. They were all waiting for Yankee to comment.

He said nothing. He thought. The Patriarchy already had a distributed military apparatus. With sub-light transport, centralized response to a threat was impossible. And so kzinti factories were everywhere. The ratcats had outposts in places where no hyperdrive-based civilization would bother to maintain a base. Thus given hyperdrive technology the kzin inherited an automatic advantage. They were immune to a centralized knock-out blow. At the same time they could mount an offensive from many directions. Not an easy threat to counter.

"I'm impressed with your tactical know-how. What you want from me, I suppose, is to teach you the art of Grand Strategy."

The look in their eyes said yes.

Yankee sighed. "I'm a poor excuse for a strategist. But I suppose we could work on it together." Just the thought delighted him. This trip was going to be a pleasure.

Eight days later, the Wunderland crewed frigate approached its target star cautiously, R'hshssira still a point of red. Military junk from the old battle tumbled on the telescopic screens, each a potential ambush. No hurry. They had days to scan and evaluate. It would be kzin strategy to lure them as deeply inside the singularity as possible before attacking. The sensors showed nothing from a distance, no power spots, no sudden acceleration changes. It did look like a dead system. Circumspectly they moved in closer. Still nothing.

Only when this runt of a stillborn star was hugely round in the sky did they spot a whole ship. It rose over the roiling reds of R'hshssira, clearly of kzinti design, spherical, huge, motherly, with all the grappling accouterments of a floating drydock. The *Nesting-Slashtooth-Bitch*. They knew what they were looking for.

The Wunderland captain kept weapons trained from a distance while adjusting velocity.

"Wrong radiation characteristics for an active ship," said one of Yankee's men from the sensor couch.

The captain was now asking for suggestions. He craned his head toward Yankee. "How close do you want to get?"

"It's all right to keep your distance. No hurry. She looks dead. But I'm not assuming she *is* dead." She could be dead but boobytrapped. He was hoping for crazy luck, hoping that the *Shark* would be there in the *Bitch's* womb. He didn't expect that kind of luck.

They tried hailing the ship on all kzinti communication frequencies. Nothing. If she wasn't dead, she was playing dead.

"We could send our kzin over," came a voice in their helmet phones.

"Not a chance!" Yankee snapped. "That hairy fighting machine stays confined!" He sent over two marines in armor with robot inspection ants, little hand-sized creatures that were programmed with the curiosity to crawl everywhere and record everything.

They were three hours reaching the ship and boarding. It was routine—but the long suspense kept everyone on edge and on alert.

"All their shuttles are gone," reported one marine in a tinny voice. Five minutes later the second marine reported that there was no *Shark* and no air. That was the last move they made for eight hours while the robo-ants sniffed about, crawled in holes, zoomed down corridors, disassembled light fixtures and air ducts. Bits of news came in from ant sensors. No food stores. Hibernation locks empty. Fuel tanks empty. Atmosphere rechargers dead. Gravitic polarizers dead. The ship had been abandoned.

Only then did Yankee take the trip himself. His team's headlamps found things that the robo-ants were not programmed to sense. In the airlock, which had no air to recycle, some desiccated leaves turned out to be Jotok fodder. On the floor of the empty spacesuit locker, Yankee found a kzin's currying brush, worn out at one end, still clogged with kzin fur.

Bolder penetration took them for a quick glide along

cold corridors of unhoused pipes and snaking power cables and gravityless catwalks. Their marine escorts loped ahead of them, lamps off, weapons ready, covering each other, signaling them forward, signaling them to freeze. When the group came to the unpowered bridge, its outer-armor was rolled open to the sky with interior layout illuminated darkly by the ruddy rays of R'hshssira. White beamlight from human heads moved silhouettes across the command center. It was jerry-rigged for operation by one kzin. Interesting. The ship had been ordered into battle with a full crew.

A scanning search by beamlight across the shadows found a porcelain fragment of a long-necked bird that had once been part of a unique Wunderland piece—a war trophy which had not survived the war. Navigation instruments were set up ready to be used. The team's kzinti electronics expert found the command brains, wiped. In the snack-bar there wasn't even a stick of kzinti jerky. Monkey curiosity caused Yankee to punch a button that normally provided drink. Nothing. But underneath the tap was the top of a human child's skull that had been converted to a drinking cup.

Moving on, they located the main machine shops. Some of the tools had been ripped out. The quality of the tools was amazing. But that's the way the kzinti fought. They couldn't call home for spare parts. They had to build them while the battle was going on. These tools weren't instruments for mass production. They were versatile, designed to turn out one of a kind of anything.

"Hey, sir. Come here. Some of this stuff isn't kzinti scrap."

He swung his beam toward the stalls and went in. They were looking at racks for old parts to be rebuilt or replaced.

His engineer was pointing with his beam. "These neatly

cataloged pieces are right off the *Shark*. They're badly damaged pieces. Frame, not motor. The *Shark* must have taken some heavy hits. It wouldn't be operational after that kind of damage."

"Could the crew have survived?"

"Dunno. You can die by breathing a rose petal into your windpipe and you can be standing in just the right place when a nuke goes off. The *Shark* was the smallest hyperdrive ship made. There would be injuries."

He was trying to imagine his cousin under attack. She *had* survived. His kzin *had* verified that. But how much did the kzinti know about healing humans? How much did they care? How long would an injured prisoner last? A day? A week? *Sixteen years?*

Reluctantly he turned back to the tools. He loved his cousin. Still she wasn't his primary concern—never forget the hypershunt. The tools all about him were of extraordinary sophistication; given clever hands, were they enough to rebuild a hyperdrive motor? He doubted it, but you never knew.

Leave that question for a later team. Now there was a ship to explore.

They explored. One tiny room was equipped as a torture chamber. A hot needle of inquiry. Restraints. Nervestim. Stretchers. Desocketers. A strip skin-flayer. He had to leave the room in a rage. *Poor Nora.* Then, in what had once been a storage area, human-sized cages were locked together. His horror increased.

In another place they found slave quarters with the kind of climbing-bar furniture you might associate with tree dwellers. Jotoki again. Yankee nodded. "That solves the mystery of how one kzin could operate a ship like this. He had a Jotoki crew. Does anyone know anything about those beasts?"

"Major Clandeboye, sir." The voice of one of the

marines resonated from his phones. "On your starboard, sir. Take a look at this."

It looked like a prison. It hadn't been built with the ship. Extra plates had been welded into place, armor plating. The surface was plastered with alarm electronics.

"Well, well, well," said Yankee. "Whatever fiend was held in there was something that terrified the fur off a kzin." He laughed. "Maybe we shouldn't open it."

"There's no air in there, sir. Nothing could be alive."

"If it would scare a kzin, maybe it doesn't need air."

"Sir, this is no time for ghost stories. I'm edgy enough as it is."

One of the marines replied, a touch of a smile to his voice. "Nothin to worry a man. By the size of the room— whatever's in there—it just cain't be no bigger'n ten kzin, if that."

"Can you crack it?" Yankee asked his electronics man. He was staring at the floor-to-ceiling lock.

The men waited silently, listening to each other breathe over the phones while their expert probed with his instruments.

"Sorry, sir. That's *secure*. From both sides. Maybe it's not a jail. Maybe it's a vault. We need a safe cracker. Gonna have to bring in some torches."

A weapons man popped over from the frigate and cut a neat hole out of the door, leaving hinges and lock in place. The width of the cut was less than a millimeter and its depth was regulated by a sonic signal so that the electron cutting beam wouldn't fry what was inside. Yankee made the mistake of trying to look in first. He was rudely moved out of the way by a marine sergeant. "Sir, where there's monsters, its my job to show head." He took a peek in, weapon at the ready. "Finagle's Dropping Jaw!" was all the sergeant could say.

Yankee got the second look. It was a woman's boudoir.

He just stood there in the hole not believing what he was seeing. *It's her*, he thought.

He recognized Lieutenant Argamentine's taste in furniture. She adored the rococo excesses of the eighteenth century's *Ancien Régime* which she tended to combine with the excesses of the late twenty-second century Turbulence style. Here was a Turbulent–Rococo bed with kzinti touches, even a hint of the classical baroque. It had a satin canopy and adjustable gravity controls. On the headboard golden cherubs flexed their bows in the direction of the King of France and his bevy of acrobatic mistresses. The king sat on a Roman throne.

Trance and Dance musicians clambered up the bedposts in a frenzy. Some of them had human heads on the bodies of Kzin animals. A chimera with a rat's tail and eagle's wings carried his violin like a bandolier while he climbed. At the top of the posts this frantic ascent was blocked by seashells upon which stood bosomed caryatids who held up the canopy.

One tended not to notice the rest of the room. There was an expansive futon for lounging. A deep pile rug. An inlaid, two drawer commode. A mirror with rococo frame. A small secretary.

Cousin Nora had spent more than a few of her teenage hours telling him what kind of furniture her husband was going to have to buy her. She had a file, thicker than her thumb, of 2D images collected from decorating mags and catalogs. She had disks of 3D display images that you could zap to change the inlay trim or furniture color or wood finish or upholstery pattern or cabinet style. In wartime one dreamed of peace.

Through thick gloves he tried to examine the delicate secretary by concentrated beamlight. Where had such pieces come from? No Wunderland cabinet maker had ever assembled anything like it! He pulled down his

helmet scope and in magnification saw foamed metal/
plastic of the kind that appealed to kzinti engineers looking for light weight and strength. Somehow the foam had
been laid down in layers that came out like wood grain.
The inlay pattern was an exuberant Flemish floral design.
All of it must have been made in the *Bitch*'s machine shop.
Still—the time! Ah, but on a subluminal voyage there
was always time.

He well knew that his Nora was a con artist—but her
magic was for men. How could it work on a kzin? He
went to the bedposts. Nora wouldn't have known how to
carve like that in metal, nor had the patience, nor the
models. They showed evidence of having been variable-
form extruded, not carved. Probably from a 3D template
based on Nora's sketches. An alien mind had fleshed out
the template. The animal bodies weren't human, weren't
even of Earth. Less of Earth, even, than the gargoyles of
the French cathedrals. Why would a kzin have done this
for her? And at the same time held her in such a formidable brig? Whoever had built such a prison had both
been terrified of Nora Argamentine and deeply under
her spell.

It didn't make sense. The Nora he knew would stand
on a stool and scream if you brought a ratcat into the
same room with her. For that matter, Yankee knew that if
he ever had to face an armed kzin at anything less than a
couple of light-minutes, *he* would stand on a stool and
scream.

It got worse. The marines found the neural lab—almost
stripped of its equipment, but not of its displays. The electronic records were gone. Yet conveniently near the op-
erating table was a collected bundle of notes on what kzinti
used for paper. The script was meticulous. This kzin jot-
ted down real-time remarks during his experiments. His
comments were in chronological order.

Back on the frigate their Wunderland kzinti specialist wasn't optimistic about a translation. He had worked in the kzinti bureaucracy most of his adult life. "It's technicalese. Even the technicalese of a standardized scientific language like English is hard to decode if you're just a linguist. This is the Hero's Tongue all right, and I can get the words and the dates and the sense of it—but the content of it is another matter. The chemical symbolism is all there—but we don't really understand how they *think* about biochemistry. It's like trying to read a scientific paper from Newton's time. But the mere fact that we know it is chemistry and medicine gives us a leg up. We'll figure out something. Don't know how far we'll get."

The initial analysis did reveal that they were dealing with experiments on many different humans; one of them was Lieutenant Nora Argamentine. Her genetic makeup was on her military records—and whoever this kzin was he had been entering in his experiments genetic codes that belonged uniquely to Argamentine.

"Can you tell what he's been trying to do to her?"

"Yeah, but I had to check it. Grow hair."

"What?"

"He was adjusting her body to grow a full coat of fur. Don't know the full outcome. The record ends suddenly, maybe when they left for Hssin."

Yankee wasn't ready for the surface just yet. The evidence was that kzin and slaves had abandoned ship for residence on Hssin, and Yankee needed to know all he could find before trying to stalk them through the wreckage of a dead city. If Nora was still alive down there he didn't want her killed as a hostage just because of failed preparations.

Yankee let Hwass Hwasschoaw loose in the *Bitch*— with a marine and a robo-ant escort. And with an explosive charge attached to Hwass's spinal cord at the point on his back which a kzin couldn't reach with his hands. Some of Yankee's men gently chided their boss for being paranoid. "Better paranoid than destroyed," was his motto. He was honest with the kzin. "I don't trust you."

The kzin accepted such directness graciously. He had made an open bargain with Clandeboye that he was keeping faithfully. Yankee was under no illusions; he suspected that his kzin had an agenda beyond any bargain—Hwass was as much interested in the fate of the hypershunt motor as was the UNSN, though the subject was never mentioned. They talked about Nora Argamentine, a screen to cover their mutual interest in the *Shark*'s fate.

In his report Hwass claimed to have put together the sequence of events which had brought the *Nesting-Slashtooth-Bitch* to Hssin, though the logs no longer existed. Yankee was surprised at the competence of the kzin's observations. They were on a level that made him dangerous. The report was thorough, but the damn ratcat was assuming too much. Hwass seemed to be having a hard time with the idea of a slave revolt. Yankee was just having a hard time with the idea of five-limbed slaves.

He did some research. The ARM's database didn't have much on the Jotok.

They were born the size of minnows. The race lacked any kind of sexual conflict because when five minnow-arms wedded during their pond phase they were always of different sexes. Divorce to a fused Jotok was as unthinkable as divorcing a heart or a liver. During childhood they were scurrying, unthinking animals of no great bulk, surviving in their forested habitat more by the laws of large numbers than by their wits—like toads or fish, the prey of carnivores. Only adolescence brought on an endocrinal sea-change in their nervous system. Half-grown, they now had the bulk and the digestive capacity to support the development of their five networked brains.

(At this point Yankee noted wryly that human intelligence was limited by the pelvic size of the human female; until not so long ago the mother of a super-genius died in childbirth.) The Jotoki had no such limitation.

Left in the wild they never learned to talk but became very clever. The wild, unparented Jotok made a cunning forest foe and a tasty meal and for that reason was widely stocked in kzinti hunting parks. To talk they needed to be adopted by a speaking adult. How had it been in the eons before they became slaves of the kzin? Had an adult Jotok taken a walk in the forest and picked out a ripe teenager to become his bond servant? Was there still a free Jotok world out there among the stars? Within the Patriarchy it was only an adult kzin who was allowed to adopt a maturing Jotok.

The ARM researcher had left an open question at the end of his essay. Full-named kzin, who had their harems and their sons to raise, told glowing tales of Jotok hunts, how cleverly this animal evaded pursuit and how dangerous he could be. There were poems to the taste of fresh-caught Jotok. But these animals were plainly thought to make vicious, unreliable slaves. Yet kzinti who had been denied harems by their more aggressive rivals, who could afford not even a single female, were the ones who adopted and raised Jotoki as slaves, praising their virtues.

Yankee called upon Hwass for clarifications to his summary of events. This kzin's command of English sometimes lacked clarity. He took for granted things that Yankee did not know. And perhaps he was being evasive about fine points.

"Let's go over it from the beginning so that I can be sure I have it straight. We'll concentrate on Nora and the slave revolt."

Hwass began his exposition from an oblique angle, too shocked by his own discoveries to be direct. "Yess. I iss deduce captive Argamentine iss first kept in cages."

"You kzin seem to have a cavalier way of treating your prisoners of war!" Yankee was angry but he was diplomat enough not to mention the torture or the experiments.

"She iss animal," explained Hwass.

"She is an intelligent being, not an animal!" snapped Yankee, his rage getting the better of him.

"Many animal iss intelligent. Not right criterion. God iss created many kinds animals. Dumb animals. Smart animals. Foolish animals. Food animals. Unclean animals. Dishonest animals. All iss got place in God's universe."

"And you're not an animal?"

"No."

"We'll agree to disagree. Let's get back on track. Nora is in the cages. What then? What you've dug up looks like a mutiny to me."

"There iss major fight battle inside *Bitch* at Wunderland. You iss not notice the spoor. Clever cleanup." He went over his documentation of the erased dents, the electronic equipment which had been rigged and then derigged, including a control room network tap. "Evidence toolroom jigs iss hasty set to shape-out weapons not good for any use except fight inside ship." Hwass was able to reconstruct the battle almost from the original dormitory gassings to the final killings in the corridors.

"Jotoki against ratcat?"

Hwass obviously had difficulty with Yankee's phrasing. "Slave against master," he corrected stiffly.

"Does that happen often?"

Hwass smiled at the insult, waiting to calm himself before he continued. "Never. Iss work of ruthless traitor, Trainer-of-Slaves. Death penalty by chopped-liver for what he iss do."

"Sounds familiar."

"You iss must understand. Dominance/dominated roles

established iss what make war profitable. Sometimes produce conundrum puzzle.

"Number one conundrum: Trainer-of-Slaves iss ordered to battle. Iss his heroic duty. As dominated-one, he sees himself make glorious obedience. All piece of puzzles fit right action. Iss good approvable solution. Thus conundrum puzzle complete.

"But Hwakkss! He iss notice piece protrude. Many ways to put conundrum back together—but iss only one way with no piece protrude. Hwakkss, this sticking-out-piece iss battle loss of important captive and all special knowledge!

"Number two: Trainer-of-Slaves iss has other excellent duty. Captive gifted to Patriarch so her big knowledge iss war profit. Such good aftermath iss golden desire. But conundrum puzzle completed new way iss has new piece sticking out.

"Hwakkss! New sticking-out-piece iss mean must break dominance bond/word/honor—run from battle—kill warriors who iss trekking duty bound. Bad smell.

"Puzzle put together one way, Trainer-of-Slaves iss traitor. Puzzle put together other way, Trainer-of-Slaves iss traitor. What iss your monkey idiom: rock and hard place?"

"Sounds like a recipe for mutiny," said Yankee. "That I understand." But he wasn't convinced. "So this Trainer-of-Slaves waves his *wtsai* in the air and his slaves swarm over the ship, killing kzin?" Put that way it didn't even sound likely.

Hwass was pained. It wasn't that simple.

First he had to explain the peculiar nature of the slaves commanded by Trainer-of-Slaves. No Jotok could or would revolt. (Hwass was absolutely sure of that.) Any Jotok, he explained, was a hopeless strategist because it was an animal with five minds. These spiderlike vegetarians were subject to five-way internal arguments. Each mind had absolute control over only one arm and one eye though each could grant control to another mind. Depending upon which minds were awake and which were asleep, a Jotok went through a kaleidoscope of daily personality changes. He could not *create* orders—but a properly trained Jotok would *obey* orders!

"I've been led to understand that many kzin refuse to own Jotoki because they can be vicious and unpredictable. That doesn't sound like obeying orders to me."

"You iss must understand the mystical order that God iss place upon His creations. When you know God's mind all iss revealed. The secret of Jotoki loyalty iss simple. Never *buy* a Jotok. He iss will serve you well or maybe not—but he iss be *loyal* to his trainer. Never to accept Jotok as *gift*. He iss will work hard—but he iss be *loyal* only to his trainer." Hwass thumped his tail. It was irritating to have to explain such elementary realities to an animal. "Trainer-of-Slaves iss have no sons to raise. He iss have time to train Jotoki. The worst he sells, the best he keeps. You iss understand now?"

"Not really."

Hwass continued his impatient lecture. He had deduced the only possible scenario. When Trainer-of-Slaves learned that the *Nesting-Slashtooth-Bitch* was to be committed to a deadly battle he laid out a plan of action for his disciplined corps of Jotoki slaves *before* being arrested for insubordination and confined to hibernation. All they had to do was carry out his brilliant plan.

"Trainer-of-Slaves iss master strategist."

First the deadly gas attack on the dormitory to kill all sleeping kzin. Hwass was unaware of the nature of the gas but was certain that Trainer knew enough chemistry to manufacture it. Then the failed attack directly at the command center which had sent the now alert kzin scurrying to battle stations. This had set up a cascade of killing traps, each one propelling the surviving kzinti into the next.

"If he's such a brilliant strategist, why was he so afraid of Lieutenant Argamentine?"

"Trainer-of-Slaves iss known coward. Mocking name iss 'Eater-of-Grass.' Lieutenant-Observer iss once escape. Iss try kill Trainer." Hwass's ears were wiggling in mirth. "Trainer pisses vegetable broth. Iss has made big mistake. Was assume female human iss feminine."

"He got that right."

"Iss wrong. Human females is all dyke." Hwass's ears were wiggling again.

"You're asking to be spaced."

"Iss joke," said Hwass, grinning. "Spacing me iss breaking honorable contract."

"Take it easy. I'm just being sarcastic. You've earned your passage back to Kzin."

"Twice," growled Hwass.

It might be a good idea to space him, thought Yankee, contract be damned. He knew too much. But it didn't really matter. If the *Shark* had been repaired, the Patriarch already knew, and if it hadn't made it, learning that Trainer had failed wasn't going to help the Patriarch. And Hwass *would* be carrying a peace message from Commissioner Markham.

"My word is good," he said.

"Contract iss not finish yet. You iss need guide to Hssin."

The ratcat was thinking that the *Shark* might be down there. "Suppose we found the ship down there? What would you do?"

"Iss interesting hypothetical question."

Later Yankee grumbled about Hwasschoaw when he was discussing the details of the coming Hssin landing party with their captain. "Every time I talk to him he gives me the heebie-jeebies. He's planning to kill us all."

"Of course. He's a kzin. But he can't."

"I didn't like the way he was looking at my air-conditioning grille. He had a glint in his eye when he talked about how Trainer had gassed the crew of the *Bitch*. Why did he notice that detail? It was on his mind."

"We've got eight separate life-support systems on this ship. The air conditioners lock up the second they sense fire or toxic gas."

"I think I'm going to keep at least two men in suits at all times."

"What about food poisoning?" the captain teased.

"I'll think about it."

"We billet him in what amounts to a cage. When he's out, he's under guard."

"He'll escape. He's going to try to kill us all and steal the ship."

The captain laughed. "Not a chance."

"Don't count on it."

• Chapter 12

(2437 A.D.)

Grraf-Nig's plan to steal the *Shark* and escape to Kzin was proceeding without a flaw. His team of W'kkai engineers had rebuilt the *Shark* to his specifications, saving the internal structures he was sure were necessary for the hyperfield build-up, replacing the rest with a kzinti design that was far in advance of any standard kzin technology. He'd been in maintenance at Wunderland, adept at implementing illegal ship modifications in fighters; he knew he had at his disposal the most deadly small fighting craft ever fielded by the kzinti. It would be able to outmaneuver *any* ship of the old W'kkai Standard Spec Attack Fleet. *If* it was in operational condition.

Cautious testing had uncovered only minor problems. Of course, there had, as yet, been no tests of the hyperdrive in the new configuration—all experimentation outside the singularity had to be carefully hidden from UNSN patrol surveillance. But the *Shark*'s new hyperspace performance did not really worry Grraf-Nig; he had spent thirteen years overhauling its motor. This particular hypershunt had brought him from Hssin to W'kkai and had never showed any of the instabilities of the W'kkai copies which were giving them so much trouble.

In the early tests of the modified *Shark* he'd always had an overdressed W'kkai warrior with him as test pilot. For this "final" test (which was only number three in a series of eight-plus-one) he had managed to arrive early, by priority shuttle, bringing with him his Jotok slave, Long-Reach, "for a special pre-flight installation." Some officer would be skinned alive for not noticing the irregularity.

The *Shark* was now loaded and flight-checked, minus only its perfumed Ship-Tester, who had been conveniently delayed on W'kkai but who was probably already puzzled by the special priority shuttle that had preceded him to the test craft. He would not yet be alarmed. The test sequence commands were to be delivered electromagnetically by the research station and could be overridden *only* by Ship-Tester and *only* in an emergency. So everyone thought.

By the time Ship-Tester was on his way, the five arms of Long-Reach had rewired the controls. It was too late to stop the escape.

Grraf-Nig turned his attention to the space around him. The research station was only a glint in the sky, but W'kkai was still a large disk. W'kkaisun was so large at a hundred light-seconds that it had to be blotted out by the sun-screens. He and Long-Reach had a lengthy maneuver ahead of them. Because the singularity around W'kkaisun extended out for three light hours it would take at least a day at maximum gravitic polarizer acceleration before they could disappear via hypershunt. They had a good chance to beat pursuit. A sphere three light hours in radius was an enormous volume to defend, and the W'kkai navy was of necessity deployed to defend priority installations, not to prevent defections.

The worst danger came from the fleet close to W'kkai, who would get their pursuit orders immediately with a minimum of light-lag delay. The improved *Shark* still had a twelve-g acceleration edge on the best of the *Scream-of-Vengeance* fighters available to intercept them. Grraf-Nig glanced warily at the brilliant point of light that was cold Hrotish, six times as massive as W'kkai with its important W'kkai-sized moon. There was a fleet there, too, and they were only six light minutes away.

Several "cones of escape" looked very good, though the desperado was not underestimating the risks. The Fanged God threw his bones carelessly. Grraf-Nig recalled the biggest coincidence of his lifetime—how he came to be testing illegal modifications of Kr-Captain's *Scream-of-Vengeance* fighter at just the right time and place. Chance alone had placed them at a location from which they were able to destroy the human ramscoop *Yamamoto* as it passed through the Alpha Centauri system. Luck might be with them now—and it might not.

Briefly he relished his memories of Grraf-Hromfi, the greatest strategist he had ever known, the warrior he had honored by taking half his name. "Look before you leap," reminded the master constantly. Grraf-Nig had programmed a randomly curving path through the cone of escape so that W'kkai sensors, handicapped by light-lag, would give an ever less accurate prediction of his real position.

A wary Hero scanned his instruments. He looked at the glint of the research station and looked straight at Hrotish before he grinned—and *leaped*. A rebuilt *Shark* shot off at an acceleration that human technology could not match.

Missile attack would be the best way to stop him, but he doubted that they would use it against their only reliably operational hypershunt motor. If they did, he had beam-armament and a very good "Weapons-Officer" in Long-Reach who had always played that part while they were illegally modifying fighter craft for the Fifth-Fleet's Black Pride at Centauri. To call his *slave* "Weapons-Officer" aloud would not do—but he could *think* it. Long-Reach's five networked brains made him the fastest Weapons-Officer Grraf-Nig had ever met.

Beam attack was another danger but he did not doubt that he could sidestep any offensive beam-weapon launched against him, never having met a W'kkai warrior who understood beam evasion. *He* understood. He had been trained by Grraf-Hromfi, who had been trained by Chuut-Riit. Beam-weapons were a favorite of the humans, who had used them in ingenious fashions while defending themselves at Man-sun. Never one to overlook details, Chuut-Riit analyzed their monkey-tricks and formalized a defensive dance against them. The weakness of beam weapons was the light-lag. They were useful against fixed targets. They were useful for a long-distance surprise assault. They were useful for light-second infighting. Otherwise they could be defended against.

"Zap-p-p-p-p!" harmonized Long-Reach in an exclamation from the five mouths of his lunged arms. He had taken out his first closing missile with a beam bolt.

Grraf-Nig roared something in the Hero's Tongue that translated roughly as, "Mate with sthondats!" Fortunately the robo-assassins were *chasing* them; none were attacking from the forward direction, which would have been really dangerous. He had been wrong about his comrades' willingness to attack him with missiles. They weren't going to limit themselves to boarding; they were killing mad. Manually he began to add fillips to the automatic evasions. Long-Reach got two more in a row, pause, then five, the last one right on their tail—blossoms as the polarizer fields collapsed. An individual missile had little chance of making it through—but Long-Reach could be overwhelmed. Grraf-Nig wished he was in fighter formation with *several* beams protecting their rear. This, however, was more exciting.

As quickly as it began, the missile attack ceased. That was good. As time passed, their pursuers' ability to estimate their present position was seriously degrading. But

Grraf-Nig watched his instruments with the intensity of a predator anticipating a flock of dangerous prey. It was to the advantage of a cluster of missiles to talk to each other and coordinate their attack for the same moment. The light-lag in the "talk" probably doomed that kind of blow, but any possibility had to be watched for.

When it came, the second missile attack was of an entirely different kind. The missiles began to detonate in front of them. It was a strategy of desperation since their pursuers knew only where they *had* been. If the explosion erupted behind them, it posed no danger. If it was *just* beyond them, the fireball of fragments presented too small a cross-section to be dangerous. And if the warhead detonated too far ahead of them, the fireball was too diffuse to do damage when they passed through it. After all, the kzin had been traveling through interstellar space at eighty percent of light-speed for thousands of years. The fierce gravitic polarizer fields that they used to move their ships were quite good enough to protect them from normal interstellar debris.

Nevertheless Grraf-Nig dodged cautiously among the fireballs, careful not to let himself be herded toward an ambush point. The adventure reminded him of a jerky video he had viewed on Wunderland. The Revolutionary American Air Claw was bombing Hamburg in winged B-TwoEights+Ones, thousands strong. Hamburg's Prince of Huns had been sending mercenaries to the English to fight on American soil, and the American man-beasts had become annoyed. Alarmed, the Hun animals tried to defend themselves by tossing exploding cylinders into the sky. But the berserker monkeys just flew through the black flak puffs yelling their Rebel cry of vengeance against the English, blowing up Huns along the way.

The kzin ran for his life until, gradually, the fireballs of "flak" faded as the *Shark*'s probable position began to be smeared over too vast a volume to make a scatter-shot attack plausible. But new attackers would now be converging from the sides. Long-Reach was keeping track of the pursuers with a Weapons-Officer's wide-angle telescopic sensors.

"Eleven pursuers visible," said one of Long-Reach's arms.

Grraf-Nig was more worried about what was coming from the direction of Hrotish than he was about the group that had already fired on him. But nothing happened. They lost track of their pursuers by outrunning them. That was unnerving, not to know where the enemy was, or whether they were accelerating headlong into a trap. They continued maximum evasion shifts as a precaution.

After uneventful hours, he began a methodical re-programming of the escape. They had lost him, but he knew exactly where he was—by now well above the thin asteroid ring of W'kkaisun. He had a good idea of where each W'kkai warship had been at the beginning of his escape and what their probable moves would be. His computations (based on pre-escape intelligence, probably inadequate) showed him that there were five warships up ahead that he need worry about, one of them a carrier of eight fast *Scream-of-Vengeance* fighters. If they made contact with him, his advantage would be hours of acceleration lead time. They could only attack him in a single fast flyby. It would be like stealing mother's milk. He'd be moving at something like an eighth the velocity of light.

But once he crossed the singularity, evading the UNSN patrol was going to be a special challenge. There was only one hyperspace warship out there now but the monkeys had hyperwave radio and could quickly call in reinforcements from light years away. Surely its captain had sat bolt upright at that fireworks display of flak and might already be calling for help. It didn't matter that his patrol ship was on the other side of the singularity—in a hop, skip, and jump he could be on top of the *Shark*. The UNSN had perfected the art of hunting down and killing the gravitic ships of the kzinti in interstellar space.

None of this was in the manuals—not even Chuut-Riit's manuals. Grraf-Nig needed to give his moves heavy thought in the few hours of peace left to him. The major problem with equipping a hypershunt ship like the *Shark* with a gravitic drive was that the gravitic polarizer, when in use, created its own hyperspace singularity. He was going to have to collapse his gravitic field *before* he disappeared into hyperspace—an action that was equivalent to decelerating down to his rest velocity. If he burst through the singularity at twenty percent of light speed, he'd be vulnerable to the UNSN *for a full day* before he could evade them by hypershunt.

He began his deceleration early. It was risky. On the other claw, it meant that the W'kkai fleet would overshoot him and, while penetrating the singularity in front of him, become a decoy fleet masking his escape—if they didn't find and kill him before the UNSN found and killed them. It was a melee he hoped wasn't going to start a new war—no world of the Patriarch was ready for that yet!

By the time the *Shark* passed through the singularity, much later than his original planning, he was still traveling fast—but slow enough so that he was flying into a swarm of W'kkai warriors. His sensors began to pick up more and more of them until he located twenty at about maximum range. It wasn't the formation he expected to see. There were already four UNSN warships on the scene. Neither fleet was attacking the other. Both were wary and moving in defensive array. Because of light-lag he was well behind on the true situation.

It looked like the monkeys were holding back in a

blocking formation, waiting for reinforcement. It looked like the W'kkai fleet was well on the way to a conservative interception which would not threaten the UNSN warships. Such precautions were all in the *Shark*'s favor. Grraf-Nig began to pick up frantic bits of communication between Hero and Man-beast.

He was being sold as a renegade. The W'kkai commander was giving the beasts permission to vaporize him, promising no retaliation if they did. They were offering to take out the *Shark* themselves if the United Nations would stand aside. All the niceties of the MacDonald-Rishshi treaty were being observed. Only the light-minutes were keeping the opponents from each other's throats.

Grraf-Nig was enormously relieved. He had timed everything perfectly. His luck as a survivor had held. Before anyone could get to them, the *Shark* would disappear into hyperspace and reappear alone inside an interstellar sphere of stars.

The gravitic field died. The *Shark* had come to rest relative to its starting frame of reference—minus the velocity of escape from W'kkai's orbital distance. Grraf-Nig wiggled his ears and cut in the phase-change for the hypershunt build-up. Nothing happened.

For a stunned moment the giant kzin thought that Long-Reach had made a mistake when he rewired the controls, but Long-Reach himself had no such doubts. He had worked with this motor a good part of his life. Instantly he was at the motor housing and hit the clamps. The housing popped away and floated off to the wall. A cast iron dummy of the correct weight and balance sat where the hypershunt should have been.

It was something to think about—but death was only minutes away. There was no time to yowl in anguish. There was no time even to curse High Admiral Si-Kish's paranoia.

Outward from W'kkaisun, the UNSN waited. The W'kkai fleet was moving in on their renegade cautiously—of course, cautiously because they already knew that the *Shark* couldn't escape into hyperspace.

"Battle stations!" Grraf-Nig screamed at Long-Reach.

A second later they were moving at full acceleration toward W'kkai. There was no escape. No matter how frantically his mind panicked through the alternatives, there was no reasonable way out. It was either fight to an honorable death or suffer the humiliation of surrender. He sat at the controls, brilliantly evading attack, but numb. He could no longer think of himself as the noble Grraf-Nig. He remembered a terrible day from his past when a gang of Hssin kits had cornered him for an easy kill—and he had saved his life by eating grass. What honor was there for a kit out to prove his warrior skills who carried the ears of a grass-eater on his belt?

Grass-Eater negotiated the surrender of the *Shark* through electronic static and violent maneuvers. He knew they wanted to save the ship because it was the prototype of a deadly fighter that was intended to spearhead W'kkai ambition, but he wasn't sure they would spare his life once the *Shark* was secure. It didn't matter. Better that W'kkai should triumph over Kzinhome with a reinvigorated Patriarchy than for Heroes to languish as the slaves of squabbling monkeys. Let them have their prototype.

There wasn't room enough for a warrior to board the *Shark*. Long-Reach and his defeated master met their captors in space and were taken back to a warship. The slave disappeared into its slave quarters; the mortified one was stripped inside the airlock. Undressed, a warrior of W'kkai was a nameless animal without power. No W'kkai Hero among those who had captured him called him by name. He had no name. They could not even look at him.

• Chapter 13

(2437 A.D.)

The landing party came down at dawn in the plains outside of what they all called Fort Hssin. In his brief glimpse of Hssin's ruins from high descent, Yankee had seen the widespread damage; sections of the city were crumpled or gone—but from the ground it looked almost whole. The ruddy light of a huge R'hshssira on the horizon had been further reddened by an oblique passage through the poisonous air, the general gloom and the low angle of their landing site obscuring the injury to the sprawling, once airtight buildings. A steady wind was whipping a thin drift of snow in the direction of the city and the dawn-bright mountains.

"Godforsaken place."

They had maps of Hssin made by the naval force that destroyed it, and they could run these 3D plots inside their helmets along with marine battle films of the ground assault, keyed to the battle locations. Still, once they had slipped into the city through the breached atmospheric barrier, they were lost tourists in a huge necropolis without any friendly local residents to set them straight—only mummified kzinti who lay in the dark where they had suffocated.

The size of the rooms and corridors was intimidating—built for two-hundred-kilogram, two-and-a-half-meter-tall kzinti. War damage was an obstacle to mobility. One grisly room contained racks of improvised hospital beds for badly wounded warriors who had died with their masks on, waiting for medical help that never came, now preserved for posterity. Some of the roofs were open to the sky, exposed corridors drifting in snow. Some corridors looked down into a well of rubble. Yankee's beamlight caught the upside down head of a kzin grinning at them from a hole in a half-collapsed ceiling. One corridor was filled with the fallen wreckage of four stories. Some of the caverns that Yankee wanted to explore were declared off-limits by the team's cautious structural engineer.

"Nobody could be living here now!" exclaimed one of Yankee's companions.

"You're a flatlander." Yankee's eyes and lamp were picking out the details of the strange kzinti air seals with the fascination of a man who had spent half his life in the Belt and in spaceships. "When you've lived in space a while you know a city like this is so compartmentalized against failure that even several blowouts won't knock it out of commission. Life support could be restored in pieces of it. I wouldn't want the job. But it could be done. That's what we're looking for."

They found nothing. They were afraid to call in their kept kzin, afraid the devastation would send him into a rage, but he had passed through this city with Chuut-Riit's armada and knew the ways of kzin when they were forced to live together. They needed his insight.

In one of the least damaged of Hssin's public spaces Clandeboye set up an inflatable command center, hardly more than a balloon with portable airlock and life support and communications interfaces. He added instruments that allowed him to follow Hwass by remote sensing, then brought down the kzin and let him loose with his marine escort.

Whatever the warrior felt in this world where the evidence of massacre was everywhere, he maintained an icy professional calm. He was a bloodhound looking for the lost trail. Almost the first place he searched was the old Hssin hunting park.

"Iss where I hunted with Chuut-Riit my first humans."

"Why don't we just cut that flea-bitten cat's throat," whispered one of Yankee's men on the monitoring team, two-way comm off. He was a fashionable Belter with delicately carved combs in his mohawk, a postwar hair style that the older generation of Belters considered effete. Mohawks were designed to keep the head shaved and the hair out of the way in space. Adding combs, grumbled parents, was an insubordinate generation's defiance of practicality.

Yankee had his eyes on the tiny color screen whose image bobbed and whizzed with Hwass's head motions. "He's getting even with us for shoving his muzzle into the massacre of his people. Be patient. He's going to lead us right to this Trainer-of-Slaves."

"Why would he do that?" asked the logician among Yankee's companions. "It's not in his best interest."

"You think. Hwass is a gambler. If he finds the *Shark* before we do, he's probably going to try to kill us all. Maybe teamed up with Trainer and his slaves he can capture the *Erfolg* and take it to Kzin. He can't do that alone. Why wouldn't he want to find Trainer?"

"For a pessimist, you're in a strangely sanguine mood!" snapped the Belter.

Another of Yankee's men commented wryly, "He just wants us to keep our terrified eyes glued to the screen."

"If that ratcat's going to kill us, why don't we kill him now?" The Belter was back to his theme song.

"We don't *know* that he's going to kill us," said Yankee happily, watching Hwass's camera eye move through a hunting park turned to petrified forest. A poisonous snow had drifted in from the open sky.

"So we wait till he does before we object?" grumbled the coiffured Belter sarcastically.

"No. We draw first."

"Nero fiddles while Rome burns. Yankee draws pictures while Rome burns? You aren't making sense."

Yankee smiled. "A 'fast draw' is just an old flatlander expression in use before you floaters corrupted the language with 'nano-swat.' "

"We're going to nano-swat him? You could have fooled me. Old man switches don't swat."

"You aren't making sense," said Yankee. "I ain't old yet; I'm a spring chicken baby-sitting toddlers."

Their kzin had picked up his spoor. He was moving out of a pattern of random search and into a quick lope.

"What's he doing?"

"Hwass thinks Trainer would have gone right to the hunting park. It was a Jotoki run when he was an apprentice slave-master. That's where he recruited his slaves. Sentimental attachment. We revisit those places we are sentimentally attached to and leave spoor for Hwass to sniff at."

"A kzin is sentimental?"

"Who knows? I'm just simianizing their emotions. I'm sentimental so that's what I understand. I once cut short a frantically urgent trip just to stop at a motel and rent the same room where I first got laid. Number 27. The wallpaper was bamboo and stars. Over the room's comp was a huge animation of a deer in the forest done by one of those production line programmers—it just kept wandering through the forest. I remember everything about my lady but her eyes; she was wearing VR goggles plugged into the comp, morphing me into Finagle knows what. Maybe kzinti are sentimental about their first slave. Who knows?"

"Iss used path of travel," commented Hwass over the phones.

The camera eye was moving now with the speed of one who wasn't bollixed by sudden rubble intrusions that shouldn't be there. It wasn't that Hwass knew where he was going; he was following the trail of someone who did. Once he stopped to examine kzin boot tracks across snow that had taken years to drift in through some breached barrier.

Yankee quickly uploaded a message to the *Erfolg.* "We've got him." He switched to one of the marine cameras to check that the explosive charge was still attached to Hwass's upper spine, then followed the lead camera in fascination as it routed itself around the damage.

Suddenly Hwass stopped. One of the internal airlocks was shut. He cycled through it manually into a sector where the telemetry said the air was good, though too cold for comfort. Hwass's perceptive eyes spotted exactly where the war-made breaches had been sealed. He found an emergency power plant that matched a missing unit from the *Bitch.* When he turned it on, the lights faded in and the air conditioner began to recycle the stale atmosphere. The system had been left on standby, as if someone had anticipated that he might have to return.

Images began to shift in staccato rhythm. Yankee had no clear idea of why the camera moved to look where it did, except that the glances were quick and purposeful as if Hwass was clicking down a checksheet of his own devising. He hastened through the few sealed rooms, checking this and checking that. He was memorizing detail that he wasn't sure his human masters would give him a second chance to see. Finally he just stopped in the middle of examining a row of machine tools. They could not see his face—but they could hear his voice. "You iss defeated, Major Yankee Clandeboye. They iss *gone*. The *Shark*'s motor iss has be here but iss *gone*."

Yankee switched his mike back to the frigate. He got

the comm officer. "Send a message by hyperwave directly to General Fry, Sol, Gibraltar Base." (They had dropped off a hyperwave buoy outside of R'hshssira's singularity and could communicate with it electromagnetically. It would take longer for the message to reach the buoy than to travel the 5.3 light years from R'hshssira to Sol.)

"Quote: 'The *Shark* has been delivered to the Patriarchy.' Unquote."

The captain came on line. "What's this? What have you got?"

"No details yet."

"What's the verification?"

"None. Hwass just told us and *he* seems sure. Get that message off! I don't want him deciding that we know too much. He might think we're all worth killing to keep the news quiet. We can send the rest later as it comes in. I told you, I don't trust that kzin."

"There's such a thing as overcaution," the captain chided.

"Captain, why does a man have tits?"

"You got me, Yankee. Why?"

"Just in case."

Later that day, Yankee's team began its painstaking assessment of the find.

On a separate floor, below the main working area that Trainer-of-Slaves had salvaged for himself, Yankee discovered a suite of luxurious apartments with its own airlock and life support. It had been repaired. Once inside he recognized it for what it had once been in the heyday of Hssin's power—the harem quarters of some consequential kzin.

The interior was all stone (or structurally enhanced stone) of abnormally large proportions even for a kzin dwelling. Spaciousness meant power and wealth—and a full name. On the floor was a tapestry-like rug, round as the world, woven with scenes of the hunt: here a kzin stalking through the orange grass, there a magnificent kzin head between the leaves of a forest. And everywhere the brilliant colors of animals of the hunt, fleeing, hushed, flying, hiding in the branches. The rug was cuddly soft. It was just right for games of coy chase and play.

There were no hanging weapons or trophies, yet it was a male's hall. Carved into the eastern wall, an august glyph glorified some noble family: a dozen kzinti in profile, the faces of conquerors. An arched niche held a crotch of polished wood, half tree, half tale of nature transformed by sculptor's power. Next to the niche a floor-to-ceiling tapestry cut a narrow window into the gray stone to a colorful landscape on some unconquered planet of fantastic imagination. A final touch to the male decor might have been lithe kzinrretti moving through the hall to entertain and serve.

An arched entrance at the back of the hall led to the living quarters of individual kzinrretti: kitchens, birthing chambers, nurseries for the kits and Yankee couldn't guess what-all. There was no trace that a whole harem might have died here. Its most recent occupants had been human. The auburn hairs in the rug were of Lieutenant Argamentine's genotype. He remembered the way she used to pull at a curl of that hair when she was agitated. *Damn, damn, damn.*

In the tunnels and caves shaped for romping kits they found a box of crudely made toys, alien—perhaps a kzin's idea (a Jotok's idea?) of what a human child would play with—perhaps leftovers from an earlier time. The only food stocks in the kitchen were formulated for a human child. Somebody had manufactured a stack of diapers. One of the leather-bound picture books wore not only the tooth marks of a kzinrret but what looked like the practice scribbles of a two-year-old child. There were enough organic bits and pieces to establish that Argamentine was the mother of the children. They didn't seem to have a common father. Frozen sperm from Wunderland?

The discards from the machine shop, hundreds of them, were all attempts to duplicate the same hypershunt part. Yankee took samples to the frigate's engineer who tested them and had a good laugh.

"Does he know what he's doing?" asked Yankee.

"Can't tell. He might be trying random variations to see what works, but I doubt it. That's like trying random variations in a quantum effect chip and expecting the hundredth one to be a fully operational computer. I suspect he knows what he's doing but is working at the outer limits of his equipment."

Yankee was still trying to grasp the implications of a functional hyperdrive in the claws of the Patriarchy. "It seems he made one that was good enough."

"Maybe not. The specs are tough. Maybe they took one jump and they are stuck out there in interstellar space freezing to death. I rebuilt a motor once and it checked out perfect. Died on the first jump, though. The navy never would have found us if our hyperwave had gone, too."

Yankee kept going back to the kzinrretti palazzo. He was looking for something that didn't seem to be there. He brooded about his cousin. She wasn't the type to just live in a place. She needed people. If you locked her up, she'd go to the phones. If you cut the phone lines, she'd chat on the net. If you took away her infocomp she'd start to write letters. Yankee still had her letters from that boarding school she had attended after her dad got killed at Ceres. She'd meet a little old lady in the grocery and start up a conversation about the brands of coffee—and remember three months later to send the little old lady a birthday card. He was sure General Fry had love letters from her tucked away somewhere.

She had a pen. There were those scribbles in the picture book, done by one of her babies who was sure to have been imitating mother. Yankee *knew* that Nora couldn't escape the temptations that came from owning a pen.

He was tearing up a fur rug in one of the least likely of the kzinrretti rooms looking for a hiding place when his back pocket got caught in loose molding. While unhooking himself, a panel slipped open—just a crack. He pounced. What he found amazed him. It was a kzinrret-built hiding place, something a dog might have made for bones if a dog had hands. Inside was mostly a vulgar collection of baubles, charming. A three-year-old might have prized them. Sitting with the gewgaws was one of the small kzinrretti picture books. He opened it, and there, written across the pictures in Nora's fine hand, was a diary.

She had no one to talk to, so she was talking to herself.

Almost the first thing he saw when he flipped through the pages was the capitalized: "THIS IS MY MEMORY." He back-skipped and read, "Nora-From-My-Future, if you are reading this over and do not understand it, I am writing it because my memory is going."

He was too impatient to wait until he got back to the inflatable command center so he sat on the rug in the great hall of the palazzo and read straight through starting from the first page where her writing squiggled around the picture, seeking white space.

• Chapter 14

(2437 A.D.)

The kzin, bare in his yellow-orange fur, was escorted by armed guards into the chambers of Si-Kish, who was admiring his raiment in a gold-tinted mirror, his tail motionless. The nameless prisoner noticed the lean tail. Ornamented—with a miniature silver mace. *That son-of-a-vegetable can probably use it, too.* With lashing swiftness. He glanced at the furniture of this splendarium, lit by diffuse skylight. All of it looked too fragile to make a good hand weapon and too far away to grab.

The guards left. That meant that Si-Kish held the naked kzin's fighting ability in contempt. Not a wise decision—but no W'kkaikzin could imagine physical power without its trappings. They needed some sobering time on the frontier where kzin lives were cavalierly squandered on the most trivial points of honor—and prisoners never behaved with humility. Nevertheless the nameless one waited for his new name which would contain his fate. If it was something like "Walking-Dead" he was doomed. He hoped it wouldn't be as awful as "Grass-Eater."

"I am not as angry with you as some of our lesser nobles."

He's keeping me suspended.

Si-Kish was arranging his collar lace, not yet deeming to notice the nameless one. "You have been useful to W'kkai. In fact, I admire your loyalty to the present Patriarch, whose slothful ways have brought us so much failure.

You honor our heroic traditions. I will not insult your honor by suggesting that your loyalty is misplaced. In my view it is the Patriarchy which must survive—not the Patriarch. When the son sees himself as a more able warrior than the father it is his duty to challenge his sire. This principle is the foundation of the continual renewal of the Patriarchy."

Si-Kish turned and the naked kzin knew that he was about to receive his new name—and fate. "We may need you again, *Conundrum-Prisoner*. My physicists have not yet wholly mastered their hunt through hyperspace. They say they no longer need you—but *I* don't believe them. If we have more questions, you may volunteer your answers. If volunteering doesn't appeal to you, telepathy might. Perhaps even the hot needle of inquiry."

"Thank you for the name," said Conundrum-Prisoner. His sarcasm was muted by the requirements of the Dominated Tense. So . . . they were delivering him to the Conundrum Priests for safekeeping.

Nobody had ever told Monkeyshine that as the eldest male he was bound by a special responsibility to his kin. It seemed like it was something he had always known from the time back on Hssin when he had saved mother and siblings by understanding a faulty atmosphere-lock mechanism that was baffling his frantic mother while their lives lay in forfeit to noxious gases—kzin master and Jotoki mechanics being absent at the time.

Mellow Yellow was often gone on trips, but why was there a new master? W'kkai was shock after shock. Get used to it, learn the new ways, feel safe—and then *boom*, a new shock. It had seemed so easy when he was young and there were so few of them living in their little world and skittering from bubble to bubble, from ship to shored-up ruin. Then the worst omen of doom had been a grumble in the air machine.

W'kkai was so vast! Space was so tiny! He still relished his memory of the day he had discovered that the sky wasn't a roof. He had had to lie down on the ground and pile bricks on his stomach as high as he could to understand that it was just the weight of the air that kept the air in! Weird. But vastness meant that too much was happening.

He was always toilet training a baby or rescuing a young brother from a ditch or stealing fruit for his mother. Sometimes he was too interested in fun and forgot about his duties. Furlessface got her head stuck between boards and had been crying for half a workshift before he found her. She was *so* dumb! He felt guilty but a man had to have fun sometimes. There was too much work to do. It wasn't easy being a slave. He wanted real clothes like a W'kkaikzin!

Kzinti constantly grumbled about the laziness of their slaves. Slaves were too indolent to survive by themselves. They had to be "induced" to work for their survival by a watchful eye. It was true. Monkeyshine avoided work with careful cunning which mostly meant when he was beyond observation. On W'kkai he had to learn new ways of avoiding work, mainly because there were so many more kzin overseers, none of them as easygoing as his mother's Mellow Yellow.

It was a game. If he got caught, he worked very very hard. If no one was looking he didn't work at all. He liked the long W'kkai nights. They were cool and no one could see him. Oh joy! The stars peeked out to announce the night before the clouds came. He liked the night insects because they were big and some had glowy segments on their bellies!

For now, two things made work-avoidance tolerably

easy. The kzin were used to servants like the Jotoki for which they had hundreds of generations of training experience. Mellow Yellow had been a trainer of slaves, specializing in the Jotoki, and knew of dozens of machines and thousands of virtual-world training modes that would shape a Jotok to almost any skill. But for monkeys there were no training artifacts. And the kzinti weren't patient with eyeball-to-eyeball training. When a kzin caught him idle, he respectfully asked for immediate training, and that was usually that.

He had painfully figured it out for himself during his sly wanderings about the estate. He couldn't explain these ideas to his brothers. The slave language he knew was too simple to express such complicated ruminations. He understood what he was thinking but there was no way to share these thoughts by the method of *saying*. His was a special duty because if he failed, then doom would befall his monkey family. Fun got in the way of his serious thinking, but he could always make it up while he worked.

The best job was currying kzinrretti. Sthondat thigh-bones, were they dumb!

Instinctively, he never broached his tortuous questions to any kzin, not even lord Grraf-Nig—who was his teacher, his master and defender, his peculiar friend who had tussled and played with him since he was an infant. He dared to call his kzin lord "Mellow Yellow," a bite's distance from those carnivorous, flesh-odored teeth, but nothing in kzindom would have induced Monkeyshine to tease that mighty machine of flesh with images of monkeys who lolled about on kzin-hide rugs and fanned themselves with kzin ears. Such amusing thoughts had to be locked in absolute privacy.

In the course of his serving duties, he *had* overheard kzintosh boasting about the deeds of conquering Heroes, but the slave races appeared in the stories only as stilted background to the glory of kzin victories. Only the kzin had a history.

Monkeyshine would never have thought to share his curiosity with his mother, though he chatted with her in monologue mode often. She, being female, did not have the wits to tell him of her origins. His father, who could, he supposed was dead. He assumed that monkeys, unlike Jotoki, did have fathers because Mellow Yellow addressed him and his brothers in the male tense and referred to his mother and her daughters in the same female tense with which he spoke of his kzinrretti wives.

Of course, he wasn't older than his befuddled sister, who was just as tall as he was, but she didn't count as a partner in responsibility because she couldn't think, could hardly make herself understood in the limited hisses and purrs of her tiny vocabulary. He had to protect her all the time; it was annoying. His brothers were of little help—after all, they were only babies and they had to contend with *their* twin sisters who were *really* stupid brats.

He adored his mother. She wasn't very bright either, and he had to protect her, too, as well as all of his siblings. But she was bigger than he was and quicker and it made Monkeyshine grin when she caught him being foolish. With the grip of her powerful hand she could restrain his greatest enthusiasm. She always grinned back at him—but would never let go until he started to *think* about the careless thing he was doing.

That was his greatest puzzle: she was so dumb, how did she always know when he was being dangerously stupid? Such a mystery impressed him. He could be ferociously fond of his mother, especially when he was assisting her during her frequent childbearing, and had to chase away her five-legged Jotoki midwives. What did they know about childbearing? They crawled out of ponds, whatever a pond was.

He didn't know whether he was grown-up or not. He felt big and it seemed like he knew everything but he kept growing. A kzin male was about twice as large as a kzinrret. If he was going to grow up twice as large as his mother he had a long way to go. He wasn't even as big as she was yet. When he got bigger, the work would be easier.

Things began to get stranger. He was currying a kzinrret one morning and her fur was standing on end in anger. She snarled at him and he was afraid of her but she seemed to like his attentions. There were hissing matches in the harem. It got worse every day until the harem was in an uproar. All the alliances between the kzinrretti were changing. He found one of them digging a den in the hillside.

Monkeyshine was proud of the way he got along with Mellow Yellow's females. He could understand their gestures and their moods, when they wanted to be groomed, when they wanted to play, and when they wanted to be left alone. He knew what gifts to bring them—pretty stones and colored leaves—and he could understand their talk-talk and even chatter with them while he played. So he took the trouble to find out what was wrong.

Their new master smelled peculiar and they were afraid he was going to eat their kits. What had happened to Mellow Yellow? Why was the new master beginning to reorganize the slave quarters?

It was just curiosity and caution that was driving him toward answers—until Long-Reach returned from somewhere in an almost catatonic state, only one of his arms articulate. Then the boy's curiosity became an intense case of anxiety. His Jotoki friends abandoned him to babble hysterically in their tree huts. Only Joker crawled down to comfort Monkeyshine and all he would say was that something terrible had happened to Mellow Yellow. He couldn't say more; he didn't have a calm arm.

For the next thirty hours Monkeyshine did not let his family out of sight. He watched his mother and made all sorts of excuses to help her while she worked. He herded his sisters. He kept his brothers out of trouble and as much out of sight of any kzin as possible.

Nightfall on W'kkai is a slow dimming and it takes forever for the darkness to overlay the land, but at first-darkness a Jotoki delegation called Monkeyshine into the tree huts for a council. He had never before been treated with such respect. Monkeyshine was a child at that unique stage in human development where he was observant enough to notice the richness of his universe yet wise enough to understand that he knew nothing.

To him the Jotoki were the fonts of all wisdom. Mellow Yellow was too busy to answer his questions, though Monkeyshine knew how to bring out the father in him for a sparring match, a thing he wouldn't have dared do with any other kzin. Mellow Yellow's kzin retainers thought only of work and not why "washers" were round. The Jotoki, on the other hand, knew everything about how machines worked and were only too willing to take them apart to show you why a washer *had* to be round. They could make a ship fly between the stars—and that *awed* Monkeyshine. He had only two arms and it made him feel like an inferior slave.

In the trees, the Jotoki crowd were very serious about their council. Nervously munching leaves that one arm stuffed into his underside mouth, and talking through the lungs of his others arms, Long-Reach told him that Mellow Yellow was in confinement. "We have a new master who owns all."

The other Jotoki keened their distress and the five shoulder eyes of each one of them stared at Monkeyshine. He looked at the eyes glinting in the night lights and uneasily glanced back at Long-Reach—and then at his toes. He knew they wanted something. "Why is he confined?"

"He is a warrior."

That, of course, was supposed to explain everything. Fighting was warriors' work and some fights were lost and others won. Monkeyshine was not satisfied with the explanation. Warring led to honorable death, not to confinement. "Warriors die!" he said disdainfully.

"No." Long-Reach was collectively sad. "Sometimes warriors are confined after a loss. Mellow Yellow has been confined before. Then it is the duty of another warrior to free him."

"A warrior *must* free him," said one of Creepy's arms. "We insist," reiterated Creepy's thinnest arm.

Monkeyshine was aware that his friends were setting him up. They had a message for him to deliver to some great warrior kzin. "I'll get lost," he replied defensively. "I've hardly been off the estate."

"A great warrior freed him during the Battle of Wunderland," intoned Long-Reach, his five voices resonating together.

"Will his friend help him now?" Monkeyshine asked slyly, hoping to stay out of the discussion.

"No. But it is the duty of the son of a crippled warrior to carry on his father's purpose."

Monkeyshine giggled. Slaves would be beaten even for *talking* like that. "Is this Hero son aware of his father's noble cause?" If such a warrior was just a few hours away, he *might* be able to sneak a message through at night to tell him of Grraf-Nig's dire need. Monkeyshine was scared already just thinking about it even if he was good at sneaking. And then he thought of his dim-witted mother. What would they all do without Mellow Yellow? The situation was desperate. "I'm only a little boy!" He was crying.

"You are the son of a warrior!" Long-Reach insisted sonorously in a collective voice that was followed by a squeaking from the most sympathetic of Long-Reach's arms in defiance of the other four. "Leave him alone! He's not a warrior yet."

"I'm *not* Mellow Yellow's son!" lamented Monkeyshine, only now wakening to the purpose of this cabal. "I only spar with him! It's pretend!"

"You come of a warrior race," said Long-Reach gently.

Were they hinting about his unknown father? "Was my father a warrior?" The mere thought terrified him.

"We know nothing of your father. Your mother was a great warrior."

Monkeyshine rebelled. *That again.* They had hinted at such foolishness before, in their multiple babblings. He was angry. "My mother is my foolish mother!" he shouted.

"Your mother killed thirteen kzin warriors," came a slow melodious reply.

The other Jotoki had folded up their stalklike limbs to protect their heads and were sitting defensively on their undermouths, arm-lungs fixed in the mode that allowed soft breathing but silenced the voice. The remembrance of the horrible crime gripped the council and only one tiny voice had the courage to justify it. "She was saving Mellow Yellow . . . from confinement," it piped.

Monkeyshine was just as frightened by the tale as his hosts.

They told the story in bits and pieces, sharing the details to share the guilt, exaggerating to impress the boy. The account wasn't always coherent for it was told in a slave language poorly designed to discuss revolt and war strategy. They had to make up words and string words together and build explanations around their compound words to define them. They had to make analogies to machines and slave work. They had to tell this to an eight-year-old-boy who had only half the language abilities of a human adult. Totally unaware of the human developmental cycle, they thought of Monkeyshine as the full intellectual equal of the Lieutenant Nora Argamentine they had once known.

They had once convinced the kzinti war captive to lead a rebellion against the crew of the *Nesting-Slashtooth-Bitch* to save their master, and they were fully convinced that they could do the same now. Guilt and horror had long suppressed their memories of the mutiny. Now it was necessary to save their master again and they argued and squabbled back and forth, arm to arm, Jotok to Jotok, to revive the details so that Monkeyshine might profit from them. Nora's warrior deeds seemed clear to them—but they argued long and hotly about how she had *planned* her campaign. Military strategy was still a mystery to them. What they couldn't understand they expected Monkeyshine to understand for them because he was of a *warrior* race.

When Monkeyshine, in an effort to understand, pointed out his mother's obvious mental failings, they spoke evasively of "wounds" or "injuries." None of them dared tell Monkeyshine of their part in betraying her. After she had masterminded the destruction of the crew of the *Bitch* they had been afraid that she would also destroy their beloved master, too. Nor did they dare tell Monkeyshine of their collaboration while Mellow Yellow delicately destroyed Nora's memories and her ability to manipulate language. To make her safe. To make her over into something he could understand.

The household learned that the name Grraf-Nig was never to be mentioned again. They learned from their authoritarian new master that their old master was being sent to the Conundrum Priests of the Rival's Range. They were told that they would have to work harder. A new factory to assemble delicate naval components was to be built on the estate.

I'm a slave; I'm a slave; I'm a slave, Monkeyshine kept telling himself. He treated his mother with a new respect when he came to curry her with his kzinrretti brush. Grinning while he combed the knots out of her long auburn mane, he imagined that her kzin opponents had died of *surprise* when she growled. He curried her fur vigorously, the way she liked, never even wondering why female monkeys had fur and males didn't; that's the way it had always been. He buried his head in her hair, afraid, hugging her.

He was not used to thinking of himself as a warrior. It was safer to be a slave. He'd have to be *angry* when he grinned. What would he do for claws? His teeth weren't sharp. Something stubborn in him was resisting his Jotoki comrades. They were ready to rescue Mellow Yellow tomorrow. He wasn't. He knew the difference between *being* and *pretending*. *Being* something could get you killed. *Pretending* let you repeat yourself. For now he was only willing to *pretend* to rescue Mellow Yellow.

Eight+One acolytes guided the naked kzin at pike point, pleased to have duty away from their studies. He would remain naked no matter how cold it got. They wore weavings of yellow and gold done in maze design. The claspings were a ring-puzzle and let the Fanged God help the acolyte who forgot the untwining sequence. Their tall headdresses of multiple heads made them bob and loom like the giants of mythology.

The tidal action of W'kkaisun kept the crust of W'kkai active even though that leisurely planet had a week-long day. There were plenty of mountains and upwelled plateaus. It was middle morning in the Rival's Range but the

evening's snow still lay on the northern slopes. The steps
to the Heart of Paradox were brilliant in the sunlight and
wet with melting snow. Where was the entrance to this
Temple carved high along the cliff? Even that was an
enigma.

Conundrum-Prisoner could not see the roof of the
Temple but it was the floor of the plateau. Conundrum
Priests had carved there in the stone for millennia, building themselves a maze of prisons so wonderful that no
warden ever needed keys. The balanced stones just closed
around their victims. A finger's push along the magic vec-
tors would open the prison again, perhaps—or cause a
rumbling that would close the cell down to the size of a
coffin.

In the Temple they were led by a gray-furred warden,
stooped, with a scar across his face that had removed half
his nose. It wasn't a corridor of cells they followed, it was
a terrifying forest of stones and pillars and blocks and
paving that had all the solidity of a master juggler's cli-
mactic act at the Patriarch's Palace. One looked around
in desperation for the hand that was rushing around keeping it all from collapsing, but there was no such hand—
only the occasional soft paving or pillar that swayed or
monolith that swung down to block their way while it
opened another. The Priests *said* it was earthquake proof.

Conundrum-Prisoner did not recognize his cell when
they came upon it. It was like a field of cut stone, or some
bizarre world from the eye of an electron microscope. It
had been opened for him the day before. The acolytes
gathered up the bones of the previous occupant. The
warden pulled a hood over his head and wove it shut. All
the prisoner heard was the slight whisperings and low
rumble as the walls shifted and the plugs fell into place.

He tore at the hood with his claws, uselessly. Then he
began to work at the lacings. Was this another kind of

puzzle? Finally he smelled the slight odor of oxidation. The hood gradually disintegrated in strength until he could tear it off, and finally it turned to ash. The cell was ample, though of no sane geometric shape. There were openings, some of them large enough for a kzin to crawl into. Death traps. He could control light or darkness. He could control smell. He had a tap for liquid food. And he had a hose to wash away his excrement.

He thought of the cages in which he had kept the experimental monkeys procured from Wunderland for his studies of the man-beast's nervous system.

He felt rage.

But the Conundrum Priests weren't impressed by rage. Every item and action of their philosophy was designed to control rage. No amount of rage against these walls would move them by a claw's breadth. Only reason would open them. The panicked reason of "try everything" wouldn't work, either. There would be Sixtyfour+One ways of moving those stones—and Sixtyfour of them would collapse his cell to the volume of a coffin, and he'd die in some distorted pretzel shape.

He remembered a time of boredom when he had been stationed at Centauri's Aarku base; he had found himself a W'kkai Conundrum Puzzle and stayed awake three days and nights trying to solve it. It had driven him mad!

Now he was trapped *in* the puzzle. Controlling his rage was going to drive him mad. Restraining his reason was going to drive him mad. No matter how good his hypothesis about the geometry of his cell, he couldn't test it with shove and push until *all* of the consequences had been reasoned out in his head. Madness, every alternative was madness! And there wasn't even any grass to eat!

Conundrum-Prisoner was his name.

• Chapter 15

(2437 A.D.)

The diary of Lieutenant Nora Argamentine was fed into the handwriting analyzer and posted on the Wunderland frigate's server, access denied only to Hwass-Hwasschoaw. Their kzin had been right about a lot of the details of the insurrection aboard the *Bitch*, including the loyalty of the Jotoki slaves to their trainer, but he had been *wrong* about its leader. Yankee grinned. Even the most paranoid of the kzin wouldn't believe in a *female* opponent.

Of course, Clandeboye was seeing some consternation among his own men on that score. Taking out a kzin warship at a distance of light-seconds required skill and bravery—taking one from the *inside* in what amounted to hand-to-claw combat, with only unarmed slaves for allies, was a remarkable feat. Yankee caught his Wunderland marines in the briefing room replaying the contest in loud agitation and debate.

These men had actually fought on the ground, in the city, during the Hssin mop-up operation in 2422. They had a full simulation of the *Bitch*'s interior displayed on the main lecture screen. Nora's diary was on multiple infocomps—even floating around in paper copies—and Hwass's analysis of the battle was being annotated with excerpts from Nora's diary. And argue, argue, argue. They were re-creating the battle, blow by blow. A heroic myth was in the making.

Through introspective monologues Yankee drafted his conclusions, even his feelings, into frantic missives that he threw out by hyperwave to General Fry, one after the other without waiting for replies. The general wrote back expansively, in a less formal manner than his usual terse style. He was astonished by Nora's feat and begged more details. Just knowing what had happened to her healed some wounds, but what had happened was not pleasant. Even the noblest of heroes does not always win.

If she was still alive, which they doubted, her mind had been wiped clean and the only language that was left to her was a primitive female form of the Hero's Tongue. And worse, from a strategic point of view, brave Nora had not prevented the delivery of the *Shark* into Patriarch hands. Yankee's worst nightmare had come true. And General Fry was no longer a man covering his bets by exploring all scenarios—he was Yankee's open ally.

The ARM, as usual, suppressed the Hssin expedition's news. Rear Admiral Blumenhandler's voice was sealed. His marines were shipped to Barnard's Starbase. The repatriation of Hwass-Hwasschoaw was so accelerated that upon the kzin's return to Wunderland he was not even allowed to contact his fellow Wunderkzin; he had a final meeting with Interworld Space Commissioner Ulf Reichstein Markham and then was gone. Yankee was warned not to publish. Somehow the major saw the hand of Admiral Jenkins in all this.

Back at Gibraltar Base in Sol System, Yankee spent hours in discussion with General Fry in his small asteroid apartment. They were good friends by now. Yankee was appalled at the navy's reaction to the *Shark* capture. In spite of the fact that there was "no news," the news was getting around by rumor and gross speculation. The prevailing opinion was that the kzinti were too incompetent technically to duplicate a captured hypershunt.

An alien race had sold them their technology eons ago and it hadn't improved since then because they had no engineers.

They were all brawn and no brain—and brawn was never enough. Who had wiped out the big cats and the whales and the mammoths?

They were technologically stagnant and no longer had the will or the ability to change.

The Patriarchy was the degenerate remains of an ancient civilization. What would they do with the *Shark*? Who had ever heard of a curious kzin?

It would take them a millennium to duplicate the hyperdrive. Haw, haw, the kzinti were so dumb that when they got the hyperdrive they would ship all their warriors into hyperspace and not be able to bring them back! Half the time, a kzin had to stand on his head to screw in a lightbulb because he could never remember the direction of the screw.

"How long do *you* think it will take?" asked Fry.

"My odds are that they are tooling up a prototype out there right now. We'll be hit with our tanks empty."

"Progress takes time. A lot of the younger officers are coming around to your viewpoint. It takes time, Yankee. Politics takes time."

"Forget the kzin. How many *men* does it take to screw in a lightbulb?"

"Granted that this younger generation knows what a bulb is. Yeah, tell me."

"A thousand and one—five hundred with their hands on the bulb turning it counter-clockwise, and five hundred and one with their hands on the bulb turning it clockwise."

"Yeah."

"I'm sorry I lost Nora's trail. If we knew where the *Shark* jumped to, we could blow the hell out of the place," grumbled Yankee.

"And risk another war? No way."

Yankee took on a distant look. "I've been meaning to ask you about something. Our informant, that Hwass Hwasschoaw, never did take his repatriation to Kzin. I hear rumors that he had himself dropped off at W'kkai. Do you suppose he picked up something I didn't?"

The general grinned. "I arranged that behind Markham's back—as a favor to Hwass and maybe as a favor to myself. My file has our kzin *born* on W'kkai. I'm not sure he wanted to be repatriated to Kzin. That was Markham's idea. Did you meet Markham?"

"Yeah. Tough old buzzard. I don't think he's happy with the turmoil on Wunderland. It's against his sense of order. He has weird ideas of promoting a universal peace with Kzin and any other alien races we might meet out there. Maybe he's feeling guilty about his bloody past. I don't think his peace plan is very realistic." Yankee paused, as if he were contemplating something incredible. "I hear he was using Hwass as a *peace* emissary between man and kzin."

"That's right. It is not so strange as you might think. Markham has information that he is a very religious kzin. He has dreams of proselytizing the galaxy. Markham thinks he is a secret convert to Christianity."

The major was amused. "Hwass as a peace emissary, that's got to be the laugh of the century. Don't get me wrong. That old kitten and I got along. Shall we say we understood each other; he knew I'd order him killed if he stepped out of line, and I knew he'd kill me first chance he got. Peace emissary! Murphy have mercy on us!"

"He decided at the last minute that he wanted to go to W'kkai. So I arranged it. I thought we might just learn something if we let him follow his own nose. Just a shot in the dark. I gave him protocols and some unclassified equipment so that he could keep in touch. Did you ever tell that proud warrior about Nora? I mean Nora as kzin-killing terror."

"Naw. I didn't want to upset him while I was in the same room."

"My little sweetheart clerk," Fry reminisced with a smile, "going around upsetting a kzin's macho sensibilities. I'll tell you some good news. It is Nora who's getting out the news about the *Shark* in spite of . . ." The general pointed his finger at the ceiling in the general direction of The Powers That Be and rolled his eyes. "Even though the ARM is keeping the lid on the story, it *is* getting around via the bilge water. It's all over Barnard's Starbase. Who can resist the story? The kzin captured themselves a hypershunt with no one to stop them but a determined little woman. Without an official ARM account, the story gets wilder by the minute. Last time I heard it Nora killed *thirty* kzin on her way to the powder room. Each day the cats grow an inch taller, and she gets more beautiful. Those space cadets are making a warrior saint out of her."

"She was no saint," said Yankee, who remembered when she was ten years old.

"Couldn't hold her down," complained Fry. "I tried. I wanted to. Some women won't let you keep them under control." There was regret in the general's voice.

"Maybe we'll pick up her trail again," said Yankee sadly.

"Maybe," agreed General Fry, lost in old memories of romance.

• Chapter 16

(2438 A.D.)

Hwass-Hwasschoaw was a celebrity when he was first delivered to the W'kkai's singularity boundary by UNSN treaty warship and fetched home by a kzin patrol. For a while he gave long blunt talks on the Battle of Wunderland to whomever of the military cared to listen. When he learned what he most wanted to know, he disappeared as a wandering Truth-Preacher.

Hwass found the W'kkai coterie of the Patriarch's Eye in the form of an ancient kzin of his father's acquaintance who was still part of the old network. The Eye was in disarray, saved only by its inbred loyalty and ability to tolerate long delays. It had always needed a steady trickle of funds and talent from Kzin to keep it purposeful. And it had always needed fire-eaters like his father, who should never have left the organization to underlings while he took off on a wild adventure with the dashing Chuut-Riit.

Hwass could barely contain his claws when learning that the Eye was unaware of any hypership sneaking through the blockade. A blind Eye? An outrage! Then doubt possessed him. He *had* found Trainer-of-Slaves's navigation notes (without revealing them to Clandeboye) proving that this yellow devil *had* planned to take his captured UNSN ship to W'kkai! But had he ever *arrived*?

A little more sniffing was in order. He traveled to pastoral places as Truth-Preacher, his intent to "dig a few watering holes" that might prove useful in a Kdapt reformation. Hustling never hurt. A better class of kzinti stayed away from the cities and, being less crowded, were more open of mind and favors. Preaching brought in the little money he needed and provided ample opportunity for gossip. Two things he learned: (1) for a defeated power, W'kkai was too confident and (2) a new schism was dividing the navy.

The overconfidence could be attributed to the arrogance of the haughty Patriarch's Voice who wouldn't know defeat if his severed head was floating in a wine barrel. Overconfidence is contagious and no one was untouched by the taste of the Voice. But what of Admiral Si-Kish? He was quietly building a navy—and it smelled like a navy more powerful than anything W'kkai had ever fielded. But why such a navy unless there was a hypershunt motor to power it? Why such secrecy? Why weren't the old naval warriors being brought into this new hunting ground? Odd smells for a humbled regime.

The buildup was being hidden from the Eye. Si-Kish shouldn't even know that the Eye existed.

One thing at a time. After lecturing with great tact to some country squires about the nature of the God of the True Form, and passing a pleasant day hunting with his hosts, he spent time by himself with a cup of fermented milk and the local slavery poop sheets. Truth-Preacher wasn't interested in buying slaves, and had no need for a personal slave—but he was looking for the spoor of Trainer-of-Slaves.

That yellow devil would have abandoned his trade for a more lucrative life, perhaps hidden behind some self-important title of his own devising—but he would leave traces. Greed. How could he wholly abandon that sideline about which he knew so much?

. . . and there it was. A tiny advertisement for a tribe of handsome, hardworking, truly unique *human* slaves to be sacrificed by their despondent owner at auction for any reasonable price. Five members of the Eye as well as Hwass were at that auction. Among the beasts for sale was one furred female man and a host of bewildered youngsters.

The fine fur on her body left him certain. He had owned human slaves and knew that human females were not furred, even if the auctioneer did not. Trainer-of-Slaves had experimented on his females and one of his favorite experiments had been a technique for activating the latent fur genes of the man-beasts. This was Lieutenant Nora Argamentine, had to be, mind-wiped, late of the United Nations Space Navy. A very valuable prize indeed.

Hwass encouraged one of his associates to examine the firmness of her musculature and the condition of her teeth. He was instructed to be subtly indelicate. She bit his finger while it was still in her mouth. (Any high quality kzinrret, breeder of warriors, would have done the same.) It was a slave-buying trick Hwass knew—it served the purpose of lowering her price.

The auctioneer and Hwass's ringer had an altercation. The auctioneer, in a reckless rage, swore by the sharpness of the teeth of his merchandise while the ringer stalked away with his bloody finger in the air, complaining loudly about the quality of the slaves to all the buyers who would listen. Hwass and his cohorts bought the entire lot of humans for a price that the impoverished Eye could afford.

Now he had a weapon he could use against Clandeboye. The God of the True Form had favored him mightily. All his supplications and prayers and sacrifice had born fresh meat. The treasure would be complete once his slaves led him to the hypershunt. Where was Trainer-of-Slaves? Trainer would not have let these slaves go so cheaply.

The female was a useless source of information, but

her eldest male probably knew something. It was the boy who was most afraid of him, the boy who watched him, the boy who stood ready to protect his mother and siblings. A mind he could use. Perhaps he could even make a Kdaptist of him, to plead the kzin case before God.

A long journey by gravity car took them along the coast. He tried a few words of English on the terrified boy, but the little monkey clearly did not understand. He tried a kzin's version of that odd mixture of Danish and Plattdeutsch that had passed for a language among his Wunderland slaves. Still nothing. Hard to find the right language for a slave muted by terror.

He watched the sea go by beyond a rocky shoreline of wet boulders, glancing sometimes into the dark interior of the car where his slaves cowered bravely. There was always a way to work fear. In the meantime, soothe your prey before its taste went bad. He noticed that the Nora-beast was thirsty. An opportunity. He held out water to the boy and spoke the kzin word for water and then gestured at the boy's mother. Thirst and hunger could reach through terror. Politely, in the dominated tense, the boy asked for water for his mother. His accent and grammar were atrocious; he seemed to speak some form of the Jotoki slave patois, but he could be understood. Progress.

They reached their isolated retreat of massive stone, once the fortress of some mighty kzin, now a safe house for the Eye. He took the boy to the newly designated slave rooms and put him in charge of the settling of his family. He gave the boy control over the food. In that way he seduced Monkeyshine to his cause.

Hwass chose mealtime to talk to his slave, just before the boy was ready to feed his family. He didn't make a big issue of it, but a slave doesn't deny his master a few civil words if that's what it takes to get the food on the table. The conversations grew longer. Monkeyshine grew less afraid.

One day Monkeyshine told him all about Hssin, and Hwass reminded him about special places among the rubble that he knew about too. Monkeyshine remembered the rug in the palazzo. Hwass described the scenes of the hunt woven all through the rug. It wasn't long before Monkeyshine was avidly telling about his adventures in hyperspace with Mellow Yellow while Hwass listened with ardent attention.

"And where *is* your Mellow Yellow? He seems to be missing."

Monkeyshine went white at his mistake. He hadn't realized that he had used the *Jotoki* name for the master. "I'm so sorry, sire. My abject apologies. I will not forget henceforth to use the title Grraf-Nig."

"Ah, yes. Hshumph. His title. Of course. But since he is not here we can call him what we please. On Wunderland we called him Grass-Eater behind his back."

"Oh, no, sire!" said a shocked Monkeyshine.

"What happened to him? Did he forget his waistcoat at the Palace? Pick his nose?"

Monkeyshine was now very wary of a kzin who would use a name like Grass-Eater for his Mellow Yellow. "Do you want him in prison?"

"So that's where he is! No, I don't want him in prison! He's the only hyperspace pilot I know. What prison? Have you heard?"

"In the Rival's Range. The Conundrum Priests have him."

"Who told you?"

"My master."

"*I'm* your master!"

"The kzin who sold us," Monkeyshine amended quickly.

"If the Conundrum Priests have him, I'll probably have to look elsewhere for a pilot," grumbled Hwass in irritation.

"You won't help him escape? I promised myself I'd be a warrior and cut off the heads of the Conundrum Priests one by one until they let him go."

Hwass threw up his hands in a very frightening way. "If you use the word 'warrior' one more time in the wrong tense, I'll have you for lunch, Walking-Meal."

"Yes, sire!" Monkeyshine came to attention.

"On the other claw, our yellow devil is probably the only hyperspace pilot on all of W'kkai. Do you know what happened to his ship?"

Monkeyshine shook his head warily.

The Patriarch's Eye had infiltrated the Conundrum Priests many Patriarchs ago. The Eye had in its secret archives a complete simulation of the Conundrum Prisons with one flaw—the pieces were only shown in their closed configuration. One of the Eye's planted acolytes, now a feeble old priest who carved wood, was still there. He was able to tell them in which puzzle Conundrum-Prisoner was bound, but had neither the way nor the puzzler's skill to liberate him.

In the basement of the reclusive fortress, by the glow of a giant tri-D screen, the best minds of the local Patriarch's Eye pondered the innards of the prison. They could slice right into Grraf-Nig's cell and see its workings, which was more than Grraf-Nig could do, but that did not help—it was still a conundrum. The Conundrum Priests devoted their lives to puzzle making. There were simple ones for the education of kits. There were puzzles to expand the mind and tame the emotions. There were puzzles that were works of art, and puzzles to hold valuables. All ranges of difficulty. But the Priest's masterpieces were their prisons. Each cell had a solution that would free its prisoner. The solution was always too difficult to find.

The cell could be opened from the inside onto the plateau. No guard was stationed there to stop an escapee. Any prisoner who could so escape was deemed to have used his intellect in a way that erased all sin. That didn't help conspirators who wanted to break *into* the cell to free a friend.

The cell could be opened from the outside by the warden—into an armed camp of fierce warriors who considered that cheating at puzzles was the most heinous of capital crimes.

Hwass-Hwasschoaw was considering brute-force entry. The model showed crawl spaces between the moving parts, all too small for a kzin but not too small for a half-grown human slave. Monkeyshine was even at the screen showing them bravely how he could squiggle in *here* and scrunch around *that*. In principle they could just melt a hole down to Grraf-Nig, lift him out, and run like a thrintun was after them.

In practice the cell was built around multiple potential energy wells of various depth, each holding its puzzle pieces. The shallow wells, the easiest ones to trigger with a shove or a pull or a kick, had the bad habit of triggering the *collapse* of the cell. Avalanche as art form. The prisoner would be squashed by tons of rock. Brute force would never be "clever" enough to trigger the sequence of events that would *open* the cell.

Back they went to trying to solve the conundrum. Hwass's mates were from W'kkai. They had been solving Conundrum Puzzles all their lives. It was an addiction. It worked off rage. It whiled away the time as the evening snow melted in the dawn light. And though brute force entrance was the only rational solution to their problem, they couldn't figure out how to make brute force work without killing their kzin, so every time they tried—and failed—they were seduced by the thought that, somehow, if they were clever enough they could solve the conundrum together. Just one more try and they'd have it.

Monkeyshine brought refreshments to his bleary-eyed masters. Just out of curiosity, because he had been pretending for so long to be the great warrior who saved Mellow Yellow, he said, "Why don't we *glue* it all together?" He knew the difference between *being* and *pretending* and knew that pretending was safe because pretending didn't kill you. But he had *already* saved Mellow Yellow a thousand times in sixty-four different ways by *pretending* and Mellow Yellow was still inside a puzzle and Monkeyshine *still* didn't know what flaws might lurk in his pretend-plans. He wanted someone to tell him—and there were no Jotoki to ask.

Hwass-Hwasschoaw came awake. One of the Eyes began to explain to Monkeyshine why you couldn't glue together the pieces of a Conundrum Prison. "Of course you can glue the pieces!" Hwass shouted.

At sunset, before the night of their covert strike, Monkeyshine was taken to a chapel. Hwass had already told him how to give homage to the God of the True Shape. It was better that he prayed, and not Hwass, because man-beasts possessed the True Shape. While candles flickered over the three crosses, he prayed to the Grandfather and the Father and the Son for the Revival of the Patriarchy, for a kzin victory; he prayed for them to find the lost hypershunt motor of the *Shark*. Fervently he prayed for the salvation of Mellow Yellow. And just in case, though not aloud, he prayed to the Fanged God, who looked like a kzin, that he might become a great warrior and do honor to the Patriarch on this evening's adventure.

It was night, before the coming of the snow. Six kzinti and one slave dropped down onto the plateau silently in black uniforms, elegantly styled in the W'kkai fashion. An ominous machine floated out of their truck on its gravity lifters, moving into position like a giant carnivorous leech.

The leech whirred, flickers of light where its teeth gripped the ground. Bubbling lava frothed and snapped behind the guard rims. With an animal cry the machine leech rose into the air—a flash of heat—and aside to discard a basaltic core gripped in its claws. It leaped back to the attack. It cut, rose, burped, and attacked, again and again to cut out its cylindrical nest. A spinning arm lining the hole with insulation.

Then almost gently, it took Monkeyshine and inserted him in the nest, food for whatever was down there. It was warm. Even the insulation was hot. A tank came after him, with hose. He had goggles that showed him every shape he would meet and where he should crawl. He lugged the tank behind him, took out the spray-wand and filled up cracks. He was scared. He got stuck. Warriors had to do silly things. It was better being a slave. He sprayed and sprayed and found more cracks and went back for another tank and got lost and sprayed and wiggled and cried and crawled out into the night air where he shivered.

The Heroes ate lunch. The cement, his kzin friends told him, had to set.

Under an overcast sky, they rebuilt the eating mouth, positioning it to bore an even larger plug—kzin-sized. They cut straight into the prison. An insulated elevator went down, waited, rose again with a puff of vapor—and out came Mellow Yellow. Monkeyshine's friends didn't seem scared—their ears were wiggling. Quickly they returned most of the cores to the hole, covering it roughly with turf and a few of the kzin-high bushes that clung to the wind-swept plateau. They piled into the truck, pulling Monkeyshine inside with a jerk, and just dropped over the cliff's edge and skedaddled.

The boy watched Mellow Yellow, his face pressed hardly more than a hand's breadth apart from the fangs of his old master. Whiskers twitched, fan ears were wilted. He seemed dazed. The boy wanted to touch this only warrior who had ever sparred with him. He didn't dare. "It was my idea to glue the pieces of the puzzle so they wouldn't crush you," he said shyly.

Mellow Yellow didn't come out of his daze. He just licked the dirt off Monkeyshine's face.

Hwass sat on some hard machinery and teased his newfound interstellar pilot. "You've got a racket. You don't have to be a warrior. You just sit around in your hotel and wait for your well-trained slaves to come around and curry the knots out of your fur." He nudged the shining-faced Monkeyshine.

The boy was proud. It was good to be a warrior. Of course, it was no fun being a *human* warrior. He was having such a hard time keeping a grin off his face.

• Chapter 17

(2438 A.D.)

Back at the Eye's safe retreat, Hwass-Hwasschoaw was not pleased when he learned about the fate of the *Shark*. On the spot he invented a fur-raising plot to recapture the *Shark* by surprise and brute force.

"No!" growled Grraf-Nig, prowling around the stone ramparts. For the first time he was really comprehending that he was free and he wanted no part of another flawed adventure. "There's nothing you can do now to stop Si-Kish. We don't need the *Shark*. It is all in my head. We have to get *my head* to Kzin."

"The *Shark* is our *transportation*, you sthondat ganglion!" spat Hwass.

How did one teach cunning patience? "We will have to wait until Si-Kish has equipped his fleet with production hypershunts, then by cunning get ourselves to Kzin. Are you fresh from your mother's womb, needing the glop licked from your eyes?"

"That will be too late!" stormed Hwass. "Kzin will be helpless if W'kkai owns hyperspace and they do not!"

"We wait!"

"If we wait, the Patriarch will have his throat clawed open! I am Hwass-Hwasschoaw and you take orders from me—Trainer-of-Slaves."

Grraf-Nig moved into a grinning crouch at this insulting use of a former name. He switched to the menacing tense of the Hero's Tongue and laid his fan-like ears flat.

"All I have to do is buy bright brass buttons to outrank you." He hissed and Hwass hissed, raging. *I am the one with the patience*, thought the smaller, yellower kzin. Too much was at bay for them to kill each other now over such trivialities. He stalked down the narrow stairs and spent his energy chasing rodents among the stately hairwhip trees.

Calmer, sitting on an outcropping where he had trapped the rodent, he spat out the fur and bones of a tasteless meal, trying to crack the skull in his teeth for the taste of brains. Monkeyshine had followed him, too afraid to approach closer than the shelter of some saplings. Grraf-Nig smelled his fear—but the boy wasn't hiding. *A great Trainer-of-Slaves I am*, he thought. *I breed for docile servants and get warriors!* He shuddered for a moment to think about his kzin-killing Jotoki. And now his humans were going wild!

That little monkey animal over there in the saplings loved nothing better than to spar. He had the most ferocious grin when he attacked, arms flailing. One whack would have killed him. Why did he dare? He was the son of that Nora-beast, that's why. It would take centuries to breed out that streak of ferocity. He thought of the little "kit" crawling around among the stones of the prison conundrum with its rollers and levers and slipways and hidden polarizers, determined to save his master.

"Come here, monkey," he growled.

The boy came instantly, and with a ready comb began to curry him industriously. It felt good. He wondered what would happen to his real sons. The new kzintosh would save his little kzinrretti, but what would be the fate of the males? "I'm not angry at you," he said. "I'm angry at that lice-infested, pissed upon, dung-eating son of a fop." He jerked his teeth in the general direction of the fortress. "Come for a walk."

They wandered through the trees together until they came to a meadow of green, streaked with the rushes of a small stream's swamp, their bulbs open to the sun, storing energy for the long night. Mellow Yellow muttered and kicked at the grass. "Different kind of grass here than on Hssin. When I was your age, I once ate the grass on Hssin. Tastes terrible!"

"You never! Hshumpfss! Grass. Yeach!"

"When I was your age, I wasn't as brave as you are."

Monkeyshine loved compliments like that. Grinning, he attacked Mellow Yellow with an immediate grand leap and a punch to the belly. The kzin had to fling him to the grass—gently. It didn't stop the boy-beast. He rolled to an erect position and was attacking again the instant his feet hit the turf. Mellow Yellow had to take a real fighting crouch to protect himself. They hissed and spat at each other, circling, charging, whacking, kicking. The kzin kept at the sparring longer than he usually did with this slave, but he was angry and it felt good. The boy was bleeding from scratches but still he fought without letup, the grin wide across his furless face.

Finally Mellow Yellow had had enough, but the monkey hadn't—so he just stood there and let the boy try to tackle him, shaking the child away with spasms of his leg. "What kind of nonsense is this?" he growled. "Where did you get your warrior's liver?"

"Long-Reach said my mother was a warrior. That's not true, is it?"

"It shouldn't be! Females don't fight well!"

"Unless you poke them!" said Monkeyshine happily, who had practice at poking.

"Well, there's that. Then you have to run like a herd of sthondats are after you!"

"Long-Reach told me to save you," said Monkeyshine gravely.

"My Long-Reach has been a faithful valet. You did well. The Patriarchy is the better for it."

Hwass-Hwasschoaw was no longer angry when they got back. He had another mad scheme of conquest to propose. They would attack and capture a human ship—another long argument that would end in frayed tempers, thought Grraf-Nig. He had no choice but to listen. Hwass was a *font* of leaps. In the middle of a leap he was so impatient that he would begin a new leap. Sometimes he would jump from the most serious of discussions to a lecture on the latest fashions. While debating a favorite plot (that might cost them their lives if misplanned) he could suddenly begin an arcane discourse broadly covering the finest points of religion—or of sheep ranching on Wunderland. He held the strange belief that God was manifest in the shape of the man-beasts. With his philosophical training Grraf-Nig was wryly sure that Hwass could have proved that God was manifest in the shape of a sheep.

Slyly Hwass began by mentioning the research on the human nervous system that Grraf-Nig had done as Trainer-of-Slaves, costing the lives of hundreds of experimental animals imported from the Wunderland orphanages. "Among your discoveries there was a nerve gas that will disable a human immediately and then kill him by inhibiting the transmission of neural impulses."

"Several of them. But the discovery was not mine. I got the formula from a human disc that came to Wunderland with the first slowboat in the luggage of a beast hunted by the ARM."

"It could kill the crew of a ship before they could defend themselves?"

"In principle. On a larger ship such as the *Nesting-Slashtooth-Bitch* the same weapon, using a slightly slower-acting gas that attacks the kzinti neural system, was not as effective."

"You planned that attack," said Hwass grimly, "and your slaves executed the plan on your instructions. It was successful."

"Yes." Grraf-Nig did not dare reveal that his slaves had also done the *planning*.

"So it can be done."

"I wouldn't advise trying it in a larger ship."

"Then we will attract and ambush a small human ship."

This was going to be a long hunt, thought Grraf-Nig. He'd have to track his energetic prey with probing questions that would tire until finally, in the end, Hwass understood the stupidity of his latest scheme. "And if we appear in sartorial splendor at Si-Kish's manor, he will be delighted to give us ships to ambush some UNSN patrol?"

"You think of me as an impractical dreamer. But you have also seen my practical talents. There is no lock that can stop my fingers. Did I not reach into a Conundrum Cell and pick you out, a feat that has never before been done in the entire history of W'kkai? I have the old navy in my livery. Why do you think Si-Kish is building his *new* navy from the ground up? The old navy is full of old kzin loyal to the legitimate Patriarch. A covert ride to the edge of the singularity can be arranged as a routine patrol."

"And from there it is only a matter of inviting ourselves to tea in the monkeys' mess?"

Hwass grinned with a battle eagerness. The grin did not challenge or offend Grraf-Nig because the eyes of this malevolent kzin were directed inward at some internal vision. "I know a Major Yankee Clandeboye who will be only too willing to bring us our ship and welcome us inside so that we may take it as a prize of war."

• Chapter 18

(2438 A.D.)

Chloe Blumenhandler had joined the Young Woman's Auxiliary on her seventeenth birthday. A significant sector of Wunderland society believed in early military training for the young and there were dozens of semi-military corps, militias, stellar scouts, rangers, and young guardians. It wasn't just an underlying unease about the kzin that fostered these groups.

Wunderland's culture had been founded on a sense of profound interstellar isolation from its root stock. Then . . . Warriors descending from the empty black. Subjugation for a people who had left Sol honoring their freedom more than comfort. Loss of land. Confiscation of property, relatives, children. Terror. Taxes. Death. Running like a fox in the hunting parks. Soul-breaking work in slave camps with strange imported slave races. And Outsiders selling military might. Wunderland had suffered a fundamental reality shock.

No parents want their children to be as naive as they once were when they were young. And so the older generation founded quasi-military groups and inducted their children—building hard-won wisdom into institutions that couldn't forget. "Will our children be ready for *them*?" Were there *others* out there?

Chloe was not interested in a military career. She had grown up in a military family without a mother. Her babysitters had been petty officers and sometimes burly marine sergeants. Her fantasies were about a landholder's castle on Wunderland, or a run-down artist's studio in a twenty-second-century ranch house on the French Somme. (She'd walked through a virtual seventeenth-century French house and didn't like the plumbing.)

In her dreams she fell in love with Wunderland statesmen, or crashlander explorers, or Jinxian scientists or deep space artists. In one of her recurring fantasies she lived with a musician who worked with his instruments in a great house on Plateau at the void edge of Mount Lookitthat overlooking the Long Fall River where it broke out into the tallest waterfall in Known Space. The man with a view.

Flatlanders both repelled and fascinated her. Earth was so crowded! It was like Tiamat turned into a whole planet! And flatlanders had such odd jobs—like reconstructing ancient Portuguese caravels dredged up from a watery Pacific grave. Her best flatlander fantasy was filled with the laughing Romans and Italians of a rosy Naples where the sun was always setting on a golden bay; she was one of a saucy menagerie of teen-aged girls held prisoner by a gay old Neapolitan classics scholar who was a sexual athlete and wit. The fantasy had lasted her a delicious week until she got bored with Italian men and moved on to the Chinese Imperial Court.

Whatever her dreams of civilian splendor, in real life she fell madly in love with military men. And so it was natural that at the age of seventeen, in total revolt against her father's military life, she should declare her independence by joining a military organization so that she could pursue her one-sided love affair with a handsome older officer of the UNSN.

Chloe was devastated when Major Yankee Clandeboye was transferred to Barnard's Starbase, something that Admiral Jenkins had demanded and something that fitted nicely into one of General Fry's more nefarious schemes. She sent her major letters, five in all. He replied once. That short note was signed with the scrawl, "Fondly, Yankee." It was all the encouragement she needed.

In a state of euphoria, with his short note tucked in her bra, she just happened to notice a recruiting ad. The Young Woman's Auxiliary needed twenty girls who were looking for a disciplined and rewarding experience at Barnard's Starbase. The "discipline" didn't appeal to her but the "rewarding experience" did. Being only seventeen, she needed her father's permission. The rear admiral objected and fought a losing war for three days before surrendering. He signed her away for a two-year contract and groaned.

Chloe, of course, had not told her father about her intentions toward the forty-nine-year-old Yankee, knowing that there were limits to Admiral Blumenhandler's permissiveness. To her father Yankee was just another one of those men upon whom she practiced her flirtation skills. The rear admiral, used to command, and respecting Yankee as a competent officer and gentleman, sent the major an almost pleading letter to take his daughter under his wing and see that no harm befell her. In effect the plea amounted to an order.

So at Barnard's Starbase it was very easy for her to find a need for counseling and to fall into small mishaps for which she needed extracting. Often they ate in the cafeteria together, a bleak humongous hut of "temporary" wartime construction. She told him horror stories of the matron who was her first officer and he sneaked her into some of the private beer parties, where she flirted outrageously with all of the men. That made him feel safe.

Barnard's Starbase was not Known Space's best posting. It was built hastily in secret during the war as a staging area for raids into kzinti space, at a time when a major worry was that the Outsiders might go on and sell hyperdrive technology to the Patriarchy for a handsome sum. The UNSN needed safe bases about which the kzinti knew nothing.

It was built on a rocky Mars-sized world glaciated with ices and dark hydrocarbons, the moon of an inhospitable planet of about eight Earth masses. The Base was conveniently at the edge of the Barnard's Star system, far enough inside Barnard's singularity to be immune from surprise hyperdrive attack, but close enough to it so that UNSN ships could quickly reach hyperspace launching distance. Inward there were two gas giants for an ample supply of hydrogen and helium, and a thin belt of rubble for heavier metals. The original intent had been to make Barnard's Starbase an independent manufacturing center but other priorities and the end of the war left the manufacturing centers incomplete. Postwar budget restraints meant that temporary facilities were still in use, even the original construction bunkers.

Yankee's main job, again, was training. General Fry had singled out Barnard's Star as a nucleus for fomenting dissatisfaction with ARM policies. Without a kzinti threat there was little purpose in Barnard's Starbase. Men need a purpose. Where better to do some long-range thinking than on a base which had been *designed* with a possible hyperdrive kzinti threat in mind? Here men were liable to find their purpose in preparing for a hyperarmed Patriarchy.

Yankee found his charge to be an often pleasant diversion. She listened to his worries and never hesitated to give an off-the-wall opinion on any subject. That irritated him but it often forced him to explain strategic concepts about which he was not himself clear. He began giving her research assignments, even requisitioning some of her official on-the-job time. He was delighted to find that she had inherited her father's sense of strategic thoroughness. What she had inherited from her mother, he did not know. Her mother had been killed swinging an axe at a kzin, and she certainly seemed to have that kind of aggressiveness.

The crisis in their relationship came unexpectedly. They were in the Starbase's honor library—their infocomps were not powerful enough to do the particularly difficult and tedious weapons tradeoff analysis that Yankee needed. He was in a bad mood, which killed her enthusiasm. She only meant to tease him enough until he laughed so that they could get back to work. It was easier to be gay and irreverent than bored.

Glibly she began to mutate the weapons discussion into free-flowing nonsense. It eventually blossomed into a free-for-all about ancient Japanese pornography. She was doing her brush strokes in the air and faking geisha flirtations about which she knew nothing—and he was richly enjoying himself pretending to be a sake-saturated teen-aged samurai on his first groping visit to the pillow world of a light-gravity planet. At least he was giggling like a teenager. She was so fascinated—she'd never seen him so wonderfully foolish—that she couldn't stop provoking him. It was true, she thought, that being alone in a public place brings out the devil in men. The devil keeps whispering that someone may walk in and that makes it impossible not to be silly. Even she felt silly and dangerously bold.

Though the eight terminal booths were empty, the library was heavily used—but mostly accessed from distant terminals. They were alone and they were likely to remain alone. For no sane reason they decided to rob the library of Kakabuni's Instructive Erotica, though robbing was entirely unnecessary in a library that took less than a second to copy a chip into a personal infocomp. Their crazy mood told them that they *had* to own the Starbase's *only* copy of Kakabuni. To get at it they needed to unlock and pull out one of the hundred sliding ROM doors—something that only the librarian was supposed to do. They managed to slide out the chip-rack but their chip was near the floor and required a chip-puller that they didn't have so they made love on the floor with their clothes on instead. He even put his arm around her when he walked her back up through the maze to her dorm.

The next day she woke up anxiously because she'd never done something so stupid in her life! On the floor! In her clothes! She faked sickness and did not report for work. All morning on the day after the next day she kept telling herself that her mother was brave enough to swing an axe at a kzin (even though her bravery had killed her). She found a way to wander up and down a corridor that Yankee would have to pass through, carrying a package so that she could pretend to be delivering messages.

She saw him coming before he saw her and tried to duck behind a support pillar but it was too thin. The package stuck out. She looked the other way in panic.

"Hi, Chloe," he said.

"Oh. You." She tried to bat her eyes but they froze. "I've been sick." Sick? She saw him seeing her wan and in crutches and desperately cast around for a more appropriate bright conversation. Yankee, damn him, wasn't saying anything. Food was all she could think of. Even Murphy couldn't get you in trouble with food. "Lunch?"

He seemed almost relieved. "Thirteen-hundred at the Caf?"

"Sure. I'll bring my teeth." She was outraged at herself for saying such a stupid thing but it was already out of her mouth. *I'll bring my teeth!* She cringed. And she was outraged at the way he had crawled back inside his straitlaced self. She wanted to shout *Kakabuni!* at his hastily retreating back but she didn't dare. Growing up wasn't pleasant. She'd never had any trouble with sex when she was thirteen.

Lunch was terrible. They had ground guinea-pig steak and veggies that had been programmed with the wrong spice. They had nothing to talk about. They had come to that horrible time in their relationship when they had already said everything that they had to say to each other. Finagle's Eyes, they were talking about the *color* of the veggies!

"You know what this parsnip looks like? It looks like one of those old brass naval cannons of the seventeenth century."

That saved them. It reminded her of weapons tradeoff analysis. Soon they were comfortable old friends again discussing the impact that hyperdrive ships might have on a millennia-old kzinti military tradition. That culture was based on a bedrock of subluminal assumptions. Supply depots were dispersed. Manufacturing was dispersed. A son could be executed for not carrying out the orders issued to his father—unto the fourth generation. Local conquest commanders had wide authority. The military kzin valued truth so highly because that was the only way of keeping messages from degrading over the centuries.

Chloe became resigned to a Yankee stuck back in his old shell. She knew she was never going to get him to talk about love, not in the Caf. He was more like a cozy confrere than a lover. Her damn father had *ordered* him to take care of her and that's what that damn Yankee was doing. Maybe he didn't even like her. Here she had gone to all the damn trouble of chasing down a damn romantic hero of the war and he'd turned out to be just another awkward damn adolescent like the damned boys she'd been trying to avoid.

Two days later everything was back to normal and she could even tease him without having him go stiff on her.

"Kakabuni" remained a taboo word. They never talked about sex. Worse, they never even talked about *relationships*. Having an admiral for a father was like having an anchor chained to her neck. She was six and a half light-years from Alpha Centauri and she was *still* winched to her father.

Four days later he actually put his arm around her and gave her a quick squeeze.

Two weeks later "fellow-prisoner" Jinny of the Young Woman's Auxiliary invited her on a double date. Her date turned out to be intellectually challenged so she left Jinny to manage both their dates and found her own double date. It was fun to wit-lash young men who were in such good shape physically that their brains recovered in minutes—not like a certain senile old man of her acquaintance.

A month later she missed her period. She thought about that for a few days and then went to the pharmacy for a pregnancy patch. It was positive. She returned for a more expensive test in the pharmacy's autodoc booth. It too was positive, predicting a completely normal pregnancy. That meant she could ask the autodoc for a non-prescription abortion right then. It was between her and the autodoc. No one had to know.

Chloe took a walk instead. She didn't believe that a human life started at conception. Your life didn't start until you got out of the womb and began to make your own decisions—like whether you wanted to breathe or not and which rattle to bang. So she wasn't thinking about the fetus. She was thinking about whether she was ready to be a mother. She hadn't built a nest yet. She was on a military base. She thought a lot about the problems of her father, a lone parent during the time of troubles just after the Battle of Wunderland with the devastation of war all about them and the economy in a shambles.

She'd been such a brat to him, pushing, demanding, and learning how to con each of her new caretakers. She was still looking for a mother even now. She walked to the very center of Starbase, a seven-story atrium where you could catch your breath at a vista of balconies and get away from the claustrophobia of corridors. The bench in the central rock garden was an inviting place to sit. One of the cacti was flowering: a rare sight. On the bench she cried silently and watched the people go by in the shallow ethereal glides of low gravity. Chloe slipped her mother's iron wedding ring out of her blouse, still on its chain where it had always been, forgotten, and thought about the mother she had never known.

At headquarters, where she seldom went, she wandered among the desks of busy men and women in uniform. Some nodded. No one stopped her—they all knew she was the daughter of a powerful admiral. She peeked into Yankee's cubbyhole with its clutter of screens and plotters, a VR helmet on his cabinet, another on the plotter, and another on the floor.

"Hi, stranger," she said.

He took her hand and pulled her inside. The unexpected touch of his hand made her eyes water and she couldn't finish what she had started to say. She let him fill the void. "Good to see you today," he said brightly. "The problems have been coming in all morning and you're a breath of fresh air. I'd ask you to sit, but there isn't any room."

"Problems seem to make you happy," she said bravely.

"We found my cousin. A flash came in from Gibraltar this morning."

"Nora? Is she alive?"

"Yeah. Nora and all of her babies. She has six babies!" Yankee seemed both stunned and excited.

Chloe burst out sobbing—it gave her an excuse.

"That doesn't sound like a problem to me! That's wonderful! I mean about finding her," she said after quickly
recovering.

He took both her hands. "You've got something on your
mind."

"Just a little problem. I came to talk to you about it. It
can wait."

"Can it wait till this evening? How about dinner?"

"Dinner is fine." She was relieved. That put off the
awful moment. "If you've got time." She began to hope
that he had a good excuse to put it off even longer.
Tomorrow she'd be more herself.

Yankee continued. "My problem is that even though
we've found Nora, she's on W'kkai and we'll have to extract
her. Do you know W'kkai? That's seventeen light-years
from here deep inside kzin space. It's a major kzin stronghold. They've given me Jay Mazzetta and my old side-
kick, Beany Heinmann, to help with planning. We've got
to do some fancy juggling in the next few hours."

"We could talk tomorrow."

"Tonight. I might not even be here tomorrow. Not dinner at the Caf—at my place. I saw a drum of apples in the
hydroponics market. Get some. I make a good flatlander
apple pie. Think up something for the main course. Make
it simple—marinated rabbit stew with onions or something. At seventeen hundred." He gave her his key. "Since
you don't have my fingerprints to get in."

"We could postpone it."

"Girls don't cry for nothing."

Chloe fled.

She had to hurry, and bustle kept her mind off what
she was going to say at dinner. She didn't want to get the
meat from the Caf's lockers, which was where they usually got it when they cooked at his apartment, so she took
the maglev to the ranch where Honest Al raised chickens,

turkeys, guinea pigs, and rabbits on an assembly line in the caves. Al was thinking of getting into real pigs, midget pigs, but he wasn't sure how they'd take to cages. "Any pig I ever knowed could snort and root his way out of any cage ever built."

She thought about turkey but Al and his sons were butchering rabbits for freezing, so she took two because she was short on time and she was damned if she was going to pluck her own turkey! Bypassing the autochef was Yankee's hobby but she'd already plucked and cleaned one chicken for him and enough was enough!

At hydroponics she picked up the usual potatoes and onions, but they had some kohlrabi and peppers and leeks so she bought those, too. And a peck of green apples. The nice thing about a stew was that you could make it out of anything. In his apartment she piled up the groceries and went straight to the autochef. Yankee laughed at her, but she *needed* the autochef for advice. It was a baseline military model—except for the luxury spice attachment—and it was a terrible cook but it gave very good advice.

She told it what she had bought and asked for a good recipe. It started with a lecture on how to prepare kohlrabi without ruining its taste. "But I want a *stew*." It suggested stews. "But I want to marinate the rabbit! And I haven't got time because he's going to be here at seventeen hundred!" It provided her with an enzyme-enhanced sauce for quick marinating. She chopped up the rabbit and mixed it in a bowl with the sauce before attacking the vegetables. She didn't know anything about spices. "What spices do I use, and they better be *perfect* or I'll kill you!" It recommended five combinations and manufactured a pinch of each for her to taste with a wet finger. "Number two," she ordered. It all went into the pot and the stew was simmering when Yankee arrived, late.

His eyes lit up and he grabbed a green apple to taste it

before he gave her his usual brotherly kiss. "A Grandma, no less!" He began to chop up each apple with six quick whacks. He never bothered to peel them. "Stew smells good. Did you fight with autochef?"

"No. We had a very civil discussion. I had to shut him up sometimes."

"Watch him. He doesn't get angry. He just poisons you when you push him too far." Yankee was already mixing up the dough for the pie crust.

"How come he doesn't make pie crust? I wanted everything ready for you when you came."

"Thank Murphy for small blessings! Have you ever tasted one of his pies?" Yankee was grinning. He ordered lemon-cinnamon and the machine produced a brown powder—manufactured, of course. Starbase wasn't on the spice trade-routes. She marveled that he knew what to ask for.

"How did it go at work today?"

He waited to answer until the pie was in the oven and he was seated and relaxed. "You remember that crazy kzin we took to Hssin? That ratcat found out more than he was telling me. Fry thought as much and left him with a covert beamer."

"You gave him hyperwave!" she exclaimed incredulously.

"No way. Electromagnetic. He sends out a message. Our patrol relays it. We just got the relay that he found Nora."

"You're sure?" She was skeptical.

"Hwass-Hwasschoaw sent us data about her DNA that he couldn't know. He has her. He wants to exchange her and her children for a ride to Kzin, and I've been elected taximan."

"It's a trap! You be careful. He's lying!"

"Kzinti don't lie."

"That's what the alien psychologists say, but *I* don't believe in kzin honesty for a minute! Do you? You're a *boy*! You're just like all the *dumb* adolescent boys I know! Do you really *believe* a kzin can't lie?"

Yankee smiled and made the yes-no nodding gesture with his hand and head. "What is truth? There are endless ways to tell a *half*-truth—and *no* way that any finite language is capable of telling the *whole* truth. For instance, I can call you up from across town and tell you that your apartment door is unlocked, and that's true, but what you really need to *know* is that I slagged your lock with a laser pistol and kicked the door off its hinges and stole your Tang Dynasty urns."

"You told me that Hwass hates you."

"He does."

"So now he tells you that he has Nora and to come get him! It's a *trap*. He doesn't want to go to Kzin. He's lying! He wants to kill you!"

"No, he's not lying. He *does* want a ride to Kzin. He's in some kind of political hot water. He needs to be met at the singularity boundary by a little ship that won't attract the whole W'kkai navy. He needs to get the hell out of there and he's using my cousin as his ticket. I believe that. It's what he is *not* telling us that worries me."

"So you *admit* he's lying?"

"In a culture where you are executed for lying, lying becomes a fine art indistinguishable from telling the truth."

"No wonder the navy hates you!" She was exasperated. "You reach into black and pull out white!"

"Let's get back to the subject." He was watching her eyes, waiting for the moment when she made eye contact with him. "And what have you been lying to *me* about?"

That made her furious. "I've always told you the truth! Always! You know that!"

"As honest as a kzin."

"Oh," she said. "You mean the things I *haven't* told you about."

"Yeah."

"That's not fair. You're older than I am. How about some rabbit stew first."

He dished out two heaping plates and they ate. "Good stew. Great recipe."

"Liar!"

The conversation died so he tried again. "I'm waiting."

"There's one thing I've never been able to say to you and it's eating my heart out." She looked at him, begging permission to go on, a forlorn waif.

"Go on."

"Kakabuni!" And she was her old mischievous self again.

He grunted from this blow to his solar plexus. "You've floored me. Yeah. We haven't been able to talk about that." The taboo word. And he concentrated on his stew for a while before he had the courage to look her grin in the teeth. "I'll be a man and take my medicine. What else?"

"You want more? Let's have some apple pie first," she said miserably.

Somehow the conversation turned back to Nora Argamentine. The topic was safe and they each had a lot to say. The chime went off for the pie. He put on his mitts and took it out of the oven. He cut her a slice. "It's hot," he said.

Chloe took a forkful and blew on it. "I'm pregnant."

Yankee was half-expecting that. He had forgotten to make his offering to Murphy. *Whatever can go wrong, will go wrong.* Murphy was a hard god who expected you to tend to the smallest details of your life. Fail him once and his wrath was upon you. Murphy, judge and executioner—and Kakabuni, tempter.

"You're more worried that my father is going to chop your head off than you are about me," she sulked.

"I *did* promise him I'd take care of you."

"You've taken very good care of me considering what a pest I am. You can marry me. Otherwise I have to have an abortion."

"Before now, have you ever thought about marrying me?" he asked.

"You know I have—unless you're blind. I've chased you mercilessly."

"You chase all men mercilessly."

"Those are just *boys*. I keep looking for a man, and all I find are adolescent *boys* like you who do things on the floor and then run away."

"It's a fantasy, Chloe. I'm *thirty-two* years older than you are."

"You're lying like a kzin," she said. "What you *mean* to say is that I'm thirty-two years *younger* than you are. You're telling me that I'm too immature to understand you, too young to fit in your life, that I giggle too much, and that I run you ragged around your stuffy old edges."

"Well, yeah."

"You're just afraid my father's going to kill you!"

"There's that."

"Haven't you ever even *once* thought about how nice it would be to be married to me?"

"More than you can imagine. I'm very fond of you. But it's a fantasy."

"Why?"

"The military life is hell."

"I'm used to it. What am I supposed to do? Marry a painter and live in a Chinese junk in the San Francisco Bay slums? Marry a Wunderland sheep rancher?"

"I'm too old."

"I'll be 178 when you are 210. Big deal. You're such an

ooze! You defy the whole navy but you're terrified that your shipmates will laugh at you for marrying a gangly pubescent!"

"But I *am* too old for you."

"I'd eat another slice of your superior pie but I'm too mad. Sit down. I'm prepared for you. I do my research." She dragged him over to the couch and pushed him into a seat. She pulled out her infocomp and made a directory out of the word "aging" and a subdirectory out of the word "Jinx." "I have an article for you." She didn't trust him to read it by himself so she read it to him.

More than forty years ago the Jinxian laboratory at Sirius had produced something they called "boosterspice." The new varieties were enormous improvements on the first product. It could run around in cells repairing DNA. It regulated the growth of cell types that had stopped reproducing—without inducing cancer. Some of the oldest test subjects were still alive.

Yankee put his arm around her soberly with the tender affection of a man who is trying to tell a youngster that they have rediscovered the wheel. "I know all about boosterspice. I've been reading up on it since before you were born. Every year Jinx turns out a better product and there is more ballyhoo. They are gradually nailing down all the side effects. Do you know what happens in your brain when neurons start to reproduce and connect up at the wrong places? Do you have any idea how expensive that stuff is? And what do you get for your money? Boosterspice has been known to extend lives. Or it might cripple you. Maybe even kill you. One of the richest old men on Earth jumped on the Boosterspice bandwagon. Now he's very young—but he's a mentally retarded youth and slightly musclebound."

"That's what rich people are for," she said petulantly. "They are very useful experimental animals for us poor military types and carpenters. The rich pay through the nose for all the fancy new technology when it isn't very good. They're desperate to live so they pay thousands of crazy witch-doctors to kill them in fancy new ways. When the rich people stop dying, we know the product is ready for market and can be mass produced cheaply."

"Chloe!"

"It's like being a king and having a food-taster. The reason I want to marry an older man is so you can test out the boosterspice for me. If you die, I get your money. If you stay young, I'll know its safe to start taking boosterspice."

"Chloe, how come you taste my pies for me? Through thick crust and thin?"

She snuggled. "How come you never tell me that you love me?"

"I love you."

"That's better. How come you never make love to me? I haven't been a virgin since I was thirteen."

"That's why. When I was thirteen, seventeen-year-old girls were old crones. Every year since then they've been getting younger. It has gotten so that I can't keep track of how old a seventeen-year-old girl is anymore."

"That's silly! Are we in a Kakabuni mood yet?"

"I have to decide whether you are grown-up or not."

"I'm grown-up. I'm pregnant, remember. I'm in the army. My father is six light-years away." She undid his belt.

"All right. You're grown-up. I can't go wrong. You're getting older every year." He picked her up, mostly to keep her from undressing him. He carried her across the threshold of his bedroom door and let her float dream-like to the small navy bed in the light gravity. He sat down on its edge and began to undress her.

She grabbed his hand in both of hers, stopping him.

She wasn't wearing a bra. "How come we are afraid of each other?"

He let her fingers stay with his hand. "Who knows? Maybe you're afraid of yourself and I'm afraid of your father."

She kissed his hand. "Are you a virgin? I mean before you met me."

"Not likely. I'm a navy man—and I used to be handsome. I even had a flatlander marriage contract once."

"You seem shy to me."

"It depends upon whom I'm with."

"How many women?"

"You ask too many questions, young lady." He kissed the tip of her nose.

She sat up. "I can undress myself. I've had lots of men, too, you know. I sexed with your crashlander friend, Brobding What's-his-Name." She wasn't used to her uniform—it didn't come off gracefully, futz! "You can't take off my wedding ring." She fingered the iron ring hanging between her breasts. "I always wear it."

"Was your mother as beautiful as you?"

"No. I'm prettier. I take after my father. Do I have to give you orders to strip? It's a Wunderland custom for a man to make sex when he's properly *naked*."

He was smiling. "It's a flatlander custom that love-partners help each other with their clothes. Unless, of course, when proceeding by the rules of unpremeditated Kakabuni."

"You're a pervert! I feel like a baby in diapers when a man tries to undress me. Is Clandeboye an Italian name?"

"I think it comes from a gloomy Scottish castle." He said that to the ceiling because she was ripping his pants off. "Wait. I'll help you with the shirt!"

Premeditated Kakabuni took over. The pleasure of flesh against flesh. Fond glances that cloak the human face in unnatural beauty. A hormonal passion driving bodies far past their design limits. "Had enough?" "No." "Me neither." It was strange to love a man who had no sweet talk.

Sleeping in a man's arms was an unnatural thing to do unless you were in love with him. One had no choice in a navy bed. Her rump was pressed against the wall and a foot twisted by some kind of bar. She couldn't sleep. She was both comfortable and frightened. He didn't talk. He hadn't said anything. She rapped him on the skull with her knuckles. "Knock, knock. Are you there?"

"Mmmpf. Yah."

"You haven't proposed to me," she accused.

He moved his head between her breasts and went back to sleep.

"Men *always* propose to me before they make love to me whether they are sincere or not. How come you haven't proposed to me?"

"Formality . . . protocol . . . etiquette . . . propriety," he muttered.

She crawled over him and sat on the edge of the bed. "I'm not feeling secure. We could get married right now." She was looking down at him. "Hey, you're awake! I woke you up!" She switched on the glow light.

"Hey, you're beautiful. You look like a woman. What's happening to my mind?"

"Don't change the subject. We're talking about marriage."

"Never tried it."

"Did you like my rabbit stew?"

"Yah."

"It went very well with your pie so we should get married right now."

"Our wedding guests would be appalled by our dishabille!"

"Are you going to propose to me?

"I don't know how."

"You're supposed to propose to a woman *before* you make love to her. Don't they teach you any manners on Earth? I've never been treated so inconsiderately in my life." She lifted the chain from her neck and stared at the ring. The iron had been formed under high pressure and it was full of bright little diamond crystals. She liberated her talisman from its chain. "Do you want to try it on?"

"It wouldn't fit."

"It's a Swiss precision telescoping ring. It will fit any finger." She slipped it on his special finger. "See. It fits. Now we're married. And oh, I forgot . . . it has an inscription that reads 'forever.' "

"It must have been made before boosterspice." He held up his hand to look at it. "You're supposed to wear one of these things, too, you know."

"Then I couldn't flirt with the boys." She crawled back in bed, hip-whacking Yankee in order to make some room for herself. "Love, I forgot to ask you—do you snore? If you snore I'm getting an abortion right now."

"With you around I just stop breathing. How about a trip to Kzin for our honeymoon? I've got the tickets."

"No, thank you! If you want a honeymoon on Kzin I'm filing for divorce in the morning." She kissed him good night and went to sleep happier than she had ever been.

Chloe dreamed about a wedding feast on Kzin in an ancient manorial hall with Major Yankee Clandeboye as the main course and Nora Argamentine and her children as dessert. She was watching from a cage that swung from the ceiling. Yankee dreamed of Earth and the ancient Royal Navy. He was being keelhauled across the barnacles of a shipbottom by a very irate British admiral.

• Chapter 19

(2438 A.D.)

It was very difficult for Hwass-Hwasschoaw to manage the rescue from W'kkai. The signals *sent* from his UNSN-supplied beamer to the UNSN patrol vessel had to be masked by the normal electromagnetic radiation from W'kkai. He had his beamer set up on a mountain in his hunting range among the cluttered equipment of an amateur astronomical observatory. Still he dared not fire it at a low angle.

Worse, he had to *receive* redundantly generated signals broadcast by the UNSN along the vector of an interstellar radio source. It was no easy task to clean away the camouflaging noise from the weak carrier.

Then each of the outgoing messages had to be acknowledged by the UNSN and each incoming message had to be acknowledged by a burst from W'kkai. Tedious.

His political skills were taxed. He had to make judicious use of the Patriarch's Eye, its amateur astronomers, its spies among the priests and government and navy. He had to seduce loyal warriors to arrange safe transportation to the singularity boundary. If it had been just himself and Grraf-Nig, there would have been no problems. But he also had to smuggle out his bait, the Nora-beast and her six whelps.

A crippled kzin, whose two sons had been killed years ago in combat with Si-Kish, designed Hwass a container cleverly outfitted for human hibernation. Grraf-Nig, their expert on human physiology, was consulted. More arguments. More snarling. But they had to get it right. There could be no tricks here. If Hwass did not deliver the Nora-beast alive, he knew there would be no transportation to Kzin; indeed, the Yankee-beast would then try to kill him. There was no sense in provoking premature suspicion.

Endless petty knots had to be curried from the plan's fur. Originally Hwass hoped that many years of W'kkai observations could be smuggled past W'kkai and human eyes inside the "diplomatic" pouch Interworld Space Commissioner Markham had given him at Tiamat. The contents of the pouch were, after all, *intended* for Kzin. But in one of his messages the Clandeboye-animal instructed him to destroy the old pouch. A duplicate would be supplied and delivered to him as he left the UNSN vessel at Kzin. So much for that. Interstellar mail was too precious to allow time for argument with monkeys.

Outlook spawned the biggest carcass of contention in this adventure. Hwass was a bold strategist, willing to take high risks because of his great skill and fleet feet. Grraf-Nig was by nature a coward. He did not like risks. Unfortunately he was essential to any plan to capture Clandeboye's mercy ship. Grraf-Nig knew how to pilot a hyperdrive vessel; Hwass did not. Grraf-Nig understood hypershunt construction; Hwass did not. Grraf-Nig knew the poisons that would destroy a monkey mind; Hwass did not.

They snarled and yowled at each other over the details of their planned theft but the coward always prevailed because he knew his worth. Hwass tried importing exotic animals for their hunts. He tried playing scent-ball with this eater-of-grass on the local meadows—and letting him win. No amount of flattery penetrated this coward's fur. Exasperating. Hwass had to work out his rage during the dinner chases.

It was fifteen light-years from W'kkai to Kzin. That distance couldn't be covered in one hyperspace jump. Hwass craved to release the nerve gas after the first jump, killing the crew instantly, then to broadcast false hyperwave distress signals. If the UNSN suspected a lethal drive malfunction, blame would not fall upon Kzin.

Grraf-Nig, in his cowardly mien, argued that some unforeseen event *might* strand them—losing both the ship and whatever service they could provide the Patriarch. Timidly he pleaded that the gas be released *after* they had reached Kzin, *after* the exchange of slave for warrior had been completed. Then if bad luck befell them, Grraf-Nig's *precious* brain (and neck) would have survived.

Dealing with this robber-of-names filled Hwass's stomach with rotten meat. His partner did not understand the strategic importance of a gas that could kill a human crew instantly without touching any kzinti on board. In the forest Hwass practiced twisting the bark off trees with his bare hands. Boulders came apart when he smashed them against stony outcrops. Rodents were squashed to a pulp in his grip.

But Grraf-Nig remained adamant: if the gas did its job at Kzin, warriors could board the hypership, and take it, no one the wiser; if the gas failed, and the man-beasts became enraged, the whole of the Kzin fleet would be there, alert and ready to protect Kzin-home. It had already been proved that a human fleet could not take a major system of the Patriarchy. All the advantages were with the defense. And it was ninety days by hyperdrive from Man-sun to Kzin. Kzinti were adapted to slow supply lines; humans were not.

Grraf-Nig had his own way of handling his rage at the wasted time invested in argument with his liver-driven co-conspirator. He was absolutely sure that, unarmed, he could kill Hwass, probably quickly. His instructor in Heroic Combat and name-sake, Grraf-Hromfi of the Black Pride, had given him years of personal training—and in the end had trusted the martial training of his sons to Grraf-Nig. It was not strength that counted in combat. But killing Hwass would strand him on W'kkai.

He took out his anger in controlled combat—by exercising the rules of tournament. He had a student. Monkeyshine liked to fight. It gave the outcast kzin a way to use up his rage and learn to control it at the same time. The old trainer-of-slaves in him was still curious about the limits of slaves. His ears wiggled to see the tiny boy charge him with a full-faced grin.

Part of Grraf-Nig was still furious about the fate of his own male kits. He had daughters but the sons were dead, murdered, probably devoured, by the scarless kzin who had taken over his harem. Monkeyshine was probably the only son he'd ever have. Was there any harm in teaching him a few fancy tricks? The little slave would be dead himself soon enough. He would die for the Patriarch. Sometimes fathers had to sacrifice their sons for the triumph of the Patriarchy.

It was a day of heavy wind. The final batch of nerve gas was being synthesized under less than ideal conditions. There was no threat to kzinti but Grraf-Nig took the whole family of man-beasts upwind for a picnic to keep them out of possible danger. Almost tenderly he spent the time with Monkeyshine in the dry orange grass of the field, teaching him how to sidestep an oncoming blow, then reverse-kick for a deadly riposte.

In time the whole operation was in place. A UNSN vessel arrived to patrol the singularity—a flea of a ship that aroused no passionate feeling on W'kkai. Friends of the Eye were ready with a small kzin corvette. Its captain requested—and was given—the mission to shadow the new ghostship. His cargo of human slaves were first tranquilized (while sleeping) and each administered a sealed suppository of nerve gas. They were drugged with the metabolic retardants Grraf-Nig had developed during those long gone days when an adequate supply of manbeast experimental animals were coming to him from the Wunderland orphanages. Suspended, the slaves were stored in their specialized container and smuggled to the spaceport.

To Grraf-Nig's immense relief, the enterprise went smoothly. There was no wild chase by Si-Kish's elite units. Hwass was a superb organizer—just as he boasted—a hunter who could pass silently over twigs in the driest of summers. Even the transfer from W'kkai corvette to UNSN flea was a model of smooth cooperation. Only the mistrust made it uncomfortable. Grraf-Nig, allergic to prisons, was outraged at their prisoner status. Hwass, who had been caged before by Major Yankee Clandeboye, delighted in his associate's discomfort. He knew how to use the formidable weaponry afforded by the Mocking Tense of the Hero's Tongue. A murderous Grraf-Nig decided that it was fortunate for Hwass that there were *two* cages.

They were in no danger. As arranged by Hwass, they were allowed a "dead-kzin" switch; the death of a kzin would trigger the explosive death of the slaves. It amused Grraf-Nig that Hwass hadn't counted on a "dead-man" switch rigged by the efficient Captain Jay Mazzetta. If any of the slaves died, the UNSN's kzinti guests would be administered a lethal injection. Grraf-Nig wiggled his ears in slow fan-like waves, which was his own way of retaliatory mocking. The gesture plainly said, "I told you so!"— Hwass's original plan to take over the UNSN's vessel would not have worked.

***

It was a tense journey. Three humans; two kzin; seven sleeping slaves. It lasted forty-five days. The time wasn't altogether unproductive. Yankee taught his kzinti gin rummy. Since they had no common currency, the winnings were paid off in ethnic jokes. The Hero's Tongue is the richest language for insults in Known Space and so the caged ratcats never ran out of monkey putdowns. Translated into butchered English, the odor of the jokes was sanitized but at the same time turned into a bizarrely hilarious travesty of which the kzin could not be aware.

Hwass enjoyed showing off his knowledge of man-beast history. "Iss German monkey self-named Hitler-Führer. Iss think to win thousand-year victory on Jewish slaves by mustache and salute." Hwass imitated Hitler with a black finger under the nose of his muzzle and an outstretched furry arm. His German accent was atrocious, the point of his story incomprehensible. Still, Yankee and Jay and Beany cracked up in helpless laughter. Hitler-Führer had his Germans by the tens, by the hundreds, by the thousands, and then by the millions marching off into the stupidest of monkey adventures imaginable.

The kzinti, in turn, taught their simian chauffeurs how to play a pentagonal card game called tournament which they were convinced no mere animal could master because no money or lies exchanged hands, only honor. The Heroes became very good at gin rummy. The humans never won a single game of tournament. They had to listen to much humor at their expense.

When it was Grraf-Nig's turn to tell an ethnic joke he was more impressed by human technical stupidity than by their sorry history. He loved simple observations about the intelligence of man-females. Once he had observed, he said, a blond woman (one of his experimental animals) repair an electrical appliance. She carefully joined the severed power-source wires, input to input, output to output. She pressed the input and output wires together because she didn't like lumps. Then, because she knew about insulation, she wrapped everything in tape until no copper was showing. She plugged it in. Grraf-Nig imitated the female scream that followed the explosive vaporization of copper. His ears flapped at the jolly memory.

Yankee and Jay and Beany enjoyed Grraf-Nig's blond "manrret" jokes but they didn't really find his admiral-monkey jokes very funny at all. The jibes were impossibly unfair—human admirals were always jumping into battle without doing their homework, or drinking kzin piss out of bottles labeled as boosterspice, or seducing young lieutenants.

The terms of reception at Kzin had been coordinated by hyperwave and electromagnetic haggling. Grraf-Nig set the strategy, Hwass the tactic. Hwass cleverly suggested to the incorrigibly naive monkeys, and the UNSN accepted, a protocol that might sound friendly to a human but would inevitably sound hostile to a kzin. It was a protocol evolved over thousands of years of interstellar squabbling to settle disputes between rival Conquest Commanders of different star systems. After an exchange of prisoners—the exchange more desired by one side than the other—the carriers were expected to admit wrongdoing in the Dominated Tense—or accept a boarding party and a fight to the death.

Hwass knew, and Grraf-Nig conceded, that this particular protocol would make no sense to the Heroes of Kzin—the UNSN was *enemy* not rival, *animal* not warrior. But the elite warriors of Kzin were the best in the Patriarchy. They would smell the wind while listening to the words—and know what the protocol was telling them across the light-years. A boarding party would be hidden in the Heroes' exchange ship, ready for Hwass to command when he was no longer a prisoner.

The barter was carried out in Kzin space with the efficiency of a demolition team disassembling a time-bomb. Kzinsun was the brightest star in the sky, Kzinhome invisible in its glare. Kzin's great gas giant Hgrall was brilliant by reflected light, but to find it a kzin had to know where it was against the backdrop of the Fanged God's constellations. Grraf-Nig was in a state of fear he hadn't felt since his failed escape from W'kkai. The tiny craft shuttling between warships was too small, too vulnerable. These critical moments after the disarming of the "dead-hand" switches were the most dangerous. He could smell his own fear inside his suit.

Hwass-Hwasschoaw was feeling no such alarm; he who believed in the God of the True Shape had nothing to fear from these divine pets. God needed the culling skills of the kzin to control His pets' disloyal impiety. With a Kdapt reformation, He would get just that. All was going according to plan.

Their shuttle gracefully docked with the kzin ship. Free, Hwass sent the shuttle back out into space, pilotless, carrying the replacement diplomatic pouch and whatever treachery it might carry besides whinings about peace. He thrust his grass-eating companion into the maw of the airlock. Machinery cycled. The inner entrance dilated. Before he was out of his suit, Hwass was ushering a black-spotted captain toward his command center, leaving Grraf-Nig to fend for himself.

"Do we have warriors trained in boarding?"

The captain, striding to keep up, hissed qualified agreement, even enthusiasm. The war against the ghostships had been going badly for too long, the humiliation of being member to a *treaty* roared out the need of vengeful retaliation—but he was a professional who wanted to know more than Hwass had been able to tell him.

"Communicator!" Hwass motioned the crewkzin out of his seat; the comm equipment was standard over the whole of the Patriarchy and he was too impatient to explain his needs. He punched in a signal from memory and beamed it at the distant UNSN ghostship. Then he counted heartbeats. Now! The gas would be erupting from the suppositories of the slaves in a flatulence of death. In the null-gee human ships, air supply was circulated by machine. It was a small ship. Grraf-Nig's test-animals from the Wunderland orphanage had died within *seconds* after exposure to the gas.

When there was no response from the ghostship, he rose from the communicator's station and turned to the captain. "They are dead. The entire crew, slaves, all. Send your boarding party! Instantly! We have captured a hyperdrive!"

Sixteen warriors, in readiness for hours, swarmed out of the kzin warship, angry wasps. Cautious at first, they were deployed so they couldn't all be slaughtered at once. They were ready to return fire with a fire that would surgically remove any weapons that the ghostship might use. But there was no return fire. Two warriors were about to open their prey like a can of rations when . . . it disappeared. Fourteen warriors had nothing to attack.

Hwass-Hwasschoaw reacted in stunned surprise. At that moment, Grraf-Nig took control, almost as if he were a trainer-of-slaves again and these warriors were suddenly his by right of a higher bid. "Honored Captain! *I* know what has happened! Call the navy. Bring up support! In the meantime, full acceleration perpendicular to the hyperboundry. Down!"

"My warriors!" wailed the captain.

"They are safe," he hissed urgently. "Pick them up later.

They'll still be there. It is absolutely *vital* that this ship not be attacked! We carry the secret of the hyperdrive to the Patriarch—in my head! Get us down!" Then more calmly Grraf-Nig turned to a recovering Hwass. "The beasts were on automatic pilot. We should have expected that. The crew is dead but their ship flies itself." He made a gesture of respect to the captain. "You will be remembered as the Hero who delivered the hyperdrive technology to our valiant Patriarch. The secret is *on board*! Get out of monkey range!"

Calmly, the captain gave the orders.

As an aside to Hwass, but in a voice loud enough for the captain to hear, Grraf-Nig added, "Plans have a life of their own. We gambled that not only could we bring the secret of the hyperdrive to Kzin, but also an actual ship. We lost."

The Patriarch's Eye tried to hide his disappointment by growling out his anger in mangled English, vocally—but only to himself. "Major Yankee Clandeboye iss not alive he!" The monkey who had humiliated him, broken Markham's word, toyed with him, kept him in a cage—was dead at last, culled by the God of the True Form. That reminded him of his diplomatic pouch and the mission Clandeboye had interrupted by his arrival at Tiamat.

He arranged with the captain that the pouch on the discarded shuttle be retrieved by the same ship that was retrieving the stranded warriors, that it be inspected by a device expert, and returned to him as soon as it was certifiably safe. *Peace!* He was bringing *peace!* What a disappointment this trip had been. A molting yellow coward would get all the glory.

• Chapter 20

(2438 A.D.)

The domain of the Patriarch was sparse, austere, even gloomy when compared with W'kkai. The granite walls were ancient and of a cruder stone masonry than one might expect at the center of galactic power. Spiraling stone stairs to the attic guest rooms had depressions where thousands of years of feet had polished them. The decorations were simple. Tapestries. Ancient, fragile weapons. Armor of beads and woven metal. A collection of *wtsai* blades. Vases from an age when fire was the mightiest of energies.

Grraf-Nig was guided everywhere by a kdatlyno slave who had strict orders; thus he saw but a small portion of the Palace. He didn't even know which Riit Palace he was in. He had glimpses of passages. From his room he could see a rotunda's dome and on a distant hill the ruin of the old Palace destroyed more than eight millennia ago by the Jotok traders who had been annoyed by the murder of an accountant. Few kzin could any longer imagine their spiderlike Jotok slaves as fierce merchants. An old trainer-of-slaves could. Their fierceness had not altogether been bred out of them.

When his kdatlyno led him to his endless interviews with the science bureaucrats of the Palace, he took quick peeks into chambers, galleries, and into a fascinating maze where an earless snow-furred kzintosh led a bevy of silent kzinrretti in flowing lace. He longed to sneak off on his

own but in this awesome seat of power he had no intention of disobeying even a slave's suggestion. Everywhere
there were signs that the slightest infraction meant an
instant death.

His guide had orders to give his life to stop any trans-
gression—or face death himself. Who knew in what black
arts the beast had been trained? His arms were huge,
even in proportion to a height that was taller than any
kzin. The hands were strangler's hands that brushed his
knees as he led, eight retractile claws at the knuckles.
Horns marked his knees and elbows. Attack him? They
were filed sharp and then buffed to a polished glow. His
brown hide would have stopped a knife. With only his
radar sense to shape his surroundings, he had nothing
resembling eyes. His face was marked only by a gash of a
mouth and by a lumped region above it where the skin
was stretched taut.

On the fourth day his kdatlyno made an awkward gesture of obeisance, a bow that forced the beast to lift his
hands slightly so that his fingers would not touch the floor.
A machine strapped to his body spoke in the Hero's
Tongue. "Make ready for your audience with the Patriarch."

Jotok slaves dressed him. One of them was propped
on three hands while two other hands cut and sewed.
The other sat on its underbelly mouth to free five hands
for rapid hem-work. They produced a heavy, flowing robe
that would have hampered any fighting; indeed, guards
attacking him could have used it to wrap him into a sack.
It looked good in the mirror, though not up to W'kkai
flamboyance. Grraf-Nig followed the kdatlyno through
keeps he had never seen. A pride of kzinti guards let them
pass into the sanctuary of the Patriarch's lair.

It was a huge room, furnished simply in slashtooth fur
and kudlotlin hide rugs, wooden chairs, tables. The ceiling

frescoes blazed from curved arches that rivaled the sky. A gravitic sleeper, elaborately inlaid, peeked from behind a screen—he was clearly equipped to work here for long periods. A huge flatplate dominated his desk, wooden, cluttered. Ostentatious kzinrretti tents filled a distant corner. An orange and yellow striped kzinrret lounged before the flaming hearth that fed into its chimney's giant tower.

Nobody had given Grraf-Nig instructions. His inclination was to crawl forth on his belly, but the Patriarch stood and beckoned him forward across that great expanse of territory with the age-old sign of well-met in the wilderness. The grizzly old kzin next to him did not move. That would be High Admiral Ress-Chiuu.

It took all his willpower not to crawl but he did stop at a distance to give his snappiest slashing claw-across-the-face, first to the Patriarch and then to Ress-Chiuu. The impatient Patriarch summoned him again. The Riit did not even bother to introduce himself or the admiral. Instead he turned with happy ears to the reclining kzinrret by the fire. "My gift to you. From my harem. Well trained, docile. She will serve your every need. She's been trained to do an extraordinary number of tricks. Lismichi."

At the sound of her name, Lismichi looked up with large yellow eyes that peered out between her languid ears. The ears waved sensually.

"Come here, wench. Meet your new mount." She rose and came. "Lie." The Patriarch indicated a chair for Grraf-Nig—and Lismichi lay beside it, ready to have her back scratched or not. "Horowrrr!" exclaimed the Patriarch, "I believe you are more comfortable now than when you entered my lair. I smell more raunch than fear!" His ears were flapping, not nearly such beautiful ears as those of Lismichi.

Grraf-Nig remained speechless.

Ress-Chiuu was ready to begin serious discussion. "My engineers have interviewed you and believe that you *can* help us to build one of those ghostships that come and go. They've been a fearsome puzzle to us. I understand from Hwass-Hwasschoaw that you worked on a similar program at W'kkai. If we give you the whole of our resources, can we catch up? I dread to see those W'kkaikzin in a position of dominance. A brash, superficial culture ignorant of its birthing nest. Hwass tells us that W'kkai will field a major ghost fleet within an octalyear. Is this truth or fantasy? In these grim days we have few sources of good information."

"Truth. When I first arrived at W'kkai I thought in hopeful despair that it would take us an octal-squared of years to achieve our goal, and only then if we could draw upon the smuggled covert creativity of the entire Patriarchal realm. W'kkai's naturalists astonished me with their technical powers. My best estimate is that Si-Kish's arm is as long as his ambition. His numbers, you see, are the very numbers *I* gave him. I will add that I expect *your* naturalists to astonish me, too."

The Patriarch cleaned his fangs with black claws. "We have different strengths. The W'kkaikzin have always enjoyed puzzles and the abstract whim of symbol. Our muscle lies more in the practical, though we do have a mathematical tradition that extends back to the time of Chmeee the Blind. You've never been to Kzin? You must visit the caves of the Mooncatcher Mountains where the Weirdmind-Hunters chiseled the tenets of their geometry into the walls. They flayed their better theorems onto the pelts of enemies but unfortunately few such hides survived the coming of the Jotok."

Lismichi was placidly out of the conversation but she was winding her tail up between his legs and flicking its tip. The sensation was very distracting.

Ress-Chiuu had more on his mind. "Hwass brought us an analysis of the situation on W'kkai that is disturbing, but he also brought us another very peculiar document that may mean something to you. It means nothing to any of our engineers—who claim that only a major research project can translate it into something they can even read. You were present during the humiliation at Ka'ashi. Did you ever smell the urine of Ulf Reichstein Markham?"

"On a distant breeze. He was a feral-slave who preyed in the Serpent Swarm. There was a reward offered to any kzin who brought in his head."

"He is now Interworld Space Commissioner for the man-beasts. We have had very peculiar dealings with him. He sent us messages via Wunderland repatriates. We ignored him." Ress-Chiuu switched into the Mocking Tense. "But he will not be ignored; we are to conquer the galaxy together with animal curiosity and Heroic discipline." The admiral paused, as if trying to comprehend something incomprehensible. "Lately he begins to suggest that he might be able to cooperate with us—against Man-home. Monkeys delight in betraying each other. What could we lose by encouraging such folly?"

"You have contact with the tree-swingers? At W'kkai there is none."

"At W'kkai they are wasps, swarming at every prod. We have no choice but to make contact and restrain our patrols. The MacDonald-Rishshi Treaty was written here. It needs adjusting, discussion, concession. Markham has helped us with some commercial deals. We are cut off by the blockade and are forced to use human ships for trade. Our trade is stifled, theirs prospers. They *forge* wealth at our expense. We tinker a little money, too, with cooling iron castoffs in a cold corner of the mongery—but it is *their* money which must, in the end, be spent on *them*.

We sent Markham some money to grease our pitiful trade interests. Strangely, he has just sent us a document via Hwass."

"Hwass mentioned some nonsense. I mean no offense—was the Markham-beast offering human subservience and tribute to the Patriarchy?"

Ress-Chiuu stood up to pace. " 'Subservience and tribute' is not the correct translation of the word"—he butchered his attempt at English—" 'peace.' I refer you to the linguists. But let us not deal with incomprehensible alien psychology. Let us deal with this manuscript that our engineers cannot understand." He pulled out a thick sheath of paper. "The document is also available electronically for quick scan, but I want you to sniff through the paper version and give me a quick opinion. What is it?"

"Now?"

"Yes, now!" snarled Ress-Chiuu impatiently.

Grraf-Nig read bits and pieces, skipping pages. "It is pedantic and in the high formal English grammar," he said. "I have my troubles speaking the language but no trouble reading it."

"Good. Does it amount to gibberish about alien harmony and the music of the spheres and astrological farting among the thistles of prescient weeds—or does it have any red meat? My engineers say it contains equations but the notation is unfamiliar to them. I understand that the monkey astrological texts also contain equations."

Moments later Grraf-Nig lifted his muzzle in astonishment. "It's a discussion of hyperspace mechanics!"

"Markham's meanderings said as much but we are not altogether ready to believe a monkey who makes his way across the battlefield singing to birds!"

"What now?"

"Read on, you begat of a lice-infested female kshat. Is this meat or is it mushroom?"

Grraf-Nig read, all the while wishing he could nail Shakespeare-Newton to Hwass's Kdapt cross so that he might save himself from the agony of their notational sins. Patriarch and admiral waited as if they could hear approaching prey in the bushes. Lismichi rubbed her head against his leg. He located a likely-looking equation and painfully translated it into kzinti script. It still didn't make sense but it was exactly the equation one would use for a rotation into hyperspace if such a thing had meaning.

While he worked, the Patriarch called for a snack of vatach. Servants released the little animals in the lair and the Patriarch sicked Lismichi on them. She chased them down with clever pounces and swivels, skidding on rugs and overturning a few chairs. She brought her first catch to the Patriarch in her teeth and dumped it upon his golden plate, where he ripped it apart, devouring the tidbit, bones and all, before licking his chin and licking his fur where the blood had spattered. The next delicacy came to the admiral, who was not as neat. Lismichi licked him clean.

Then after a frantic chase, she brought to Grraf-Nig the last vatach, squealing unharmed in her teeth. Gently she crushed its skull with her jaws before she laid it carefully on his plate. He was too excited to be hungry. He scratched her head, and put the plate on the floor for her. She thanked him with a whack of her hips against his leg, pushed aside a rug so that she wouldn't bloody it, and devoured her catch on the floor, daintily getting no blood on her fur.

"She's so well trained," marveled the ex-slave-trainer, who could appreciate such niceties.

"For a female," bellowed the Patriarch.

When Grraf-Nig followed his kdatlyno guide back to his quarters with his new wife on a leash, he saw none of the marvels of the Palace. His mind was racing over his new duties. He was the Hssin barbarian who held the fate of the Patriarchy in his decisions. Where would it go? Another war for sure, with W'kkai and Kzin fighting over the territory recovered from the ephemeral man-beasts.

In his room Lismichi sniffed about her unfamiliar surroundings. He called up a map of Kzin on the flatplate, zooming in on the design daedal that was to be his new home. Power and responsibility and respect like he'd never known. It frightened him to the point where he could hardly think.

I'm too old to be afraid, he thought.

He took his wife by the scruff of the neck and threw her on the bed which had once seemed too large and now seemed too small. After those horrible months in that conundrum cell with only liquid meal and a water hose to keep him alive and a stone floor to sleep on, having a kzinrret again, and such a pleasant one, was a real pleasure. No use trying to sex with her. She wasn't in estrus and wouldn't be in the mood. It was always more exciting when they had that delicious smell about them and were full of desire. A Hero really needed five wives with their periods properly staggered to enjoy life.

He dimmed the lights and took one last look at the ruins of the old palace against the mountainside, undressed, and brought his great body down on the bed to snuggle with his petite wife. What an honor to be given a kzinrret from the Patriarch's harem! He would cherish her. She was licking his face affectionately and he had to dodge out of the way of her tongue. The pleasures of life! He nibbled at her huge floppy ears! He didn't deserve such a beauty.

She went to sleep in his arms, still smelling slightly of wood smoke. He didn't sleep. He had too much to ponder. He was remembering the desperate loneliness of space. *I was mad then.* He had his malfunctioning hypershunt motor, and his slaves, and a mangled world to remind him of the deadly beasts from Man-sun. Cuddling with Lismichi nostalgically reminded him of his days with the Nora-beast in that dimly remembered palazzo of the nightmare Hssin.

She had been under control then, the memory of her past gone, her language capability gone, no longer a fearsome warrior who had killed the entire crew of a kzin warship and had nearly killed her Trainer-of-Slaves. Peaceful. She was like a young kzinrret curiously learning about her unknown world, learning how to hiss, to get angry, to groom her fur, to beg for food and affection. In many ways like a young kzinrret with a fierce loyalty to her children—but not like a kzinrret. Different. Odd the way one grew fond of slaves.

He had slept with her all that time, cuddling like he was cuddling with Lismichi now in the dark. A strange relationship. There had never been any sex—sex between man-beast and kzin was impossible, as much as sex was impossible between kzin and Jotok. She never went into estrus and she smelled wrong so he had never desired her. She had the ugliest ears of any beast he had ever seen. But he had needed her. He loved to stroke her soft fur. She needed him, growing up fresh in a dangerous world surrounded by poisonous gases. When she began to learn to speak again, with the limited language apparatus he had left her, her first words in broken patois were, "My Hero." The Nora-beast had followed him everywhere as loyal and naive as only a slave can be.

He thought about killing slaves. Lying on his bed in this sacred place where Jotoki had once ruthlessly killed their enslaved kzinti, he tried to imagine being a slave who was being killed by his master. It was impossible. As impossible as to imagine being an animal. Many a kzin killed his slave. Jotoki were delicious. Kdatlyno hide made the finest couch leather. Once on Kzin, Hwass-Hwasschoaw had immediately located a source of human slaves who had long ago been imported from Wunderland as exotic luxuries—and he would skin them to make masks for the rituals of supplication to his Only God. Expensive masks, but that was his taste.

There was no moral reason not to kill a slave.

Yet, Grraf-Nig had been very fond of his Nora-beast. Even on W'kkai she had spent hours taking the burrs out of his fur. Her Monkeyshine was probably the only son he'd ever have, a warrior in his liver. A kzin could miss not having sons. He could be enraged when another kzin murdered his helpless sons as if they were no more than slaves. Some of his best friends had carried the ears of other friends on their belt. The Nora-beast was a kzin killer and she terrified him to the point where he might have eaten grass for her. Her son was a warrior. He had been conceited as a youth to suppose that he was such an expert at training slaves. It would take ten generations of culling to make a human slave whose docility would breed true. It would be done—but not in Grraf-Nig's lifetime.

An image came to him of Monkeyshine charging him across the grass. He caressed his sleeping kzinrret. Maybe he would have other sons. He was pleased that he had substituted carbon dioxide for the nerve gas in the suppositories. He told himself that he had only done it because Hwass's plan had been stupid to the end. Capturing a hyperdrive ship at the boundaries of Kzinsun by perfidious treachery would have brought a million warriors twice the size of Monkeyshine raging down upon Kzin at a time when the Patriarchy was weak.

Grraf-Nig was a coward.

• Chapter 21

(2438 A.D.)

The ship was in hyperspace. Major Clandeboye's pilots were in command and beaming like kids in a drag race. Somehow the three of them had finagled the exchange. Nora and the children remained with them. All were safe from the two terrifying kzin—giving them a spare room behind the cabin. Still, Yankee had a sense of foreboding. Hwass would never cool his hatred so easily. There could be a lethal joker somewhere. And if there was a joker, he had to find it—now.

Nora's life-monitors read out their signals—green. The kids' monitors were in the green. Everyone was breathing in slow motion. The air was good, a little high in carbon dioxide but it always was on such a small ship. It was a little high on kzin body odor, too. It was the *hibernation* that worried him even though it did not involve freezing. This was a *kzin* technology and who knew how well it had been adapted to the human metabolism?

He *had* to see Nora conscious. It was an obsession. And so he began revival procedures, slowly, carefully. Her temperature went up. Her heart rate gradually increased. Her breathing became deeper, less sluggish. All exactly as the yellow kzin had predicted. His claim was that humans couldn't go under as deeply as kzin, and so revived more quickly. If the mechanical muscle toners were used, no physiotherapy would be needed. The mind drugs duplicated the refreshing functions of sleep but stabilized memory. They would wake up, disoriented, because of the time discontinuity, but clear of the normal dulling load of saturated multitasking. At revival, colors would be bright, senses strong, mind ready to focus on the first problem that presented itself.

Too good to be true. The kzin, of course, had been using hibernation for thousands of years.

When the monitors read normal, he lifted her out, mixtures of emotions tearing at him. He knew she was wounded but there was no sign of it in her sleeping form. Her nakedness embarrassed him but the toners required it. What horrified him was the fur. A light down swathed her face where a man had a beard. Her body was endowed with a rich auburn fur in the same places where fur might be found on a chimpanzee.

He didn't see her when she first awoke but when he did, he wasn't looking into the eyes of a retarded woman, he was looking into calm serene eyes that scanned the cabin and became bewildered and then terrified. Before he could react she was in deep adrenaline flight. With kzin-swift reflexes she flashed to the safest corner, where she eyed him with a profound and hostile suspicion, arms ready to defend herself. It disoriented him. This was the cousin he had known all his life, her face older but still young—the same luxurious mane of hair, the same dimples, only the fur unnatural. Clearly she did not recognize him. He felt strangely snubbed—but that was absurd. He already *knew* that she had been mind-wiped.

"Nora," he said as gently as he could.

She hissed at him. She was threatening him, ready to attack, afraid but brave.

Jay spoke with a sudden quiet earnestness, calmly, no threat in his voice. "Yankee, you've let an angry tigress loose in here. Do something. Toss her some clothes."

"Nora, everything is all right."

By now Beany had also swiveled his couch. "It's not all right, Yankee. You've never been a mother. She's frantic with worry about her kids. She's ready to kill us."

Yankee made a quick decision. He moved slowly to the hibernation cells. He'd have to show her that the children were all right. Her eyes watched every move he made. Carefully he activated the sequence to revive the oldest boy. It took forever. She never broke her battle stance. As soon as he could, he pulled out the drawer so that she could see her son breathing. Then he lifted the boy—he looked about eight years old—and gently seated him.

Still as a statue, she snarled some kind of warning cry.

Monkeyshine didn't know where he was. W'kkai? But no. Some kind of a ship, closed in from the stars. Mellow Yellow's fabled hyperspace? The strong smell of kzin. But it was *not* a kzin shuttle. His beloved Prrt was here and very afraid. And so were three monsters of the True Shape. No Mellow Yellow. Why wasn't he able to make a connection between the past and the present? His mother's warning cry was still ringing in his ears.

He was on adrenaline alert, aware of everything, every threat, ready to pounce. The monster enemies in the True Shape were all bigger than he was, bigger than his helpless mother, one standing, two seated, all making soft slave-like sounds. They were surprised and not ready for him. That meant a very narrow window of attack. They were in freefall. He breathed deeply, remembering everything that Mellow Yellow had ever taught him. How to kill. He breathed again and spoke a simple Kdapt prayer to himself. These were enemies of the kzin. He leaped.

In one graceful motion of grabbed hair he cracked the skulls of the pilots and on the rebound was strangling the third, elbow around his neck, crack, until he went unconscious. Warrior strength. He had already seen that the acceleration couches made perfect trusses. When the enemies woke up they would not be able to move. He made the Hero's cry of triumph. Victory to the Patriarch! Then he went over to comfort his mother.

When Yankee recovered consciousness with a sore windpipe he found himself hogtied. He could see everything. With monkey curiosity, Nora was examining the hibernation machines. Touching this, twiddling with that. When the boy tried to help her, she growled a warning at her son.

"Nora. We're your friends," Yankee implored.

She spit-threatened him. Carefully, remembering every gesture she had seen, she liberated each of her children—aged from about four to eight. By then the cabin was a howling pandemonium of seven savages and three officers strapped helplessly into their couches. Yankee tried out English on the warrior boy. Jay and Beany tried other languages. The naked boy replied in something that both did/didn't sound like the Hero's Tongue.

Yankee, who was the only one of the three who understood anything in the Hero's Tongue, told his pilots what he thought he had heard. "He was telling us that he's going to kill us. I think he wants to know what has happened to his kzinti friends. If we don't produce them, we're lunch."

"Hey, guy. Can't you see we're human?" pleaded Jay Mazzetta.

"That's the trouble; he *does* see that we are human."

Nora found the food. That was a very good distraction. All kids get hungry. But the food wasn't going to last very long. They were ninety days by hyperdrive from Barnard's Starbase. The ship was too small. They were supposed to drop out of hyperspace, send out a hyperwave "yahoo" and be picked up by the *Abraham Lincoln*. In time they did drop out of hyperspace on automatic. They might drift there until the end of time.

Monkeyshine was sure they had been in hyperspace when the blinds opened to the stars. He knew the sky of W'kkai both from space and from the ground. He had recently spent time with Mellow Yellow at the observatory. He recognized the sky, scanning it with a professional interest. The brighter stars were more or less where they should be, some of the lesser ones were missing. They were not at W'kkai. He looked along the Pointers to find the most important star in the sky—Kzin. It was not there. It was not close. Ah, that meant they were near Kzin. His heart leaped. Maybe they had a chance!

Carefully he scanned the sky, looking for the brighter stars. He found one to the stern, bright, bright, which should not be there. That one would be Kzin! Now he knew his destination. His captives mewed in their funny sounds. He paid no attention. Hwass, the savior of Mellow Yellow, had told him about these sinners!

For a moment he was caught up in a squabble with the babies. He assigned Fastanimal to organize their care. Furlessface, his twin, was uselessly clinging to her mother's footsteps. His mother was a helpless nuisance but it was his duty to protect her. He watched her in amusement. She was poking around at the prisoners' crotches to see their genitals. Monkeyshine growled a warning at her. Poking was one thing; liberation was another. She growled back. Impudent mother!

Now all he had to do was learn to pilot the ship. Long-Reach had taught him all the mechanics he knew. He was proud that he could repair anything even if he didn't have five arms. He stared at the controls, trying to deduce their functions. He was not tempted to push and pull and twiddle things at random. He knew better than that. He began to take the controls apart to see how they worked.

His *kz'eerkt* prisoners had a fit—but there was nothing they could do to stop him. He kept working, puzzling, careful not to break or short anything. This was no more than a W'kkai conundrum puzzle. What he didn't understand at all, he left alone. Get the machine pointed at Kzin. Start it.

Hours later he was still at work, concentrating like he had never before concentrated in his life. The babies were getting out of control. Still he understood nothing. His mother had been squirting water into the mouths of the prisoners and watching to see if it turned yellow and came out of their oversize penises like it did with her sons. She had to wait too long. In the meantime she became fascinated by the fur that was starting to grow on their faces. She interrupted Monkeyshine to show him. He growled at her.

No matter how much he tried, he couldn't make sense of the wires and little boxes and mechanical linkages. He couldn't even read the instruments or make the screens light up. He wanted Long-Reach to explain it all to him. Even Mellow Yellow would answer his questions. He didn't understand anything! He was angry and had to control his rage like Mellow Yellow had shown him how to do in a fight. It was important that he not break anything. He knew that if he did, he would kill his family. He knew where he had to take them—but he didn't know how!

The tears started to pool in his eyes and he had to shake them away. He couldn't help himself. He was sobbing.

His mother lost interest in the face-fur. She glided over and put her arms around him. He tried to push her away, but he didn't really want her to go. She was very stupid but she was good at comforting. He let her hold him and he sobbed.

***

Yankee completely understood the boy's frustration. Yankee was trussed so tight that his feet had gradually gone to sleep. Tears came to his eyes, pooling in sympathy until the major was seeing from a watery world of blindness. He had been watching the boy, first with dread, then with admiration. The kid was a mechanical genius. It didn't matter, of course. He didn't know the codes. The ship was kzin-proof. No stranger could have piloted it. What was going to happen to them?

Nora was a soft focus blur holding her son's head to her breasts and staring at Yankee. Gently she left her calmer son with soothing purrs. She came over to Yankee and stared into his eyes, perhaps bewildered that the water was coming out of *them* and not his penis. She touched a finger to his tears and tasted them. Then, with her tongue, she licked his eyes clear. The fear had returned to her face, but cunning fear. She was smiling. It wasn't the kzin grin of ferocity, it was a human smile, dimples and all. This woman wanted something from the man she feared and she wasn't sure she was going to get it so she poured on the charm.

She began to undo Yankee's bonds with the intelligence of a mind that knows it can never ask for help. The boy, sober now, leaped in to stop her. She whacked him away with a snarl. Yankee, not yet free, watched in amazement as the boy began to plead with her in quick kzinti yappings. He could tell that she didn't understand a single word her son was saying. Still she worked at the strapping. Alternately she smiled at Yankee and snarled like a kzin at her son.

The boy went off with his brothers and sisters to sulk. Yankee tested his legs. They were numb and painful when he tried to use their muscles. He didn't need them in null-gee. He inspected the control panel—no damage at all. The boy hadn't tried to be smarter than he was. Because of that he called him over to help in the job of reassembly. He smiled at the boy—human instinct was the only working language they had in common. The boy helped him fearfully but did not smile back.

"Hey, get us out of these cocoons," complained Jay.

"Hold your horses!" Idioms survive forever in a language. Yankee powered up the hyperwave and called their pickup ship which had to be sitting out there somewhere less than a tenth of a light-year away. That had been pre-arranged. He made contact. The reply was excited, stellar reference points exchanged. They were on their way.

Now to tend to the boy. He set all the screens to run a game called *Brick Bradford's Shrinking Sphere*. The screen put you inside a porous fractile sponge of incredible colors and shapes. Brick Bradford could float his sphere anywhere among the pores, and since each surface was also porous, he could penetrate any wall by shrinking into the finer sponge. The demonstration mesmerized the shaken child.

Yankee needed a name for the boy but asking for a name in the Hero's Tongue was a very delicate matter of the proper protocol. If a kzin had a name, you took your life in your hand to ask him his profession. Yet if he had a profession, you were not even allowed the *assumption* that he might have earned a name. Who knew the proper protocol for a slave?

Yankee put on his headphones and consulted the ship's translator. The machine gave vague advice. He tried anyway in his best hiss-and-spits. "You have the honor of speaking to Yankee-Clandeboye." No use being modest. "And I shall need to speak with you."

The boy wasn't a warrior anymore. He looked at Yankee. "Kz'eerkttt," he said timidly with a chopped glottal bray at the end. He had the voice of a confused slave who was unsure of his station in life or whether he still had a life. The machine seemed to think his whisper translated as, "the tricks of a monkey."

Yankee couldn't tell if that was a swear word in the Hero's Tongue or the boy's name, probably both. "Okay. We'll call you Sir Monk Argamentine." He took the boy's hand and showed it how to wave fingers in the "command space" above the keyboard to move the screen viewpoint around inside the variegated sponge, and how he could shrink to pass into the pores of any wall. Yankee was giving him back a little bit of the control he'd lost. Monk might not be able to handle a hyperdrive—but he could fly a mathematical ship into the depths of fractile space.

Then Yankee unstrapped Jay and Beany, much to their relief. Lieutenant Nora Argamentine watched his every move. *She's very smart*, he thought. *She just negotiated the settlement of a lethal impasse.* But she wasn't the Nora he knew. It broke his heart.

• Chapter 22

(2438 A.D.)

The UNSN *Abraham Lincoln* slipped slowly into its berth in orbit above the bleak surface of Barnard's Starbase, the news of its arrival classified by the ARM. Chloe Blumenhandler sat with a very nervous General Lucas Fry in the reception area down-planet, watching the docking through the controller's camera. She was very pregnant and had not seen her husband for seven months. Hyperspace travel was fast but not that fast—three days to cross a light-year. Fry had not seen Nora for eighteen years.

A phone chimed a few chords from Beethoven's Fifth. "That's me," said Fry pulling out the comm from his belt infocomp. "Lucas here." He listened for a second, then turned to Chloe. "It's Yankee." He switched on the sound. "Great operation! Smooth. We're going to gild you and set you on top of the UN building!"

"Finagle hasn't told you half of it! I'm just calling up to warn you. Nora isn't going to recognize you when she sees you."

"I know that," said the general gruffly.

"It's still a shock. I felt snubbed after all the trouble I'd taken to rescue her. I was outraged—just for a second. She used to do that to me when we were kids. She'd snub me when she was mad at me. I hated it."

"Yah, well I'm made of sterner stuff than you flabby flatlanders. How is she?"

"Healthy as a kzin. We're having a little trouble at the moment. She's ripping off her clothes as fast as we can put her into them. Stubborn. She doesn't like clothes. For the reception, we're going to have to sew her into a jumpsuit."

"Sounds like Nora."

"That's what I'm trying to tell you, Lucas. It's not Nora. I've been with her for three months now. I don't know who the hell she is!"

"Is the brain damage bad?"

Yankee changed the subject. "I hear they brought in Dr. Hunker for her. Is he there?" Dr. Hunker was from the Institute of Knowledge on Jinx. He was the man on the boosterspice team who studied neural-aging reversal.

"Yah, he's here. How bad is the damage?"

"It hasn't effected her intelligence at all. Bright as a brass button. She just doesn't think with words, that's all. Whatever intelligence is, it's not language."

"You can't think without words, Yankee."

"That so? Try *catching a ball* with words. What you mean is: words facilitate communication. A hermit never needs words."

"She has no words at all?"

"I haven't been able to teach her a single word of English. She has some kzinti chitchat, not much. She calls me 'Hairless Hero.' That's a grievous insult but she says it with a smile. She's still got her dimples."

"She can smile?" General Fry was reaching for straws.

"You bet. Her specialty is practical jokes. It's Nora's smile because the face is the same, but it isn't Nora's smile. It's less inhibited. Nora was coy. This lady hasn't got a drop of coyness in her body. When we met she was more interested in my funny-looking penis than me."

Chloe giggled and put both hands over her mouth, sputtering.

"General, you have a eunuch's giggle," complained Yankee.

Chloe grabbed the comm. "It's me, silly. Do you think I'm not down here waiting for you?"

"As long as your father's not there. It's so *good* to hear your voice. How's the kid?"

"Thumping," she said proudly.

"They grow up to be monsters, you know. I have one eight-year-old here who is half as big as the general, and twice as smart. He damn near threw me over his shoulders and hauled me off to Kzin."

"What are you talking about?"

"Just one of my misadventures. I'll tell you about it someday."

The general wrestled with Chloe to take back his comm. "How are Nora's brats?"

"The three boys are fine. The three girls are a bit spacy—brain damage. Now put my sweetheart back on the line."

"Stop talking!" Chloe complained. "Come down here instantly!"

"I'll have to jump out of the *Lincoln* and come down on beam power."

It was ARM guards who brought Nora to the surface. They had "restricted" quarters for her set up, spacious for Starbase. Yankee had called ahead to see that Nora's strange boudoir furniture from the *Nesting-Slashtooth-Bitch* was used. The medical staff and equipment were in place. And teachers, psychologists, nursery staff. But no press. Absolute censorship.

Chloe took over to become one of the few people with easy access to Nora. She was attracted to this heroine of the wars. Here was the mother she had never had—a woman brave enough to attack kzinti with what amounted to bare hands. One mother had died. This "surrogate" mother was only wounded. Chloe was absolutely determined to be her friend, even find a way to talk to her.

Nora, in turn, was attracted to Chloe. Pregnancy had been a large part of Nora's remembered life; she couldn't recall a time before she had been pregnant. In her mind she was the only child-bearing woman in the universe. That her daughters might someday bear children was unreal. Her first reaction to Chloe was to try to pull off those maternity clothes to *see* the belly. Nora was not fond of clothes.

The guards restrained her, but Chloe knew how to handle the situation and when they met again a few hours later, in privacy, the expectant mother showed the experienced mother what she wanted to see and held the woman's hand where it could feel the baby kicking. From that magical moment on, there was a bond between them. Chloe was the only one able to reassure Nora when her fur began to fall out.

The psychologists left around many objects so they might observe their patient's interaction modes. Nora loved picture books and discovering new ones with Chloe. Her favorites she shared with her children. She loved to play Russian-egg games with her four-year-old daughter. She'd pop off a layer of egg and hand it to her daughter. Her daughter would pop off the next layer of egg and hand it back. When they got down to the tiny chicken, they'd both laugh, put the chicken back in the tiniest egg, and begin to reassemble the eggs again. Over and over.

Nora liked to pile up chairs against the door to keep the psychologists out, take off her clothes and chase Chloe around the four-posted bed with a pair of VR goggles until she had them firmly on Chloe's head so they could gallivant together in a virtual reality game called *Other Worlds*. It was hide-and-seek in a booby-trapped landscape whose rules of physics changed with each game.

The booby traps didn't "kill" you—but they did do things like change the frequency of your visual spectrum, or change your size, or change the coefficient of friction of your skin, or your permeability to stone. When the two friends found themselves in one world where some objects had positive mass while others had negative mass, Chloe learned a major lesson about intelligence. Nora adapted to the strange forces. Chloe floundered, desperately trying to figure out what was going to happen by solving Newtonian equations like $F = -ma$.

Nora was generally just a good-natured child-woman who liked to play practical jokes on the psychologists and doctors who were studying her, but she had a terrible temper. Once, when the ARM was tightening up security, the maintenance men came in and put a lock on the door between her room and the nursery. ARM wasn't thinking of the nursery when they specified *all* doors. Nora improvised tools out of broken furniture and smashed the lock to bits, spitting and snarling like a kzin the whole while.

Of course, Nora and Chloe had their fights. Nora began to avoid Chloe, sulk, pretend she didn't exist, hide Chloe's goggles and retreat into their virtual world alone. "What's the matter?" She knew she wasn't going to get an answer, but she kept asking it. *I've got to teach her to talk!* She sat down with Nora's favorite picture book. She let Nora turn the pages, but she was very firm about pointing at things and naming them. That afternoon Nora painted the book with mayonnaise.

All of this had been observed. Chloe knew that one-way mirrors were in the walls but they were so unobtrusive that they were easy to forget. The staff who watched was invisible, even socially. But one day Lura Hsi invited Yankee's wife to lunch. She was the wife of Dr. Hunker, the boosterspice expert who was in charge of repairing Nora's brain—if that turned out to be possible. Lura was petite for a Jinxian, shorter even than most Jinxians, but she had the round powerful muscles of an ox on a neck thick enough to have pulled a yoke. She was a psychologist.

"Let me tell you what Nora can't."

"But I *love* her! I'm doing everything I can to help. She's just misunderstanding. I've *got* to talk to her. Communication solves everything. Yankee and I have this wonderful way of settling our problems because we can *talk* it out!"

"She's not going to talk," said Lura.

Chloe slumped. "I know. She growls at me, though. Sometimes she cusses me out in kzinti. I know because my translator told me."

"She has a vocabulary about the size of a chimp's."

"She must be able to learn something, just a few words. She's so bright! I *hate* the kzin who did that to her!" Chloe was trying to hold back her tears.

"Let's focus. State the problem."

"She can't learn to talk," said Chloe.

"I see." Lura smiled. "Is that *your* problem, or *her* problem?"

"It's *her* problem. Yankee says *I* talk too much."

"If you could ask her, she would agree with Yankee. You talk too much."

"How else is she going to learn to talk!"

"Chloe, think. You are running on automatic instinct. When mothers teach their children to talk—they chatter. They point at things and say words. They open doors and say 'open.' A normal child has the machinery to process that and that's the way you *should* teach them. Nora has a great soul—but souls don't learn to talk; it's neural machinery that learns to talk." She paused to make her point.

"She's angry at you for trying so hard to make her talk. She *can't* talk. People have been insisting that she do what she can't do ever since the first day she boarded the *Abraham Lincoln*. For Finagle's sake have pity on her! Everyone who meets her sees a sweet two-year-old and they fall in love with her—and go into an automatic language teaching mode. 'See the *doggie*. Isn't he a *nice* doggie? Doggie *won't* hurt. Do you like *black* doggies? Old Rover, here, is *black* or do you like *brown* doggies like this one in this book? See the *brown* doggie. Oh, look at the *red* retriever.' "

Chloe thought about all this silently.

"Let me make an analogy. I had the sweetest father in the world. He was just as sweet as you are."

"Lucky you."

"But all he ever talked about to me was Riemannian Metrics and Gödel Recursives and Fiechbacker Hyperspaces—since I was two. He might be having an interesting discussion with my mother about ancient Roman politics or about ice cream flavors with his brother but whenever I would walk in the room his eyes would glaze over and he'd go into his *education-of-Lura* mode. He had his mind set on making a mathematician out of me. He was a research mathist at the Institute because he was a hopeless teacher. He lectured and little me listened. I couldn't stop him, I couldn't ask questions.

"No matter how hard I listened it was all gibberish. I loved that man but he *expected* me to do the differential geometry of n-space before I could count, let alone add. I *wanted* to be a math genius, I was desperate to please him but I wasn't at all sure of what he did. I thought he laid kitchen floors because of a very famous piece of mathematics called Kitchener's Tiling that he was working on when I was three. I wanted him to stop and start over, but

I was too shy to tell him. He was uninterruptable! I was a very angry young girl."

"I'm talking too much?"

"Yes."

"But she's going to *have* to learn how to communicate."

"Oh, she can communicate, all right. A very word-oriented Chloe just isn't listening. Didn't Nora brush mayonnaise all over your pretty book today? How else is a non-verbal person going to tell a verbal person to *shut up*?"

"Should I stop seeing her?"

"Darling, you're doing great. But I have an exercise for you to try with her that will make all the difference in the world. I'm forbidding you to use words around her—except words like 'yikes' or 'ouch' or 'wowie' or 'damn'; she'll understand those."

"Talk like a brainless teen-ager?" Chloe was horrified.

Lura smiled and broke out a second beer for herself, offering one to Chloe without saying a word.

"Oh wow!" said Chloe taking one and popping the top, comprehension dawning. She took a swig.

"Remember when she was playing the Russian-egg game with her little girl? What was she saying? 'Watch me open the pretty egg. Look at the prettier egg inside! Take the egg. Copy what I did! Now give me the egg and I'll copy what *you* did.' All without using any words. You can't tell me that's not communication."

Chloe was conceding the argument with her facial expression, if reluctantly. "She's not ever going to learn differential geometry that way," she said glumly.

"Yes. And she can't wish her mother in Iowa City a happy birthday. And she has a very hard time telling a chatterbox like you to stop trying to teach her how to talk. She tries so hard to be human—but we humans insist on thinking that only language is what makes us human."

"I'll be good," said Chloe. "Yikes! I forgot to tell you; we just got a box from Iowa City. Her mother sent us all her old homework. We even have her nursery school crayon stick figures with arms coming out of the ears! She drew this fantastic picture of a kzin when she was in the second grade. It is so tall it has to stoop under the top of the page. It scared me cross-eyed! I *am* a chatterbox, aren't I?"

• Chapter 23

(2438 A.D.)

One morning Tam Claukski eased himself into Yankee's office, warily stepping around a wobbly pile of books, Adam's apple bobbing. He had big plans. Before he had even found secure footing, he was proposing a gigantic simulation of a future Second Man-Kzin War that he had just thought up.

It was Tam's immoderate imagination which had induced Yankee to steal him from Admiral Blumenhandler. Like most enthusiastic young men this prodigy was totally unaware of the size and scope of the tasks he took upon himself. Yankee liked to describe such gargantuan efforts in terms of "gallons," an ancient flatlander measure of the amount of midnight oil that had to be burned in a whale oil lamp to get the job done. The major kept a straight face. "Well, don't just stand there pontificating, sit down!"

"Where?"

Yankee motioned for Tam to move the VR helmet onto the pile of books. Then he took assorted reports off the controller for the wall screen so that Tam would have a way to show off. "Fire away. You have five minutes."

In response, Tam moved the helmet to its pedestal, balanced it, and recklessly rolled his chair up to the controller, smiling the whole while. What appeared on the screen was "several gallons" worth of an incomprehensible organization chart. Tam was rapturous. "I got hit by this bolt of lightning. For a tactician like me, Grand Strategy is a bit awesome."

"I suppose *one* cure for awe is to grab a million volt line."

"This is the first time I've ever been able to get a handle on the whole bag." He raised his arms in supplication to the wall. "What do you think of that?"

"I don't understand a line of it," complained Yankee. "It looks like the command structure of a military org. That's *not* the way ARM is organized."

"But the ARM is peacekeeping," admonished Tam. "We're talking about a real *war*, here."

"You realize, of course, that we'll be well into a third war by the time you get the ARM to consider the idea that it might be a good idea to set up a study commission to plan an approach to reorganizing for the second war."

Tam looked at his diagram in consternation. "You're misunderstanding me, sir! That's not a military reorganization chart. I've just arranged my *ideas* into manageable lumps. Strategy is complicated. It takes a lot of praying to Murphy. I just want to know if I've left anything out before Murphy clobbers me for my neglect."

"Leave it on the wall and I'll stare at it for a while." Yankee stared at the wall. "I hope you're not in a hurry!"

"No, sir. You'll have a couple of days with my masterpiece. Tonight I have to make up a strategy chart for the *kzinti* High Command. That's going to be hard because they are used to making their major decisions at the local level. And we don't have enough information on the Far Side." He meant the worlds at the far side of the Patriarchy.

"So, you're appointing kzinti admirals too, eh?"

"With your permission, sir."

"That's quite all right with me. Make sure we have a

worthy Patriarch to oppose us—and put the VR helmet back on the chair when you leave."

From time to time during the day, Yankee called up various different files that were attached to the wall screen's boxes. He couldn't get the idea out of his head that these were all job descriptions. Poor Tam thought like a Von Neumann machine; he was going to linearize the graph, and then continually cycle through it, doing everything himself, Finagle help the boy.

Chloe called in to chat—a pleasant interlude. Her gossip about the Brozik industrial family primed him to turn from his routine screenwork to read up on the current economic outlook of We Made It. Military budgets were tight. He had been trying to determine for a long time how much strain the crashlander civilian economy could take doing military research under the table.

The Broziks seemed to be putting all their efforts into a set of basic spaceship shells that could be finished either for civilian use or as warcraft. That meant that, in case of war, the naval assembly lines would already be in place—though Yankee wasn't sure how much good that would do; Procyon was sitting up there with its head in the Patriarch's jaws. Chloe's news, direct from her father, was that Barnard's Starbase was receiving, for test and finishing, one of the Brozik shells equipped with a Wunderland salvaged kzinti gravitic drive, courtesy of Admiral Blumenhandler. Gossip through hyperspace was faster than the military command line.

He called up his naval architect specialist to meet him for a coffee and salad. If Stefan Brozik wasn't continually getting the right military feedback, his project could be a disaster. It was going to be damn good to get their hands on one of his shells. They could give it a workout, shake down the problems.

When he returned from the snack he rearranged some

of the book piles on his floor so that he would have pacing space. The chart on the wall kept staring at him. He sighed at its supreme logic. If only he belonged to such a rationally structured org, he could get something done. It seemed like everything that had to be done was being done out of channels if it got done at all.

General Fry was a master at that. He didn't even have a command at Starbase but he was essentially acting as its staffing officer from distant Gibraltar—quietly pulling out the men from Barnard who weren't wanted here, or didn't jibe with Starbase's aggressive philosophy, and as quietly arranging for the inflow of people who were inclined to take the Patriarchy as a real threat. Yankee had learned a few tricks from his mentor. He was already making tough hardware decisions—and hardware wasn't even part of his training duties. And there was Tam who didn't even know that he was doing the work of a chief of staff's adjutant.

The strain of thinking was sometimes physically exhausting. Yankee stopped pacing. He flopped into his chair, confronting Tam's electronic glyphs. Unbelievable, the number of things that had to be done just to position mankind against a new assault. In a dream world he would have real power to assign names to the boxes on the wall! They were job descriptions and jobs had to be carried out by men, didn't they?

The dream took on a life of its own. Reverie transported his spirit to Sol, where, in a fanciful office as the biggest black gorilla at ARM, he made endless profound decisions. He put Blumenhandler in charge of patrols. Jay Mazzetta became his top trouble-shooter. Fry was, of course, chief of staff. It was a pleasant power fantasy. Names for his mythical duty roster came like the flow of a bursting dam.

The shock of that brought him back to Starbase. The

dream had been an astonishing exercise of his imagination. He hadn't realized just how *many* competent people
he knew. When had that happened? That old bastard Fry
had been doing things to him.

He peered into his past. One must look back to have
the wisdom to look forward. What had Fry seen in him, a
misfit who was challenging every petty mind with words,
even fists? What exactly had Fry done to transform him
into a man who felt comfortable with the people who did
the real work of the world? It was a bit of a puzzle.

A liberating idea was forming in Yankee's head as he
continued to stare at Tam's chart. Why not set up a General Staff-In-Exile and *really* get ready for the Patriarch's
next move. What had the sergeant said to the soldier who
found himself recruited into an incompetent army? "Complaining will only kill you—fast; start recruiting your own
good men!"

Chloe was now very pregnant. One of her more devious schemes involved deceiving her obstetrician. She
planned it very carefully without Nora's help. Nora wasn't
very good with lists and lying. She thought of the idea
when Nora started to plan for the birth in her own way—
everything they'd need, water for washing the baby, swaddling clothes, makeshift tools to cut and tie the cord.

"How does she know these things?" Chloe asked in
bed with Yankee that night. "I can't believe it. Look. What
do you think this is?"

"It looks like a piece of wood." He pinched it. "Hardwood."

"It's for me to bite on when I'm in labor! She made me
test it."

"What's so surprising about that?"

"She doesn't remember anything about Earth!"

"Her kzin taught her."

"Those male-centered strutters! What would they know about women?"

"He was a *professional* slave trainer, remember. In her diary Nora thought he wanted to set up a business breeding human slaves. He taught her everything she'd need to know to teach her daughters how to bear healthy babies."

"You're joking! A kzin?"

"Who do you think was Nora's midwife? According to our xenologists, kzinti males are wiser about birthing than human males. Their females bear and nourish, even protect. The males have to handle the emergencies and the cultural transmission. Fathering one's male kits is a very serious business."

"They are warriors who go off to war and abandon their young!"

"Chloe. You were pregnant. I abandoned you to go off on a wild military cloak-and-dagger adventure to W'kkai that some young firebrand could have done just as well. If the kzin had killed me, you would have born our child and probably done a very good job of raising the tyke, teaching, nourishing. That's *human* society. Men have abandoned women all through history—and the women have raised their children. Why do you think, willy-nilly, that kzin society works the same?"

"They're warriors! They run off to battle the minute they hear a shot fired!"

"You're anthropomorphizing."

"What?"

"Seeing man in kzin. Think about this. In a kzin warship there is no age barrier to service. If a kzin cannot find a baby-sitter for his sons, or a creche, or a brother to take care of them, he takes them to battle with him. They fight—just like the four-year-old son of one of your farmer ancestors milked the cows."

"Child labor on a warship? That's horrible!"

"Think about this. Suppose a kzin leaves or sells a wife. Suppose she runs away. Suppose a mightier kzin is attracted to her and takes her by force. Who gets the kits? Always, always, always the father. Suppose he is killed or goes to prison or abandons his kits. The male who takes over the family of a kzinrret who is left with young kits *kills* her male offspring. That is hell on the patriarchal line of any kzin who doesn't have very strong fathering genes. Now a monkey like me, I can sow my wild oats, abandon my woman and know that some other man will bring up my kid, or she will."

Chloe switched on the night light. She rose in the bed like a Valkyrie who had chosen a warrior about to die. "You wouldn't do that to me!"

"I already have. I have a boy on Earth, about your age. He was raised by another man—successfully, so far as I know."

She was shocked. "You never told me."

He smiled wanly. "You never told me about the first boy you seduced when you were thirteen."

"You ratcat!" She smashed a pillow down on his face.

"Mumflpuf," he said.

She lifted the pillow off because she wanted to hear the rest of the story. "Well?" she said.

"It's a long story. I'll tell you someday. It was war. The kzinti were at our gates. Who knew? The next fleet might be the end of the human race. The hyperdrive was new. I had a chance at a deep space attack, maybe farther than any man had ever gone. It seemed like the thing to do."

"You just abandoned him?"

"Chloe, I never got back to Earth. The mail to 59 Virginis is very slow."

When the first of the labor pangs came to Chloe, she sneaked up to Nora's apartment. She was worried about the one-way mirrors so she began to pile couches and different pieces of furniture into a cave with a crooked entrance. Nora helped. (She thought she knew what was going on. At Mellow Yellow's estate on W'kkai she had seen some of his kzinrretti go into a nesting frenzy.) Chloe had no intention of depending upon Nora. Nora might be a mother. She might have been trained by a kzin midwife—shudder—but Chloe had read *books*. She had her infocomp loaded with obstetric advice, with its comm ready to call out. In case. And she had a flashlight.

She crawled into her cave and began to deliver the baby. It was a strange sort of bonding gift that she wanted to give to Nora. Besides, she was curious about what it had been like to give birth in a kzinrret nest deep in the plundered city of Hssin, poisonous gases swirling outside, protected only by makeshift seals and a refurbished life-support machine, with no human company for light-years. It took hours. After nearly biting through her hardwood chip, she was beginning to decide that she was crazy.

The baby came out with a plop, and Nora knew what to do faster than Chloe could remember what she had read. The baby cried to fill its lungs. Nora tied off the umbilical cord while Chloe was looking up the right picture in her infocomp. They washed her tiny body in temperate water. And there she lay cuddled in swaddling clothes, a sleepy, exhausted baby girl. They watched her by flashlight in the cave of furniture, two grinning women.

Yankee was furious. He rushed her and the baby off to the infirmary. Her obstetrician was furious and she rushed the very healthy baby into an infant's autodoc for a careful checkout. The baby woke up and wanted to be fed.

Yankee got over being mad. He was getting used to being married to a teen-ager. In many ways he was the father of nine children, varying in age from Nora down to his own newborn. It was quite an experience dealing with an adult child, a wild teen, three silent daughters, two shy boys, a baby, and Monk.

Sir Monk, as Yankee called him, helped out enthusiastically. Monk had always thought of himself as the man of the family when his family had been the whole human race. In that way he thought like a kzin. He had gross problems: when in control he acted kzinish, when unsure or overwhelmed he turned into a slave. He had a frightful time with English grammar and idiom but loved the computer that patiently taught him. He was happy to have an uncle. Politics confused him. His first real conversation with Yankee was about master Mellow Yellow, told in a broken mixture of spitting-hisses and English that never quite jelled into grammatical sentences—how he had saved his friend from the dungeons of W'kkai. Yankee didn't have the heart to tell him that it was Mellow Yellow who had mind-wiped his mother and eaten boys like Monkeyshine for lunch after finishing up his experiments.

As a reward for working so hard, Yankee sneaked Monk into the Starbase simulators and taught him how to fly a starship in virtual space. There was no stopping this kid. He was a born warrior—and eventually his kzinti accent would wear off. What Yankee dreaded was the lessons in kzinti martial arts that Monk insisted on giving him, claw to claw.

So it always came as a welcome relief to change diapers and feed the tiny girl whom Chloe insisted on naming Valiance. Val pursued the simple things of life such as sleeping in her father's arms.

• Chapter 24

(2439 A.D.)

The interstellar game of "Trolls & Bridges" became an instant success among a certain group of the military. Major Yankee Clandeboye had toyed with the name "General Staff-In-Exile" but went chicken before typing such blasphemy into the net. He put it down to his new maturity. After all, he had just turned fifty.

The game developed a different structure than he had originally imagined. It proved impossibly complicated to set up a "shadow" ARM. Instead, "Trolls & Bridges" evolved into a "command patch." There were a lot of isolated officers out there for whom the command lines had failed, who were looking for the kind of "work-around" that the structure of T&B provided.

Normally, bypassing command lines in a military organization is a bad habit because it leads to contradictions and inconsistencies in practice. Nothing destroys an army faster than captains who have to carry out the orders of generals who aren't speaking to each other. Nevertheless command lines are bypassed all the time through what has been called for centuries "the old boy's network." Bypassing command lines is an art form with definite strategies, rules, and protocols.

Young men under sixty are not adept practitioners of this arcane art and are advised to seek counsel from a mentor. The game of T&B, in its first naive implementation, presently put its players in conflict with powerful men. Admiral Jenkins had a fit when one of his patrols received two sets of orders. He suspected the hand of Fry—though Fry was innocent—and moved in for the kill, demanding a full investigation of Starbase shenanigans.

Fry, caught off guard, did his own instant investigation and found out that he had been elevated to Grand Vizier of a very weird caper that had been going on under his nose for months. He studied the rules in shock, penned a scathing rejoinder to all Starbase nitwits, reconsidered, remembered that he needed an excuse to see Nora and hastily hitched a ride to Barnard's Star. Immediately on arrival he lectured his young fans in the sternest terms. But by then he was amused, even elated.

As Grand Vizier of T&B, he sat his boys down and showed them how their game really worked. With one hand he arranged to have Admiral Jenkins promoted to head up the "Jenkins Commission on Military Ethics." Writing that report would take up at least five years of the admiral's life. In case Jenkins got too pushy . . . well, there were ethical issues from his own past that he had forgotten about. With the other hand Fry used some contacts in the Wunderland House of Patricians to outmaneuver the ARM and push Rear Admiral Blumenhandler into Jenkins' old job.

While these promotions were going through, Fry suspected that a quick review of patrol methods, desk ready, might please Blumenhandler when he moved into Jenkins office to take over. The current T&B Grand Kzin Strategy model was laid on the table. It called for new kinds of patrol information. Then a document was compiled out of recent T&B items sent in by patrol officers who felt that certain unacknowledged reports needed a critical second ear. Fry added his own wish list. Gibraltar was stumbling for lack of an aggressive assessment of the

Patriarchy's smaller worlds. Finally, synthesis produced a
written policy that Blumenhandler could take seriously.

"That was a lot of work." Fry was enjoying teaching his
students. He was coming to like his maverick major. "But
is your stuffy father-in-law going to read it? We need an
insurance policy. A personal touch. I'm going to ask him a
favor. That sets me up in his debt so later on, when he
needs it, he can ask *me* a favor."

With Blumenhandler's biases in mind Fry made a special request, in his own name, for patrol time to seek out
the rumored kzinti stronghold, Warhead. Perhaps, while
finding it, they could also locate the rumored Pierin aliens,
who might then become mankind's ally. He implied that
Wunderland officers were best equipped to carry out such
a mission.

Lucas Fry had no authority to issue any such orders to
the UNSN patrols. But, of course, Chloe's father, in his
new capacity, did. The orders would get issued.

Over the weeks that the general was with them, Tam
Claukski watched him in awe, taking notes and codifying
what he saw. The old reprobate held seminars on everything that a devious officer should know about side-step-
ping the rules. The general was very adamant about what
should go through channels, what might profitably be
transmitted through the T&B comm lines, and what had
to be aborted.

One whole day he spent with Tam manually process-
ing messages which Tam's procedures had been editing
and routing automatically.

"Take this guy." Fry meant the message, not the sender.
He used his pen as a pointer. "These three sentences are
a lament to the gods and a whine about the sender's pow-
erlessness. The next paragraph is an outright appeal for
sympathy. Then he gets angry and we have to read what
is essentially a page of diatribe against his commanding

officer. He wraps up his case with a conspiracy theory. Only the last two lines contain the nub of a useful suggestion. If this sadsack tried to put such a missive through normal channels, he'd get head detail." Fry laughed. "But as I understand it, T&B is trying to be more than a normal channel."

Tam grimaced. "It's pretty hard to do something with that kind of ranting mess. I have a good semantic program that I'm training to sort and flush gripes like that."

"*No*," said the general. "Flushing just dumps out the gold dust with the sand." Fry used his pen to block the whining in red, then attached the note, "Delete." He recast the last two lines in a larger, bold typeface, this time attaching the message, "Expand and resubmit." He grinned. "That ought to shock the shit out of our raving victim. Make him think. Otherwise send him out on head detail."

The next day, too early, Fry held a seminar for the Starbase coterie who had signed up for "Trolls & Bridges." He combed over the T&B categories with a razor sharp ruthlessness. Tam saw his categories as a skeleton around which to build a defense strategy. Yankee saw them as an alternate command structure. Fry saw them as communication nodes that connected people in ways that command lines couldn't. The general tried to explain to them why, in two months, the T&B team had been able to make a better strategic analysis of the rising kzinti threat than the whole apparatus of expensive ARM think tanks.

Looking out over the room, he saw that these eager officers, who would probably dominate the roster of heroes of the next war, were flattered but didn't really believe him. They might make jokes about the ARM, but they had been brought up in awe of its secret dominion. The ARM had pulled some deadly tricks out of its hat when the kzinti seemed overwhelming. The ARM wore a mystique of invincibility, of endless cabalistic powers it could command if it had to.

So go back to basics. The general spent the next hour lecturing these neophytes on ARM's modus operandi. How did the ARM develop Grand Strategies? It had the resources to recruit mankind's best strategic minds. It even had a science of creative mood drugs. Inject just the right sense of danger in which to think about threat strategy. Inject just the right kind of cold concentration in which to work out logistic problems. The ARM's think tanks were high-powered places. But they weren't working—because they couldn't transfer what they knew to the grunt tacticians who had to *implement* the Grand Strategy. Why?

For four hundred years the ARM had been acting to repress the cycles of revenge that once threatened to tear the Earth apart and infect space. From immemorial time mothers had pledged their infant sons to the task of murdering their father's murderer. Men plotted revenge for the rape of daughters. Tribes massacred each other to revenge an insult. Each brooding generation laid down its sedimentary layer of pain, claiming special victim status. Revenge was gradually formalized to the level of religious dogma and elevated to an art form by technology—eventually scouring Europe with religious wars, devastating the Middle East with Holy Jihads when vengeful Christian pushed Jew into lands where prophets had elevated revenge to a way of life.

It was all nonsense. Yet none of it was easily given up. Even later thinkers of this violent era, atheists repelled by the mindlessness of a religious spirit that buried men in the mud of France's trenches, invented "class warfare" as their new spiritual cleanser. The ARM *forced* men's minds into a mold of peace, catholic in its guidance.

The centuries of effort had been so successful that these young officers of Barnard's Starbase didn't know their own history. Each one of them saw mankind as essentially benevolent. Whatever they thought, they felt that evil was an aberration, not a choice. Whatever they thought, they felt that a soldier's soul remained in mortal peril, absolution his lot.

The general spoke to shock them: whatever lurked out there, kzin or no kzin, the ARM could not permit *men* to risk their souls by thinking about war. Better that they die and go to heaven in a state of grace. The military strategists of the ARM were like the priests of the Old Catholic Church who read the Bible but did not permit their parishioners to read the Bible because it was too dangerous. Fry noted wryly that a priest who cannot talk to his flock about theology atrophies as a theologian and ends his days by harassing Galileos.

The general drove on with his analogies. Like deadly experimental viruses, the ARM kept its military strategists in sealed bottles, inside sealed labs, a fragile mankind protected from contact with the military mind through elaborate protocols. Were these strategists still virile? How dangerous could a mutating virus be after generations of isolation from its host, feeding on government pablum?

Was he making his audience hostile by laying on the heresy so thick? He had to convince these boys that *they* were mankind's main line of defense against the kzin. "The ARM's military strategists can't even talk to each other without going through rigorous *need-to-know* protocols. *I* can't talk to them without going through channels and telling the protocol keepers what I need to know and why! I could be dangerous. I might get infected and lead Earth to a rediscovery of revenge. I might resurrect the ultimate weapon and use it." Fry paused, then paced until he had his curious audience waiting for his next words. "When I tell you that Barnard's Starbase is the best

strategic think tank that humanity has right now, I mean
you to take me *seriously*."

A cocky officer in the back interrupted. "When is ARM
going to close us down?"

"Ah, we have a conspiracy theorist in the back. ARM
isn't going to close us down. Perhaps you think the ARM
is an oligarchy desperate to cling to power, even if that
means losing a war with the Patriarchy. Nonsense. The
ARM is just another tradition with a lot of social inertia.
I've talked with men high in the ARM. They know what's
wrong. We lost battles in the last war because they couldn't
bring themselves to release the tech in time—they were
genuinely afraid that we would turn the tech against ourselves. Have you ever read the Los Alamos plea to Truman
asking him not to use the first fission bomb on Japan?
The ARM struggled to make critical changes during the
war. They *did* make changes. You can't imagine the agonies they went through when the kzinti were winning.

"Then came the peace and the pre-kzin mindset all
snapped back like so much memory-plastic. How easy
was it to end slavery? How easy was it to end the Hundred Year War? How easy was it to shift from the paradigm of Biblical authority to the paradigm of science?
Right now the ARM is bigger than any man. The pre-
cepts of the ARM were already built into the hidden
assumptions of billions of people long before we met the
kzin. Shoot every member of ARM today and it would
just recreate itself out of the ashes and go about its business of wiping war from the minds of men. At Starbase
we have no traditions. We can travel light and fast. The
next war is going to be the worst war that mankind has
ever faced and we need men who can think about it
unencumbered."

At the end of the seminar, Lucas Fry turned to Yankee. "Let's sneak out. I'd like nothing better than to play

some silly game with Nora. Is there a place where I can buy her a present? Is there anything she likes?"

Yankee took the general over to a friend's house whose daughter fashioned jewelry as a hobby. "I can't think of a thing she likes better than baubles."

Lucas picked out a chain platinum headband inlaid with translucent stones from Starbase's primary. "Do you think she'll like it?"

"She probably won't wear it. She likes to squirrel away pretty things where she can dig them up and cherish them."

"Well, women don't wear their jewelry anyway. They keep all that stuff in boxes to show their girlfriends." Fry bought the headband from the young girl with praise for her workmanship.

"That was a good speech you gave us," said Yankee, gliding along the hallway and up the steel stairs. "You make a fine mentor."

"That's what Grand Viziers are for," muttered the general gruffly. "It's going to be touch and go. My biggest worry is Earth."

"Why?"

"You're a flatlander. You figure it out. I can't. But we have to bring the mass of them over to our side. They've forgotten that there ever was a war. Amnesia. Only the colonies are preparing. But once the kzinti have the factories to churn out hypershunt motors they will be converging on every human world from all over the Patriarchy. Flatlander's will have to take the brunt of the attack. Earth is the place with the population. It's where we'll have to find our cannon-fodder."

"Do you think the ARM is behind the shut down of public debate?"

"Yah. For security reasons. Old habit. They can't resist any ploy if it might *stop* people from thinking about war.

Maybe you flatlanders were buying too many toy guns. Made them nervous. They reacted. But it is not just the ARM. It's the flatlanders themselves. The ARM's message has been assimilated into the culture. War is no longer even part of the idiom. Kzinti warriors have to be marching across Kansas before . . . Oh what the hell. I want to see Nora's face when she sees my bauble. You don't think she is afraid of me, do you?"

Yankee had all of his cousin's old papers. Her high school yearbooks. Her many attempts at writing a diary. Her letters to her father. School essays. Drawings. Her photo album. Her anguished, and finally angry, exchange with the war department. Her patriotic newspaper essays that had been franchised for a while on the net. Drafts of the many love letters she wrote to boys. First drafts of letters never sent—embarrassments that she had neglected to erase. One of them was a mushy love letter to a certain Yankee Clandeboye. He had never known, from the way she treated him, that she had ever had a crush on him.

For no particular reason he began to organize this unsorted mess. They all hoped Nora might recover her use of words. She would *never* recover her memories. She would always be the woman who had grown up half-slave, half-kzinrret, born on Hssin. Those were the only memories she had. But maybe, if she ever learned to read and talk again, she might find an interest in these papers by the woman she once had been—like a granddaughter reading the musty diary of a heroic grandmother never known.

Gradually, as Yankee got involved, as memories reminded him of the charmer who had twiddled compulsively with the same strand of hair for all the years he had known her, he started to write about her. He had a need to organize his thoughts. He wanted other people to *understand* this heroine. It was a story that grew on him, built around her Hssin diaries.

Something that stirred inside him told him it was a way to talk to the flatlander soul.

He began his story while Lieutenant Nora Argamentine was living as a kzinrret in the dungeon of a wrecked interstellar fortress beside a dying star, totally dependent upon a kzin who thought that it was natural for females to tend their males and young without the aid of an independent self—a kzin who had the biotechnical power, and the inclination, to take away her mind so that she might more easily fit into his world and serve him.

He built the legend around her hidden diary. With each brain operation it became more urgent for her to record what she was afraid she was losing forever. Yankee lovingly annotated her entries with her pictures, with other things she had written, with his own personal memories. On far-off Hssin she'd wistfully remember a boy she had once known on Earth. Yankee would include her love letter to that boy in a fourteen-year-old's grammar.

Very carefully he wove through the book the saga of the hypershunt motor that had been captured at the Battle of Wunderland, and of Lieutenant Argamentine's valiant attempts to destroy it. An almost successful mutiny. The killing of the kzinti crew. The last kzin. The recapture. The attempts to kill the last kzin. The failure. Her captor could have killed her but he found her useful, yet too dangerous to be left with a mind. Human heroes aren't defined by their wins. A hero is the one who remains committed to principles. A hero is the one who never stops trying and never stops learning.

Why did Lieutenant Nora Argamentine try so hard to destroy that motor when she could have played it cool, been non-threatening, and perhaps saved her mind? Yankee hinted to his reader the chilling truth. Wasn't it because she could see what a reverse-engineered hypershunt would mean to the Patriarchy? Had she seen the assembly lines on a hundred kzin worlds building a new and greater fleet to launch against Sol with *all* the resources of the Patriarchy behind it?

Her father died in the desperate days of the Ceres conflagration defending mankind against a fleet that had *nearly* brought the race to slavery—yet the enemy was only an adventurer's ragtag knock-together manned by border barbarians whose resource base depended wholly upon the factories of Wunderland. In the next war light-lag would not protect Sol from a sluggish giant driven to anger by swarms of alien gnats who had penetrated its *territory* with impunity on wings that might be plucked out and turned to better use by *warriors* who knew what to do with such speeded reflexes.

To teach his readers how to see the man-kzin conflict with the eyes of Nora Argamentine, that was Yankee's hope.

It was a mad project and he worked too hard on it, after his other duties. Sometimes a man just had to stop and go home.

"You're late," said Chloe, happy to see him. She was breast-feeding Val on the bed.

"Let me hold her."

"After she's fed, dummy."

"How was your day?"

"I was with Nora and the kids again. Her boys are too much for me. They still don't know what to make of a woman who can talk. Yankee," she added sadly, "Nora isn't getting better."

"She might be." He stripped and crawled under the covers. All he wanted was to close his eyes and sink his head deep into the pillow, but you lose wives you ignore. He reached a hand out and switched on the bedroom flatscreen, fiddling with it until it networked with his office.

He called up a picture that was an obvious brain scan.

"One of Dr. Hunker's pictures. See the white fuzz inside that gray area? Let me contrast it in false color." He made adjustments. "Those are baby neurons."

"She's going to talk?"

"Hunker doesn't know, but he's giving it his best shot. It will be easier with the girls because of their age."

"Didn't *that kzin* grow a lot of neurons in her head?"

"He sure did. He killed a lot, too. And played around with dendritic growth like a yo-yo. Hunker has studied Trainer-of-Slaves' notes. He's incorporating bits and pieces of kzin biotechnology into some of his tailor-made boosterspices."

"Is he going to make one for you so I can have a nice giggling teen-aged husband?"

"No. But I'm trying to convince him to cook up a reverse boosterspice that I can sneak into your soup. Imagine the glories of waking up to a mature wife."

"You've never liked boosterspice."

"Scares me out of my mind," said Yankee. "Especially after I've talked to Hunker for a while about some of the weird side-effects that can turn up."

"... on his rich old playboy experimental animals. Is he experimenting on Nora?"

"Yah. He's being careful. Taking it easy. A little at a time. It's a tough problem. Construction and repair don't go by the same rules. It is easier to build something that *can't* be repaired than it is to build something that *can* be repaired. Humans weren't built to be repaired. We come in disposable containers. If we last long enough to see our children live through the terrible teens, our genes don't see the need to have us repaired."

"My poor daddy is ready for the junkyard?"

"You haven't made it out of your teens yet, kid. You might still need him."

"Men think of women as disposable containers," said Chloe.

"Aw, no we don't. Neither of you." And he kissed the baby. "*I* didn't design humans as disposable containers; God did. Suppose you build a gizmo and it wears out and you have to repair it. What do you do? If it is cheaper to build a new one than repair the old one, you throw away your gizmo. If it is cheaper to repair than replace, you repair it. Humans are too hard to repair so they have evolved in disposable format. They are cheap to make."

"Just wave your magic wand and say 'Kakabuni,' right?" She grinned.

"Not *that* easy." He took Val and laid her on his chest where she burbled. "You've got to factor in the price of raising the little buggers until they are smart enough to leave home. There's a bit of expense in that. You and I don't know the worst of it yet. But still, for the price of one boosterspice shot I can raise ten teen-agers. At prices like that, what is a company going to do? They can hire a freshly weaned kid out of university, train him and bury the worn-out worker, or they can buy a boosterspice shot for the older worker. At present prices they have no choice."

"Is it costing so much to help Nora?"

"It's costing a fortune. The Institute of Knowledge is footing the bill. They expect to learn a lot. The information in our genes tells us how to build a brain and not a damn thing about repairing it because the genetic cost of carrying that information is greater than the going price for a teen-ager, you being the exception."

"You're into *buying* me now!"

"I'm into going to sleep—and *your* little darling just pissed on me."

At breakfast, refreshed, Yankee continued the discussion. He printed out pictures of Nora's brain with

enlargements of critical segments. Breakfast consisted of
guinea pig jerky and flapjacks with cultured maple syrup.

"When Hunker tells me about brain repair my eyes go
into orbit. That's why nature knows enough not to try. Brain
cells die and that's it. We can't activate the genes that grow
the brain because Nora already has a brain. We can't just
plant the right kind of baby neurons where Nora's language
processor used to be because they have to grow and connect—and the rules for connecting them in an adult are
different than the rules for connecting them in a baby.
Hunker has to design the language-repair protocols and
program it into the spice. Boosterspice already has in it half
the information of the whole human genome. That's a lot."

"Yankee, I'm miserable. You don't come home at night.
Don't you love me anymore?"

"Just another one of my damn projects."

"What project! A new one? You don't tell me anything!
Is it a military secret?"

"No. I'm too involved in this Nora thing."

"So am I! You're supposed to talk to me. We're supposed to work together."

"I thought you might be jealous. It's almost like I'm
caught up in an old love."

"Oh Yankee!"

"You're right." He took her into the bedroom and transferred the whole Nora file in from his work computer.
"Read it. It'll take all day. Tell me what you think."

Chloe had rabbit stew for dinner and he came home
early. She was happy again. "It's marvelous. Now what
are you going to do with it? *They*'ll kill you. You never
change."

"I'll publish it."

"On Earth? Over the ARM's dead body you will! You'll
never get clearance!"

"Did I lay it on that thick? I guess I did. I want to tell Nora's story, but I'm also trying to use her as a political club."

"Neither of the Noras would mind and you know it!"

"I'm not going to try for clearance. I'm not going to publish with a copyright. I'm going to make a thousand chip copies and hide them under rocks. Then I'm going to smuggle one copy to Earth and put it on the nets, free. The ARM can *try* to suppress the story. It will be like running around with cans of antiweed, spraying the dandelions."

Chloe was wide-eyed. "Defy them? They haven't let anyone write about Nora. They'll kill you. They'll put you in the brig. They'll send you to the other side of Kzin. They'll feed you tranquilizers!" What would become of Val? Happiness was supposed to last—at least forever. But it never did.

"Nah."

"Nah!" she imitated angrily. "Why do I fall in love with brave men? I'm such a damn fool."

"Chloe. Listen carefully to an old man's advice. I've been in trouble since I was a kid. Suppressive people have one great weakness. They believe their own stories. They hint darkly at what they'll do to you when you speak up. Naive people believe them and get afraid and, being afraid, *suppress themselves*. The suppressors are stupid enough to think that *they* are doing the suppressing. I don't have anything to worry about from the ARM. I just have to dodge all those poor people who are afraid."

"Will General Fry protect you?"

"Sure. And so will your father. The *best* people are my friends. You'd be surprised at how large that group has become."

"After reading your story I feel brave myself. But I'm still one of those people who are afraid."

"It's okay. For us it'll be a roller-coaster ride for a few years. Outrage and argument. No big deal. Then in about five years some poor schmuck will come back bloodied by an encounter with a kzinti hyperdrive warship. Then instantly, I'll be a prophet and a hero. But it is Nora they'll remember. When the going gets rough and the starscape is full of grinning kzinti and monkey-life looks hopeless, they'll remember the Heroic Myth of Lieutenant Nora Argamentine, and they'll say, 'What the hell, if Nora could do a little kzin bashing, so can I.' "

"Why do you call it a myth? Yankee, she *did* all of those things."

"Chloe. Look at me. All writers are liars. I'm a political writer. Humanity hasn't been at war for hundreds of years. We're short of heroes. We're going to need them. So I took this story and built Nora up larger than life. I wrapped it around all the old archetypes. That's a myth. My only excuse is that I was inspired. Stories just grow. This one will become humongous. I'm sorry to do it to my sweet Nora but I couldn't help myself. Guys in cans being shot at by kzinti hypershunt dreadnoughts will take courage from this crazy story. That's what myth is all about."

TROJAN CAT

*Mark O. Martin and
Gregory Benford*

• Chapter One
Relativistic Hunt

We were only a half light-year out from Sol, but it took me a moment to find that bright point among so many other suns. Somehow it looked no warmer than the other brilliant dots. Probably my imagination.

The more immediate target was obvious. A finger pointed straight at it—a radiant finger a hundred thousand klicks long.

The slowboat was huge, even by the standards of the kzin troopship that had carried me across four light-years. Distant stars glittered coldly around the image-enhanced shape on the viewscreen. It was a relief to see a starscape not distorted and squashed by relativity, fore and aft. The Doppler shift was almost imperceptible at 10 percent of lightspeed.

I felt an itching sensation all over my body, but I didn't look away from the viewscreen to scratch. My little singleship had to be within their sensor range by now, and the crew had no way to determine if I was friend or foe.

I waited to die. I almost hoped for it.

No such luck, of course. Not that I was special. All of humanity was running out of luck.

Goosing the viewscreen magnification up a bit, I studied the target across two hundred kilometers of deep space. The slowboat was a fat cylinder sitting on the hard white blaze of a fusion drive. Even with the jury-rigged gravitic polarizer, it had taken me an hour to maneuver far around the deadly plume of the drive wash pushing the *R. P. Feynman* back to Sol. Getting anywhere near that column of fusion fire would have fried me thoroughly.

Reaction drives can be effective weapons, in direct proportion to their power. Such was the kzinti lesson, according to rumors overheard from the singed-tailed ratcats returning from at least two attempts on Sol. I frowned. *If only . . .*

Too bad Centauri system hadn't gotten more large fusion drive units in place a few decades back, when the kzin first arrived. Things might have gone very differently for both Serpent Swarmer and Wunderlander. My whole life would have been different, and I would never have ended up here and now.

The singleship control board began to ping. That meant the first faint lines of magnetic force were brushing by the main sensory array of my singleship. I keyed up a false color display of the magnetic field structure at the front and flank of *Feynman*. Stark crimson lines stretched across my viewscreen into a huge and intricate pattern.

The ramscoop field reached invisible fingers outward for hundreds of kilometers, an invisible throat. It funneled interstellar hydrogen and icy dust microparticles into the fusion drive section at the core of the slowboat. Anything with a slight electrical charge, the mags picked up and gobbled.

Like any good Belter, I sat very still and studied the viewscreen with great care, trying to find a clear path through the closely packed field lines. The ramscoop fueling the slowboat wasn't a big belcher, like the unmanned ramrobots that could run up to nearly 0.9 lights. This one was pushing hard to make 0.1. The exhaust plume's ion excitations showed it was at ram-limited cruising velocity.

Slowboat, indeed, despite its incandescent power

scratching across the starscape. It was ridiculous, compared to the kzin spacedrive. A trip time of forty years, Wunderland to Sol.

Which is why the passengers in there were stacked up in cryo like canned goods. It had been a long way back, this close to Sol. The *Feynman* crew must have traded off cruise watches with their sleepers through several shifts now.

Desperate people. And they weren't going to make it.

The slowboat looked to be in good shape on extreme mag. The awake crew must have done repairs on the fly; the slowboats were meant for one-way trips, Earth to Wunderland.

And *Feynman* looked *old*. Pitted, blotchy. Even the most recent of the colony ships had orbited Wunderland, empty and ignored, for over fifty years.

It had been a near thing, getting all of the old colony slowboats repaired, crewed, and on emergency boost outsystem. Prole and Herrenmann and Belter, working together for once, before the ratcats arrived in victory. But all three of the slowboats had made it. The kzin made only a half-hearted attempt to stop them.

And for what? I reminded myself bitterly. The rest of us had lost almost everything—rights, dignity, property, countless lives—to let a few Herrenmannen lords and ladies run away from the kzin.

And I knew that better than most. Knew it in my guts.

Feynman's magnetic funnel was not as lethal as a ramrobot's, but plenty dangerous to any living thing with a notochord. I would have to be careful, maneuvering closer to the plasma tongue. Mag vortices curled and licked and ate each other there. High turbulence. It could reach out with rubber fingers and strum this little ship like a guitar string. At 0.1 lights, not recommended by the manufacturer.

As if anybody, even a kzin, had ever tried this before.

The navigational computer held my position relative to *Feynman* as I studied the field line intensities more closely, and plotted a weaving path through the invisible macramé of magnetic force. The ripping-cloth sound of the gravitic polarizer muted to a low crackle. I rubbed my forehead for a moment, then inhaled deeply. The kzin had installed a minimal space drive in my singleship, nothing like their warships or transports. It warped space unevenly, the unbalanced gravitic emissions always giving me a splitting headache.

It was show time.

I took a long sip of tepid water from my suit collar nipple. I cleared my throat and keyed the omnidirectional commlink.

"*Feynman, Feynman,*" I sang out crisply, forcing a professional tone into my voice. "This is Free Wunderland Navy emissary spacecraft *Victrix*. Code Ajax. Do you copy?"

The lie felt thick and bitter on my tongue, like bad coffee. *Trojan Horse* or *Judas Goat* would have been better names for my peaceful-looking converted singleship. I steeled myself. No Wunderlander, ground pounder or Belter, owed these running cowards a thing.

It still didn't feel right. It never would.

But I had little choice. I had my reasons for serving the kzin. Four of them, in fact.

But I'm no Jacobi.

I had been telling myself that for months, over and over, like a mantra.

Again I waited for my sensors to bleat their alarms. That would be the first warning as the slowboat's signal laser blasted my singleship to vapor. The only warning, maybe a half-second of it.

No reply to my transmission. Just a faint lonely hiss

over the shipboard commlink. Backwash emission at the plume's plasma frequency. The stars looked very far away, cold and uncaring. Sol looked warm, unreachable. Why had we ever left her?

I repeated the transmission. Nothing. I set the commlink to autorepeat, left the receiver volume amped, and waited. I peeled a ration bar, and chewed the fibrous lump slowly. Swallowed. Tried not to think about the damned ratcat holo in my pocket, and my four good reasons to serve the kzin.

I took another bite, the ration bar even more tasteless than usual. *Slave fodder. Monkeyfood.*

Maybe the crew were all dead and had left the slowboat on autopilot. Yet repairs and modifications had been carried out on the old colony ship at some point after its escape. The scope image enhancers showed fresh-looking weld stains, jury-rigged antennas, replaced flux generators with sloppy seals.

They were in there, all right, sitting fat and happy while the rest of us were slaves to the damned ratcats.

I crumpled the ration bar peel in anger. First trouble insystem, and the Herrenmann ruling elite abandoned their high and mighty code of honor. They ran back to their Solward brethren, like any common Prole.

I couldn't understand why they had bolted in the first place, other than cowardice. Wunderlanders had quickly learned that the kzin gravitic polarizers changed the strategies of warfare. The tabbies could get it up to 0.8 lights within a week or two, and could hull the slowboats anytime the whim took them. It would have been better to fight, to take a few tabbies with them. But the Herrenmann cowards cut and ran.

The noble slogans meant nothing. *Honor.* I frowned in distaste, remembering. They were just saving their own precious hides.

The autorepeat dragged on. No reply. The music of the spheres remained mostly static with dead spaces. I finished my ration bar and ate the wrapper, not that there was much difference in taste or texture.

Now I hoped that the crew were all dead onboard. It would make my job a little easier. Not much, but a little. Best be done and gone. . . .

Did I have a choice? I swallowed past a foul taste in my mouth that had nothing to do with salvaged singleship rations. The shipboard commlink suddenly hissed to life. "*Victrix, Victrix.* This is *Feynman.* Return signal on tightbeam at once, both visual and multiplex datalink."

They didn't need to actually threaten me directly. It was all implicit. A slight change in the ramscoop fluxnet configuration, and the magnetic field would scramble every nonoptical byte in my shipboard computers. Probably burn out my brain, too.

If that wasn't enough, I was certainly in range of their main laser array. It was designed to punch messages across light years, but was equally suited to vaporizing unwanted visitors.

I took another sip of warm flat water and got to work.

The singleship computer quickly gave me a fix on the transmitter they were using. Standard five-meter mica dish setup, tucked into the back third of the slowboat. Snug in its prowbay, a phased array. The modulated laserlink was standard too, at 420 nanometers. I tweaked my signal laser frequency to that wavelength and targeted the dish in the crosshairs. I thumbed on the data handshake subroutine. My own signal laser hunted a bit, then settled on the dish array. *Lock*—and I was still alive.

Communications data flashed across the main screens, and a low tone sounded. Transmission datalink belted in.

It was time to move to the next act.

I thumbed the channel open. Weak color, jittery fuzz

all over. But it showed a youngish man with the idiotic asymmetric beard worn by Herrenmann dandies back in München on Wunderland. Either he had been in coldsleep for most of the trip or he had carried along a supply of very expensive anti-aging drugs.

After all, they had been en route for over thirty-five years. His face was immobile with the typical arrogant expression of the ruling class, the Nineteen Families. Prunefaced and straight backed in his crashcouch. That asshole expression was no longer common in München, even on collaborationist faces. Things had changed, courtesy of our kzin masters.

Come on. Can't let any of that show. A lot is riding on this. I forced my expression into a friendly smile. The hybrid Germanic tongue of Wunderland nobility sliding easily across my lips. "*Guten Gross-Tag, Herrenmann. Ich heissen . . .*"

"There is no cause," he interrupted, "to speak Wunderlander." His eyes were hard and proud and suspicious. No trace of an accent in his clipped voice. "You are clearly a Serpent Swarmer, and should not put on airs to which you are not entitled. Speak Belter Standard, if you please."

"As you wish." I smiled. Arrogant fool. How would he like his children to become hunt-toys for some kzin noble's young sons? "I was merely going to introduce myself in a polite fashion."

I paused and waited for my haughty little friend to gesture me to continue. "My name is Karl Friedrich Höchte. I bring you good news."

Fake, of course. My real name would have surprised him, made him instantly suspicious. So I had selected another good noble name to reassure the Herrenmann crew of the *Feynman*. An extended member of the Nineteen Families, by the sound of it. Just the kind of purse-mouthed dandy who'd use his middle name when introducing himself. A convincing little touch, that. Maybe.

He was good, I had to give him that much. No hint of curiosity as to how I had arrived at his slowboat, only a little over half a light-year from Sol. Even his long Herrenmann ears did not twitch.

"My name is Klaus Bergen," he replied, still expressionless. "You were mentioning news? I remind you that we do have defenses."

I leaned forward. Earnest expression, enthusiastic. "Klaus, my friend, we beat them."

"Impossible."

Okay, so he wasn't profoundly stupid. "We were lucky. Most of them left—we still aren't sure why—and we took the garrison force they left behind. And most of us died. But we did it, drove them out of Wunderlander space."

Now Bergen's ears twitched with interest. He raised a haughty eyebrow in disbelief. Might as well stick to the prepared story, I figured. Don't improvise more than you have to. "And we follow them all the way, flaming their rat tails as we go, I can assure you."

"You exaggerate, surely." His eyes were flat and hard.

"It's true," I insisted. "I have come out to *Feynman* on behalf of the rest of Wunderland. We cracked the secret of the ratcat gravitic polarizer drive, and the Serpent Swarm Resistance" —I paused and patted my control console affectionately— "learned to build warcraft of our own to match the tabbies. There were a lot more of us than of them, after all."

There was a long pause. Here was the worst point. If he didn't buy it . . .

Bergen stared, still without expression other than a cocked eyebrow. He looked to one side, out of range of his camera eye, and listened intently. He nodded once and turned back to me.

"You will understand our suspicions." The same clipped, up-yours tone, but a hint of excitement got through. Good. "I presume that you have proofs for our inspection."

I grinned harmlessly, gesturing behind me at the cramped lifebubble. "*Herr* Bergen, you can see that *Victrix* is unarmed, and I am the sole occupant. Even now I am at your mercy, my friend. A larger ship waits farther out to install a gravitic drive and make other modifications to *Feynman*. We felt that *Victrix* would be less threatening, so I came to you as an emissary."

I held back a grimace at the way the words tasted. There was at least a kernel of truth in what I said.

The Herrenmann said nothing. I was getting worried.

"After all," I continued, "you're poking along. Once *Feynman* is retrofitted, you can be at Sol in a matter of weeks."

He blinked. It must be pretty foul in there. The prospect of reaching Earth's opulence so soon . . . That's what I had working for me. Herrenmannen will be Herrenmannen.

I changed the subject. "As for *bona fides*, I would think that *Victrix*'s own gravitic polarizer would be proof enough. But I do have holos and datadisks for your inspection, sir. They detail our victories against the ratcats."

"I would like to see them," replied my arrogant little friend across the empty kilometers. He did not sound convinced.

Time to play my trump card.

As if on sudden impulse I laid it down. "I do have one further piece of evidence you may find more persuasive," I said in a carefully cheerful tone, reaching into the clear organiform bag I had kept clipped next to my crashcouch. "Or, more accurately, pieces of evidence."

Smiling into the camera eye, I held up the engraved metal ring. Dozens of mummified kzinti ears swung gently in the slight breeze from the airplant ventilator grill. I selected one ear in particular, stretching it like an old fashioned Chinese parasol, displaying the crimson tattoos scrawled across the dried white tissue.

"*Herr* Bergen, my friend, you are familiar with tabby rank? This particular ear was taken from a fleet captain, as you can see from the tattoo pattern." I paused, flicking the edge of the ear with a finger for emphasis. "He did not approve of its removal, but I was indifferent to his remonstrations."

Again, I had not lied.

Bergen's voice was hoarse, and no longer haughty. "How many do you have on that trophy ring?"

I could see many emotions in his eyes, thawing of Herrenmann reserve. They had not left the dried ears.

"Thirty-one. And your unspoken guess is quite correct, as well. It's a kzin trophy ring."

"How could you possibly—"

"Taken from yet another ratcat captain. Again against his will. Many of us in the Free Wunderland Space Navy have taken similar souvenirs. I thought that my own small trophy was an appropriate item for its present purpose, *nicht wahr?*"

The Wunderlander once more looked off camera for a moment, then squared his jaw. "I confess I find your evidence persuasive. And anyway, a ratcat warship would not *bother* with such a shadow play. They would hull us from outside our fields and have done." His eyes became once again hard, making his asymmetric beard look still more ludicrous. "*Herr* Höchte, you may now negotiate through the ramscoop field lines to our main airlock—"

"*Viel dank.*" It is always best to let the customer draw the desired conclusions.

"—where you will be met. We remind you that you

are being watched most carefully, and we have . . . resources . . . with which *Feynman* can be protected."

Try to look concerned. "You still harbor suspicions, then?" I got it out calmly, with the slightest trace of sarcasm flavoring my words.

"We mean no insult—*if* you are who you claim to be."

"I'm telling—"

"You must understand us, *Herr* Höchte. We carry the hope of Wunderland with us, and can take no chances with such a precious cargo." He paused, his features once more unreadable.

Time for the icy, insulted manner. "I am a fellow human, as you know."

He ignored it. "You understand that we cannot reduce or shape out our magnetics?"

"I know your specs, *ja*." I let more irritation show in my tone and face. *Careful* . . .

Bergen paused for a moment, his iron Herrenmann expression softening just a bit. "*Herr* Höchte, I believe your story. After all, anyone meaning us ill could easily destroy us from a distance, is it not so?"

Yes, I thought to myself, *that is one way to think of it*. I nodded at Bergen with false satisfaction.

Bergen nodded back once in reply, his face again tight and haughty. "*Feynman* out."

So far, so good, I thought grimly.

The viewscreen dissolved to holographic snow. I had been dismissed. No matter that I was supposedly saving his ass, I was still just a ground-grubber Prole in his book.

I took a few deep breaths to calm my nerves. Then back to work, careful work. No room for mistakes.

It took half an hour, just optimizing the gravitic polarizer to full power. Then I laid in my macros, routines which would take me slipping through magnetic field lines. My now-familiar headache began to pound once again as the polarizer came fully on line, and carried me toward the slowboat.

It took over an hour to gingerly navigate among the magnetic field lines, headed toward the main airlock of *Feynman*. The fields here were strumming with tension—ten kiloGauss, easy. Magnetic field lines are like rubber bands that can never break—but you can stretch them. I had to worm my way through the steep gradients, while plasma hailed against my hull. The field lines stretch, all right—and they can snap back. That would not be good.

Each klick I slithered through felt like it took a day. I knew the slowboat crew could kill me instantly with the slightest change in the fluxline configuration. Or boil me to vapor with the signal laser, if they wanted to make a nice gaudy splash.

Not that it would be so damn bad. At least it would be over then. And why wait for them to make a move? Part of me wanted to die, vectoring right in under full acceleration, say, into the white-hot plasma plume—

But I knew what Kraach-Captain would then do. Who would really suffer as a result of my oh-so-noble gesture?

I was a traitor, yes, but not like Jacobi. Nothing like Jacobi. I had my reasons for serving the damned ratcats, four very good reasons: Sharna, Gretha, Henry, and Hilda.

Kraach-Captain would keep his side of the bargain, if I kept mine. Maybe that was the only good side to the kzin. Come hell or high water, they kept their word. Predator's honor.

Unlike almost any human—especially unlike Jacobi. Horrible to know that I could trust the word of an alien monster more than a fellow human.

Burnt-gold plasma curled and lashed around me. I kept away from the drive wash but errant coils fought up and down the field lines, bow turbulence. The gravitic polarizer whined with a thrumming effort. *Careful, careful* . . . My target loomed large, a huge hull, raked and burned.

A slight jar as I grounded *Victrix* next to the main airlock. It loomed huge through the viewscreen, as did every visible aspect of the slowboat. I activated the magnetic grapnels. A hollow boom startled me—I was that tense—as we locked firmly against the slowboat.

On the viewscreen I could see the crew tunnel slowly arching toward my own airlock. Like an elephant's trunk from an old history holocube, from a time when there had been elephants.

Clunk, whir—the slowboat airlock adapted to the geometry of my singleship airlock. The status board winked green and I keyed the airlock cycle.

You're on, kid. This first part was easy. . . .

I popped a stimulant to take the ragged edge from my fatigue. Everything depended on the next few hours. Everything.

The singleship airlock chimed and swung open silently. My ears popped a bit with a slight pressure drop. I left my helmet open in what I intended to be a demonstration of harmlessness. Yawning, concentrating on my lines, I grabbed access loops, and swung hand over hand into the dimly lit crew tunnel.

The far end of the crew tunnel was closed, of course. Final inspection time. *Try to look like Karl Friedrich Höchte.*

I crouched casually, bracing a foot and hand against the microgravity, and smiled directly into the camera eye next to the airlock. The slowboat air in the crew tunnel smelled oily and slightly rank. I doubted that many of *Feynman's* systems worked optimally. Here was the first proof.

The lock slowly irised open. Here I was, and all I had wanted to do was get in one last bit of smuggling, a million years ago. . . .

• Chapter Two
Smuggler's Blues

The asteroid swimming in *Victrix*'s viewscreen had no official name on the navigation charts. The distant glint was listed as 2121–21, the twenty first asteroid catalogued during the 2121 A.D. survey of the Serpent Swarm. To the temporary rockjack crews living there, the asteroid had also developed an obvious nickname: Blackjack.

Blackjack was a slow-spinning oblong of stone twenty kilometers across its long axis. Rich veins of water ice and nickel-iron riddled it, along with deposits of carbonaceous chondrite. Pockmarked and battered by other asteroids in the Serpent Swarm over the eons, it had slowly swung in its orbit, half a billion kilometers from Alpha Centauri A. The rock had raw materials, access to energy, and was in an orbit easily accessible to singleships.

There were many thousands of rocks just like it in the Swarm, but Blackjack was a little different. For a few weeks, this whirling piece of an unformed planet would be home to the few human beings still resisting the iron claws and sharp teeth of the kzin.

I intended to do my part to help them, at least this one last time. Sure, some of the rebels were more pirate than freedom fighter, more interested in lining their pockets than collecting kzinti ears. But an old Earther saying came to mind: "The enemy of my enemy is a friend."

If only it were always true.

I unlimbered the signal laser remotes. Squinting against

the sun glare, I set the aiming crosshairs on the tiny flash of the receiver dish a thousand kilometers away. The laser guide prowled slowly in a small arc, seeking. A thin beep— a target lock.

I paused before I set up the recognition signal trigger, and eyed the highly illegal monopole detector array mounted above my control console. I studied it with great care, as if my life depended on it.

Which it did.

Three rows of amber lights shone steadily at me in the cramped lifebubble. All clear. No ratcat ships were within range of the detector. I made a few adjustments, increasing the range, and studied the lights again.

The kzin gravitic polarizers used large quantities of magnetic monopoles. Easily identified—if you had access to the now-illegal tech, that is. Our kzin masters were many things, but stupid was not one of them. The detector array pinged sleepily after a moment, confirming that no large monopole sources were within at least a hundred thousand klicks of Blackjack.

Opening the commlink port, I carefully inserted the tiny chip I had been given at the Nipponese restaurant in Tiamat. The ready lights blinked green. I triggered the downlink recognition code sequence. Multicolored lights rippled across the readout as the signal laser downloaded its smuggler's message.

Caution was everything in my business. It really wouldn't do for our mighty felinoid masters to be in the neighborhood while I carried out my last smuggling run for that Prole bastard Jacobi. One more load of equipment that the Resistance needed: monopole detectors, submolar assemblies, nano units, fusion point components. I had carefully double-recorded the cargo back in Tiamat, then loaded the contraband along with my own completely legal cargo.

The kzin were not good at accounting; it did not fit with their ideal of the Warrior Heart. How could a Hero scream and leap his way to a Full Name while recording a long series of cargo manifests onto a handlink?

Their five-eyed, five-armed, warty Jotoki monsters, ever watchful and nosy, were another matter. I had waited until I was unsupervised on my loading dock shift, then covered the computer traces most carefully. It was easy; men and women had designed and programmed those computers, not aliens. And what a Jotok can't see or hear, it can't report to its furry rat-tailed masters.

Contraband stowed and hidden, I had hitched the cargo pod to *Victrix*, and started on my kzin-approved trade and delivery route, zigzagging across the Swarm. Tiamat to Avalon. Avalon to Lodestar. Lodestar to Archangel. Now an undocumented stop at nearby Blackjack, the dicey part. Then I'd shape orbit back for Tiamat. It had been five long months, and I was lonely for Sharna and the children.

The route would have taken days with the ratcat gravitic polarizers instead of my fusion drive, but such kzin tech was not for "slave races."

The commlink warbled in response to the recognition signal. Smuggler's handshake. Everything was going according to plan—which worried me a little.

Still, I followed my instructions. No overt communications traffic, even by tightbeam. I tuned up the fusion drive. It thrummed and headed *Victrix* down to Blackjack at a nice sedate vector. It never pays to stand out, even when you are not being watched. On the screen, the asteroid swelled from a glint to a toy pebble to an irregular brick.

Not long after the initial kzin assault on Wunderland, Blackjack had been abandoned. Immediately after suppressing military resistance there, the kzinti had moved on the Serpent Swarm, but most of the Belters had focused on protecting Tiamat, with its shipyards and bubblefarms.

Not that it mattered a damn in the long run. Singleship fusion drives were no match for the ratcat space drive. The damage to the densely colonized asteroids like Tiamat and Thule was heavy, and took time to repair. The smaller rocks, like Blackjack, were left relatively intact—very useful to smugglers and pirates. Or as the noble kzin called them, "feral humans."

As Blackjack slowly filled the viewscreen, I organized the cargo manifest and thought about how to spend my ill-gotten gains. My smuggler's money had kept my family well insulated from the ratcats, and I intended to keep it that way. Jacobi had gone so far as to suggest that this delivery could earn enough credits to buy my children a billet in the Proxima cometary manufacturing plants.

Kzin almost never went to Proxima. It was not sufficiently Heroic.

About two kilometers above Blackjack, I saw the rhythmic blinking of the landing beacon next to a bubble-domed minehead. I switched to chemical jets so that I wouldn't have to hike in the microgravity to the airlock. As we slipped in I closed my suit helmet and started pumping the lifebubble air back into the tanks. No sense wasting even a few lungfuls when I popped the airlock.

Wan sunlight gleamed on solar collectors and vacuum fractionating columns near the minehead. I drifted closer to the landing beacon. You don't land on an asteroid as small as Blackjack; you rendezvous. Attitude jets held my singleship steady as I carefully shot a mooring line through a landing loop, then made *Victrix* fast against the bulk of Blackjack.

A few minutes later I was in the minehead airlock, listening to the deepening whistle of pressure building up.

All according to plan, smooth as water ice. The airlock telltales finally winked green, and the inner door cycled open.

The first thing I saw was Jacobi's sneering smile. But even before that image fully registered, I smelled the spicy-sour scent of excited kzinti. Which had to be imaginary, since my suit helmet was still sealed and dogged down.

Jacobi stood braced in front of the airlock door, dart pistol in hand, eyes bright in his scarred face. Flanking him were two kzin in combat armor—predator fangs bared in identical smile-threats. Before I could make a move to hit the cycle keypad in the airlock, something slammed into my upper right arm. I swung my body in response as Belter micrograv reflexes kept me on my feet.

I looked down. A large, hollow dart, designed to foil the suit's self-sealing mechanism, protruded from my shipsuit. Crimson spheres of blood began floating out of the wound. They wobbled slowly away in the microgravity. If I cycled the lock now, with my ruptured suit, I would be breathing vacuum in seconds. Pain suddenly flooded my arm and into my gut, folding me in two, my feet leaving the deck.

"So good to see you again, *Herr* Upton-Schleisser," I heard Jacobi hiss with irony.

I swore to myself as the snarling figures in battle armor, each over two meters tall, snatched me from midair like kittens batting at yarn. Black spots clouded my vision. I did the only reasonable thing. I passed out.

The bite of a stimulant slapshot in my neck brought me to my senses. My shipsuit and helmet were gone. I was dressed in a standard falling jumper. My right arm throbbed badly, but I could see a ratcat field dressing on the wound. The bandage was easily three times larger than necessary; medicine on a kzin-sized scale. Bindings cut into my ankles and wrists, holding me securely to a packing crate.

I looked up and saw Jacobi seated on air a few meters away, a thin line mooring him in place against the ventilator breeze. We were in a small storage room, lit with glaring mining lights. The cold air smelled of oil and steel. And of kzin, of course. I shook my head to clear my thoughts. It didn't help.

"Jacobi," I said as calmly as I could, my neck still stinging from the drug, "I had no idea that you were a pussy-kisser collabo."

He made no reply, just stared at me. It was hard to read any expression on the ruins of his face. When I was a boy, Tomás Jacobi had been a leader among the Serpent Swarmers during the kzin invasion. His forces had held back the invasion troopships from Tiamat for most of a week. Then his lifebubble had been lasered open during the final assault, searing his face and giving him decompression scars. Later, Jacobi had become one of the major smugglers in the Swarm and a supplier to the Resistance. A criminal, but a human criminal.

Just like me.

How could he of all people become a collaborationist?

Jacobi's eyes were ice blue, and peered impassively from the runnels and scars of his face. He made a clucking sound with his tongue. In my years of dealing with Jacobi, he had always tried to act like a kindly uncle to me. I knew better.

"Kenneth, Kenneth," he said softly, "there is no reason to be insulting. I had to make sure that you didn't leave suddenly, didn't I? An impression had to be made on my, ah, employers as well. In any event, I tended to your wound myself. No real harm done."

I kept all expression from my face, my tone level. "Valve

that sewage. You sold me out to the kzin." I took a deep breath, thinking of my family. "You might as well kill me, Jacobi. I won't go collabo and work for the damn ratcat tabbies."

"Hush." He made a throat-cutting gesture with his free hand. "Kraach-Captain speaks Belter Standard, Wunderlander, Jotok, and Principle knows what else. Do not insult his honor or his person." He looked sternly at me out of that ruined face. "As for selling anyone out, I do not need to justify my decisions to a petty small-time smuggler."

I allowed my expression to show how I felt then and Jacobi sighed in exasperation. He reached down with a free hand and untied his mooring line. Both of his legs were missing; another legacy from the kzin armory. He reached out to a wall-ring, pushed off, and floated down next to me. His grip was very strong. Jacobi's mouth was centimeters from my ear.

"Kenneth, my friend," he whispered, "you are to be taken before Kraach-Captain. So this can go one of two ways after I untie you. The first is for you to overpower me, which would not be difficult for you. Yet if you do, what will you then do?"

"Break your neck."

"And then? There are over fifty Heroes here on Black-jack. Will you fight them all? And if so, to what purpose?"

He paused for a moment, looking at me carefully. It was that look he used when dickering over contraband cargoes. Shrewd and knowing. I said nothing.

"On the other hand," he continued, "I can call a few Heroes to escort you to Kraach-Captain person-ally. But I do not wish to do so. It is better, more dig-nified, that we go to the Captain together. Better for both of us. Surely you would prefer to go under your own power, not as an unconscious lump carried by kzinti guards." Jacobi waited for my response, scarred lips twisted.

Finally, I nodded curtly. Deftly, Jacobi untied my bonds. I grasped a wall ring to keep from floating off the deck in the tiny gravity of Blackjack. He gestured me to follow, and pushed off for the doorway.

"Just tell me one thing," I asked Jacobi's back. "Why would *you* work for the ratcats? You have spent your entire life fighting them. And even if you are a traitor by nature, still they *crippled* you, Finagle take it!"

His back stiffened at my words, but he did not reply.

We carefully leaped from wall-ring to wall-ring through the corridors of the minehead station. The legless Jacobi was graceful in the microgravity, using just the tips of his fingers to correct each jump. As I followed him from handhold to handhold, I swallowed back my anger and tried to think of a way out of this. Nothing occurred to me.

The low-grav conditions might become yet another problem in considering options and choices. Kzinti hated microgravity, having used gravitic polarizers for centuries; once their monopole-laden ships returned to Blackjack, they could provide some artificial gravity.

Kzinti didn't deal well with the fluid buildup caused by microgravity; they got a little . . . short tempered, even for kzinti.

It was a silent five-minute trip to the unused comm center. Jacobi knocked once, the hatch opened, and I followed him into a large room. The ceilings were tall enough to allow a kzin to stand upright. Three kzinti in full space armor stood guard at the doorway, weapons glittering in the orange filtered lamps. As we passed them they hissed softly.

A very large table was fixed to the floor in the center of the room. Clips held holocubes and data platters in neat arrays within easy reach of the obviously high-ranking kzin who sat there working, giving no sign that we had been noticed. Jacobi and I crouched motionless in front of the table, eyes averted, waiting. I could feel the collective gaze of the kzinti at the door on me. The air was cold and very dry.

Finally, one of the guards growled softly.

The kzin behind the makeshift desk looked up from a portable thinscreen display, and blinked at us. His black nose sniffed wetly in our direction. Enormous violet eyes held mine for a moment, weighing and judging. His short muzzle was shot with gray, and I could see the ridged battle scars on his face and arms. Very old for a kzin. There were no old, stupid kzinti.

Jacobi began to hiss and spit in the falsetto human version of the kzin language. I wasn't surprised that he knew it, given recent events. But the kzin at the desk bared his teeth and roared for silence. The room seemed to echo for a moment.

"Better," the seated alien rasped in passable Belter Standard. His voice was octaves lower than human. "Except under necessity, humans should not defile the Hero's Tongue. No Warrior Heart. No honor. I tell you when to speak." He paused. We remained silent. Satisfied, he continued.

"I am named Kraach-Captain," the old kzin grated. His eyes speared me. "How are you called, slave who may soon be meat?"

"I am called Kenneth Upton-Schleisser," I said slowly, knowing better than to meet the kzin's eyes directly. My word choice was intentional; to a kzin, names are earned, not given.

"Sssoo," Kraach-Captain rumbled. "It is as the legless monkey says. The Jacobi beast is as without honor as legs, but at least on this occasion truth issues from his slave mouth. Your two fathers, they fight Heroes when we first come to *Ka'ashi*?" I shook my head, not understanding. The old kzin finally snarled a hissing oath and gestured at Jacobi with a careless hand, claws glittering.

Jacobi leaned close and whispered in my ear. "Kraach-Captain means your father and mother, Kenneth. Kzin females aren't sentient. . . ."

"I know that," I interrupted loudly, still feeling confused. I shut my mouth abruptly as one of the guards growled a warning behind me. I could smell fear-sweat on the other man.

"Don't do that again. They expect me to have explained all of this to you." Jacobi urged me to continued silence with a hard glare. "Explaining details to slaves is a duty for slaves, not for a Hero. Now, listen carefully. They know about your father and mother, Kenneth, but their females aren't intelligent, so I told them—"

"I get it," I whispered back, cutting Jacobi's explanation short. I was not interested in whatever bizarre rationale had led to gender morphing of my female parent.

I took a deep breath, feeling a familiar, almost comforting anger rise in my guts, partially displacing the roil of emotions already churning there. My parents. Henry Upton had been a good rockjack Belter in the Swarm, a humanitarian interested in promoting better Swarm–Wunderland relations. It worked so well that he had married the ice queen Herrenmann daughter of the First Family, Helga Schleisser. I had been their only child, five years old when the kzin came. My father died holding off the ratcats.

My mother left with the slowboats. In the chaos of the invasion, I ended up as indentured labor.

I looked back up at Kraach-Captain. "Yes," I said. "My . . . fathers . . . did battle with Heroes at that time."

His huge eyes were searching my face again. Apparently he was familiar enough with humans to at least attempt to read expressions. "You seem a clever beast. Perhaps you shall be allowed to live."

I said nothing, eyes partially averted. It was safer not to volunteer anything to a kzin, unless an actual question was asked. Part of me was surprised at how quickly I recalled the manners appropriate to staying alive around a kzin. Slave manners were reemerging, a hated reflex.

"I have need of a slave-human—one with knowledge of the feral-human ways," the kzin added.

"Dominant One," I said slowly and distinctly, hating the servility, hating my desire to keep on breathing, "Jacobi is much wiser in the ways of the feral-humans." Jacobi sucked in his breath.

The old kzin looked at me for a moment, blinking. Then he coughed ratcat laughter, licking his thin black lips with a lolling tongue. "Most amusing, human. Jacobi is *crippled*. Worse than a cull from the sickliest litter of the most lowborn monkey. Useless for a Valiant One's plan."

"I do not understand," I said.

"The Jacobi-beast will now explain to you my Hero's plan. You will serve me in its execution, indeed you will." Kraach-Captain began to methodically groom his pelt. Chinese parasol ears unfolded to listen better.

Jacobi leaned closer. "Kraach-Captain wishes to regain his full Name. He has permission from the Conquest Governor to take a small troopship to one of the slowboats on the way back to Sol."

"Doesn't make sense," I said. The slowboats were almost to Sol by now. The ratcats could have destroyed them at any time. For some reason, they had chosen not to bother. Perhaps it just wasn't worth their time to do so. Why now, when the costs would be significant?

He didn't respond to my reaction, just continued emotionlessly, refusing to look at me. "The kzin have gotten bloodied trying to penetrate Sol's perimeter defense. Kraach-Captain wants to put a crack force of kzinti and weaponry inside a commandeered slowboat. He will then use the slowboat in a surprise attack on perimeter defenses, allowing a follow-on kzin fleet into solar space." Jacobi paused. "A Trojan Cat, as it were."

Shock kept my voice low. "You Judas!"

Kraach-Captain stopped grooming for a moment and looked at me closely. Perhaps I had raised my voice a bit after all. He scented the air wetly and rumbled.

Jacobi continued to speak softly. "Kenneth—we owe the Earthers nothing."

"We're still—"

"They've left us to the kzin for nearly forty years. What have they done for us? And the Herrenmannen in the slowboats . . . well, you have even more reason than most to hate them."

"I'm no Prole, Jacobi," I told him firmly.

"I've left out a few details, Kenneth." Jacobi said nothing for a moment. "The slowboat that the kzin have targeted is the *R. P. Feynman*."

My mother had left Wunderland space aboard *Feynman*.

It was too much. Jacobi had always been a sadistic bastard at his core. If he was to be Judas, then he intended to use me as a Judas goat. Using my own hated past as a bargaining chip. I braced myself carefully with my hands, face blank. I leaned down, then kicked Jacobi as hard as I could. Alas, less a stranger to micro-g combat than I, he managed to rotate slightly on his vertical axis; in reaction, I floated across the room toward the opposite wall. One of the kzin guards launched himself at me like a three-meter furry orange missile.

Kraach-Captain shrieked a banshee wail. The guard streaked past me, rebounded against the wall, and came

to attention. The old kzin then hissed and spat orders to
the other growling guards.

In a few moments, Jacobi and I were in front of Kraach-
Captain's desk again. The guards stood over us this time,
ready to cuff any more slave outbursts. Jacobi wheezed a
bit and moved to ease the sprained ribs that had taken
the blow intended for vertebrae.

"Upton-Schleisser," Kraach-Captain growled, "I
approve of your spirit. The Jacobi-beast is indeed an eater
of grass. Still, we will reward him with the legs and face
he wishes, if our quest is successful. And wealth and
females, of course." He blinked, heavy-lidded. "None of
this will give him even monkey honor, however."

My brain whirled. When the kzin invaded, one of the
first things shut down were the organ banks. To the kzinti,
an organ bank was a restaurant.

Jacobi was selling out humans for a pair of legs and a
new face.

I sat tight, thinking. There wasn't anything to do. Jacobi
had sewed up things too thoroughly. He must have
planned this years in advance. There was only one option.
I looked up at Kraach-Captain and stared him directly in
the eye. The guards began to rumble with menace at my
intentional rudeness.

"You cannot make me serve you," I said. "I have one
thing to say, Kraach-Captain."

The kzin blinked in curiosity. Time to take my shot.

"*Ch'rowl* you!" I shouted in falsetto kzin at the top of
my lungs. The kzinti curse would surely be my death sentence, but at least I would go clean. The room was deathly
silent as I thought of my wife and children, so far away in
Tiamat. I felt the guards' huge hands clamping down on
my shoulders, holding me in place, and prepared to die.

Nothing happened. I could hear blood singing in my
ears.

Even the guards were silent.

Finally, Kraach-Captain coughed in laughter. "The Jacobi-beast is correct yet again!" He pointed an ebony clawtip at Jacobi. "This slave did exactly as you predicted. You indeed deserve your legs." In a burst of generosity he added, "And I will see that they are taken from a well-muscled youthful specimen of precisely your height or a little taller. Fresh killed, of course. It is well worth the loss of a Hero's meal!"

Jacobi said nothing, simply stared straight ahead at a blank wall.

The kzin turned his head toward me. In what passed among kzinti for warm benignity he said, "Again I salute your courage, little slave. It is like that of an undisciplined kitten, but courage just the same." His violet eyes turned suddenly hard and opaque. He hissed, "But know this, slave: you *will* serve us." Kraach-Captain jabbed a claw at a small cryobox on his makeshift desk. "Open it."

I reached forward and pulled the cryobox free of the velcro strip holding it down. It was the kind of container used to store low-temperature medicinals for autodoc supplies. Numbly I toggled the keypad. Seals hissed and unlocked. The lid to the box slid smoothly open.

There was a human hand in the container.

A left hand.

Then I recognized the ring on the third finger. The one I had placed there. On Sharna's hand.

I could not speak. My eyes would not focus.

From very far away, I heard Jacobi's voice. "She is still alive, Kenneth. It was I who convinced them that your wife would be more useful alive than dead. Remember that, boy."

I said nothing, still staring into the box. Frost gleamed on my wife's severed hand. Then a giant, four-fingered black hand eclipsed the smaller one and took the box from my grasp. Kraach-Captain sat back in his seat, fixing the cryobox back to its velcro strip.

Jacobi continued, his voice almost drowned out by the pounding in my temples. "It's still viable. They'll reattach it if you work for them. Just like they are going to give me new legs and a new face."

My lips were numb. "My children?"

The scarred little man next to me was quiet for a moment. "Kenneth," he said at last, "Kraach-Captain will do nothing to you or your family if you work with him. He'll even make you a member of his household. Protection, see?" He cleared his throat, continued. "Refuse, and he'll . . . eat your wife. His teeth will be the last thing she sees."

I was just breathing, taking it in. There was a ringing in my ears.

"Your children will attend. Then they will be hunted for sport by Kraach-Captain's sons."

I dared not look at Jacobi. I would try to kill him if I did. Someday, some way, he would pay for his treachery. But for now I turned my attention back to the captain. I had to be clear, for their sake.

"Kraach-Captain," I said, the words dead and empty in my mouth, "how do I know you will abide by this . . . agreement?"

The guards growled and grumbled at the implication, but the old kzin merely blinked at me. "Little slave," he rumbled, "a Hero's Word is binding. I stake my Name on it, my lands, and my sons."

Kraach-Captain did the kzinti equivalent of a shrug. "Do not fail."

Kraach-Captain tapped a clawtip on an innocuous-looking holocube sitting on his desk. He picked it up and extended it to me. "Take this recording. Watch it, then carry it with you as a reminder."

"What is it?" I asked dully, taking it. But I knew the answer.

"It is a recording of my session with your mate, when I removed her hand," the old kzin rasped. "This interview is concluded."

The guards' hands released my shoulders, and Jacobi murmured in my ear. "Come on, Kenneth. Kraach-Captain has laid in everything we need. There is much to plan."

I let Jacobi lead me away.

• Chapter Three
Catspaw Gambit

Lies. They made a sour lump in my chest as I stood waiting in *Feynman*'s airlock.

Control was everything at this point, but it was difficult to stay focused. I thought of my children. My wife. I thought of the cryobox on that huge table back at Blackjack. I thought of Kraach-Captain's oath, delivered four light-years away. My children's faces swam in my memory. Did little Gretha remember me? She was not so little now, it occurred to me suddenly; it had been four years in absolute time, a few weeks to me.

The damned holocube seemed a massive weight in my inner pocket, reminding me of what was at stake. I could not let any of my children become a plaything in a kzin hunting park. Not even to save elitist, cowardly Herrenmann lives. *No choice.* So I swallowed my bile and looked at the opening inner lock with false calm.

The hatch to *Feynman* finished sliding open with a metallic grinding and a blast of compressed air. My little Herrenmann friend stood just inside the lock, a welding laser held meaningfully in his hands. Not much of a weapon, but one that would do the job, yes. His eyes flicked swiftly from side to side, scanning the airlock behind me. A young Herrenmann woman stood near a doorway about ten meters away and watched us intently.

"Ah, *Herr* Bergen, I presume," I said, forcing a smile

to my lips and tone. Hard to do, but what choice did I have?

Act like Jacobi, yes, perhaps—but don't *become* like him.

Bergen pointed the big laser at my chest and waved me inside with his free hand. "You are to please keep your hands away from your body, where I might see them." The little dyed tufts of his asymmetric beard made Bergen look like a goat I had once seen at a zoo in Tiamat.

"I understand your caution," I said. Reassuring tone, bland face. All the while, my wife's voice and children's faces were in my heart like a knife. I spread my hands carefully and stepped inside the slowboat. The airlock cycled shut behind me, sealing with a hiss like an angry kzin.

Bergen watched me and took a few steps backward. He handed the welding laser to the woman. She braced herself in marksman position, trim and efficient. He whispered to her, then came toward me again, magnetic soles of his shipshoes clicking on the deck. He reached into a toolpouch on his belt.

"It is good to see you again, my friend," I said easily. *Too friendly? Got to get the right tone.*

Bergen ran a small box with blinking lights over the outlines of my shipsuit and carryall, looking for energy weapons or inappropriate electronics. He grunted approval and put the box away. The woman with the welding laser did not relax.

"Trust is a wonderful thing," I observed. Ironic? Witty? What character was I playing here? No one replied.

I popped my helmet and left it on a velcro patch near the airlock. I picked up my carryall and raised an eyebrow at Bergen in question. A nod. He escorted me toward the doorway. The silent woman came behind us. I could feel the itch of a laser sight in the small of my back. The shot would flash-boil the water in me like a steam jet.

Suspicious elitists, yes. But then, they would soon discover that they had reason to be suspicious. Not that the fact made me feel any better.

Feynman had been designed to run nearly automatically. Crew of three to five, carrying well over three hundred coldsleepers, with a sizable cargo bay. The life support sections we walked through were therefore small and cramped. Huge slowboat, tiny lifebubble. Well kept, though, even neat. Large wallscreens with complex automated monitoring readouts caught my eye as we passed.

The 0.1 *g* was enough for a strong up-and-down orientation. Magnetic shipboots kept us from leaping like Wunderland *zithraras* down the hallways. Soon, I could see the slight curve to the main ring corridor, which gave true perspective to the size and bulk of *Feynman*.

It felt huge, empty, lonely. Dim corridor lights, chilly echoing halls. Walls stained by time, stinks flavoring the air, aromas both biological and mechanical. Only a few crew could be awake on *Feynman*; life support systems couldn't handle more. Many doors and hatches were closed along the main ring corridor, some with oxidized seals. Some led to the cargo bay, I knew, and others to ship function areas. A few would lead to the liquid nitrogen chambers.

Coldsleep. There had to be a passenger manifest somewhere. I had sworn to myself that I would have a little talk with my cryogenically suspended mother at some point soon. I wanted her to see where her cowardice had led.

We stooped through one low hatchway and down a short corridor. It opened to the small control room for the slowboat. An old woman sat in front of a console, her face dimly lit from the control boards. On one of her screens I could see a wide spectrum scan of *Victrix* running. The old woman looked up, eyes tired.

"You are Höchte?" she snapped. A voice cracked and brittle. Her hair was ice-white and thin. This woman had taken no anti-aging drugs. Time had carved deep lines into her face, which was dark and leathery with a fusion drive tan. She must have spent too much time at the core of *Feynman*, monitoring the fire fed by the ramscoop fields. But her eyes were bright and alive.

I kept my smile intact. "That is correct, Madame. And to whom have I the pleasure to speak?" She carried herself like an old-school Herrenmann women, like the great aunts I met while my parents were alive, or some of the collaborationist doyennes I had seen in München. No jewelry, a wiry frame in a simple shipsuit. Her expression was more than merely haughty, though. There was another quality to it, one I could not quite name. Disturbing.

She stared at me coolly for a moment, then chuckled low in her throat. "I am Freya Svensdottir. I command on this shift. You have met Klaus Bergen, and his silent but efficient wife, Madchen Franke."

"I am pleased to make your acquaintance." Murmured pseudo-formalities took a moment while our eyes assessed each other. There could only be one or two more crew awake, if that. The lifesystem capacity was *small*. This would be simpler than I had planned. But something about the woman made me edgy, eager to get it over with as quickly as possible.

Her expression did not change. "And you bring us news that the ratcat kzinti have been defeated? Driven from Wunderland?"

I nodded. "It is my distinct pleasure to tell you so." Gesture with the carryall. "May I?"

She nodded. I opened it and removed the items that Jacobi and Kraach-Captain had so carefully prepared during the voyage out to *Feynman*. Holocubes. False historical records. Even the loop of kzinti ears I had shown

Bergen earlier over tightbeam. Kraach-Captain had earned those himself, dueling for authorization to form his expedition to the slowboat.

For the next hour, I explained about the mythical Free Wunderland Navy, and its equally mythical victories. About driving the ratcats out of Wunderlander space. Great stories. I had spent plenty of time on them.

If only they had been true.

The crew had no way of knowing the truth, after all. There had been no attempt by the slowboats to contact Wunderland. Sol had not been in contact either, so far as any human knew. Hard to do, through the plasma plume and the forward bow shock.

We Wunderlanders had been left on our own by our so-wise Solar brethren. This slowboat was in the same predicament.

Bergen grew slowly enthusiastic as I told my stories. His wife simply stared at me. Maybe the isolation of the slowboat crew shift did not agree with her psyche. Svensdottir stared at me, too, but with a weighing gaze; she was clearly in command, the one to convince.

I told my hosts about the vessel some distance out from *Feynman* that had carried me here. I explained how it would retrofit *Feynman* with a gravitic polarizer drive, allowing the slowboat to make it the rest of the way to Sol in a matter of weeks.

Bergen stroked his chin thoughtfully. "So we would need to deactivate the ramscoop fields, yes?"

I nodded agreement. "The tender vessel is large. I don't think that it could work its way through the fluxlines, even with the protective field from the gravitic polarizers."

"This would take time," Svensdottir said. "We must avoid instability of the field as it is being shut down. The fusion drive is most delicately balanced." She stood. "I will go below and begin programming the shutdown mode."

I blinked. I had anticipated some more doubt, maybe even opposition, debate. But then, they were desperate in here. The long years had worn them. Then I knocked on their door, bringing safety, freedom, hope.

I swallowed what I was feeling. Concentrated on images of innocent faces, a woman's severed hand.

After the old gray woman left I looked over at Bergen. "She seems a bit hard edged."

"That is true. But she has kept *Feynman* going, all this time." He smiled a bit, against his innate Herrenmann sobriety.

"You mean she's been on duty the entire trip?"

He nodded. "From the time we boosted away from Wunderland, just ahead of the kzin. She took one look at the destruction of the Serpent Swarmer fleet behind her, and refused coldsleep." Bergen looked pensive. "Since the lifesystems on board don't work terribly well, we take frequent shifts. But the old woman . . . well, she has stayed on shift for nearly forty years."

"Odd," I replied.

"Space is deep, Herr Höchte. We are the same age, she and I," Bergen said. "I slept most of the time."

"Could you have not talked her into shifts? After all, spending one's life this way . . . " I pursed my lips, gestured around me at the slowboat.

He shrugged. "She insists."

Typical Herrenmannen behavior.

I nodded. "A formidable woman. You have all been brave. Earth will hail you." Might as well hand out the compliments. It relaxed people. Madchen Franke smiled, clearly a rare expression for her.

I shrugged. "Well, while your estimable leader is looking over the fusion drive shutdown parameters, we have one more order of business." I reached into my carryall and very casually removed a stylus. I wanted to take care of this as quickly as possible, just in case there were further complications. I did not want anyone doing anything to ship systems without my supervision. Too much risk.

Careful to breathe through my nose I twisted at the cylinder I was holding. An invisible, inaudible puff: complete surprise. An incipient shock on Bergen's face glazed to a sleeping mask. The welding laser thumped uselessly on the floor below Franke's nerveless fingers. Her expression was little different, awake or asleep.

Quick and neat.

Invisible nose filters no longer needed—the gas degraded to harmlessness in less than thirty seconds—I heaved a great gasp of the ship's pungent air. Pocketing the stylus, I carefully laid them out flat on the control room floor. Then I reached for the welding laser. Time to do a little hunting.

"I knew it." Suddenly I realized that I had half expected the voice from the hatchway—but why? I turned around to face the fragile old woman. The laser would not be necessary. Svensdottir, unarmed, ignored me completely. She was looking at the bodies of Bergen and Franke.

I said nothing. She ignored it.

Her eyes finally raised to mine. "Are they alive?"

"Yes," I told her calmly. Soothing. "A simple nerve gas. It will wear off in a few hours."

"You are working for the kzin." Not a question.

I nodded again, removing the nose filters and stuffing them into a pocket. I didn't want to insult her or myself by explaining my actions. How could she possibly understand?

"I suppose that you will put me down now, like some kind of inconvenient pet." I could see the harsh lines deepen around Svensdottir's mouth in the control-room light. Disapproval carved those features, like a great-aunt surveying some broken dishes left by a clumsy toddler on an unwanted visit.

"Hardly," I told her. "My ... employers ... will need you left alive, as guides and teachers."

Her eyes narrowed, then widened. She seemed to instantly grasp the Trojan Cat gambit. *"Never."*

"That is what I said," I said softly, almost kindly. "Now look at me."

"Well, what is next, traitor?" I couldn't look at her eyes. Didn't want to see the accusation peering from that old face.

I paused, wet my lips. The words were difficult. "There is something you can do for me."

The old woman said nothing, stony-faced. I could see that she was a hard woman, had always been a hard woman. She fairly vibrated with her hatred at my betrayal.

"Tante," I said softly.

She looked up at me sharply, face gone rigid. Her pale eyes stared into mine, studying, studying. Her wrinkles seemed etched deep by pain and loss. I knew how she felt. She raised a wisp of an eyebrow, her Herrenmann ears long and incongruous on her thin face. "You shouldn't call me your auntie," the old woman said at last, her tone almost gentle. "You are a traitor."

"Did you know Helga Schleisser?" I finally asked, ignoring her insult.

Another long silence, then she sighed. *"Ja.* She was a proud woman; perhaps too proud." Dry, crackling precision. "She had her duty and honor to carry out. It was a heavy burden for her to bear." Svensdottir considered it for a moment. "Perhaps too heavy."

I snorted in derision.

The old woman poked me hard with a gnarled, fearless finger. "Do not make light of honor and duty, nor their weight, *Herr* Höchte. They are qualities that set us apart from the beasts." A frown deepened her wrinkles. "Yet too much attention to those qualities makes us little different than the ratcat *teufels*, is it not so?"

I nodded. I couldn't stand much more of this. The stylus was a burning weight in my pocket. I suddenly remembered Sharna's bell-like laugh in the welcoming darkness of our compartment.

"What happened to Helga Schleisser?" I persisted.

"I'll show you," the old woman replied, and motioned me toward the corridor. I let Svensdottir lead the way. She was unarmed. My micrograv reflexes were better than hers. I had nothing to fear.

The curving corridor finally led to a sealed hatch, which the old woman unlocked with an identikey from around her neck. The hatch sighed and slid aside, releasing foggy, bitterly cold air into the corridor. I shivered. A chilly brush of the liquid nitrogen at 77 degrees Absolute. A touch of the grave—though a temporary one. Dim lights flickered on inside the ceramic chamber.

I followed her into a connected series of cargo holds, filled from floor to ceiling with row after row of identical cryosuspension bunks. Svensdottir seemed to know exactly where she was going as she passed the stacked ranks of coffinlike containers. Finally, she stood in front of one lower-tier coldsleep bunk, gestured. I could see the name illuminated by glowing lights on the case: HELGA YAKOBSON SCHLEISSER.

The coldsleep bunk was empty.

I looked back at Svensdottir in confusion. Just in time for the magneto wrench to catch me in the pit of my stomach.

I drifted to my knees in the low gravity, gasping, grabbed for her legs—and she clubbed me again, behind the ear this time. Sharp pain. Contracting vision.

"I couldn't do it, my son," she told me sadly. When I

could open my eyes, bright lights swam before them.

Somehow she had gotten a welding laser and was pointing it at me. Cool, stern. She had set all of this up. Set *me* up, smooth as water ice. "Uh, I—"

"I thought that it was wrong to sleep away the decades, to let others bear my burdens. I had lost Henry, you . . . everything. All I had left was keeping *Feynman* going, and reaching Sol. Just honor and duty." She gestured at the stacks of coldsleep bunks. "These are all the experts we could find on the kzin, people who knew what little we had learned about fighting them. We even have some kzinti warship wreckage as cargo. Maybe the Earthers can do a better job at understanding the ratcat tech."

I tried hard to catch my breath, my mind racing. "You knew it was me all along." The laser did not waver.

My mother nodded. "The years have not been kind to me, watching the fusion fires of *Feynman* burn, and keeping the systems functioning. Useful work, but it had its price. But you, Kenneth, have become the image of your father; how could I not know you?"

She stared at me for a long time. Her eyes were deep, unyielding. Yet I could remember them now from other, ancient days. An imperious weight on me.

I did nothing. What was there to say?

"We have a few coldsleep bunks open. I will put you into one, and deal with this trouble at Sol." She gestured with the laser for me to get up. "The kzin can kill us, but they will not board us." I believed her utterly.

"Don't you want to know why?" I asked her.

She shook her head, bird-quick. "Not particularly. I had expected a possibility like this one. Just not a son of mine leading the betrayal. We can sort all of that out in six months or so. There is no time now. I have preparations to make, to deal with your masters."

My mother paused for a beat, then continued. "The

signal laser has been down since the kzin near-miss when
Feynman left Wunderland. We don't have the spare parts
to fix it. So I cannot tell the status of Sol, Wunderland, or
the kzin. I had to be careful. It was well I had prepared."

I started to get to my feet, reaching out a hand for
support.

"Easy now," she warned, backing away from me.

"Without the signal laser, you couldn't have stopped
the kzin from boarding *Feynman*." I was angry, suddenly.
My sacrifice was not even needed. All of this, for nothing!

A cold smile. "Perhaps it would be worth trying for the
kzin, but with the ramscoop fields and fusion drive, I think
we could keep the ratcats at bay." She gestured more
insistently with the laser. "Get up."

"You don't understand," I told her, standing upright. "I
had no choice."

The lines in her face deepened. I could see her flush
beneath her fusion tan. She snorted, features sharpening
in a sneer. "You were only following orders, I suppose?"

"Hardly."

She gestured at me once more with the welding laser,
toward one of the coldsleep chambers. Once inside, the
autodoc routines would sedate me and start the chill-down
cycle. I didn't have long to think of something. Her right
hand covering me with the laser, my mother's left danced
across the keypad. She stood out of the way as the readouts beeped musically.

The panel in front of me hissed as a series of lights
blinked green across its diagnostic readout display. The
coldsleep bunk access opened, like a sideways coffin lid. I
paused.

"Mother. Please listen." I met her icy gaze sideways. It
was my last chance.

She said nothing, but neither did she shoot me. If I
failed, Kraach-Captain would send his message back to

Wunderland, and my family would die. An image of sharp white teeth, designed to shear through living flesh, came into my head unbidden.

"This means nothing to you, perhaps," I found myself saying urgently. "The ratcats have my family. Your grandchildren. I had no choice."

It was time. Bet a little, bet it all.

I leaped backward. The laser spat a high-energy pulse where I had been a moment before. Where it hit the coldsleep bunk electronics fried and sputtered. An alarm shrieked.

I swept the welding laser from my mother's grasp. It pinwheeled across the chamber. I ducked with Belter reflexes, rolled, and came up with the gas stylus in my hand.

"Sorry," I said, the words out of my mouth a surprise. My mother looked at me, shock and resignation tightening her face. She didn't beg. I'll give her that.

"Is it true?" she asked.

"What?"

"About your family?"

Her question surprised me. "Of course. Any other threat I could have answered with suicide." I reached into my shipsuit pocket and pulled out the nose filters, pushed them in, breathed deeply—and the stylus hissed. The gas puff cloaked her face instantly.

She shook her head as if to clear it of cobwebs, and slowly slid to the deck. "Not your fault," she muttered. "Never had the chance . . . to raise you as . . . a Herrenmann." Her eyes flickered, closed. The lined mummy face smoothed with unconsciousness.

I recovered the welding laser and slung it over my shoulder. I picked her up and carried her to the control room. She was feather-light in the microgravity.

Around me the ship hummed on. *Anybody home?* It

would be like her to hide a backup crew member, or booby traps. I was angry, jittery with reaction.

I kept the laser ready but the corridors stayed empty. In the control room I put her on the floor with the other two and did some quick analysis with the shipboard computers. They were little different from the computers in the Swarm; the kzin discouraged innovation.

INTERNAL INVENTORY: ACTIVE: IR. No other infrared radiators at 37° C in *Feynman*. No movement other than small cleaning and maintenance autobots. Good. I'd had enough surprises for one watch.

Time to complete my job. I looked at the three bodies at my feet and breathed heavily. It had been a very near thing. I checked them over quickly again. Vital signs were all strong and steady, even my mother's. Jacobi had not lied about the nerve gas. The three of them would be needed in good health by my ratcat masters, to explain the operation of *Feynman*.

I hated the way those thoughts sounded in my head. The deck thrummed under my feet. It was very quiet in the control room. Was this triumph? I thought of what my treachery had bought. I was different from Jacobi; I did what I had to for my wife and my children. My mother's stern, weathered face accused me even while unconscious.

Jacobi was buying legs and a face. What had I bought?

I was delivering my children's children, and their children, into slavery to the kzin. But at least they would be alive. There comes a time, I realized, to do what is *right*. Not what is best, actually. Nor what one would prefer to do.

What is *right*.

I thought of slavery and defeat and my family. Of honor. Of empty platitudes about freedom versus the harsh reality of a frost-rimed severed hand in a cryobox. I thought of orange striped shapes flashing through a forest, pursuing human children.

My children.

It was time to send for Kraach-Captain and his Heroes, to turn *Feynman* into a Trojan Cat full of kzin hardware, soldiers, and weapons. To help that Trojan Cat prepare to break the back of the defense perimeter around Sol, to allow the next kzin fleet to destroy and conquer as they had at Wunderland. But at least I was not helping the aliens in exchange for a new pair of legs, no.

I was better than Jacobi . . . yet a tiny voice jibed in my head. *Nicht wahr? How, exactly?*

My body seemed on autopilot as I walked away from the sleeping bodies, down the main ring corridor. The holocube felt very heavy in my inner pocket as I walked back to the airlock and I re-entered the singleship. My fingers automatically went so far as to orient *Victrix's* signal laser correctly. I could tightbeam the message directly. . . .

My fingers paused. First, it would take me some time to unravel the shipboard instructions for shutting down the ramscoop fields and fusion drive.

In my mind's eye, I could see the kzin armada breaking the back of Sol. Tightening their grip over all of human space like a clenching fist. I could see my great-great-grandchildren, close-mouthed slaves in some kzin household, wielding blowdryers and brushes on their indolent predator masters.

Just another slave race, eventually no better than a degenerate Jotok.

The image sickened me. I could imagine those future generations reviling my name in private, slaves whispering to other slaves in low voices while their masters slept. Tiny humans scurrying around huge kzin households, secretly cursing the names of the humans who had sold their birthright, their future. My descendants would not remember them. But I did. The hated names flowed easily over the tongue, echoing in my mind.

Arnold.

Quisling.

Chien.

Easterhouse.

Upton-Schleisser.

I turned away from the commset. Quickly, not thinking any more, I left my singleship. Back into *Feynman*. I walked to the three lying in a drugged stupor. I looked down at them, emotions warring within me.

My wife, my children: they would die if I failed, yes. All life's sweetness, gone.

But they would at least know that I, husband and father—and most of all, human—finally believed in things larger than myself.

One human *can* make a difference, no matter what people like Jacobi said.

And perhaps it was not too late.

I made my decision. Swearing gently, I reached into my pouch for the antidote ampules to the nerve gas. My fingers shook a little, but I ignored it. I stabbed my mother's wrinkled neck with the drug and waited for her to wake up.

This was going to be hard. Owning up to who you are usually is.

My mother had been right, damn her stern soul. Once a Herrenmann, always a Herrenmann.

She coughed once, her eyes fluttering, and tried to sit up.

When she finally became coherent, I told her everything.

• Chapter Four
Punica Fides

Go out like a rocket, boy, not like a fizzled, wet match.
My mother had said that. It had a certain dark ring
that appealed to me.

Once again I made the journey from the kzin troopship to *Feynman*, across the Deep between stars. This
time, though, I did so in a small kzin fighter, not my tiny
singleship *Victrix*. The ship interior was huge, orange-lit,
built on a scale for kzin. The air was cold and dry, making
my sinuses ache. I moved unobtrusively to one of the
gunners' stations, the straps at their tightest ludicrously
loose on me. Jacobi was strapped in across from me. I
refused to look at him.

The engines thrummed softly, and I could hear Kraach-
Captain and Alien-Technologist hissing and spitting from
the control cockpit forward. The sour-spicy smell of anger
filled the cabin. I tried to ignore the angry sounds. At
least this gravitic polarizer didn't give me a hammering
headache.

Victrix had been left just outside the kzin vessel, under
heavy guard. I had told the kzinti by tightbeam that the
fusion point generators were different than those used in
the Swarm, and that I was bringing a sample for their
Alien-Technologists to study.

Which was true, in a manner of speaking.

At the same time, I told Kraach-Captain that I could
not torture information out of the humans onboard

Feynman. Nor could I determine how to shut the system down myself. I needed expert help. I suspected sabotage, and booby traps, as well.

Jacobi didn't trust me, but Kraach-Captain saw me as a reliable beast-slave. The kzin thought that he understood the nature of the leash around my neck. Still, he had brought Jacobi along to keep an eye on me.

Up front, Kraach-Captain and Alien-Technologist sat huddled over their thinscreens. They snarled arguments about the ramscoop fields and our route through the tangled web of force. Kzin do not care for close quarters, and the differential in rank made Kraach-Captain's temper quite short. It was his place of honor as Conquest Hero, though, to board and deactivate *Feynman* in person. I believed that he would have insisted on this, even if I had reported it possible to shut down the slowboat by myself.

None of this would work without the kzin worship of the Warrior Heart. Gamble after gamble after gamble, but the only game in town. . . .

Jacobi and I could see little from where we were packed next to one another in the back of the ratcat fighter. He smelled sour with fear, sweaty. What had broken in the kzin fighter to turn him into what he had become? I ignored him as best I could, and looked at the dots-and-comma script of the kzin language on various pieces of ratcat tech in my field of vision.

"Kenneth," he whispered to me quietly.

I didn't look at him. Instead I continued to scan the interior of the spacecraft, lit in garish orange. I doubted that any humans had seen as much of kzinti spacecraft as the two of us had over the last few months.

I for one didn't understand much of what we had seen. Kraach-Captain had kept us in a largish cabin during the trip out to *Feynman,* with our own supplies and autodoc.

The occasional trip outside the cabin looked like the kzin fighter ship around us: cavernous spaces, orange lit. Oddly shaped devices, flickering thinscreens. Could that kind of information ever be of use? I shook my head, trying to make sense of the alien spaces around me. I was a singleship pilot and part-time smuggler, not a genius.

Jacobi's voice was an insistent whisper, like a pesky insect. "Did you find your mother, boy?"

Now I turned and looked at him. "Yeah," I grated. *Stay in character.* "I did what I must. I do not thank you for it."

Jacobi nodded. "In the coming years, Kenneth," he replied, "you will come to see that I had your best interests at heart." Jacobi started to reach out to me, perhaps to pat my arm.

My expression stopped him cold, as I studied his ruined face, and smiled like a kzin. "I give you respect of sorts, Jacobi, even as a traitor. Because of the scars you earned fighting the kzin. But don't push me."

Outrage glinted in his eyes. "And what are you? A saint?"

"I am nothing like you, Jacobi. *Nothing.* Now seal it and lock it down, before I see how long it would take Kraach-Captain to get back here and pull my hands from around your miserable throat."

He fell silent.

The rest of the trip was quiet, except for more unintelligible snarling arguments in the Hero's Tongue from the command cockpit. From Jacobi I could have found out what Kraach-Captain and Alien-Technologist were saying, but I think that I understood the gist. Irritation seems quite universal among sentient beings.

I had left the outer airlock open when I had departed *Feynman* in *Victrix*. That way the kzin crew tunnel mechanism could adapt and seal the two vessels together. We were instructed to leave our helmets open and to come along. The old kzin was clearly impatient, ready to get started on the real job.

Kraach-Captain paused for a moment before we left the kzin airlock. He bent nearly double and put his face near mine, rasped, "Think of your cubs and your mate. Their fate is in your hands."

"I know that, Kraach-Captain." I studiously looked to one side of his huge eyes.

He coughed and spat in reply, then he and Alien-Technologist herded us into *Feynman*. Alien-Technologist had a complicated device clipped to his forearm. It beeped at intervals.

I felt a heavy weight on my shoulder. A four-fingered black hand squeezed like a vise. "Lead us to the control lair," Kraach-Captain rumbled. I walked them along the main ring corridor. The kzinti had to stoop. I thought that I heard Alien-Technologist hiss-spit something at Kraach-Captain, who coughed kzin laughter in reply. Perhaps a joke about the edibility of the passengers in cryo-suspension.

I lead them into the cramped control room, feeling the tension build. I pointed to the sleeping bodies on the floor. *Careful, careful* . . .

"Your sources of information, Kraach-Captain," I said. "They altered the ship systems such that I cannot turn off the ramscoop."

Kraach-Captain sniffed through his open faceplate, looking around the control room. "We will deal with them in a moment," he rasped. "Show us these ship systems."

I smoothly called up the various subroutines on the main viewscreen. Jacobi was leaning over my shoulder to see better. First, the safety interlocks. Since the fusion drive used interstellar matter swept up by ramscoop fields, shutting the fields down was a delicate matter. I showed them encrypted block after encrypted block at every step of the shutdown commands. The kzinti rumbled and hissed their impatience. Claws tapped at keypads as they called up diagnostic subroutines far more quickly than I had expected.

I snuck a glance at the chronometer above the central console. It was almost time.

Kraach-Captain turned to me. "Prepare one of these for interrogation." A claw flicked at the three sleeping bodies.

I carefully lifted the body of my mother, and moved to put her in a chair.

"No," thundered Kraach-Captain. "That one would be too fragile." He hissed and spat at Alien-Technologist, who yowled in reply.

Jacobi looked thoughtful. "Dominant One, may I speak?"

A careless wave of unsheathed claws.

"It could be," Jacobi continued, "that an older human would be a better choice. Heroes have . . . ah, a tendency to overestimate human tolerances. The writhings of a young male might be misinterpreted as defiance." He carefully looked away.

"Hrrrr . . ." mused Kraach-Captain. "You could well be right, cull. Prepare her."

I moved to tie my mother down in the chair.

There was a sudden broad-band squeal across all commlink frequencies. The two aliens shrieked in pain and surprise at the sound. It was loudest from the huge wristband on Alien-Technologist. Kraach-Captain looked at the main viewscreen in time to see a multi-colored bloom of ionized gas fluorescing where his vessel waited.

The kzin stared at the screen, not breathing. The cloud of gas glowed, changing from blue to yellow to reddish as it cooled and expanded. Behind their backs, quick as an eyeblink, my mother shot from the chair into the corridor, bounding in the low gravity.

Kraach-Captain's impressive ears drooped suddenly, then folded tightly into knots. The orange ruff visible around his helmet seal puffed out in rage. "Death Cry," he growled past thin black lips.

The old kzin turned and looked at me, smiling like a . . . like a kzin. "What have you done?"

I looked him back in the eye, carefully moving to one side. "The fusion-point generator I brought back in *Victrix* was sabotaged. It just fried the inside of your troopship, Kraach-Captain."

Alien-Technologist started to snarl something, but Kraach-Captain slashed a gesture for quiet. His claws unsheathed, he gathered himself to leap. Nervously I prepared myself as best I could to dodge the elderly kzin's attack.

From behind the huge alien, Klaus Bergen suddenly leaped up like a child's toy from his false sleep in the microgravity. He thrust a sharpened power conduit into Kraach-Captain's massive back. The kzin spread his huge arms in an enormous embrace, his scream going up and up in frequency—

—into silence. He hung limply in midair as his pelt began to smoke.

Madchen Franke shoved an electrode into Alien-Technologist. She was quick, but the kzin caught her with one spasming swipe, tearing her arm off. As she slammed into a bulkhead, blood spurting from a fleshy gaping socket, Alien-Technologist roared and collapsed in convulsions.

Bergen's face was a mask of grief, but he never eased his grip on the electrode lodged in Kraach-Captain's back.

My mother peered into the control room, a laser aimed and ready. She looked around quickly, tossed me the laser.

Quickly, she grabbed the electrode piercing Alien-Technologist, standing above the concussed woman lying on the deck.

Jacobi looked wildly from side to side at the twitching kzinti. At two crew carefully holding the electrodes steady. His eyes jerked toward me.

"You," he exclaimed.

"Me," I replied, putting down the laser.

Then I broke his neck with my own hands. I felt nothing.

We had Trojan Horsed the Trojan Cat. Or perhaps Trojan Monkeyed the Trojan Cat.

My mother stood over us with the welding laser while Bergen and I quickly but very carefully bound the two unconscious kzin. Franke had lost consciousness immediately. We could leave her for a few minutes without risking significant further damage. If there was one thing the crew of *Feynman* knew, it was cryo-suspension.

I entered the kzin fighter ship in search of medical supplies. I was careful not to touch anything. This fighter was a very important prize now. There could be booby traps anywhere. Strange devices, complicated controls. I couldn't make sense of it. Perhaps wiser heads than mine could.

"Well done, my son," I heard my mother say to me as I sealed the kzin ship behind me. "I am proud."

I smiled tightly, but shook my head a little. I did what I had to do. Still, I would never know the price I paid, nor what I had bought.

But at least it felt *right*.

Later, I stood in the tiny control room of the *Feynman*. Stars filled the screen, a riot of gaudy pinpoints against velvet blackness. With some thought and careful orientation, I was able to pick out Sol. The sight still didn't warm me, nor make me feel victorious.

I heard a voice behind me. "Son?"

"Yes, mother?" I replied, not needing to turn around.

"It's time." Her voice was old, yes, but it still crackled and burned with a trace of Herrenmann command.

I felt the familiar argument rise in my throat. "I don't see why we can't at least try to understand the ratcat drive. If we succeed, we would . . ."

"If, if, if," she interrupted softly. "You know perfectly well that the kzin booby trap their devices to keep them out of slave-race hands. And we dare not risk either of our captives to explain the failsafes here and now."

She was right, irritatingly right. Both Kraach-Captain and Alien-Technologist would be invaluable to unlocking the secrets of kzin technology when we reached Sol. But the aliens were far too large and strong to keep conscious. That was an unacceptable risk in a small lifebubble. Life support was already beginning to break down on *Feynman*. It stank. We had rigged two coldsleep chambers for our alien captives and iced them down for the trip.

But only after we had carefully deep-suspended Madchen Franke. She would reawaken on Earth intact and healed.

Kraach-Captain had never really wakened before we chilled him down. His kzin physiology had put his body into hibernation state without the biochemical tricks we humans needed for suspension. I never had the chance to explain to the alien ratcat about human honor.

Or human vengeance.

My mother and I watched the stars together for a time in silence.

I said nothing. Why should victory taste of ashes?

Finally she spoke. "Remember this, my son. Had you succeeded in the original plan, you would have saved their lives, true. But as slaves." She gestured Solward. "Perhaps, with our new cargo, we have a chance at leveling the playing field with the kzin. We can start to erase their technological advantage, to drive them back." She was right. An intact kzin fighter and crew was a prize indeed. *But still* . . .

I felt my mouth form a tense line across my face. "It isn't enough. Sharna and the children—they need to *know* that I did not betray them."

"They cannot—and must not—know. The kzin must think that their Trojan Horse expedition failed utterly." I heard an ironic smile in her voice. "But think, Kenneth: you judged me yourself, did you not? A coward and a traitor, I believe. Both of us did what we did. What we had to do."

Would Sharna have faith in me? Would my children see me as pawn to the kzin, or as a hero? Would they ever know how I really felt, what I had done?

Deal with it. My mother's words echoed in my head. This was honor, the thin reassurance that I had done the right thing? It could not compare to seeing my wife and children again. To telling them in person.

I felt a tugging at my arm, and looked down to see a gnarled, blue-veined hand at my elbow. I could see how the long years of exposure to the ramscoop fusion drive had aged her, burning away everything but her devotion to a cause. And I knew how empty victory could make you feel.

"It is time for you to take the coldsleep," she said simply. "You will awaken at Sol, a hero. Perhaps you can convince the Earthers to let you return to Wunderland, to battle for what you believe." There was a sly smile playing about her aged face.

Even smiling, the face seemed stern. A mirror to my own, as I had recently discovered. How had I not seen it? I had been blinded by my own knotty conflicts.

"No," I told her. "I'll stay awake—with you."

A slight squeeze on my arm. "Kenneth, Bergen knows *Feynman* far better than you."

"There is nothing Bergen knows that I cannot learn."

She smiled wanly. "No, there is nothing you cannot learn. But still, you must sleep."

"*You* deserve to sleep, then."

"As for me, I am too old to take the rigors of coldsleep, except for deep suspension." She chuckled a bit. "But do not worry, Kenneth. Klaus and I, we make quite the team."

I couldn't find the words in my Herrenmann mouth to express how I felt. I nodded agreement.

"It is all right," she soothed, standing up a bit straighter. "I may be feeble, but never confuse that with weakness. Do not forget that I am Herrenmann, as are you." A chuckle in the dim control room. "I will be there to waken you at Sol, my son, as I used to do when you were a child. I never expected to have that honor again."

Finally I simply nodded. I had no words.

I started to adjust the viewscreen, to get a last glimpse of Alpha Centauri before leaving the control room. To see the faint glimmer of light that four years ago had shone on my wife and children, Principle willing. But even as I began to touch the keypads, my mother's hands gently turned me around. She peered intently into my face.

"Never backward, Kenneth." Her voice was old, yes, but very strong. "Always look forward. That is what every Herrenmann must do."

That is what Herrenmannen do. I nodded tightly. The future had to be focus, for now.

We walked together away from the warm lights of the control room. Toward the coldsleep chambers. I thought of the sunny seas of Earth, the salty waters, and tried to ignore the images flitting behind my eyes, images of small pale shadows fleeing hopelessly through leafy glades.

Niven • Pournelle • Flynn
FALLEN ANGELS

In 1995 Earth finally had its act together. There were two manned spacc stations orbiting, one from the former Soviet Union, one from the United States. Even better, the human race had finally agreed that something had to be done about the environment—and was doing it, one green law after another. By the year 2020 the Greenhouse Effect was just a bad memory, and the air was a clean green dream.

There was only one problem. All that pollution, all that CO_2—the Greenhouse Effect itself—was the only thing holding off the next, regularly scheduled ice age! With the carbon dioxide gone the glaciers came, and came down fast. In the mid-21st century, the icebergs had reached North Dakota and weren't slowing down.

But by then an alliance of the most extreme "deep ecology" Greens and the zaniest of religious fundamentalists had taken over in the winter-bound U.S.—and they weren't about to give up their power merely because they were destroying civilization. And they needed a scapegoat. So they decided that it was the "air thievery" of the folks they left stranded in the orbiting space stations that was causing the New Ice Age.

FALLEN ANGELS is the story of two spacemen. Shot down and stranded on a hostile Earth, they think there is no hope for them. But they're wrong. Help is on the way. Help from the one nationally organized pro-technology group left on Earth; the only ones who would dare fly in the face of their unforgiving authoritarian government; the only ones foolish enough to risk everything to help two strangers from space. Science fiction fandom. *Angels* down. *Fans to the rescue!*

72052-X • 384 pp. • $5.95